The window was open on the driver's side...

Joe had never seen a car like it—and the keys were in the dashboard. He opened the door, got in. He could feel the shift in balance as the splendid machine accepted him like a lover. He closed the door, reached for the key, turned it. There was a soft purring sound, and the window at his left slid up. Joe grunted in surprise and turned the key again. Nothing.

He looked down. There wasn't a starter anywhere.

For a split second he glanced forlornly at his glorious vision of flight and power, then forever let it go. He put his hand on the door control and half-rose in his seat.

The handle spun easily, uselessly around. So did that on the other door. "I can't get out," he whispered. He looked out into the dark. *"Can't!"* he cried.

"That's right," said a voice. "You sure can't."

The Latest Science Fiction and Fantasy from Dell Books

VISIONS AND VENTURERS

THEODORE STURGEON

A DELL BOOK

Published by
Dell Publishing Co., Inc.
1 Dag Hammarskjold Plaza
New York, New York 10017

Contents

THE HAG SÈLEEN

(written with James H. Beard)

It was while we were fishing one afternoon, Patty and I, that we first met our friend the River Spider. Patty was my daughter and Anjy's. Tacitly, that is. Figuratively she had originated in some hot corner of hell and had left there with such incredible violence that she had taken half of heaven with her along her trajectory and brought it with her.

I was sprawled in the canoe with the nape of my neck on the conveniently curved cedar stern piece of the canoe, with a book of short stories in my hands and my fish pole tucked under my armpit. The only muscular energy required to fish that way is in moving the eyes from the page to the float and back again, and I'd have been magnificently annoyed if I'd had a bite. Patty was far more honest about it; she was fast asleep in the bilges. The gentlest of currents kept my mooring line just less than taut between the canoe and a half-sunken snag in the middle of the bayou. Louisiana heat and swampland mosquitoes tried casually to annoy me, and casually I ignored them both.

There was a sudden thump on the canoe and I sat upright just as a slimy black something rose out of the muddy depths. It came swiftly until the bow of the canoe rested on it, and then more slowly. My end of the slender craft sank and a small cascade of blood-warm water rushed on, and down, my neck. Patty raised her

11

head with a whimper; if she moved suddenly I knew the canoe would roll over and dump us into the bayou. "Don't move!" I gasped.

She turned puzzled young eyes on me, astonished to find herself looking downward. "Why, daddy?" she asked, and sat up. So the canoe did roll over and it did dump us into the bayou.

I came up strangling, hysterical revulsion numbing my feet and legs where they had plunged into the soft ooze at the bottom. "Patty!" I screamed hoarsely.

She popped up beside me, trod water while she knuckled her eyes. "I thought we wasn't allowed to swim in the bayou, daddy," she said.

I cast about me. Both banks presented gnarled roots buried in rich green swamp growth, and I knew that the mud there was deep and sticky and soft. I knew that that kind of mud clutches and smothers. I knew that wherever we could find a handhold we could also find cottonmouth moccasins. So I knew that we had to get into our canoe again, but fast!

Turning, I saw it, one end sunken, the other high in the air, one thwart fouled in the black tentacles of the thing that had risen under us. It was black and knotted and it dripped slime down on us, and for one freezing second I thought it was alive. It bobbed ever so slowly, sluggishly, in the disturbed water. It was like breathing. But it made no further passes at us. I told Patty to stay where she was and swam over to what I could reach of the canoe and tugged. The spur that held it came away rottenly and the canoe splashed down, gunwale first, and slowly righted itself half full of water. I heard a shriek of insane laughter from somewhere in the swamp but paid no attention. I could attend to that later.

We clung to the gunwales while I tried to think of a way out. Patty kept looking up and down the bayou as

12

if she thought she hadn't enough eyes. "What are you looking for, Patty?"

"Alligators," she said.

Yeah, I mused, that's a thought. We've got to get out of here! I felt as if I were being watched and looked quickly over my shoulder. Before my eyes could focus on it, something ducked behind a bush on the bank. The bush waved its fronds at me in the still air. I looked back at Patty—

"Patty! Look out!"

The twisted black thing that had upset us was coming down, moving faster as it came, and as I shrieked my warning its tangled mass came down on the child. She yelped and went under, fighting the slippery fingers.

I lunged toward her. "Patty!" I screamed. "Pat—"

The bayou bubbled where she had been. I dived, wrenching at the filthy thing that had caught her. Later—it seemed like minutes later, but it couldn't have been more than five seconds—my frantic hand closed on her arm. I thrust the imprisoning filth back, hauled her free, and we broke surface. Patty, thank Heaven, remained perfectly still with her arms as far around me as they would go. Lord knows what might have happened if she had struggled.

We heard the roar of a bull alligator and that was about all we needed. We struck out for the bank, clawed at it. Fortunately Patty's hands fell on a root, and she scuttled up it like a little wet ape. I wasn't so lucky—it was fetid black mud that I floundered through. We lay gasping, at last on solid ground.

"Mother's gonna be mad," said Patty after a time.

"Mother's going to gnash her teeth and froth at the mouth," I said with a good deal more accuracy. We looked at each other and one of the child's eyes closed in an eloquent wink. "Oh, yeah," I said, "and how did we lose the canoe?"

Patty thought hard. "We were paddling along an' a big fella scared you with a gun and stoled our canoe."

"How you talk! I wouldn't be scared!"

"Oh, *yes* you would," she said with conviction.

I repressed an unpaternal impulse to throw her back into the bayou. "That won't do. Mother would be afraid to have a man with a gun stompin' around the bayou. Here it is. We saw some flowers and got out to pick them for mother. When we came back we found the canoe had drifted out into the bayou, and we knew she wouldn't want us to swim after it, so we walked home."

She entered into it with a will. "Silly of us, wasn't it?" she asked.

"Sure was," I said. "Now get those dungarees off so's I can wash the mud out of 'em."

A sunsuit for Patty and bathing trunks for me were our household garb; when we went out for the afternoon we pulled on blue denim shirts and slacks over them to ward off the venomous mosquitoes. We stripped off the dungarees and I searched the bank and found a root broad enough for me to squat on while I rinsed off the worst of the filth we had picked up in our scramble up the bank. Patty made herself comfortable on a bed of dry Spanish moss that she tore out of the trees. As I worked, a movement in midstream caught my eye. A black tentacle poked up out of the water, and, steadily then, the slimy branches of the thing that had foundered us came sloshing into the mottled sunlight. It was a horrible sight, the horror of which was completely dispelled by the sight of the sleek green flank of the canoe which bobbed up beside it.

I ran back up my root, tossed the wet clothes on a convenient branch, broke a long stick off a dead tree and reached out over the water. I could just reach one end of the canoe. Slowly I maneuvered it away from its black captor and pulled it to me. I went into mud up to

14

my knees in the process but managed to reach it; and then it was but the work of a moment to beach it, empty out the water and set it safely with its stern on the bank. Then I pegged out our clothes in a patch of hot sunlight and went back to Patty.

She was lying on her back with her hands on her eyes, shielding them from the light. Apparently she had not seen me rescue the canoe. I glanced at it and just then saw the slimy mass in mid-bayou start sinking again.

"Daddy," she said drowsily, "what was that awful thing that sinked us?"

"What they call a sawyer," I said. "It's the water-logged butt of a cypress tree. The bottom is heavy and the top is light, and when the roots catch in something on the bottom the current pushes the top under. Then one of the branches rots and falls off, and the top end gets light again and floats up. Then the current will push it down again. It'll keep that up for weeks."

"Oh," she said. After a long, thoughtful pause she said, "Daddy—"

"What?"

"Cover me up." I grinned and tore down masses of moss with which I buried her. Her sleepy sigh sounded from under the pile. I lay down in the shade close by, switching lazily at mosquitoes.

I must have dozed for a while. I woke with a start, fumbling through my mind for the thing that had disturbed me. My first glance was at the pile of moss; all seemed well there. I turned my head. About eight inches from my face was a pair of feet.

I stared at them. They were bare and horny and incredibly scarred. Flat, too—splayed. The third toe of each foot was ever so much longer than any of the others. They were filthy. Attached to the feet was a scrawny pair of ankles; the rest was out of my range of

15

vision. I debated sleepily whether or not I had seen enough, suddenly realized that there was something not quite right about this, and bounced to my feet.

I found myself staring into the blazing eye of the most disgusting old hag that ever surpassed imagination. She looked like a Cartier illustration. Her one good eye was jaundiced and mad; long, slanted—feline. It wasn't until long afterward that I realized that her pupil was not round but slitted—not vertically like a cat's eyes, but horizontally. Her other eye looked like—well, I'd rather not say. It couldn't possibly have been of any use to her. Her nose would have been hooked if the tip were still on it. She was snaggle-toothed, and her fangs were orange. One shoulder was higher than the other, and the jagged lump on it spoke of a permanent dislocation. She had enough skin to adequately cover a side-show fat lady, but she couldn't have weighed more than eighty pounds or so. I never saw great swinging wattles on a person's upper arms before. She was clad in a feathered jigsaw of bird and small animal skins. She was diseased and filthy and—and evil.

And she spoke to me in the most beautiful contralto voice I have ever heard.

"How you get away from River Spider?" she demanded.

"River Spider?"

She pointed, and I saw the sawyer rising slowly from the bayou. "Oh—that." I found that if I avoided that baleful eye I got my speech back. I controlled an impulse to yell at her, chase her away. If Patty woke up and saw that face—

"What's it to you?" I asked quietly, just managing to keep my voice steady.

"I send River Spider for you," she said in her Cajun accent.

"Why?" If I could mollify her—she was manifestly

16

furious at something, and it seemed to be me—perhaps she'd go her way without waking the child.

"Because you mus' go!" she said. "This my countree. This swamp belong Séleen. Séleen belong this swamp. Wan man make *p'tit cabane* in bayou, Séleen *l'enchante*. Man die far away, smash."

"You mean you haunted the man who had my cabin built and he died?" I grinned. "Don't be silly."

"Man is dead, no?"

I nodded. "That don't cut ice with me, old lady. Now look—we aren't hurting your old swamp. We'll get out of it, sure; but we'll go when we're good and ready. You leave us alone and we'll sure as hell"—I shuddered, looking at her—"leave you alone."

"You weel go *now—ce jour!*" She screamed the last words, and the pile of moss behind me rustled suddenly.

"I won't go today or tomorrow or next week," I snapped. I stepped toward her threateningly. "Now beat it!"

She crouched like an animal, her long crooked hands half raised. From behind me the moss moved briskly, and Patty's voice said, "Daddy, what . . . oh. *Ohh!*"

That does it, I said to myself, and lunged at the old woman with some crazy idea of shoving her out of the clearing. She leaped aside like a jackrabbit and I tripped and fell on my two fists, which dug into my solar plexus agonizingly. I lay there mooing "uh! uh! u-u-uh!" trying to get some wind into my lungs, and finally managed to get an elbow down and heave myself over on my side. I looked, and saw Séleen crouched beside Patty. The kid sat there, white as a corpse, rigid with terror, while the old nightmare crooned to her in her lovely voice.

"*Ah! C'est une jolie jeune fille, ça! Ah, ma petite ma fleur douce, Séleen t'aime, trop, trop—*" and she put out her hand and stroked Patty's neck and shoulder.

When I saw the track of filth her hand left on the child's flesh, a white flame exploded in my head and dazzled me from inside. When I could see again I was standing beside Patty, the back of one hand aching and stinging; and Séleen was sprawled eight feet away, spitting out blood and yellow teeth and frightful curses.

"Go away." I whispered it because my throat was all choked up. "Get—out—of—here—before—I—kill you!"

She scrambled to her knees, her blazing eye filled with hate and terror, shook her fist and tottered swearing away into the heavy swamp growth.

When she had gone I slumped to the ground, drenched with sweat, cold outside, hot inside, weak as a newborn babe from reaction. Patty crawled to me, dropped her head in my lap, pressed the back of my hand to her face and sobbed so violently that I was afraid she would hurt herself. I lifted my hand and stroked her hair. "It's all right, now, Patty—don't be a little dope, now—come on," I said more firmly, lifting her face by its pointed chin and holding it until she opened her eyes. "Who's Yehudi?"

She gulped bravely. "Wh-who?" she gasped.

"The little man who turns on the light in the refrigerator when you open the door," I said. "Let's go find out what's for dinner."

"I . . . I—" She puckered all up the way she used to do when she slept in a bassinet—what I used to call "baby's slow burn." And then she wailed the same way. "I don' want dinno-o-o!"

I thumped her on the back, picked her up and dropped her on top of her dungarees. "Put them pants on," I said, "and be a man." She did, but she cried quietly until I shook her and said gently, "Stop it now. I didn't carry on like that when I was a little girl." I got

18

into my clothes and dumped her into the bow of the canoe and shoved off.

All the way back to the cabin I forced her to play one of our pet games. I would say something—anything—and she would try to say something that rhymed with it. Then it would be her turn. She had an extraordinary rhythmic sense, and an excellent ear.

I started off with "We'll go home and eat our dinners."

"An' Lord have mercy on us sinners," she cried. Then, "Let's see you find a rhyme for 'month'!"

"I bet I'll do it . . . jutht thith onth," I replied. "I guess I did it then, by cracky."

"Course you did, but then you're wacky. Top that, mister funny-lookin'!"

I pretended I couldn't, mainly because I couldn't, and she soundly kicked my shin as a penance. By the time we reached the cabin she was her usual self, and I found myself envying the resilience of youth. And she earned my undying respect by saying nothing to Anjy about the afternoon's events, even when Anjy looked us over and said, "Just look at you two filthy kids! What have you been doing—swimming in the bayou?"

"Daddy splashed me," said Patty promptly.

"And you had to splash him back. Why did he splash you?"

" 'Cause I spit mud through my teeth at him to make him mad," said my outrageous child.

"Patty!"

"Mea culpa," I said, hanging my head. " 'Twas I who spit the mud."

Anjy threw up her hands. "Heaven knows what sort of a woman Patty's going to grow up to be," she said, half angrily.

"A broad-minded and forgiving one like her lovely mother," I said quickly.

"Nice work, bud," said Patty.

Anjy laughed. "Outnumbered again. Come in and feed the face."

On my next trip into Minette I bought a sweet little S. & W. .38 and told Anjy it was for alligators. She was relieved.

I might have forgotten about the hag Séleen if it were not for the peculiar chain of incidents which had led to our being here. We had started with some vague idea of spending a couple of months in Natchez or New Orleans, but a gas station attendant had mentioned that there was a cabin in the swamps for rent very cheap down here. On investigation we found it not only unbelievably cheap, but deep in real taboo country. Not one of the natives, hardened swamp runners all, would go within a mile of it. It had been built on order for a very wealthy Northern gentleman who had never had a chance to use it, due to a swift argument he and his car had had one day when he turned out to pass a bridge. A drunken rice farmer told me that it was all the doing of the Witch of Minette, a semimythological local character who claimed possession of that corner of the country. I had my doubts, being a writer of voodoo stories and knowing therefore that witches and sech are nonsense.

After my encounter with Séleen I no longer doubted her authenticity as a horrid old nightmare responsible for the taboo. But she could rant, chant, and ha'nt from now till a week come Michaelmas—when *is* Michaelmas, anyway?—and never pry me loose from that cabin until I was ready to go. She'd have to fall back on enchantment to do it, too—of that I was quite, quite sure. I remembered her blazing eye as it had looked when I struck her, and I knew that she would never dare to come within my reach again. If she as much as came within my sight with her magics I had a little hocus-pocus of my own that I was sure was more powerful than anything she could dream up. I carried it strapped to my waist, in a holster, and while it couldn't call up any ghosts, it was pretty good at manufacturing 'em.

As for Patty, she bounced resiliently away from the episode. Séleen she dubbed the Witch of Endor, and used her in her long and involved games as an archvillain in place of Frankenstein's monster, Adolf Hitler, or Miss McCauley, her schoolteacher. Many an afternoon I watched her from the hammock on the porch, cooking up dark plots in the witch's behalf and then foiling them in her own cold-bloodedly childish way. Once or twice I had to put a stop to it, like the time I caught her hanging the Witch of Endor in effigy, the effigy being a rag doll, its poor throat cut with benefit of much red paint. Aside from these games she never mentioned Séleen, and I respected her for it. I saw to it that she didn't stray alone into the swamp and relaxed placidly into my role of watchful skeptic. It's nice to feel oneself superior to a credulous child.

Foolish, too. I didn't suspect a thing when Patty crept up behind me and hacked off a lock of my hair with my hunting knife. She startled me and I tumbled out of the hammock onto my ear as she scuttled off. I muttered imprecations at the little demon as I got back into the hammock, and then comforted myself by the reflection that I was lucky to have an ear to fall on—that knife was sharp.

A few minutes later Anjy came out to the porch. Anjy got herself that name because she likes to wear dresses with masses of tiny pleats and things high on her throat, and great big picture hats. So *ingenue* just naturally became Anjy. She is a beautiful woman with infinite faith and infinite patience, the proof of which being that: (a) she married me and, (b) she stayed married to me.

"Jon, what sort of crazy game is your child playing?" She always said "your child" when she was referring to something about Patty she didn't like.

"S'matter?"

"Why, she just whipped out that hog-sticker of yours and made off with a hank of my hair."

"No! Son of a gun! What's she doing—taking up barbering? She just did the same thing to me. Thought she was trying to scalp me and miscalculated, but I must have been wrong—she wouldn't miss twice in a row."

"Well, I want you to take that knife away from her," said Anjy. "It's dangerous."

I got out of the hammock and stretched. "Got to catch her first. Which way'd she go?"

After a protracted hunt I found Patty engaged in some childish ritual of her own devising. She pushed something into a cleft at the foot of a tree, backed off a few feet, and spoke earnestly. Neither of us could hear a word she said. Then she backed still farther away and squatted down on her haunches, watching the hole at the foot of the tree carefully.

Anjy clasped her hands together nervously, opened her mouth. I put my hands over it. "Let me take care of it," I whispered, and went out.

"Whatcha doin', bud?" I called to Patty as I came up. She started violently and raised one finger to her lips. "Catchin' rabbits?" I asked as loudly as I could without shouting. She gestured me furiously away. I went and sat beside her.

"Please, daddy," she said, "I'm making a magic. It won't work if you stay here. Just this once—please!"

"Nuts," I said bluntly. "I chased all the magic away when I moved here."

She tried to be patient. "Will you please go away? Oh, daddy. Daddy, PLEASE!"

It was rough but I felt I had to do it. I lunged for her, swept her up, and carried her kicking and squalling back to the cabin. "Sorry, kiddo, but I don't like the sort of game you're playing. You ought to trust your dad."

I meant to leave her with Anjy while I went out to confiscate that bundle of hair. Not that I believe in such nonsense. But I'm the kind of unsuperstitious apple that won't walk under a ladder *just in case* there's something in the silly idea. But Patty really began to throw a whingding, and there was nothing for me to do but to stand by until it had run its course. Patty was a good-natured child, and only good-natured children can work themselves up into that kind of froth. She screamed and she bit, and she accused us of spoiling everything and we didn't love her and she wished she was dead and why couldn't we leave her alone—"Let me alone," she shrieked, diving under the double bed and far beyond our reach. "Take your *hands* off me!" she sobbed when she was ten feet away from us and moving fast. And then her screams became wordless and agonized when we cornered her in the kitchen. We had to be rough to hold her, and her hysteria was agony to us. It took more than an hour for her fury to run its course and leave her weeping weak apologies and protestations of love into her mother's arms. Me, I was bruised outside and in, but inside it hurt the worst. I felt like a heel.

I went out then to the tree. I reached in the cleft for the hair but it was gone. My hand closed on something far larger, and I drew it out and stood up to look at it.

It was a toy canoe, perhaps nine inches long. It was an exquisite piece of work. It had apparently been carved painstakingly from a solid piece of cedar, so carefully that nowhere was the wood any more than an eighth of an inch thick. It was symmetrical and beauti- fully finished in brilliant colors. They looked to me like

23

vegetable stains—dyes from the swamp plants that grew so riotously all around us. From stem to stern the gunwales were pierced, and three strips of brilliant bark had been laced and woven into the close-set holes. Inside the canoe were four wooden spurs projecting from the hull, the end of each having a hole drilled through it, apparently for the purpose of lashing something inside.

I puzzled over it for some minutes, turning it over and over in my hands, feeling its velvet smoothness, amazed by its metrical delicacy. Then I laid it carefully on the ground and regarded the mysterious tree.

Leafless branches told me it was dead. I got down on my knees and rummaged deep into the hole between the roots. I couldn't begin to touch the inside wall. I got up again, circled the tree. A low branch projected, growing sharply upward close to the trunk before it turned and spread outward. And around it were tiny scuff marks in the bark. I pulled myself up onto the branch, cast about for a handhold to go higher. There was none. Puzzled, I looked down—and there, completely hidden from the ground, was a gaping hole leading into the hollow trunk!

I thrust my head into it and then clutched the limb with both arms to keep from tottering out of the tree. For that hole reeked with the most sickly, noisome smell I had encountered since . . . since Patty and I—

Séleen!

I dropped to the ground and backed away from the tree. The whole world seemed in tune with my revulsion. What little breeze there had been had stopped, and the swampland was an impossible painting in which only I moved.

Never taking my eyes off the tree, I went back step by step, feeling behind me until my hand touched the wall of the cabin. My gaze still riveted to the dead hole of the tree, I felt along the wall until I came to the kitchen door. Reaching inside, I found my ax and raced back. The blade was keen and heavy, and the haft of it felt good to me. The wood was rotten, honeycombed, and the clean blade bit almost noiselessly into it. *Thunk!* How dare she, I thought. What does she mean by coming so near us! *Thunk!* I prayed that the frightful old hag would try to fight, to flee, so that I could cut her down with many strokes. It was my first experience with the killer instinct and I found it good.

At the uppermost range of my vision I could see the trunk trembling with each stroke of the ax. Soon, now—soon! I grinned and my lips crackled; every other inch of my body was soaking wet. She who would fill Patty's clean young heart with her filthy doings! Four more strokes would do it; and then I remembered that skinny hand reaching out, touching Patty's flesh; and I went cold all over. I raised the ax and heard it hiss through the thick air; and my four strokes were one. Almost without resistance that mighty stroke swished into and through the shattered trunk. The hurtling ax head swung me around as the severed tree settled onto its stump. It fell, crushing its weight into the moist earth, levering itself over on its projecting root; and the thick bole slid toward me, turned from it as I was, off balance. It caught me on the thigh, kicking out at me like a sentient, vicious thing. I turned over and over in the air and landed squashily at the edge of the bayou. But I landed with my eyes on the tree, ready to crawl, if need be, after whatever left it.

Nothing left it. Nothing. There had been nothing there, then, but the stink of her foul body. I lay there weakly, weeping with pain and reaction. And when I looked up again I saw Séleen again—or perhaps it was a crazed vision. She stood on a knoll far up the bayou, and as I watched she doubled up with silent laughter.

Then she straightened and lifted her arm; and, dangling from her fingers, I saw the tiny bundle of hair. She laughed again though I heard not a sound. I knew then that she had seen every bit of it—had stood there grinning at my frantic destruction of her accursed tree. I lunged toward her, but she was far away, and across the water; and at my movement she vanished into the swamp.

I dragged myself to my feet and limped toward the cabin. I had to pass the tree, and as I did the little canoe caught my eye. I tucked it under my arm and crept back to the cabin. I tripped on the top step of the porch and fell sprawling, and I hadn't strength to rise. My leg was an agony, and my head spun and spun.

Then I was inside and Anjy was sponging off my head, and she laughed half hysterically when I opened my eyes. "Jon, Jon, beloved, what have you done? Who did this to you?"

"Who . . . heh!" I said weakly. "A damn fool, sweetheart. Me!" I got up and stood rockily. "How's Pat?"

"Sleeping," said Anjy. "Jon, what on earth is happening?"

"I don't know," I said slowly, and looked out through the window at the fallen tree. "Anjy, the kid took that hair she swiped and probably some of her own and poked it all into that tree I just cut down. It—seems important for me to get it back. Dunno why. It . . . anyway, I got out there as soon as we had Pat quieted, but the hair had disappeared in the meantime. All I found was this." I handed her the canoe.

She took it absently. "Pat told me her story. Of course it's just silly, but she says that for the past three days that tree has been talking to her. She says it sang to her and played with her. She's convinced it's a magic tree. She says it promised her a lovely present if she

26

would poke three kinds of hair into a hole at the roots, but if she told anyone the magic wouldn't work." Anjy looked down at the little canoe and her forehead puckered. "Apparently it worked," she whispered.

I couldn't comment without saying something about Séleen, and I didn't want that on Anjy's mind, so I turned my back on her and stood looking out into the thick wet heat of the swamp.

Behind me I heard Patty stir, shriek with delight as she saw the canoe. "My present . . . my pretty present! It was a *real* magic!" And Anjy gave it to her.

I pushed down an impulse to stop her. As long as Séleen had the hair the harm was done.

Funny, how suddenly I stopped being a skeptic.

The silence of the swamp was shattered by a great cloud of birds—birds of every imaginable hue and size, screaming and cawing and chuckling and whirring frantically. They startled me and I watched them for many minutes before it dawned on me that they were all flying one way. The air grew heavier after they had gone. Anjy came and stood beside me.

I have never seen such rain, never dreamed of it. It thundered on the shingles, buckshotted the leaves of the trees, lashed the mirrored bayou and the ground alike, so that the swamp was but one vast brown steam of puckered mud.

Anjy clutched my arm. "Jon, I'm frightened!" I looked at her and knew that it wasn't the rain that had whitened her lips, lit the fires of terror in her great eyes. "Something out there—*hates* us," she said simply.

I shook her off, threw a poncho over me. "Jon— you're not—"

"I got to," I gritted. I went to the door, hesitated, turned back and pressed the revolver into her hand. "I'll be all right," I said, and flung out into the storm. Anjy didn't try to stop me.

I knew I'd find the hag Séleen. I knew I'd find her unharmed by the storm, for was it not a thing of her own devising? And I knew I must reach her—quickly, before she used that bundle of hair. Why, and how did I know? Ask away. I'm still asking myself, and I have yet to find an answer.

I stumbled and floundered, keeping to the high ground, guided, I think, by my hate. After a screaming eternity I reached a freakish rocky knoll that thrust itself out of the swamp. It was cloven and cracked, full of passages and potholes; and from an opening high on one side I saw the guttering glare of firelight. I crept up the rough slope and peered within.

She crouched over the flames, holding something to her withered breast and crooning to it. The rock walls gathered her lovely, hateful voice and threw it to me clear and strong—to me and to the turgid bayou that seethed past the cleft's lower edge.

She froze as my eyes fell upon her, sensing my presence; but like many another animal she hadn't wit enough to look upward. In a moment she visibly shrugged off the idea, and she turned and slid and shambled down toward the bayou. Above her, concealed by the split rock, I followed her until we were both at the water's edge with only a four-foot stone rampart between us. I could have reached her easily then, but I didn't dare attack until I knew where she had hidden that bundle of hair.

The wind moaned, rose an octave. The rain came in knives instead of sheets. I flattened myself against the rock while Séleen shrank back into the shelter of the crevice. I will never know how long we were there, Séleen and I, separated by a few boulders, hate a tangible thing between us. I remember only a shrieking hell of wind and rubble, and then the impact of something

28

wet and writhing and whimpering against me. It had come rolling and tumbling down the rocky slope and it lodged against me. I was filled with horror until I realized that it sheltered me a little against the blast. I found the strength to turn and look at it finally. It was Patty.

I got her a little under me and stuck it out till the wind had done its work and was gone, and with it all the deafening noise—all but the rush of the bayou and Séleen's low chuckle.

"Daddy—" She was cut and battered. "I brought my little boat!" She held it up weakly.

"Yes, butch. Sure. That's dandy. Patty—what happened to mother?"

"She's back there," whimpered Patty. "The cabin sagged, like, an' began m-movin', an' then it just fell apart an' the bits all flew away. I couldn' find her so I came after you."

I lay still, not breathing. I think even my heart stopped for a little while.

Patty's whisper sounded almost happy. "Daddy–I–hurt–all–over—"

Anjy was gone then. I took my hatred instead, embraced it and let it warm me and give me life and hope and strength the way she used to. I crawled up the rock and looked over. I could barely see the hag, but she was there. Something out in the bayou was following the rhythmic movement of her arms. Something evil, tentacled, black. Her twisted claws clutched a tiny canoe like the one she had left in the tree for Patty. And she sang:

"River Spider, black and strong,
Folks 'bout here have done me wrong.
Here's a gif' I send to you,
Got some work for you to do.

29

"If Anjy-woman miss the flood,
River Spider, drink her blood.
Little one was good to me,
Drown her quick and let her be.

"River Spider, Jon you know,
Kill that man, and—kill—him—slow!"

And Séleen bent and set the canoe on the foaming brown water. Our hair was tied inside it.

Everything happened fast then. I dived from my hiding place behind and above her, and as I did so I sensed that Patty had crept up beside me, and that she had seen and heard it all. And some strange sense warned Séleen, for she looked over her crooked shoulder, saw me in midair, and leaped into the bayou. I had the terrified, malevolent gleam of her single eye full in my face, but I struck only hard rock, and for me even that baleful glow went out.

Patty sat cross-legged with my poor old head in her lap. It was such a gray morning that the wounds on her face and head looked black to me. I wasn't comfortable, because the dear child was rolling my head back and forth frantically in an effort to rouse me. The bones in my neck creaked as she did it and I knew they could hear it in Scranton, Pennsylvania. I transmitted a cautionary syllable but what she received was a regular houn'-dawg howl.

"Owoo! Pat—"

"Daddy! Oh, you're awake!" She mercifully stopped gyrating the world about my tattered ears.

"What happened?" I moaned, half sitting up. She was so delighted to see my head move that she scrambled out from under so that when the ache inside it pounded it back down, it landed stunningly on the rock.

"Daddy darling, I'm sorry. But you got to stop layin' around like that. It's time to get up!"

"Uh. How you know?"

"I'm hungry, that's how, so there."

I managed to sit up this time. I began to remember things and they hurt so much that the physical pain didn't matter any more. "Patty! We've got to get back to the cabin!"

She puckered up. I tried to grin at her and she tried to grin back, and there is no more tragedy left in the world for me after having seen that. I did a sort of upward totter and got what was left of my feet and legs under me. Both of us were a mess, but we could navigate.

We threaded our way back over a new, wrecked landscape. It was mostly climbing and crawling and once when Patty slipped and I reached for her I knocked the little canoe out of her hand. She actually broke and ran to pick it up. "Daddy! You got to be careful of this!"

I groaned. It was the last thing in the world I ever wanted to see. But then—Anjy had said that she should have it. And when she next dropped it I picked it up and handed it back to her. And then snatched it again.

"Patty! What's this?" I pointed to the little craft's cargo: a tiny bundle of hair.

"That's the little bag from the tree, silly."

"But how . . . where . . . I thought—"

"I made a magic," she said with finality. "Now please, daddy, don't stand here and talk. We have to get back to . . . y-you know."

If you don't mind, I won't go into detail about how we dragged trees and rubbish away to find what was left of our cabin, and how we came upon the pathetic little heap of shingles and screening and furniture and how, wedged in the firm angle of two mortised two-by-fours,

31

we found Anjy. What I felt when I lifted her limp body away from the rubble, when I kissed her pale lips—that is mine to remember. And what I felt when those lips returned my kiss—oh, so faintly and so tenderly—that, too, is mine.

We rested, the three of us, for five days. I found part of our store of canned goods and a fishing line, though I'm sorry now that we ate any of the fish, after what happened. And when the delirium was over, I got Patty's part of the story. I got it piecemeal, out of sequence, and only after the most profound cross-questioning. But the general drift was this:

She had indeed seen that strange performance in the rocky cleft by the bayou; but what is more, by her childish mysticism, she understood it. At least, her explanation is better than anything I could give. Patty was sure that the River Spider that had attacked us that time in the bayou was sent by Séleen, to whom she always referred as the Witch of Endor. "She did it before, daddy, I jus' betcha. But she didn't have anythin' strong enough for to put on the canoe." I have no idea what she did use—flies, perhaps, or frogs or crayfish. "She hadda have some part of us to make the magic, an' she made me get it for her. She was goin' to put that li'l' ol' hair ball in a canoe, an' if a River Spider caught it then the Spider would get us, too."

When I made that crazed leap for the old woman she had nowhere to go but into the bayou. Pat watched neither of us. She watched the canoe. She always claimed that she hooked it to shore with a stick, but I have a hunch that the little idiot plunged in after it. "They was one o' those big black sawyer things right there," she said, "an' it almos' catched the canoe. I had a lot of trouble." I'll bet she did.

"You know," she said pensively, "I was mad at that ol' Witch of Endor. That was a mean thing she tried to do to us. So I did the same thing to her. I catched the ugliest thing I could find—all crawly and nasty an' bad like the Witch of Endor. I found a nice horrid one, too, you betcha. An' I tied him into my canoe with your shoelaces, daddy. You di'n' say not to. An' I singed to it:

> 'Ol' Witch of Endor is your name,
> An' you an' Witchie is the same;
> Don't think it's a game.' "

She showed me later what sort of creature she had caught for her little voodoo boat. Some call it a mud puppy and some call it a hellbender, but it is without doubt the homeliest thing ever created. It is a sort of aquatic salamander, anywhere from three inches to a foot and a half in length. It has a porous, tubercular skin with two lateral streamers of skin on each side; and these are always ragged and torn. The creature always looks as if it is badly hurt. It has almost infinitesimal fingered legs, and its black shoe-button eyes are smaller than the head of a hatpin. For the hag Séleen there could be no better substitute.

"Then," said Patty complacently, "I singed that song the way the Witch of Endor did:

> 'River Spider, black an' strong,
> Folks 'bout here have done me wrong.
> Here's a gif' I send to you,
> Got some work for you to do.'

"The rest of the verse was silly," said Pat, "but I had to think real fast for a rhyme for 'Witch of Endor' an' I used the first thing that I could think of quicklike. It was somepin I read on your letters, daddy, an' it was silly."

And that's all she would say for the time being. But I do remember the time she called me quietly down to the bayou and pointed out a sawyer to me, because it was the day before Carson came in a power launch from Minette to see if we had survived the hurricane; and Carson came six days after the big blow. Patty made absolutely sure that her mother was out of hearing, and then drew me by the hand down to the water's edge. "Daddy," she said, "we got to keep this from mother on account of it would upset her," and she pointed.

Three or four black twisted branches showed on the water, and as I watched they began to rise. A huge sawyer, the biggest I'd ever seen, reared up and up—and tangled in its coils was a . . . a *something*.

Séleen had not fared well, tangled in the whips of the River Spider under water for five days, in the company of all those little minnows and crawfish.

Patty regarded it critically while my stomach looped itself around violently and finally lodged between my spine and the skin of my back. "She ain't pretty a-*tall!*" said my darling daughter. "She's even homelier'n a mud puppy, I betcha."

As we walked back toward the lean-to we had built, she prattled on in this fashion: "Y'know, daddy, that was a real magic. I thought my verse was a silly one but I guess it worked out right after all. Will you laugh if I tell you what it was?"

I said I did not feel like laughing.

"Well," said Patty shyly, "I said:

'Spider, kill the Witch of Endor.
If five days lapse, return to sender.' "

That's my daughter.

THE MARTIAN
AND THE MORON

MARTIAN SIG
23 22 21 20 19 18 17

In 1924, when I was just a pup, my father was a thing currently known as a "radio bug." These creatures were wonderful. They were one part fanatic, one part genius, a dash of childlike wonderment, and two buckets full of trial-and-error. Those were the days when you could get your picture in the paper for building a crystal set in something smaller and more foolish than the character who had his picture in the paper the day before. My father had his picture in there for building a "set" on a pencil eraser with a hunk of galena in the top and about four thousand turns of No. 35 enamelled wire wrapped around it. When they came around to take his picture he dragged out another one built into a peanut. Yes, a real peanut which brought in WGBS, New York. (You see, I really do remember.) They wanted to photograph that too, but Dad thought it would be a little immodest for him to be in the paper twice. So they took Mother's picture with it. The following week they ran both pictures, and Dad got two letters from other radio bugs saying his eraser radio wouldn't work and Mother got two hundred and twenty letters forwarded from the paper, twenty-six of which contained proposals of marriage. (Of course Mother was a YL and not an OW then.)

Oddly enough, Dad never did become a radio ham. He seemed satisfied to be the first in the neighborhood to own a set, then to build a set—(after the spiderweb coil phase he built and operated a one-tube regenerative set which featured a UX-11 detector and a thing called a vario-coupler which looked like a greasy fist within a lacquered hand, and reached his triumph when he hooked it into a forty-'leven-pound "B-eliminator" and ran it right out of the socket like a four-hundred-dollar "electric" radio) and first in the state to be on the receiving end of a court-order restraining him from using his equipment (every time he touched the tuning dials—three—the neighboring radios with which Joneses were keeping up with each other, began howling unmercifully). So for a time he left his clutter of forms and wire and solder-spattered "bathtub" condensers shoved to the back of his cellar workbench, and went back to stuffing field mice and bats, which had been his original hobby. I think Mother was glad, though she hated the smells he made down there. That was after the night she went to bed early with the cramps, and he DX'd WLS in Chicago at 4:30 one morning with a crystal set, and wanted to dance. (He learned later that he had crossed aerials with Mr. Bohackus next door, and had swiped Mr. Bohackus' fourteen-tube Atwater-Kent signal right out of Mr. Bohackus' gooseneck megaphone speaker. Mr. Bohackus was just as unhappy as Mother to hear about this on the following morning. They had both been up all night.)

Dad never was one to have his leg pulled. He got very sensitive about the whole thing, and learned his lesson so well that when the last great radio fever took him, he went to another extreme. Instead of talking his progress all over the house and lot, he walled himself up. During the late war I ran up against security regulations—and who didn't—but they never bothered me. I had my training early.

He got that glint in his eyes after grunting loudly over

the evening paper one night. I remember Mother's asking him about it twice, and I remember her sigh—her famous "here we go again" sigh—when he didn't answer. He leapt up, folded the paper, got out his keys, opened the safe, put the paper in it, locked the safe, put his keys away, looked knowingly at us, strode out of the room, went down into the cellar, came up from the cellar, took out his keys, opened the safe, took out the paper, closed the safe, looked knowingly at us again, said, "Henry, your father's going to be famous," and went down into the cellar.

Mother said, "I knew it. I *knew* it! I should have thrown the paper away. Or torn out that page."

"What's he going to make, Mother?" I asked.

"Heaven knows," she sighed. "Some men are going to try to get Mars on the radio."

"Mars? You mean the star?"

"It isn't a star, dear, it's a planet. They've arranged to turn off all the big radio stations all over the world for five minutes every hour so the men can listen to Mars. I suppose your father thinks he can listen too."

"Gee," I said, "I'm going down and—"

"You're going to do no such thing," said Mother firmly. "Get yourself all covered with that nasty grease he uses in his soldering, and stay up until all hours! It's almost bedtime. And—Henry—"

"Yes, Mother?"

She put her hands on my shoulders. "Listen to me, darling. People have been—ah—teasing your father." She meant Mr. Bohackus. "Don't ask him any questions about this if he doesn't want to talk, will you, darling? Promise?"

"All right, Mother." She was a wise woman.

Dad bought a big shiny brass padlock for his workshop in the cellar, and every time Mother mentioned the cellar, or the stars, or radio to him in any connection, he would just smile knowingly at her. It drove her wild. She didn't like the key, either. It was a big brass key, and he wore it on a length of rawhide shoelace tied around his neck. He wore it day and night. Mother said it was lumpy. She also said it was dangerous, which he denied, even after the time down at Roton Point when we were running Mr. Bohackus' new gasoline-driven ice cream freezer out on the beach. Dad leaned over to watch it working. He said, "This is the way to get things done, all right. I can't wait to get into that ice cream," and next thing we knew he was face down in the brine and flopping like a banked trout. We got him out before he drowned or froze. He was bleeding freely about the nose and lips, and Mr. Bohackus was displeased because Dad's key had, in passing through the spur-gears in which it had caught, broken off nine teeth. That was six more than Dad lost, but it cost much more to fix Dad's and showed, Mother said, just how narrow-minded Mr. Bohackus was.

Anyway, Dad never would tell us what he was doing down in the cellar. He would arrive home from work with mysterious packages and go below and lock them up before dinner. He would eat abstractedly and disappear for the whole evening. Mother, bless her, bore it with fortitude. As a matter of fact, I think she encouraged it. It was better than the previous fevers, when she had to sit for hours listening to crackling noises and organ music through big, heavy, magnetic earphones—or else. At least she was left to her own devices while all this was going on. As for me, I knew when I wasn't needed, and, as I remember, managed to fill my life quite successfully with clock movements, school, and baseball, and ceased to wonder very much.

About the middle of August Dad began to look frantic. Twice he worked right through the night, and though he went to the office on the days that followed,

I doubt that he did much. On August 21—I remember the date because it was the day before my birthday, and I remember that it was a Thursday because Dad took the next day off for a "long weekend," so *it* must have been Friday—the crisis came. My bedtime was nine o'clock. At nine-twenty Dad came storming up from the cellar and demanded that I get my clothes on instantly and go out and get him two hundred feet of No. 27 silk-covered wire. Mother laid down the law and was instantly overridden. "The coil! The one coil I haven't finished!" he shouted hysterically. "Six thousand meters, and I have to run out of it. *Get* your clothes on this instant, Henry, number twenty-seven wire. Just control yourself this once Mother and you can have Henry stop standing there with your silly eyes bulging and get dressed you can have any hat on Fifth Avenue *hurry!*"

I hurried. Dad gave me some money and a list of places to go to, told me not to come back until I'd tried every one of them, and left the house with me. I went east, he went west. Mother stood on the porch and wrung her hands.

I got home about twenty after ten, weary and excited, bearing a large metal spool of wire. I put it down triumphantly while Mother caught me up and felt me all over as if she had picked me up at the foot of a cliff. She looked drawn. Dad wasn't home yet.

After she quieted down a little she took me into the kitchen and fed me some chocolate-covered doughnuts. I forget what we talked about, if we talked, but I do remember that the cellar door was ajar, and at the bottom of the steps I could see a ray of yellow light. "Mother," I said, "you know what? Dad ran out and left his workshop open."

She went to the door and looked down the stairs.

"Darling," she said after a bit, "Uh—wouldn't you like to—I mean, if he—"

41

I caught on quick. "I'll look. Will you stay up here and bump on the floor if he comes?"

She looked relieved, and nodded. I ran down the steps and cautiously entered the little shop.

Lined up across the bench were no less than six of the one-tube receivers which were the pinnacle of Dad's electronic achievement. The one at the end was turned back-to-front and had its rear shielding off; a naked coil-form dangled unashamedly out.

And I saw what had happened to the two alarm clocks which had disappeared from the bedrooms in the past six weeks. It happened that then, as now, clocks were my passion, and I can remember clearly the way he had set up pieces of the movements.

He had built a frame about four feet long on a shelf at right angles to the bench on which the radios rested. At one end of the frame was a clock mechanism designed to turn a reel on which was an endless band of paper tape about eight inches wide. The tape passed under a hooded camera—Mother's old Brownie—which was on a wall-bracket and aimed downward, on the tape. Next in line, under the tape, were six earphones, so placed that their diaphragms (the retainers had been removed) just touched the under side of the tape. And at the other end of the frame was the movement from the second alarm clock. The bell-clapper hung downwards, and attached to it was a small container of black powder.

I went to the first clock mechanism and started it by pulling out the toothpick Dad had jammed in the gears. The tape began to move. I pulled the plug on the other movement. The little container of black powder began to shake like mad and, through small holes, laid an even film of the powder over the moving tape. It stopped when it had put down about ten inches of it. The black line moved slowly across until it was over the phones.

The magnets smeared the powder, which I recognized thereby as iron fillings. Bending to peer under the tape, I saw that the whole bank of phones was levered to move downward a half an inch away from the tape. The leads from each of the six phones ran to a separate receiver.

I stood back and looked at this goldberg and scratched my head, then shook same and carefully blew away the black powder on the tape, rewound the movements, refilled the containers from a jar which stood on the bench, and put the toothpick back the way I had found it.

I was halfway up the stairs when the scream of burning rubber on the street outside coincided with Mother's sharp thumping on the floor. I got to her side as she reached the front window. Dad was outside paying off a taxi-driver. He never touched the porch steps at all, and came into the house at a dead run. He had a package under his arm.

"Fred!" said Mother.

"Can't stop now," he said, skidding into the hallway. "Couldn't get 27 anywhere. Have to use 25. Probably won't work. Everything happens to me absolutely everything." He headed for the kitchen.

"I got you a whole reel of 27, Dad."

"Don't bother me now. Tomorrow," he said, and thumped downstairs. Mother and I looked at each other. Mother sighed. Dad came bounding back up the stairs. "You *what*?"

"Here." I got the wire off the hall table and gave it to him. He snatched it up, hugged me, swore I'd get a bicycle for my birthday (he made good on that, and on Mother's Fifth Avenue hat, too, by the way) and dove back downstairs.

We waited around for half an hour and then Mother

43

sent me to bed. "You poor baby," she said, but I had the idea it wasn't me she was sorry for.

Now I'd like to be able to come up with a climax to all this, but there wasn't one. Not for years and years. Dad looked, the next morning, as if he had been up all night again—which he had—and as if he were about to close his fingers on the Holy Grail. All that day he would reappear irregularly, pace up and down, compare his watch with the living-room clock and the hall clock, and sprint downstairs again. That even went on during my birthday dinner. He had Mother call up the office and say he had Twonk's disease, a falling of the armpits (to whom do I owe this gem? Not my gag) and kept up his peregrinations all that night and all the following day until midnight. He fell into bed, so Mother told me, at one ayem Sunday morning and slept right through until suppertime. He still maintained a dazzling silence about his activities. For the following four months he walked around looking puzzled. For a year after that he looked resigned. Then he took up stuffing newts and moles. The only thing he ever said about the whole crazy business was that he was born to be disappointed, but at least, this time, no one could rib him about it. Now I'm going to tell you about Cordelia.

This happened the above-mentioned years and years later. The blow-off was only last week, as a matter of fact. I finished school and went into business with Dad and got mixed up in the war and all that. I didn't get married, though. Not yet. That's what I want to tell you about.

I met her at a party at Ferris's. I was stagging it, but I don't think it would have made any difference if I had brought someone; when I saw Cordelia I was, to understate the matter, impressed.

She came in with some guy I didn't notice at the time and, for all I know, haven't seen since. She slipped out of her light wrap with a single graceful movement; the sleeve caught in her bracelet, and she stood there, full profile, in the doorway, both arms straight and her hands together behind her as she worried the coat free, and I remember the small explosion in my throat as my indrawn breath and my gasp collided. Her hair was dark and lustrous, parted widely in a winging curve away from her brow. There were no pins in it; it shadowed the near side of her face as she bent her head and turned it down and toward the room. The cord of her neck showed columnar and clean. Her lips were parted ever so little, and showed an amused chagrin. Her lashes all but lay on her cheek. They stayed there when she was free and turned to face the room, for she threw her head back and up, flinging her hair behind her. She came across to my side of the party and sat down while the Thing who was with her went anonymously away to get her a drink and came unnoticeably back.

I said to myself, "Henry, my boy, stop staring at the lady. You'll embarrass her."

She turned to me just then and gave me a small smile. Her eyes were widely spaced, and the green of deep water. "I don't mind, really," she said, and I realized I had spoken aloud. I took refuge in a grin, which she answered, and then her left eyelid dropped briefly, and she looked away. It was a wink, but such a slight, tasteful one! If she had used both eyelids, it wouldn't have been a wink at all; she would have looked quickly down and up again. It was an understanding, we're-together little wink, a tactful, gracious, wonderful, marvellous, do you begin to see how I felt?

The party progressed. I once heard somebody decline an invitation to one of Ferris's parties on the grounds that he had *been* to one of Ferris's parties. I had to be a little more liberal than that, but tonight I could see the point. It was because of Cordelia. She sat still, her chin on the back of her hand, her fingers curled against her white throat, her eyes shifting lazily from one point in the room to another. She did not belong in this conglomeration of bubbleheads. Look at her—part Sphinx, part Pallas Athene . . .

Ferris was doing his Kasbah act, with the bath towel over his head. He will next imitate Clyde McCoy's trumpet, I thought. He will then inevitably put that lampshade on his head, curl back his upper lip, and be a rickshaw coolie. Following which he will do the adagio dance in which he will be too rough with some girl who will be too polite to protest at his big shiny wet climaxing kiss.

I looked at Cordelia and I looked at Ferris and I thought, no, Henry; that won't do. I drew a deep breath, leaned over to the girl, and said, "If there were a fire in here, do you know the quickest way out?"

She shook her head expectantly.

"I'll show you," I said, and got up. She hesitated a charming moment, rose from her chair as with helium, murmured something polite to her companion, and came to me.

There were French doors opening on to the wide terrace porch which also served the front door. We went through them. The air was fragrant and cool, and there was a moon. She said nothing about escaping from fires. The French doors shut out most of the party noises—enough so that we could hear night sounds. We looked at the sky. I did not touch her.

After a bit she said in a voice of husky silver,

> "Is the moon tired? she looks so pale
> Within her misty veil:
> She scales the sky from east to west,
> And takes no rest.

46

> *"Before the coming of the night*
> *The moon shows papery white;*
> *Before the drawing of the day*
> *She fades away."*

It was simple and it was perfect. I looked at her in wonderment. "Who wrote that?"

"Christina Rosset-ti," she said meticulously, looking at the moon. The light lay on her face like dust, and motes of it were caught in the fine down at the side of her jaw.

"I'm Henry Folwell and I know a place where we could talk for about three hours if we hurry," I said, utterly amazed at myself; I don't generally operate like this.

She looked at the moon and me, the slight deep smile playing subtlely with her lips. "I'm Cordelia Thorne, and I couldn't think of it," she said. "Do you think you could get my wrap without anyone seeing? It's a—"

"I know what it's," I said, sprinting. I went in through the front door, located her coat, bunched it up small, skinned back outside, shook it out and brought it to her. "You're still here," I said incredulously.

"Did you think I'd go back inside?"

"I thought the wind, or the gods, or my alarm clock would take you away."

"You said that beautifully," she breathed, as I put the coat around her shoulders. I thought I had too. I notched her high up in my estimation as a very discerning girl.

We went to a place called the Stroll Inn where a booth encased us away from all of the world and most of its lights. It was wonderful. I think I did most of the talking. I don't remember all that passed between us but I remember these things, and remember them well.

I was talking about Ferris and the gang he had over there every Saturday night; I checked myself, shrugged, and said, "Oh well. *Chacun à son goût,* as they say, which means—"

And she stopped me. "Please. Don't translate. It couldn't be phrased as well in English."

I had been about to say "—which means Jack's son has the gout." I felt sobered and admiring, and just sat and glowed at her.

And then there was that business with the cigarette. She stared at it as it lay in the ashtray, followed it with her gaze to my lips and back as I talked, until I asked her about it.

She said in a soft, shivery voice, "I feel just like that cigarette."

I, of course, asked her why.

"You pick it up," she whispered, watching it. "You enjoy some of it. You put it down and let it—smolder. You like it, but you hardly notice it. . . ."

I thereupon made some incredibly advanced protestations.

And there was the business about her silence—a long, faintly amused, inward-turning silence. I asked her what she was thinking about.

"I was ruminating," she said, in a self-depreciating, tragic voice, "on the futility of human endeavor," and she smiled. And when I asked her what she meant, she laughed aloud and said, "Don't you know?" And I said, "Oh. That," and worshipped her. She was deep. I'd have dropped dead before I'd have admitted I didn't know what specifically she was driving at.

And books. Music, too. When we were at the stage where I had both her hands and for minutes on end our foreheads were so close together you couldn't have slipped a swizzle stick between them, I murmured, "We seem to think so much alike. . . . Tell me, Cordelia, have you read Cabell?"

She said, "Well, really," in such a tone that, so help me, I apologized. "Lovely stuff." I said, recovering.

She looked reminiscently over my shoulder, smiling her small smile. "So lovely."

"I knew you'd read him," I said, struck with sweet thunder. "And Faulkner—have you read any of Faulkner?"

She gave me a pitying smile. I gulped and said, "Ugly, isn't it?"

She looked reminiscently over my other shoulder, a tiny frown flickering in her flawless brow. "So ugly," she said.

In between times she listened importantly to my opinions on Faulkner and Cabell. And Moussorgsky and Al Jolson. She was wonderful, and we agreed in everything.

And, hours later, when I stood with her at her door, I couldn't do a thing but shuffle my feet and haul on the hem of my jacket. She gave me her hand gravely, and I think she stopped breathing. I said, "Uh, well," and couldn't improve on it. She swept her gaze from my eyes to my mouth, from side to side across my forehead; it was a tortured "No!" her slightly turning head articulated, and her whole body moved minutely with it. She let go my hand, turned slowly toward the door, and then, with a cry which might have been a breath of laughter and which might have been a sob, she pirouetted back to me and kissed me—not on the mouth, but in the hollow at the side of my neck. My fuse blew with a snap and a bright light and, as it were, incapacitated my self-starter. She moved deftly then, and to my blurred vision, apparently changed herself into a closed door. I must have stood looking at that door for twenty minutes before I turned and walked dazedly home.

I saw her five more times. Once it was a theatre party, and we all went to her house afterward, and she showed great impartiality. Once it was a movie, and who should we run into afterward but her folks. Very nice people. I liked them and I think they liked me. Once it was the circus; we stayed very late, dancing at a pavilion, and yet the street was still crowded outside her home when we arrived there, and a handshake had to do. The fourth time was at a party to which I went alone because she had a date that night. It devolved that the date was the same party. The way she came in did things to me. It wasn't the fact that she was with somebody else; I had no claim on her, and the way she acted with me made me feel pretty confident. It was the way she came in, slipping out of her wrap, which—caught on her—bracelet, freezing her in a profile while framed in the doorway. . . . I don't want to think about it. Not now.

I did think about it; I left almost immediately so that I could. I went home and slumped down in an easy chair and convinced myself about coincidences, and was almost back to normal when Dad came into the room.

"*Argh!*" he said.

I leapt out of the chair and helped him to pick himself up off the middle of the rug. "Blast it, boy," he growled, "Why don't you turn on a light? What are you doing home? I thought you were out with your goddess. Why can't you pick up your big bony feet, or at least leave them somewhere else besides in the doorway of a dark room?" He dusted off his knees. He wasn't hurt. It's a deep-piled rug with two cushions under it. "You're a howling menace. Kicking your father." Dad had mellowed considerably with the years. "What's the matter with you anyhow? She do you something? Or are you beginning to have doubts?" He wore glasses now, but he saw plenty. He'd ribbed me about Cordelia as can only a man who can't stand ribbing himself.

"It was a lousy party," I said.

He turned on a light, "What's up, Henry?"

"Nothing," I said. "Absolutely nothing. I haven't had a fight with her, if that's what you're digging for."

"All right, then," he said, picking up the paper.

"There's nothing wrong with her. She's one of the most wonderful people I know, that's all."

"Sure she is." He began to read the paper.

"She's deep, too. A real wise head, she is. You wouldn't expect to find that in somebody as young as that. Or as good-looking." I wished he would put his eyebrows down.

"She's read everything worth reading," I added as he turned a page a minute later.

"Marvelous," he said flatly.

I glared at him. "What do you mean by that?" I barked. "What's marvellous?"

He put the paper down on his knee and smoothed it. His voice was gentle. "Why Cordelia, of course. I'm not arguing with you, Henry."

"Yes you—well, anyway, you're not saying what you think."

"You don't want to hear what I think."

"I know what I want!" I flared.

He crackled the paper nervously. "My," he said as if to himself, "this is worse than I thought." Before I could interrupt, he said, "Half of humanity doesn't know what it wants or how to find out. The other half knows what it wants, hasn't got it, and is going crazy trying to convince itself that it already has it."

"Very sound," I said acidly. "Where do you peg me?"

He ignored this. "The radio commercial which annoys me most," he said with apparent irrelevancy, "is

51

the one which begins, 'There are some things so good they don't have to be improved.' That annoys me because there isn't a thing on God's green earth which couldn't stand improvement. By the same token, if you find something which looks to you as if it's unimprovable, then either it's a mirage or you're out of your mind."

"What has that to do with Cordelia?"

"Don't snap at me, son," Dad said quietly. "Let's operate by the rule of reason here. Or must I tear your silly head off and stuff it down your throat?"

I grinned in spite of myself. "Reason prevails, Dad. Go on."

"Now, I've seen the girl, and you're right; she's striking to look at. Extraordinary. In the process of raving about that you've also told me practically every scrap of conversation you've ever had with her."

"I have?"

"You're like your mother; you talk too much," he smiled. "Don't get flustered. It was good to listen to. Shows you're healthy. But I kept noticing one thing in these mouthings—all she's read, all the languages she understands, all the music she likes—and that is that you have never quoted her yet as saying a single declarative sentence. You have never quoted her as opening a conversation, changing the subject, mentioning something you both liked *before* you mentioned it, or having a single idea that you didn't like." He shrugged. "Maybe she is a good listener. They're—"

"Now wait a minute—"

"—They're rare anywhere in the world, especially in this house," he went on smoothly. "Put your hands back in your pockets, Henry, or sit on 'em until I've finished. Now, I'm not making any charges about Cordelia. There aren't any. She's wonderful. That's the trouble. For Pete's sake get her to make a flat statement."

"She has, plenty of times," I said hotly. "You just don't know her! Why, she's the most—"

He put up his hands and turned his head as if I were aiming a bucket of water at him. "Shut up!" he roared. I shut. "Now," he said, "listen to me. If you're right, you're right and there's no use defending anything. If you're wrong you'd better find it out soon before you get hurt. But I don't want to sit here and watch the process. I know how you tick, Henry. By gosh, I ought to. You're like I was. You and I, we get a hot idea and go all out for it, all speed and no control. We spill off at the mouth until we have the whole world watching, and when the idea turns sour the whole world gets in its licks, standing around laughing. Keep your beautiful dreams to yourself. If they don't pan out you can always kick yourself effectively enough, without having every wall-eyed neighbor helping you."

A picture of Mr. Bohackus with the protruding china-blue eyes, our neighbor of along ago, crossed my mind, and I chuckled.

"That's better, Henry," said Dad. "Listen. When a fellow gets to be a big grown-up man, which is likely to happen at any age, or never, he learns to make a pile of his beloved failures and consign them to the flames, and never think of them again. But it ought to be a private bonfire."

It sounded like sense, particularly the part about not having to defend something if it was right enough to be its own defense. I said, "Thanks, Dad. I'll have to think. I don't know if I agree with you. . . . I'll tell you something, though. If Cordelia turned out to be nothing but a phonograph, I'd consider it a pleasure to spend the rest of my life buying new records for her."

"That'd be fine," said Dad, "if it was what you wanted. I seriously doubt that it is just now."

53

"Of course it isn't. Cordelia's all woman and has a wonderful mind, and that's what I want."

"Bless you, my children," Dad said, and grinned.

I knew I was right, and that Dad was simply expressing a misguided caution. The Foxy Grandpa routine, I thought, was a sign of advancing age. Dad sure was changed since the old days. On the other hand, he hadn't been the same since the mysterious frittering-out of his mysterious down-cellar project. I stopped thinking about Dad, and turned my mind to my own troubles.

I had plenty of time to think; I couldn't get a Saturday date with her for two weeks, and I wanted this session to run until it was finished with no early curfews. Not, as I have said, that I had any doubts. Far from it. All the same, I made a little list . . .

I don't think I said ten words to her until we were three blocks from her house. She quite took my breath away. She was wearing a green suit with surprising lapels that featured her fabulous profile and made me ache inside. I had not known that I was so hungry for a sight of her, and now she was more than a sight, now her warm hand had slipped into mine as we walked. "Cordelia . . ." I whispered.

She turned her face to me, and showed me the tender tuggings in the corners of her mouth. She made an interrogative sound, like a sleepy bird.

"Cordelia," I said thickly. It all came out in a monotone. "I didn't know I could miss anybody so much. There's been a hollow place in my eyes, wherever I looked; it had no color and it was shaped like you. Now you fill it and I can see again."

She dropped her eyes, and her smile was a thing to see. "You said that beautifully," she breathed.

I hadn't thought of that. What I had said was squeezed out of me like toothpaste out of a tube, with the same uniformity between what came out and what was still inside.

"We'll go to the Stroll Inn," I said. It was where we met. We didn't meet at the party. We just saw each other there. We met in that booth.

She nodded gravely and walked with me, her face asleep, its attention turned inward, deeply engaged. It was not until we turned the corner on Winter Street and faced the Inn that I thought of my list; and when I did, I felt a double, sickening impact—first, one of shame that I should dare to examine and experiment with someone like this, second, because item 5 on that list was "You said that beautifully . . ."

The Stroll Inn, as I indicated before, has all its lights, practically, on the outside. Cordelia looked at me thoughtfully as we walked into their worming neon field. "Are you all right?" she asked. "You look pale."

"How can you tell?" I asked, indicating the lights, which flickered and switched, orange and green and blue and red. She smiled appreciatively, and two voices spoke within me. One said joyfully, " 'You look pale' is a declarative statement." The other said angrily, "You're hedging. And by the way, what do you suppose that subtle smile is covering up, if anything?" Both voices spoke forcefully, combining in a jumble which left me badly confused. We went in and found a booth and ordered dinner. Cordelia said with pleasure that she would have what I ordered.

Over the appetizer I said, disliking myself intensely. "Isn't this wonderful? All we need is a moon. Can't you see it, hanging up there over us?"

She laughed and looked up, and sad sensitivity came into her face. I closed my eyes, waiting.

" *Is the moon tired? she looks so pale*—' " she began.

I started to chew again. I think it was marinated herring, and very good too, but at the moment it tasted like cold oatmeal with a dash of warm lard. I called the waiter and ordered a double rum and soda. As he turned away I called him back and asked him to bring a bottle instead. I needed help from somewhere, and pouring it out of a bottle seemed a fine idea at the time.

Over the soup I asked her what she was thinking about. "I was ruminating," she said in a self-depreciating, tragic voice, "on the futility of human endeavor." Oh, brother, me too, I thought. Me too.

Over the dessert we had converse again, the meat course having passed silently. We probably presented a lovely picture, the two of us wordlessly drinking in each other's presence, the girl radiating an understanding tenderness, the young man speechless with admiration. Look how he watches her, how his eyes travel over her face, how he sighs and shakes his head and looks back at his plate.

I looked across the Inn. In a plate-glass window a flashing neon sign said bluely, "nnI llortS. nnI llortS."

"Nnillorts," I murmured.

Cordelia looked up at me expectantly, with her questioning sound. I tensed. I filled the jigger with rum and poured two fingers into my empty highball glass. I took the jigger in one hand and the glass in the other.

I said, "You've read Kremlin von Schtunk, the Hungarian poet?" and drank the jigger.

"Well, really," she said pityingly.

"I was just thinking of his superb line 'Nni llorts, nov shmoz ka smörgasbord,' " I intoned, "which means—" and I drank the glass.

She reached across the table and touched my elbow. "Please. Don't translate. It couldn't be phrased as well in English."

Something within me curled up and died. Small, tight, cold and dense, its corpse settled under my breastbone. I could have raged at her, I supposed. I could have coldly questioned her, pinned her down, stripped from her those layers of schooled conversational reactions, leaving her ignorance in nakedness. But what for? I didn't want it. . . . And I could have talked to her about honesty and ethics and human aims—why did she do it? What did she ever hope to get? Did she think she would ever corral a man and expect him to be blind, for the rest of his life, to the fact that there was nothing behind this false front—nothing at all? Did she think that—did she think? No.

I looked at her, the way she was smiling at me, the deep shifting currents which seemed to be in her eyes. She was a monster. She was some graceful diction backed by a bare half-dozen relays. She was a card-file. She was a bubble, thin-skinned, covered with swirling, puzzling, compelling colors, filled with nothing. I was hurt and angry and, I think, a little frightened. I drank some more rum. I ordered her a drink and then another, and stayed ahead of her four to one. I'd have walked out and gone home if I had been able to summon the strength. I couldn't. I could only sit and stare at her and bathe myself in agonized astonishment. She didn't mind. She sat listening as raptly to my silence as she had to my conversation. Once she said, "We're just *being* together, aren't we?" and I recognized it as another trick from the bag. I wondered idly how many she might come up with if I just waited.

She came up with plenty.

She sat up and leaned forward abruptly. I had the distinct feeling that she was staring at me—her face was positioned right for it—but her eyes were closed. I put my glass down and stared blearily back, thinking, now what?

Her lips parted, twitched, opened wide, pursed. They uttered a glottal gurgling which was most unpleasant. I pushed my chair back, startled. "Are you sick?"

"Are you terrestrial?" she asked me.

"Am I *what?*"

"Making—contact thirty years," she said. Her voice was halting, filled with effort.

"What are you talking about?"

"Terrestrial quickly power going," she said clearly. "Many—uh—much power making contact this way very high frequencies thought. Easy radio. Not again thought. Take radio code quickly."

"Listen, toots," I said nastily, "This old nose no longer has a ring in it. Go play tricks on somebody else." I drank some more rum. An I. Q. of sixty, and crazy besides. "You're a real find, you are," I said.

"Graphic," she said. "Uh—write. Write. Write." She began to claw the table cloth. I looked at her hand. It was making scribbling motions. "Write write."

I flipped a menu over and put it in front of her and gave her my pen.

Now, I read an article once on automatic writing— you know, that spiritualist stuff. Before witnesses, a woman once wrote a long letter in trance in an unfamiliar (to her) hand, at the astonishing rate of four hundred and eight words a minute. Cordelia seemed to be out to break that record. That pen-nib was a blur. She was still leaning forward rigidly, and her eyes were still closed. But instead of a blurred scrawl, what took shape under her flying hand was a neat list or chart. There was an alphabet of sorts, although not arranged in the usual way; it was more a list of sounds. And there were the numbers one to fourteen. Beside each sound and each number was a cluster of regular dots which looked rather like Braille. The whole sheet took her not over forty-five seconds to do. And after she finished she didn't move anything except her eyelids which went up.

"I think," she said conversationally, "that I'd better get home, Henry. I feel a little dizzy."

I felt a little more than that. The rum, in rum's inevitable way, had sneaked up on me, and suddenly the room began to spin, diagonally, from the lower left to the upper right. I closed my eyes tight, opened them, fixed my gaze on a beer-tap on the bar at the end of the room, and held it still until the room slowed and stopped. "You're so right," I said, and did a press-up on the table top to assist my legs. I managed to help Cordelia on with her light coat. I put my pen back in my pocket (I found it the next morning with the cap still off and a fine color scheme in the lining of my jacket) and picked up the menu.

"What's that?" asked Cordelia.

"A souvenir," I said glumly. I had no picture, no school ring, no nothing. Only a doodle. I was too tired, twisted, and tanked to wonder much about it, or about the fact that she seemed never to have seen it before. I folded it in two and put it in my hip.

I got her home without leaning on her. I don't know if she was ready to give a repeat performance of that goodnight routine. I didn't wait to find out. I took her to the door and patted her on the cheek and went away from there. It wasn't her fault. . . .

When I got to our house, I dropped my hat on the floor in the hall and went into the dark living-room and fell into the easy-chair by the door. It was a comfortable chair. It was a comfortable room. I felt about as bad as I ever had. I remember wondering smokily whether anyone ever loves a person. People seem to love dreams instead, and for the lucky ones, the person is close to the dream. But it's a dream all the same, a sticky dream. You unload the person, and the dream stays with you.

What was it Dad had said? "When a fellow gets to be a big grown-up man . . . he learns to make a pile of his beloved failures and consign them to the flames." "Hah!" I ejaculated, and gagged. The rum tasted terrible. I had nothing to burn but memories and the lining of my stomach. The latter was flaming merrily. The former stayed where they were. The way she smiled, so deep and secret . . .

Then I remembered the doodle. Her hands had touched it, her mind had—No, her mind hadn't. It could have been anyone's mind, but not hers. The girl operated under a great handicap. No brains. I felt terrible. I got up out of the chair and wove across the room, leaning on the mantel. I put my forehead on the arm which I had put on the mantel, and with my other hand worried the menu out of my pocket. With the one hand and my teeth I tore it into small pieces and dropped the pieces in the grate, all but one. Then I heaved myself upright, braced my shoulder against the mantel, which had suddenly begun to bob and weave, got hold of my lighter, coaxed a flame out of it and lit the piece I'd saved. It burned fine. I let it slip into the grate. It flickered, dimmed, caught on another piece of paper, flared up again. I went down on one knee and carefully fed all the little pieces to the flame. When it finally went out I stirred the ashes around with my finger, got up, wiped my hands on my pants, said, "That was good advice Dad gave me," and went back to the chair. I went back into it, pushed my shoes off my feet, curled my legs under me and, feeling much better, dozed off.

I woke slowly, some time later, and with granulated eyelids and a mouth full of emory and quinine. My head was awake but my legs were asleep and my stomach had its little hands on my backbone and was trying to pull it out by the roots. I sat there groggily looking at the fire.

Fire? What fire? I blinked and winced; I could almost hear my eyelids rasping.

There was a fire in the grate. Dad was kneeling beside it, feeding it small pieces of paper. I didn't say anything; I don't think it occured to me. I just watched.

He let the fire go out after a while; then he stirred the ashes with his finger and stood up with a sigh, wiping his hands on his pants. "Good advice I gave the boy. Time I took it myself." He loomed across the shadowy room to me, turned around and sat down in my lap. He was relaxed and heavy, but he didn't stay there long enough for me to feel it. "Gah!" he said, crossed the room again in one huge bound, put his back against the mantel and said, "Don't move, you, I've got a gun."

"It's me, Dad."

"Henry! Bythelordharry, you'll be the death of me yet. That was the most inconsiderate thing you have ever done in your entire selfish life. I've a notion to bend this poker over your adam's apple, you snipe." He stamped over to the book case and turned on the light. "This is the last time I'll ever—Henry! What's the matter? You look awful! Are you all right?"

"I'll live," I said regretfully. "What were you burning?"

He grinned sheepishly. "A beloved failure. Remember my preachment a couple weeks ago? It got to working on me. I decided to take my own advice." He breathed deeply. "I feel much better, I think."

"I burned some stuff too," I croaked. "I feel better too. I think," I added.

"Cordelia?" he asked, sitting near me.

"She hasn't got brain one," I said.

"Well," he said. There was more sharing and comfort in the single syllable than in anything I have ever heard. I looked at him. He hadn't changed much over the years. A bit heavier. A bit grayer. Still intensely alive, though. And he'd learned to control those wild projects of his. I thought, quite objectively, "I like this man."

We were quiet for a warm while. Then, "Dad—what was it you burned? The Martian project?"

"Why, you young devil! How did you know?"

"I dunno. You look like I feel. Sort of—well, you've finally unloaded something, and it hurts to lose it, but you're glad you did."

"On the nose," he said, and grinned sheepishly. "Yup, Henry—I really hugged that project to me. Want to hear about it?"

Anything but Cordelia, I thought. "I saw your rig," I said, to break the ice. "The night you sent me out for the wire. You left the workshop open."

"I'll be darned. I thought I'd gotten away with it."

"Mother knew what you were up to, though she didn't know how."

"And you saw how."

"I saw that weird gimmick of yours, but it didn't mean anything to me. Mother told me never to mention it to you. She thought you'd be happier if you were left alone."

He laughed with real delight. "Bless her heart," he said. "She was a most understanding woman."

"I read about the Martian signals in the papers," I said. "Fellow named—what was it?"

"Jenkins," said Dad. "C. Francis Jenkins. He built a film-tape recorder to catch the signals. He tuned to six thousand meters and had a flashing light to record the signals. Primitive, but it worked. Dr. David Todd of Amherst was the man who organized the whole project, and got the big radio people all over the world to cooperate. They had a five-minute silence every hour during Mars' closest proximity—August 1 to 3."

"I remember," I said. "It was my birthday. 1924. What got you so teed off?"

"I got mad," said my father, folding his hands over his stomach. "Just because it had become fashionable to use radio in a certain way on earth, those simple souls had to assume that the Martian signals—if any—would come through the same way. I felt that they'd be different."

"Why should they be?"

"Why should we expect Martians to be the same? Or even think the same? I just took a wild stab at it, that's all. I tuned in on six wavelengths at the same time. I set up my rig so that anything coming through on any one wavelength would actuate a particular phone."

"I remember," I said, trying hard. "The iron filings on the paper tape, over the ear-phones."

"That's right. The phone was positioned far enough below the tape so that the magnetic field would barely contain the filings. When the diaphragm vibrated, the filings tended to cluster. I had six phones on six different wavelengths, arranged like this," and he counted them out on the palm of his hand:

$$1 \quad 2$$
$$3 \quad 4$$
$$5 \quad 6$$

"What could you get? I don't figure it, Dad. There'd be no way of separating your dots and dashes."

"Blast!" he exploded. "That's the kind of thinking that made me mad, and makes me mad to this day! No; what I was after was something completely different in transmission. Look; how much would you get out of piano music if all the strings but one were broken? Only when the pianist hit that note in the course of his transmission would you hear anything. See what I mean?

Supposing the Martians were sending in notes and chords of an established octave of frequencies? Sure—Jenkins got signals. No one's ever been able to interpret them. Well, supposing I was right—then Jenkins was recording only one of several or many 'notes' of the scale, and of course it was meaningless."

"Well, what did you get?"

"Forty-six photographs, five of which were so badly under-exposed that they were useless to me. I finally got the knack of moving the tape carefully enough and lighting it properly, and they came out pretty well. I got signals on four of the six frequencies. I got the same grouping only three or four times; I mean, sometimes there would be something on phones 1, 2, and 4, and sometimes it would only be on 4, and sometimes it would be on 2 and 6. Three and 5 never did come through; it was just fantastic luck that I picked the right frequencies, I suppose, for the other four."

"What frequencies did you use?"

He grinned. "I don't know. I really don't. It was all by guess and by Golly. I never was an engineer, Henry. I'm in the insurance business. I had no instruments—particularly not in 1924. I wound a 6000-meter coil according to specs they printed in the paper. As for the others, I worked on the knowledge that less turns of heavier wire means shorter wave-lengths. I haven't got the coils now and couldn't duplicate 'em in a million years. All I can say for sure is that they were all different, and stepped down from 6000.

"Anyway, I studied those things until I was blue in the face. It must've been the better part of a year before I called in anyone else. I wrote to Mr. Jenkins and Dr. Todd too, but who am I? A taxidermical broker with a wacky idea. They sent the pictures back with polite letters, and I can't say I blame them . . . anyway, good riddance to the things. But it was a wonderful idea, and

I wanted so much to be the man who did the job. . . . Ever want something so badly you couldn't see straight, Henry?"

"Me?" I asked, with bitterness.

"It's all over now, though. I'm through with crazy projects, for life. Never again. But gosh, I did love that project. Know what I mean?"

"No," I said with even more bitterness.

He sat straight. "Hey, I'm sorry, fellow. Those were rhetorical questions. Maybe you'd better spill it."

So I told it to him—all of it. Once I started, I couldn't stop. I told him about the moon poem and the "well, really" gimmick and the "please don't translate" routine, and the more I talked the worse I felt. He sat and listened, and didn't say "I told you so," and the idea was worming its way into the back of my mind as I talked that here sat one of the most understanding people ever created, when he screamed. He screamed as one screams at the intrusion of an ice-cube into the back of one's bathing-suit.

"What's the matter?" I asked, breaking off.

"Go on, go on," he gabbled. "Henry you idiot don't tell me you don't know what you're saying for Pete's sake boy tell it to—"

"Whoa! I don't even remember where I was."

"What she said to you—'Are you a terrestrial?' "

"Oh, don't get so excited, Dad. It doesn't mean anything. Why bother? She was trying to interest me, I suppose. I didn't let it get to me then and I won't now. She—"

"*Blast* her! I'm not talking about her. It was what she said. Go on, Henry! You say she wrote something?"

He wormed it all out of me. He forced me to go over it and over it. The windows paled and the single light by the book case looked yellow and ill in the dawn, but still

65

he pounded at me. And I finally quit. I just quit, out of compounded exhaustion and stubbornness. I lay back in the big chair and glared at him.

He strode up and down the room, trying to beat his left hand to a pulp with a right fist. "Of course, of course," he said excitedly. "That's how they'd do it. The blankest mind in the world. Blank and sensitive, like undeveloped film. *Of course!* 'Making contact thirty years' they said. 'Much power making contact this way—very high frequencies thought.' A radionic means of transmitting thought, and it uses too much power to be practical. 'Easy radio. Not again thought.' "

He stopped in front of me, blaring. " 'Not again thought,' " he growled. "You—you *dope!* How could my flesh and blood be so abjectly stupid? There in your hands you held the interplanetary Rosetta Stone, and what did you do with it?"

I glared back at him. "I was quote consigning one of my beloved failures to the flames end quote," I said nastily.

Suddenly he was slumped and tired. "So you were, son. So you were. And it was all there—like Braille, you said. A series of phonetic symbols, and almost certainly a list of the frequency-octave they use. And—and all my pictures. . . . I burned them too." He sat down.

"Henry—"

"Don't take it so hard, Dad," I said. "Your advice was good. You forget your Martians and I'll forget my moron. When a fellow gets to be a grown-up man—"

He didn't hear me. "Henry. You say her folks like you?"

I sprang to my feet. "NO!" I bellowed. "Dad, I will not, repeat, *not* under any circumstances woo that beautiful package of brainless reflexes. I have had mine. I—"

"You really mean it, don't you?"

"That I do," I said positively.

"Well," he said dejectedly, "I guess that's that."

And then that old, old fever came back into his face. "Dad—"

He slowly straightened up, that hot "Land ho!" expression in his eyes. My father is hale, handsome, and, when he wants to be, extremely persistent.

"Now, Dad," I said. "Let's be reasonable. She's very young, Dad. Now, let's talk this thing over a little more, Dad. You can't go following a girl all over the house with a notebook and pencil. They said they wouldn't use the thought contact again, Dad. Now Dad—"

"Your mother would understand if she were alive," he murmured.

"No! You can't!" I bawled. "Dad, for heaven's sake use your head! Why you—Cordelia—Dad, she'd make me call her *Mummy!*"

Now what am I going to do?

THE NAIL
AND THE ORACLE

Despite the improvements, the Pentagon in 1970 was still the Pentagon, with more places to walk than places to sit. Not that Jones had a legitimate gripe. The cubical cave they had assigned to him as an office would have been more than adequate for the two-three days he himself had estimated. But by the end of the third week it fit him like a size-6 hat and choked him like a size-12 collar. Annie's phone calls expressed eagerness to have him back, but there was an edge to the eagerness now which made him anxious. His hotel manager had wanted to shift his room after the first week and he had been stubborn about it; now he was marooned like a rock in a mushroom patch, surrounded by a back-to-rhythm convention of the Anti-Anti-Population Explosion League. He'd had to buy shirts, he'd had to buy shoes, he'd needed a type-four common-cold shot, and most of all, he couldn't find what was wrong with ORACLE.

Jones and his crew had stripped ORACLE down to its mounting bolts, checked a thousand miles of wiring and a million solid-state elements, everything but its priceless and untouchable memory banks. Then they'd rebuilt the monster, meticulously cross-checking all the way. For the past four days they had been running the recompleted computer, performance-matching with crash-priority time on other machines, while half the science boys and a third of the military wailed in anguish. He had reported to three men that the machine had nothing wrong with it, that it never had had anything wrong with it, and that there was no reason to believe there ever would be anything wrong with it. One by one these three had gone (again) into ORACLE's chamber, and bolted the door, and energized the privacy field, and then one by one they had emerged stern and disappointed, to tell Jones that it would not give them an answer: an old admiral, an ageless colonel and a piece of walking legend whom Jones called to himself the civilian.

Having sent his crew home—for thus he burned his bridges—having deprived himself of Jacquard the design genius and the 23 others, the wiring team, all the mathematicians, everyone, Jones sighed in his little office, picked up the phone again and called the three for a conference. When he put the instrument down again he felt a little pleased. Consistencies pleased Jones, even unpleasant ones, and the instant response of all three was right in line with everything they had done from the time they had first complained about ORACLE's inability to answer their questions, all through their fiddling and diddling during every second of the long diagnostic operation. The admiral had had an open line installed to Jones' office, the colonel had devised a special code word for his switchboard, the civilian had hung around personally, ignoring all firm, polite hints until he had turned his ankle on a cable, giving Jones a reason to get him out of there. In other words, these three didn't just want an answer, they *needed* it.

They came, the admiral with his old brows and brand-new steel-blue eyes, the colonel with starch in his spine and skin like a postmaneuver proving grounds, the civilian limping a bit, with his head tilted a bit, turned a bit, a captivating mannerism which always gave his audiences the feeling that history cared to listen to them. Jones let them get settled, this admiral whose whole career had consisted of greater and greater commands until his strong old hand was a twitch away from the spokes of the helm of the ship of state; this colonel who had retained his lowly rank as a mark of scorn for the academy men who scurried to obey him, whose luxurious quarters were equipped with an iron barracks bed; and this civilian with the scholarly air, with both Houses and a Cabinet rank behind him, whose political skills were as strong, and as deft, and as spiked as a logroller's feet.

"Gentlemen," said Jones, "this may well be our last meeting. There will, of course, be a written report, but I understand the—uh—practicalities of such a situation quite well, and I do not feel it necessary to go into the kind of detail in the report that is possible to us in an informal discussion." He looked at each face in turn and congratulated himself. That was just right. This is just between us boys. Nobody's going to squeal on you.

"You've dismissed your crew," said the civilian, causing a slight start in the admiral and a narrowing of the colonel's eyes and, in Jones, a flash of admiration. This one had snoopers the services hadn't even dreamed up yet. "I hope this is good news."

"Depends," said Jones. "What it means primarily is that they have done all they can. In other words, there is nothing wrong with ORACLE in any of their specialties. Their specialties include everything the computer is and does. In still other words, there's nothing wrong with the machine."

"So you told us yesterday," gritted the colonel, "but I got no results. And—I want results." The last was added as an old ritual which, apparently, had always gotten results just by being recited.

"I followed the procedures," said the admiral, intoning this as a cardinal virtue, "and also got no results." He held up a finger and suspended operations in the room while he performed some sort of internal countdown. "Had I not done so, ORACLE would have responded with an 'insufficient data' signal. Correct?"

"Quite correct," said Jones.

"And it didn't."

"That was my experience," said the civilian, and the colonel nodded.

"Gentlemen," said Jones, "neither I nor my crew—and there just is not a better one—have been able to devise a question that produced that result."

"It was not a result," snapped the colonel.

Jones ignored him. "Given the truth of my conclusion—that there is nothing wrong with the machine—and your reports, which I can have no reason to doubt, there is no area left to investigate but one, and that is in your hands, not mine. It's the one thing you have withheld from me." He paused. Two of them shifted their feet. The colonel tightened his jaw.

The admiral said softly, but with utter finality, "I can*not* divulge my question."

The colonel and the civilian spoke together: "Security——" and "This is a matter——" and then both fell silent.

"Security." Jones spread his hands. To keep from an enemy, real or potential, matters vital to the safety of the nation, that was security. And how easy it was to wrap the same blanket about the use of a helicopter to a certain haven, the presence of a surprising little package in a Congressional desk, the exact relations between a certain officer and his——*argh!* This, thought Jones, has all the earmarks of, not *our* security, but the three cases of *my* security . . . I'll try just once more.

"Thirty years ago, a writer named William Tenn wrote a brilliant story in which an Air Force moon

74

landing was made, and the expedition found an inhabited pressure dome nearby. They sent out a scout, who was prepared to die at the hands of Russians or even Martians. He returned to the ship in a paroxysm, gentlemen, of laughter. The other dome belonged to the U. S. Navy."

The admiral projected two loud syllables of a guffaw and said, "Of course." The colonel looked pained. The civilian, bright-eyed, made a small nod which clearly said, One up for you, boy.

Jones put on his used-car-salesman face. "Honestly, gentlemen, it embarrasses me to draw a parallel like that. I believe with all my heart that each of you has the best interests of our nation foremost in his thoughts. As for myself—security? Why, I wouldn't be here if I hadn't been cleared all the way back to *Pithecanthropus erectus*.

"So much for you, so much for me. Now, as for ORACLE, you know as well as I do that it is no ordinary computer. It is designed for computations, not of math, specifically, nor of strictly physical problems, though it can perform them, but for the distillation of human thought. For over a decade the contents of the Library of Congress and other sources have poured into that machine—everything: novels, philosophy, magazines, poetry, textbooks, religious tracts, comic books, even millions of personnel records. There's every shade of opinion, every quality of writing—anything and everything that an army of over a thousand microfilming technicians have been able to cram into it. As long as it's printed and in English, German, Russian, French or Japanese, ORACLE can absorb it. Esperanto is the funnel for a hundred Oriental and African languages. It's the greatest repository of human thought and thought-directed action the world has ever known, and its one most powerful barrier against error in human affairs is the sheer mass of its memory and the wide spectrum of opinion that has poured into it.

"Add to this its ability to extrapolate—to project the results of hypothetical acts—and the purposely designed privacy structure—for it's incapable of recording or reporting who asked it what question—and you have ORACLE, the one place in the world where you can get a straight answer based, not in terms of the problem itself, but on every ideological computation and cross-comparison that can be packed into it."

"The one place I couldn't get a straight answer," said the civilian gently.

"To your particular question. Sir, if you want that answer, you have got to give me that question." He checked a hopeful stir in the other two by adding quickly, "and yours. And yours. You see, gentlemen, though I am concerned for your needs in this matter, my prime concern is ORACLE. To find a way to get one of the answers isn't enough. If I had all three, I might be able to deduce a common denominator. I already have, of course, though it isn't enough: you are all high up in national affairs, and very close to the center of things. You are all of the same generation" (translation: near the end of the road) "and, I'm sure, equally determined to do the best you can for your country" (to get to the top of the heap before you cash in). "Consider *me*," he said, and smiled disarmingly. "To let me get this close to the answer *I* want; namely, what's wrong with ORACLE, and then to withhold it—isn't that sort of cruel and unusual punishment?"

"I feel for you," said the civilian, not without a twinkle. Then, sober with a coldness that would freeze helium into a block, he said, "But you ask too much."

Jones looked at him, and then at the others, sensing their unshakable agreement. "OK," he said, with all the explosive harshness he could muster, "I'm done here.

I'm sick of this place and my girl's sick of being by herself, and I'm going home. You can't call in anyone else, because there isn't anyone else: my company built ORACLE and my men were trained for it."

This kind of thing was obviously in the colonel's idiom. From far back in his throat, he issued a grinding sound that came out in words: "You'll finish the job you were ordered to do, mister, or you'll take the consequences."

Jones shouted at him, "Consequences? What consequences? You couldn't even have me fired, because I can make a damn good case that you prevented me from finishing the job. I'm not under your orders either. This seems a good time to remind you of the forgotten tradition that with this"—he took hold of the narrow lapel of his own sports jacket—"I outrank any uniform in this whole entire Pentagon." He caught the swift smile of the civilian, and therefore trained his next blast on him. "Consequences? The only consequence you can get now is to deny yourself and your country the answer to your question. The only conclusion I can come to is that something else is more important to you than that. What else?" He stood up. So did the officers.

From his chair, the civilian said sonorously, "Now, now . . . gentlemen. Surely we can resolve this problem without raising our voices. Mr. Jones, would the possession of two of these questions help you in your diagnosis? Or even one?"

Breathing hard, Jones said, "It might."

The civilian opened his long white hands. "Then there's no problem after all. If one of you gentlemen——"

"Absolutely not," said the admiral instantly.

"Not me," growled the colonel. "You want compromise, don't you? Well, go ahead—you compromise."

"In this area," said the civilian smoothly, "I possess

77

all the facts, and it is my considered judgment that the disclosure of my question would not further Mr. Jones' endeavors." (Jones thought, the admiral said the same thing in two words.) "Admiral, would you submit to my judgment the question of whether or not security would be endangered by your showing Mr. Jones your question?"

"I would not."

The civilian turned to the colonel. One look at that rock-bound countenance was sufficient to make him turn away again, which, thought Jones, puts the colonel two points ahead of the admiral in the word-economy business.

Jones said to the civilian, "No use, sir, and by my lights, that's the end of it. The simplest possible way to say it is that you gentlemen have the only tools in existence that would make it possible for me to repair this gadget, and you won't let me have them. So fix it yourself, or leave it the way it is. I'd see you out," he added, scanning the walls of the tiny room, "but I have to go to the john." He stalked out, his mind having vividly and permanently photographed the astonishment on the admiral's usually composed features, the colonel's face fury-twisted into something like the knot that binds the lashes of a whip, and the civilian grinning broadly.

Grinning broadly?

Ah well, he thought, slamming the men's-room door behind him—and infuriatingly, it wouldn't slam—Ah well, we all have our way of showing frustration. Maybe I could've been just as mad more gently.

The door moved, and someone ranged alongside at the next vertical bathtub. Jones glanced, and then said aloud, "Maybe I could've been just as mad more gently."

"Perhaps we all could have," said the civilian, and then with his free hand he did four surprising things in

78

extremely rapid succession. He put his finger to his lips, then his hand to the wall and then to his ear. Finally he whisked a small folded paper out of his breast pocket and handed it to Jones. He then finished what he was doing and went to wash up.

Shh. The walls have ears. Take this.

"All through history," said the civilian from the sink, his big old voice booming in the tiled room, "we read about the impasse, and practically every time it's mentioned, it's a sort of preface to an explanation of how it was solved. Yet I'll bet history's full of impasses that just couldn't be solved. They don't get mentioned because when it happens, everything stops. There just isn't anything to write down in the book anymore. I think we've just seen such an occasion, and I'm sorry for each of us."

The old son of a gun! "Thanks for that much, anyway, sir," Jones said, tucking the paper carefully away out of sight. The old man, wiping his hands, winked once and went out.

Back in his office, which seemed three times larger than it had been before the conference, Jones slumped behind his desk and teased himself with the small folded paper, not reading it, turning it over and over. It had to be the old man's question. Granted that it was, why had he been so willing to hand it over now, when three minutes earlier his refusal had been just about as adamant as—adamant? So, Jones, quit looking at the detail and get on the big picture. What was different in those three minutes?

Well, they were out of one room and into another. Out of one room that was damn well not bugged and into one which, the old man's pantomime had informed him, may well be. Nope—that didn't make sense.

Then—how about this? In the one room there had been witnesses. In the second, none—not after the finger on the lips. So if a man concluded that the civilian probably never had had an objection to Jones' seeing and using the question, but wanted it concealed from anyone else—maybe specifically from those other two . . . why, the man had the big picture.

What else? That the civilian had not said this, therefore would not bring himself to say it in so many words, and would not appreciate any conversation that might force him to talk it over. Finally, no matter how reluctantly he might be to let Jones see the paper, the slim chance Jones offered him of getting an answer outweighed every other consideration—except the chance of the other two finding out. So another part of the message was: I'm sitting on dynamite, Mr. Jones, and I'm handing you the detonator. Or: I trust you, Mr. Jones.

Sobeit, old man. I've got the message.

He closed his eyes and squeezed the whole situation to see if anything else would drip out of it. Nothing . . . except the faint conjecture that what worked on one might work on the other two. And as if on cue, the door opened and a bland-faced major came in a pace, stopped, said "Beg pardon, sir. I'm in the wrong room," and before Jones could finish saying "That's all right," he was gone. Jones gazed thoughtfully at the door. That major was one of the colonel's boys. That "wrong room" bit had a most unlikely flavor to it. So if the man hadn't come in for nothing, he'd come in for something. He hadn't taken anything and he hadn't left anything, so he'd come in to find something out. The only thing he could find out was whether Jones was or was not here. Oh: and whether he was or was not alone.

All Jones had to do to check that out was to sit tight.

You can find out if a man is alone in a room for now, but not for ten minutes from now, or five.

In two minutes the colonel came in.

He wore his "I don't like you, mister" expression. He placed his scarred brown hands flat on Jones' desk and rocked forward over him like a tidal wave about to break.

"It's your word against mine, and I'm prepared to call you a liar," grated the colonel. "I want you to report to me and no one else."

"All right," said Jones, and put out his hand. The colonel locked gazes with him for a fair slice of forever, which made Jones believe that the Medusa legend wasn't necessarily a legend after all. Then the officer put a small folded paper into Jones' outstretched palm. "You get the idea pretty quick, I'll say that, mister"; he straightened, about-faced and marched out.

Jones looked at the two scraps of folded paper on the desk and thought, I will be damned.

And one to go.

He picked up the papers and dropped them again, feeling like a kid who forces himself to eat all the cake before he attacks the icing. He thought, maybe the old boy wants to but just doesn't know how.

He reached for the phone and dialed for the open line, wondering if the admiral had had it canceled yet.

He had not, and he wasn't waiting for the first ring to finish itself. He knew who was calling and he knew Jones knew, so he said nothing, just picked up the phone.

Jones said, "It was kind of crowded in here."

"Precisely the point," said the admiral, with the same grudging approval the colonel had shown. There was a short pause, and then the admiral said, "Have you called anyone else?"

Into four syllables Jones put all the outraged innocence of a male soprano accused of rape. "Certainly not."

"Good man."

The Britishism amused Jones, and he almost said Gung ho, what?; but instead he concentrated on what to say next. It was easy to converse with the admiral if you supplied both sides of the conversation. Suddenly it came to him that the admiral wouldn't want to come here—he had somewhat farther to travel than the colonel had—nor would he like the looks of Jones' visiting him at this particular moment. He said, "I wouldn't mention this, but as you know, I'm leaving soon and may not see you. And I think you picked up my cigarette lighter."

"Oh," said the admiral.

"And me out of matches," said Jones ruefully. "Well—I'm going down to ORACLE now. Nice to have known you, sir." He hung up, stuck an unlit cigarette in his mouth, put the two folded papers in his left pants pocket, and began an easy stroll down the catacombs called corridors in the Pentagon.

Just this side of ORACLE's dead-end corridor, and not quite in visual range of its security post, a smiling young ensign, who otherwise gave every evidence of being about his own business, said, "Light, sir?"

"Why, thanks."

The ensign handed him a lighter. He didn't light it and proffer the flame; he handed the thing over. Jones lit his cigarette and dropped the lighter into his pocket. "Thanks."

"That's all right," smiled the ensign, and walked on.

At the security post, Jones said to the guard, "Whoppen?"

"Nothing and nobody, Mr. Jones."

"Best news I've had all day." He signed the book and accompanied the guard down the dead end. They each produced a key and together opened the door. "I shouldn't be too long."

"All the same to me," said the guard, and Jones realized he'd been wishfully thinking out loud. He shut the door, hit the inner lock switch, and walked through the little foyer and the swinging door which unveiled what the crew called ORACLE's "temple."

He looked at the computer, and it looked back at him. "Like I told you before," he said conversationally, "for something that causes so much trouble, you're awful little and awful homely."

ORACLE did not answer, because it was not aware of him. ORACLE could read and do a number of more complex and subtle things, but it had no ears. It was indeed homely as a wall, which is what the front end mostly resembled, and the immense size of its translators, receptors and the memory banks was not evident here. The temple—other people called it Suburbia Delphi— contained nothing but that animated wall, with its one everblooming amber "on" light (for the machine never ceased gulping its oceans of thought), a small desk and chair, and the mechanical typewriter with the modified Bodoni type face which was used for the reader. The reader itself was nothing more than a clipboard (though with machined guides to hold the paper exactly in place) with a large push button above it, placed on a strut which extended from the front of the computer, and lined up with a lens set flush into it. It was an eerie experience to push that button after placing your query, for ORACLE scanned so quickly and "thought" so fast that it was rapping away on its writer before you could get your thumb off the button.

Usually.

Jones sat at the desk, switched on the light and took out the admiral's lighter. It was a square one, with two parts which telescoped apart to get to the tank. The tight little roll of paper was there, sure enough, with the typescript not seriously blurred by lighter fluid. He smoothed it out, retrieved the other two, unfolded them, stacked them all neatly; and then, feeling very like Christmas morning, said gaily to the unresponsive ORACLE:

"Now!"

Seconds later, he was breathing hard. A flood of profanity welled upward within him—and dissipated itself as totally inadequate.

Wagging his head helplessly, he brought the three papers to the typewriter and wrote them out on fresh paper, staying within the guidelines printed there, and adding the correct code symbols for the admiral, the colonel and the civilian. These symbols had been assigned by ORACLE itself, and were cross-checked against the personnel records it carried in its memory banks. It was the only way in which it was possible to ask a question including that towering monosyllable "I."

Jones clipped the first paper in place, held his breath and pushed the button.

There was a small flare of light from the hood surrounding the lens as the computer automatically brought the available light to optimum. A relay clicked softly as the writer was activated. A white tongue of paper protruded. Jones tore it off. It was blank.

He grunted, then replaced the paper with the second, then the third. It seemed that on one of them there was a half-second delay in the writer relay, but it was insignificant: the paper remained blank.

"Stick your tongue out at me, will you?" he muttered at the computer, which silently gazed back at him with

84

its blank single eye. He went back to the typewriter and copied one of the questions, but with his own code identification symbols. It read:

THE ELIMINATION OF WHAT SINGLE MAN
COULD RESULT IN MY PRESIDENCY?

He clipped the paper in place and pushed the button. The relay clicked, the writer rattled and the paper protruded. He tore it off. It read (complete with quotes):

"JOHN DOE"

"A wise guy," Jones growled. He returned to the typewriter and again copied one of the queries with his own code:

IF I ELIMINATE THE PRESIDENT, HOW
CAN I ASSURE PERSONAL CONTROL?

Wryly, ORACLE answered:

DON'T EAT A BITE UNTIL YOUR EXECUTION.

It actually took Jones a couple of seconds to absorb that one, and then he uttered an almost hysterical bray of laughter.

The third question he asked, under his own identification, was:

CAN MY SUPPORT OF HENNY BRING PEACE?

The answer was a flat NO, and Jones did not laugh one bit. "And you don't find anything funny about it either," he congratulated the computer, and actually, physically shuddered.

For Henny—the Honorable Oswaldus Deeming Henny—was an automatic nightmare to the likes of Jones. His weatherbeaten saint's face, his shoulder-length white hair (oh, what genius of a public-relations man put him onto that?), his diapason voice, but most of all, his "Plan for Peace" had more than once brought Jones up out of a sound sleep into a cold sweat. Now, there was once a man who entranced a certain segment of the population with a slogan about the royalty in every man, but he could not have taken over the country, because a slogan is not a political philosophy. And there was another who was capable of turning vast numbers of his countrymen—for a while—against one another and toward him for protection: and he could not have taken over the country, because the manipulation of fear is not an economic philosophy. This Henny, however, was the man who had both, and more besides. His appearance alone gave him more nonthinking, vote-bearing adherents than Rudolph Valentino plus Albert Schweitzer. His advocacy of absolute isolation brought in the right wing, his demand for unilateral disarmament brought in the left wing, his credo that science could, with a third of munitions-size budgets, replace foreign trade through research, invention and ersatz, brought in the tech segment, and his dead certainty of lowering taxes had a thick hook in everyone else. Even the most battle-struck of the war wanters found themselves shoulder to shoulder with the peace-at-any-price extremists, because of the high moral tone of his disarmament plan, which was to turn our weapons on ourselves and present any aggressor with nothing but slag and cinders—the ultimate deterrent. It was the most marvelous blend of big bang and beneficence, able to cut chance and challenge together with openhanded Gandhiism, with an answer for everyone and a better life for all.

"All of which," complained Jones to the featureless face of the computer, "doesn't help me find out why you wouldn't answer those three guys, though I must say, I'm glad you didn't." He went and got the desk chair and put it down front and center before the computer. He sat down and folded his arms and they stared silently at each other.

At length he said, "If you were a people instead of a thing, how would I handle you? A miserable, stubborn, intelligent snob of a people?"

Just how do I handle people? he wondered. I do—I know I do. I always seem to think of the right thing to say, or to ask. I've already asked ORACLE what's wrong, and ORACLE says nothing is wrong. The way any miserable, stubborn, intelligent snob would.

What I do, he told himself, is to empathize. Crawl into their skins, feel with their fingertips, look out through their eyes.

Look out through their eyes.

He rose and got the admiral's query—the one with the admiral's own identification on it—clipped it to the board, then hunkered down on the floor with his back to the computer and his head blocking the lens.

He was seeing exactly what the computer saw.

Clipboard. Query. The small bare chamber, the far wall. The . . .

He stopped breathing. After a long astonished moment he said, when he could say anything, and because it was all he could think of to say: "Well, I . . . be . . . damned . . ."

The admiral was the first in. Jones had had a busy time of it for the 90 minutes following his great discovery, and he was feeling a little out of breath, but at the same time a little louder and quicker than the other guy, as if he had walked into the reading room after a rub-down and a needle-shower.

"Sit down, Admiral."

"Jones, did you—"

"Please, sir—sit down."

"But surely—"

"I've got your answer, Admiral. But there's something we have to do first." He made waving gestures. "Bear with me."

He wouldn't have made it, thought Jones, except for the colonel's well-timed entrance. Boy oh boy, thought Jones, look at 'm, stiff as tongs. You come on the battlefield looking just like a target. On the other hand, that's how you made your combat reputation, isn't it? The colonel was two strides into the room before he saw the admiral. He stopped, began an about-face and said over his left epaulet, "I didn't think—"

"Sit down, Colonel," said Jones in a pretty fair imitation of the man's own brass gullet. It reached the officer's muscles before it reached his brain and he sat. He turned angrily on the admiral, who said instantly, "This wasn't my idea," in a completely insulting way.

Again the door opened and old living history walked in, his head a little to one side, his eyes ready to see and understand and his famous mouth to smile, but when he saw the tableau, the eyes frosted over and the mouth also said: "I didn't think—"

"Sit down, sir," said Jones, and began spieling as the civilian was about to refuse, and kept on spieling while he changed his mind, lowered himself guardedly onto the edge of a chair and perched his old bones on its front edge as if he intended not to stay.

"Gentlemen," Jones began, "I'm happy to tell you that I have succeeded in finding out why ORACLE was unable to perform for you—thanks to certain unexpected cooperation I received." Nice touch, Jones. Each one of 'em will think he turned the trick, singlehandedly. But not for long. "Now I have a plane to catch, and you all have things to do, and I would appreciate it if you would hear me out with as little interruption as possible." Looking at these bright eager angry sullen faces, Jones let himself realize for the first time why detectives in whodunits assemble all the suspects and make speeches. Why they *personally* do it—why the author has them do it. It's because it's fun.

"In this package"—he lifted from beside his desk a brown paper parcel a yard long and 15 inches wide—"is the cause of all the trouble. My company was founded over a half century ago, and one of these has been an appurtenance of every one of the company's operations, each of its major devices and installations, all of its larger utility equipment—cranes, trucks, bulldozers, everything. You'll find them in every company office and in most company cafeterias." He put the package down flat on his desk and fondled it while he talked. "Now, gentlemen, I'm not going to go into any part of the long argument about whether or not a computer can be conscious of what it's doing, because we haven't time and we're not here to discuss metaphysics. I will, however, remind you of a childhood chant. Remember the one that runs: 'For want of a nail the shoe was lost; for want of a shoe the horse was lost; for want of a horse the message was lost; for want of the message the battle was lost; for want of the battle the kingdom was lost—and all for the want of a horseshoe nail.' "

"Mr. Jones," said the admiral, "I–we–didn't come here to—"

"I just said that," Jones said smoothly, and went right on talking until the admiral just stopped trying. "This"—he rapped the package—"is ORACLE's horseshoe nail. If it's no ordinary nail, that's because ORACLE's no ordinary computer. It isn't designed to solve problems in their own context; there are other machines that do that. ORACLE solves problems the way an educated man solves them—by bringing everything he is and has to bear on them. Lacking this one part"—he thumped the package again—"it can then answer your questions, and it accordingly did." He smiled suddenly. "I don't think ORACLE was designed this way," he added musingly. "I think it . . . became . . . this way . . ." He shook himself. "Anyway, I have your answers."

Now he could afford to pause, because he had them. At that moment, the only way any of them could have been removed was by dissection and haulage.

Jones lined up his sights on the colonel and said, "In a way, your question was the most interesting, Colonel. To me professionally, I mean. It shows to what detail ORACLE can go in answering a wide theoretical question. One might even make a case for original creative thinking, though that's always arguable. Could a totally obedient robot think if you flatly ordered it to think? When does a perfect imitation of a thing become the thing itself?"

"You're not going to discuss my question here," said the colonel as a matter of absolute, incontrovertible fact.

"Yes I am," said Jones, and raised his voice. "You listen to me, before you stick that trigger finger of yours inside that tunic, Colonel. I'm in a corny mood right now and so I've done a corny thing. Two copies of a detailed report of this whole affair are now in the mail, and, I might add, in a mailbox outside this building. One goes to my boss, who is a very big wheel and a loyal friend, with as many contacts in business and government as there are company machines operating, and that puts him on the damn moon as well as all over the world. The other goes to someone else, and when you find out who that is it'll be too late, because in two hours he can reach every paper, every wire service, every newscasting organization on earth. Naturally, consistent with the corn, I've sent these out sealed with orders to open them if I don't phone by a certain time—and I assure you it won't be from here. In other words, you can't do anything to me and you'd better not delay me. *Sit down, Admiral,*" he roared.

"I'm certainly not going to sit here and——"

"I'm going to finish what I started out to do whether you're here or not." Jones waved at the other two. "They'll be here. You want that?"

The admiral sat down. The civilian said, in a tolling of mighty sorrow, "Mr. Jones, I had what seemed to be your faithful promise——"

"There were overriding considerations," said Jones. "You know what an overriding consideration is, don't you, sir?" and he held up the unmistakable ORACLE query form. The civilian subsided.

"Let him finish," gritted the colonel. "We can—well, let him finish."

Jones instantly, like ORACLE, translated: *We can take care of him later*. He said to the colonel, "Cheer up. You can always deny everything, like you said." He fanned through the papers before him and dealt out the colonel's query. He read it aloud:

" 'IF I ELIMINATE THE PRESIDENT, HOW CAN I ASSURE PERSONAL CONTROL?' "

The colonel's face could have been shipped out, untreated, and installed on Mount Rushmore. The civilian gasped and put his knuckles in his mouth. The admiral's slitted eyes went round.

"The answer," said Jones, "makes that case for cre-

ative thinking I was talking about. ORACLE said: 'DETO-
NATE ONE BOMB WITHIN UNDERGROUND H. Q. SPEND
YOUR SUBSEQUENT TENURE LOOKING FOR OTHERS.' "

Jones put down the paper and spoke past the colonel
to the other two. "Get the big picture, gentlemen? 'UN-
DERGROUND H. Q.' could only mean the centralized control for government in the mountains. Whether or not
the President—or anyone else—was there at the time is
beside the point. If not, he'd find another way easily
enough. After that happened, our hero here would take
the posture of the national savior, the only man compe-
tent to track down a second bomb, which could be anywhere. Imagine the fear, the witch-hunts, the cordons,
the suspicion, the 'Emergency' and 'For the Duration'
orders and regulations." Suddenly savage, Jones
snarled, "I've got just one more thing to say about this
warrior and his plans. All his own strength, and the entire muscle behind everything he plans for himself, de-
rives from the finest *esprit de corps* the world has ever
known. I told you I'm in a corny mood, so I'm going to
say it just the way it strikes me. That kind of *esprit* is a
bigger thing than obedience or devotion or even faith,
it's a species of love. And there's not a hell of a lot of
that to go around in this world. Butchering the President to make himself a little tin god is a minor crime
compared to his willingness to take a quality like that
and turn it into a perversion."

The civilian, as if unconsciously, hitched his chair a
half inch away from the colonel. The admiral trained a
firing-squad kind of look at him.

"Admiral," said Jones, and the man twitched, "I'd
like to call your attention to the colonel's use of the
word 'eliminate' in his query. You don't, you know, you
just *don't* eliminate a live President." He let that sink in,
and then said, "I mention it because you, too, used it,

and it's a fair conjecture that it means the same thing. Listen: 'WHAT SINGLE MAN CAN I ELIMINATE TO BE-COME PRESIDENT?' "

"There could hardly be any *one* man," said the civilian thoughtfully, gaining Jones' great respect for his composure. Jones said, "ORACLE thinks so. It wrote your name, sir."

Slowly the civilian turned to the admiral. "Why, you sleek old son of a bitch," he enunciated carefully, "I do believe you could have made it."

"Purely a hypothetical question," explained the admiral, but no one paid the least attention.

"As for you," said Jones, rather surprised that his voice expressed so much of the regret he felt, "I do believe that you asked your question with a genuine desire to see a world at peace before you passed on. But, sir—it's like you said when you walked in here just now—and the colonel said it, too: 'I didn't think . . .' You are sitting next to two certifiable first-degree murderers; no matter what their overriding considerations, that's what they are. But what you planned is infinitely worse."

He read, " 'CAN MY SUPPORT OF HENNY BRING PEACE?' You'll be pleased to know—oh, you already know; you were just checking, right?—that the answer is Yes. Henny's position is such right now that your support would bring him in. But—you didn't *think*. That demagog can't do what he wants to do without a species of thought policing the like of which the ant-heap experts in China never even dreamed of. Unilateral disarmament and high morality scorched-earth! Why, as a nation we couldn't do that unless we meant it, and we couldn't mean it unless every man, woman and child thought alike—and with Henny running things, they would. Peace? Sure we'd have peace! I'd rather take on a Kodiak bear with boxing gloves than take my chances in that kind of a world. These guys," he said carelessly, "are prepared to murder one or two or a few thousand. You," said Jones, his voice suddenly shaking with scorn, "are prepared to murder every decent free thing this country ever stood for."

Jones rose. "I'm going now. All your answers are in the package there. Up to now it's been an integral part of ORACLE—it was placed exactly in line with the reader, and has therefore been a part of everything the machine has ever done. My recommendation is that you replace it, or ORACLE will be just another computer, answering questions in terms of themselves. I suggest that you make similar installations in your own environment . . . and quit asking questions that must be answered in terms of *your*selves. Questions which in the larger sense would be unthinkable."

The civilian rose, and did something that Jones would always remember as a decent thing. He put out his hand and said, "You are right. I needed this, and you've stopped me. What will stop *them*?"

Jones took the hand. "They're stopped. I know, because I asked ORACLE and ORACLE said this was the way to do it." He smiled briefly and went out. His last glimpse of the office was the rigid backs of the two officers, and the civilian behind his desk, slowly unwrapping the package. He walked down the endless Pentagon corridors, the skin between his shoulder blades tight all the way: ORACLE or no, there might be overriding considerations. But he made it, and got to the first outside phone booth still alive. Marvelously, wonderfully alive.

He heard Ann's voice and said, "It's a real wonderful world, you know that?"

"Jones, darling! . . . you certainly have changed your tune. Last time I talked to you it was a horrible place full of evil intentions and smelling like feet."

94

"I just found out for sure three lousy kinds of world it's not going to be," Jones said. Ann would not have been what she was to him if she had not been able to divine which questions not to ask. She said, "Well, good," and he said he was coming home.

"Oh, darling! You fix that gadget?"

"Nothing to it," Jones said. "I just took down the

sign."

She said, "I never know when you're kidding."

WON'T YOU WALK—

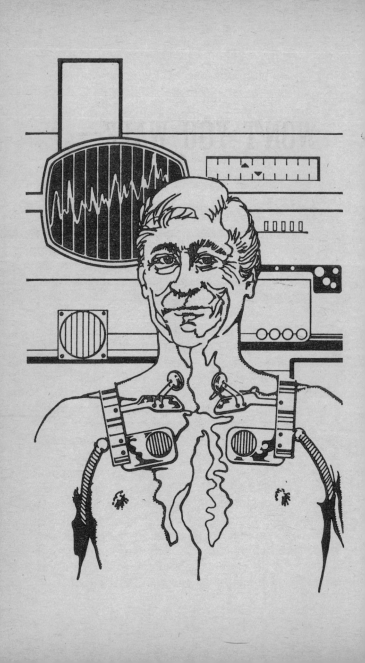

Joe Fritch walked under the moon, and behind the bridge of his nose something rose and stung him. When he was a little boy, which was better than thirty years ago, this exact sensation was the prelude to tears. There had been no tears for a long time, but the sting came to him, on its occasions, quite unchanged. There was another goad to plague him too, as demanding and insistent as the sting, but at the moment it was absent. They were mutually exclusive.

His mind was a jumble of half-curses, half-wishes, not weak or pale ones by any means, but just unfinished. He need not finish them any of them; his curses and his wishes were his personal clichés, and required only a code, a syllable for each. "He who hesitates—" people say, and that's enough. "Too many cooks—" they say wisely. "What's sauce for the goose—" Valid sagacities, every one, classic as the Parthenon and as widely known.

Such were the damnations and the prayers in the microcosm called Joe Fritch. "Oh, I wish—" he would say to himself, and "If only—" and "Some day, by God—"; and for each of these there was a wish, detailed and dramatic, so thought-out, touched-up, policed and maintained that it had everything but reality to make it real. And in the other area, the curses, the code-words expressed wide meticulous matrices: "That Barnes—"

dealt not only with his employer, a snide, selfish, sarcastic sadist with a presence like itching powder, but with every social circumstance which produced and permitted a way of life wherein a man like Joe Fritch could work for a man like Barnes. "Lutie—" was his wife's name, but as a code word it was dowdy breakfasts and I-can't-afford, that-old-dress and the finger in her ear, the hand beginning to waggle rapidly when she was annoyed; "Lutie—" said as the overture to this massive curse was that which was wanted and lost *("Joe?" "What, li'l Lutie?" "Nothing, Joe. Just . . . Joe—")* and that which was unwanted and owned, like the mortgage which would be paid off in only eighteen more years, and the single setting of expensive flowery sterling which they would never, never be able to add to.

Something had happened after dinner—he could almost not remember it now; what bursts the balloon, the last puff or air, or the air it already contains? Is the final drop the only factor in the spilling-over of a brimming glass? Something about Marie Next Door (Lutie always spoke of her that way, a name like William Jennings Bryan) and a new TV console, and something about Lutie's chances, ten years ago, of marrying no end of TV consoles, with houses free-and-clear and a car and a coat, and all these chances forsworn for the likes of Joe Fritch. It had been an evening like other evenings, through 10:13 p.m. At 10:14 something silent and scalding had burst in the back of Joe's throat; he had risen without haste and had left the house. Another man might have roared an epithet, hurled an ashtray. Some might have slammed the door, and some, more skilled in maliciousness, might have left it open so the angry wife, sooner or later, must get up and close it. Joe had simply shambled out, shrinking away from her in the mindless way an amoeba avoids a hot pin. There were things he might have said. There were things he

100

could have said to Barnes, too, time and time again, and to the elevator-starter who caught him by the elbow one morning and jammed him into a car, laughing at him through the gate before the doors slid shut. But he never said the things, not to anyone. Why not? Why not?

"They wouldn't listen," he said aloud, and again the sting came back of his nose.

He stopped and heeled water out of his left eye with the base of his thumb. This, and the sound of his own voice, brought him his lost sense of presence. He looked around like a child awakening in a strange bed.

It was a curved and sloping street, quite unlike the angled regimentation of his neighborhood. There was a huge elm arched over the street-lamp a block away, and to Joe's disoriented eye it looked like a photographic negative, a shadow-tree lit by darkness looming over a shadow of light. A tailored hedge grew on a neat stone wall beside him; across the street was a white picket fence enclosing a rolling acre and the dark mass of just the house he could never own, belonging, no doubt, to someone people listened to. Bitterly he looked at it and its two gates, its rolled white driveway, and, inevitably, the low, long coupé which stood in it. The shape of that car, the compact, obedient, directional eagerness of it, came to him like the welcome answer to some deep question within him, something he had thought too complex to have any solution. For a moment a pure, bright vision overwhelmed and exalted him; his heart, his very bones cried *well, of course!* and he crossed to the driveway, along its quiet grassy margin to the car.

He laid a hand on its cool ivory flank, and had his vision again. At the wheel of this fleetfooted dream-car, he would meet the morning somewhere far from here. There would be a high hill, and a white road winding up it, and over the brow of that hill, there would be the sea. Below, a beach, and rocks; and there would be people. Up the hill he would hurtle, through and over a stone wall at the top, and in the moment he was airborne, he would blow the horn. Louder, *bigger* than the horn would be his one bright burst of laughter. He had never laughed like that, but he would, he could, for all of him would be in it, rejoicing that they listened to him, they'd all be listening, up and down the beach and craning over the cliff. After that he'd fall, but that didn't matter. Nothing would matter, even the fact that his act was criminal and childish. All the "If only—" and "Some day, by God—" wishes, all the "That Barnes—" curses, for all their detail, lacked implementation. But this one, this one—

The window was open on the driver's side. Joe looked around; the street was deserted and the house was dark. He bent and slid his hand along the line of dimly-glowing phosphorescence that was a dashboard. Something tinkled, dangled—the keys, the keys!

He opened the door, got in. He could feel the shift in balance as the splendid machine accepted him like a lover, and they were one together. He pulled the door all but closed, checked it, then pressed it the rest of the way. It closed with a quiet, solid click, Joe grasped the steering wheel in both hands, settled himself, and quelled just the great trumpeting of laughter he had envisioned. *Later, later.* He reached for the key, turned it.

There was a soft purring deep under the hood. The window at his left slid up, nudging his elbow out of the way, seated itself in the molding above. The purring stopped. Then silence.

Joe grunted in surprise and turned the key again. Nothing. He fumbled along the dashboard, over the cowling, under its edge. He moved his feet around. Accelerator, brake. No clutch. A headlight dimmer switch.

With less and less caution he pushed, turned and pulled at the controls on the instrument panel. No lights came on. The radio did not work. Neither did the cigarette lighter, which startled him when it came out in his hand. There wasn't a starter anywhere.

Joe Fritch, who couldn't weep, very nearly did then. If a man had a car burglar-proofed with some sort of concealed switch, wasn't that enough? Why did he have to amuse himself by leaving the keys in it? Even Barnes never thought of anything quite that sadistic.

For a split second he glanced forlornly at his glorious vision, then forever let it go. Once he sniffed; then he put his hand on the door control and half rose in his seat.

The handle spun easily, uselessly around. Joe stopped it, pulled it upward. It spun just as easily that way. He tried pulling it toward him, pushing it outward. Nothing.

He bit his lower lip and dove for the other door. It had exactly the same kind of handle, which behaved exactly the same way. Suddenly Joe was panting as if from running hard.

Now take it easy. Don't try to do anything. Think. Think, Joe.

The windows!

On his door there were two buttons; on the other, one. He tried them all. "I can't get out," he whispered. "I can't—" Suddenly he spun one of the door handles. He fluttered his hands helplessly and looked out into the welcome, open dark. *"Can't!"* he cried.

"That's right," said a voice. "You sure can't."

The sting at the base of Joe Fritch's nose—that was one of the unexpressed, inexpressible pains which had plagued him ever since he was a boy. Now came the other.

103

It was a ball of ice, big as a fist, in his solar plexus; and around this ball stretched a membrane; and the ball was fury, and the membrane was fear. The more terrified he became, the tighter the membrane shrank and the more it hurt. If ever he were frightened beyond bearing, the membrane would break and let the fury out, and that must not, must not happen, for the fury was so cold and so uncaring of consequence. This was no churning confusion—there was nothing confused about it. There was only compression and stretching and a breaking point so near it could be felt in advance. There was nothing that could be done about it except to sit quite still and wait until it went away, which it did when whatever caused it went away.

This voice, though, here in the car with him, it didn't go away. Conversationally it said, "Were you thinking of breaking the glass?"

Joe just sat. The voice said, "Look in the glove compartment." It waited five seconds, and said, "Go ahead. Look in the glove compartment."

Trembling, Joe reached over and fumbled the catch of the glove compartment. He felt around inside. It seemed empty, and then something moved under his fingers. It was a rectangle of wood, about six inches by three, extremely light and soft. Balsa. "I used to use a real piece of glass as a sample," said the voice, "but one of you fools got to bashing it around and broke two of his own fingers. Anyway, that piece of wood is exactly as thick as the windshield and windows." It was nearly three quarters of an inch thick. "Bulletproof is an understatement. Which reminds me," said the voice, stifling a yawn, "if you have a gun, for Pete's sake don't use it. The slug'll ricochet. Did you ever see the wound a ricocheted bullet makes?" The yawn again. " 'Scuse me. You woke me up."

Joe licked his lips, which made him shudder. The

tongue and lip were so dry they scraped all but audibly. "Where are you?" he whispered.

"In the house. I always take that question as a compliment. You're hearing me on the car radio. Clean, hm-m-m? Flat to twenty-seven thousand cycles. Designed it myself."

Joe said, "Let me out."

"I'll let you out, but I won't let you go. You people are my bread and butter."

"Listen," said Joe, "I'm not a thief, or a . . . or a . . . or anything. I mean, this was just a sort of wild idea. Just let me go, huh? I won't *ever* . . . I mean, I promise." He scraped at his lip with his tongue again and added, "Please. I mean, please."

"Where were you going with my car, Mister I'm-not-a-thief?"

Joe was silent.

A sudden blaze of light made him wince. His eyes adjusted, and he found it was only the light over the porte cochere which bridged the driveway where it passed the house. "Come on inside," said the voice warmly.

Joe looked across the rolling lawn at the light. The car was parked in the drive near the street; the house was nearly two hundred feet away. *Catch ten times as many with it parked way out here,* he thought wildly. And, *I thought Barnes was good at making people squirm.* And, *Two hundred feet, and him in the house. He can outthink me; could he outrun me?* "What do you want me inside for?"

"Would it make any difference how I answered that question?"

Joe saw that it wouldn't. The voice was calling the shots just now, and Joe was hardly in a position to make any demands. Resignedly he asked, "You're going to call the police?"

"Absolutely not."

A wave of relief was overtaken and drowned in a flood of terror. No one knew where he was. No one had seen him get into the car. Being arrested would be unpleasant, but at least it would be a known kind of unpleasantness. But what lay in store for him in this mysterious expensive house?

"You better just call the police," he said. "I mean, have me arrested. I'll wait where I am."

"No," said the voice. It carried a new tone, and only by the change did Joe realize how—how *kind* it had been before. Joe believed that single syllable completely. Again he eyed the two hundred feet. He tensed himself, and said, "All right. I'll come."

"Good boy," said the voice, kind again. "Sleep sweet." Something went *pffft!* on the dashboard and Joe's head was enveloped in a fine, very cold mist. He fell forward and hit his mouth on the big V emblem in the hub of the steering wheel. A profound astonishment enveloped him because he felt the impact but no pain.

He blacked out.

There was a comfortable forever during which he lay in a dim place, talking lazily, on and on. Something questioned him from time to time, and perhaps he knew he was not questioning himself; he certainly didn't care. He rested in an euphoric cloud, calmly relating things he thought he had forgotten, and while an objective corner of his mind continued to operate, to look around, to feel and judge and report, it was almost completely preoccupied with an astonished delight that he could talk about his job, his marriage, his sister Anna, even about Joey—whom he'd killed when he and Joey were ten years old—without either the self-pitying twinge of unshed tears nor the painful fear which contained his rage.

106

Someone moved into his range of vision, someone with a stranger's face and a manner somehow familiar. He had something shiny in his hand. He advanced and bent over him, and Joe felt the nip of a needle in his upper arm. He lay quietly then, not talking because he had finished what he had to say, not moving because he was so comfortable, and began to feel warm from the inside out. That lasted for another immeasurable time. Then he detected movement again, and was drawn to it; the stranger crossed in front of him and sat down in an easy chair. Their faces were about at the same level, but Joe was not on an easy chair. Neither was it a couch. It was something in between. He glanced down and saw his knees, his feet. He was in one of those clumsy-looking, superbly comfortable devices known as a con-tour chair. He half-sat, half-reclined in it, looked at the other man and felt just wonderful. He smiled sleepily, and the man smiled back.

The man looked too old to be thirty, though he might be. He looked too young for fifty, though that was pos-sible, too. His hair was dark, his eyebrows flecked with gray—a combination Joe thought he had never seen be-fore. His eyes were light—in this dim room it was hard to see their color. The nose was ridiculous: it belonged to a happy fat man, and not someone with a face as long and lean as this one. The mouth was large and flexible; it was exactly what is meant by the term "gen-erous," yet its lips were thin, the upper one almost non-existent. He seemed of average height, say five, ten or eleven, but he gave the impression of being somehow too wide and too flat. Joe looked at him and at his smile, and it flashed across his mind that the French call a smile *sourire,* which means literally "under a laugh"; and surely, in any absolute scale of merriment, this smile was just exactly that. "How are you feeling?"

"I feel fine," said Joe. He really meant it.

"I'm Zeitgeist," said the man.

Joe was unquestioningly aware that the man knew him, knew all about him, so he didn't offer his name in return. He accepted the introduction and after a moment let his eyes stray from the friendly face to the wall behind him, to some sort of framed document, around to the side where a massive bookcase stood. He suddenly realized that he was in a strange room. He snapped his gaze back to the man. "Where am I?"

"In my house," said Zeitgeist. He uncrossed his legs and leaned forward. "I'm the man whose car you were stealing. Remember?"

Joe did, with a rush. An echo of his painful panic struck him, made him leap to his feet, a reflex which utterly failed. Something caught him gently and firmly around the midriff and slammed him back into the contour chair. He looked down and saw a piece of webbing like that used in aircraft safety belts, but twice as wide. It was around his waist and had no buckle; or if it had, it was behind and under the back of the chair, well out of his reach.

"It's O.K.," Zeitgeist soothed him. "You didn't actually steal it, and I understand perfectly why you tried. Let's just forget that part of it."

"Who are you? What are you trying to do? Let me out of this thing!" The memory of this man approaching him with a glittering hypodermic returned to him. "What did you do, drug me?"

Zeitgeist crossed his legs again and leaned back. "Yes, several times, and the nicest part of it is that you can't stay that excited very long just now." He smiled again, warm.

Joe heaved again against the webbing, lay back, opened his mouth to protest, closed it helplessly. Then he met the man's eyes again, and he could feel the indignation and fright draining out of him. He suddenly felt foolish, and found a smile of his own, a timid, foolish one.

"First I anaesthetized you," said Zeitgeist informatively, apparently pursuing exactly the line of thought brought out by Joe's question, "because not for a second would I trust any of you to come across that lawn just because I asked you to. Then I filled you full of what we'd call truth serum if this was a TV play. And when you'd talked enough I gave you another shot to pull you out of it. Yes, I drugged you."

"What for? What do you want from me, anyway?"

"You'll find out when you get my bill."

"Bill?"

"Sure. I have to make a living just like anybody else."

"Bill for what?"

"I'm going to fix you up."

"There's nothing the matter with me!"

Zeitgeist twitched his mobile lips. "Nothing wrong with a man who wants to take an expensive automobile and kill himself with it?"

Joe dropped his eyes. A little less pugnaciously, he demanded, "What are you, a psychiatrist or something?"

"Or something," laughed Zeitgeist. "Now listen to me," he said easily. "There are classic explanations for people doing the things they do, and you have a textbook full. You were an undersized kid who lost his mother early. You were brutalized by a big sister who just wouldn't be a mother to you. When you were ten you threw one of your tantrums and crowded another kid, and he slipped on the ice and was hit by a truck and killed. Your sister lambasted you for it until you ran away from home nine years later. You got married and didn't know how to put your wife into the mother-

109

image, so you treated her like your sister Anna instead; you obeyed, you didn't answer back, you did as little as possible to make her happy because no matter how happy she got you were subconsciously convinced it would do you no good. And by the way, the kid who was killed had the same name as you did." He smiled his kindly smile, wagged his head and *tsk-tsked*. "You should see what the textbooks say about *that* kind of thing. Identification: you are the Joey who was killed when you got mad and hit him. Ergo, don't ever let yourself get mad or you'll be dead. Joe Fritch, you know what you are? You're a mess."

"What am I supposed to say?" asked Joe in a low voice. Had he run off at the mouth that much? He was utterly disarmed. In the face of such penetrating revelation, anger would be ridiculous.

"Don't say anything. That is, don't try to explain—I already understand. How'd you like to get rid of all that garbage? I can do that for you. Will you let me?"

"Why should you?"

"I've already told you. It's my living."

"You say you're a psychiatrist?"

"I said nothing of the kind, and that's beside the point. Well?"

"Well, O.K. I mean . . . O.K."

Zeitgeist rose, smiling, and stepped behind Joe. There was a metallic click and the webbing loosened. Joe looked up at his host, thinking: *Suppose I won't? Suppose I just don't? What could he do?*

"There are lots of things I could do," said Zeitgeist with gentle cheerfulness. "Full of tricks, I am."

In spite of himself, Joe laughed. He got up. Zeitgeist steadied him, then released his elbow. Joe said, "Thanks . . . what are you, I mean, a mind reader?"

"I don't have to be."

Joe thought about it. "I guess you don't," he said.

"Come on." Zeitgeist turned away to the door. Joe reflected that anyone who would turn his back on a prisoner like that was more than just confident—he must have a secret weapon. *But at the moment confidence is enough.* He followed Zeitgeist into the next room.

It, too, was a low room, but much wider than the other, and its dimness was of quite another kind. Pools of brilliance from floating fluorescents mounted over three different laboratory benches made them like three islands in a dark sea. At about eye-level—as he stood— in the shadows over one of the benches, the bright green worm of a cathode-ray oscilloscope writhed in its twelve-inch circular prison. Ranked along the walls were instrument racks and consoles; he was sure he could not have named one in ten of them in broad daylight. The room was almost silent, but it was a living silence of almost indetectable clickings and hummings and the charged, noiseless *presence* of power. It was a waiting, busy sort of room.

"Boo," said Zeitgeist.

"I beg your . . . huh?"

Zeitgeist laughed. "You say it." He pointed. "Boooo."

Joe looked up at the oscilloscope. The worm had changed to a wiggling, scraggly child's scrawl, which, when Zeitgeist's long-drawn syllable was finished, changed into a green worm again. Zeitgeist touched a control knob on one of the benches and the worm became a straight line. "Go ahead."

"Boo," said Joe self-consciously. The line was a squiggle and then a line again. "Come on, a good loud long one," said Zeitgeist. This time Joe produced the same sort of "grass" the other man had. Or at least, it looked the same. "Good," said Zeitgeist. "What do you do for a living?"

"Advertising. You mean I didn't tell you?"

"You were more interested in talking about your boss than your work. What kind of advertising?"

"Well, I mean, it isn't advertising like in an agency. I mean, I work for the advertising section of the public relations division of a big corporation."

"You write ads? Sell them? Art, production, research—what?"

"All that. I mean, a little of all those. We're not very big. The company is, I mean, but not our office. We only advertise in trade magazines. The engineer'll come to me with something he wants to promote and I check with the . . . I mean, that Barnes, and if he O.K.'s it I write copy on it and check back with the engineer and write it again and check back with Barnes and write it again; and after that I do the layout, I mean I draft the layout just on a piece of typewriter paper, that's all, I can't draw or anything like that, I mean; and then I see it through Art and go back and check with Barnes, and then I order space for it in the magazines and—"

"You ever take a vocational analysis?"

"Yes. I mean, sure I did. I'm in the right sort of job, according to the tests. I mean, it was the Kline-Western test."

"Good test," said Zeitgeist approvingly.

"You think I'm not in the right sort of job?" He paused, and then with sudden animation, "You think I should quit that lousy job, I mean, get into something else?"

"That's your business. All right, that's enough."

The man could be as impersonal as a sixpenny nail when he wanted to be. He worked absorbedly at his controls for a while. There was a soft whine from one piece of apparatus, a clicking from another, and before

Joe knew what was happening he heard someone saying, "All that. I mean, a little of all those. We're not very big. The company is, I mean, but not our office. We only advertise—" on and on, in his exact words. His exact voice, too, he realized belatedly. He listened to it without enthusiasm. From time to time a light blazed, bright as a photo-flash but scalding red. Patiently, brilliantly, the oscilloscope traced each syllable, each pulse within each syllable. ". . . and check with Barnes, and then I order sp—" The voice ceased abruptly as Zeitgeist threw a switch.

"I didn't know you were recording," said Joe, "or I would have . . . I mean, said something different maybe."

"I know," said Zeitgeist. "That red light bother you?"

"It was pretty bright," said Joe, not wanting to complain.

"Look here." He opened the top of the recorder. Joe saw reels and more heads than he had ever seen on a recorder before, and a number of other unfamiliar components. "I don't know much about—"

"You don't have to," said Zeitgeist. "See there?" He pointed with one hand, and with the other reached for a button on the bench and pressed it. A little metal arm snapped up against the tape just where it passed over an idler. "That punched a little hole in the tape. Not enough to affect the recording." Zeitgeist turned the reel slowly by hand, moving the tape along an inch or so. Joe saw, on the moving tape, a tiny bright spot of light. When the almost invisible hole moved into it, the red light flared. "I pushed that button every time you said 'I mean.' Let's play it again."

He played it again, and Joe listened—an act of courage, because with all his heart he wanted to cover his ears, shut his eyes against that red blaze. He was consumed with embarrassment. He had never heard anything that sounded so completely idiotic. When at last it was over, Zeitgeist grinned at him. "Learn something?"

"I did," said Joe devoutly.

"O.K.," said Zeitgeist, in a tone which disposed of the matter completely as far as he was concerned, at the same time acting as prelude to something new. The man's expressiveness was extraordinary; with a single word he had Joe's gratitude and his fullest attention. "Now listen to this." He made some adjustments, threw a switch. Joe's taped voice said, ". . . go back and check it with Ba-a-a-a-a-a-ah—" with the "ah" going on and on like an all-clear signal. "That bother you?" called Zeitgeist over the noise.

"It's awful!" shouted Joe. This time he did cover his ears. It didn't help. Zeitgeist switched off the noise and laughed at him. "That's understandable. Your own voice, and it goes on and on like that. What's bothering you is, it doesn't breathe. I swear you could choke a man half to death, just by making him listen to that. Well, don't let it worry you. That thing over there"—he pointed to a massive cabinet against the wall—"is my analyzer. It breaks up your voice into all the tones and overtones it contains, finds out the energy level of each, and shoots the information to that tone-generator yonder. The generator reproduces each component exactly as received, through seventy-two band-pass filters two hundred cycles apart. All of which means that when I tell it to, it picks out a single vowel sound—in this case your 'a' in 'Barnes'—and hangs it up there on the 'scope like a photograph for as long as I want to look at it."

"All that, to do what I do when I say 'ah'?"

"All that," beamed Zeitgeist. Joe could see he was unashamedly proud of his equipment. He leaned forward and flicked Joe across the Adam's apple. "That's a hell of a compact little machine, that pharynx of yours. Just look at that wave-form."

Joe looked at the screen. "Some mess."

"A little tomato sauce and you could serve it in an Italian resturant," said Zeitgeist. "Now let's take it apart."

From another bench he carried the cable of a large control box, and plugged it into the analyzer with a many-pronged jack. The box had on it nearly a hundred keys. He fingered a control at the end of each row and the oscilloscope subsided to its single straight line. "Each one of these keys controls one of those narrow two-hundred-cycle bands I was talking about," he told Joe. "Your voice—everybody's voice—has high and low overtones, some loud, some soft. Here's one at the top, one in the middle, one at the bottom." He pressed three widely separated keys. The speaker uttered a faint breathy note, than a flat tone, the same in pitch but totally different in quality; it was a little like hearing the same note played first on a piccolo and then on a viola. The third key produced only a murmuring hiss, hardly louder than the noise of the amplifier itself. With each note, the 'scope showed a single wavy line. With the high it was a steep but even squiggle. In the middle it was a series of shallow waves like a child's drawing of an ocean. Down at the bottom it just shook itself and lay there.

"Just what I thought. I'm not saying you're a so-prano, Joe, but there's five times more energy in your high register than there is at the bottom. Ever hear the way a kid's voice climbs the scale when he's upset—whining, crying, demanding? 'Spose I told you that all the protest against life that you're afraid to express in anger, is showing up here?" He slid his fingers across the entire upper register, and the speaker bleated. "Listen to that, the poor little feller."

In abysmal self-hatred, Joe felt the sting of tears. "Cut it out," he blurted.

"Caht eet ow-oot," mimicked Zeitgeist. Joe thought he'd kill him, then and there, but couldn't because he found himself laughing. The imitation was very good. "You know, Joe, the one thing you kept droning on about in the other room was something about 'they won't listen to me. Nobody will listen.' How many times, say, in the office, have you had a really solid idea and kept it to yourself because 'nobody will listen'? How many times have you wanted to do something with your wife, go somewhere, ask her to get something from the cleaners—and then decided not to because she wouldn't listen?" He glanced around at Joe, and charitably turned away from the contorted face. "Don't answer that: you know, and it doesn't matter to me.

"Now get this, Joe. There's something in all animals just about as basic as hunger. It's the urge to attack something that's retreating, and its converse: to be wary of something that won't retreat. Next time a dog comes running up to you, growling, with his ears laid back, turn and run and see if he doesn't take a flank steak out of your southern hemisphere. After you get out of the hospital, go back and when he rushes you, laugh at him and keep going on about your business, and see him decide you're not on his calorie chart for the day. Well, the same thing works with people. No one's going to attack you unless he has you figured out—especially if he figures you'll retreat. Walk around with a big neon sign on your head that says HEY EVERYBODY I WILL RETREAT, and you're just going to get clobbered wherever you go. You've got a sign like that and it lights up every time you open your mouth. Caht eet owoot."

Joe's lower lip protruded childishly. "I can't help what kind of voice I've got."

"Probably you can't. I can, though."

"But how—"

"Shut up." Zeitgeist returned all the keys to a neutral position and listened a moment to the blaring audio. Then he switched it off and began flicking keys, some up, some down. "Mind you, this isn't a matter of changing a tenor into a baritone. New York City once had a mayor with a voice like a Punch and Judy show, and he hadn't an ounce of retreat in him. All I'm going to do is cure a symptom. Some people say that doesn't work, but ask the gimpy guy who finds himself three inches taller and walking like other people, the first time he tries his built-up shoes. Ask the guy who wears a well-made toupee." He stared for a while at the 'scope, and moved some more keys. "You want people to listen to you. All right, they will, whether they want to or not. Of course, *what* they listen to is something else again. It better be something that backs up this voice I'm giving you. That's up to you."

"I don't under—"

"You'll understand a lot quicker if we fix it so you listen and I talk. O.K.?" Zeitgeist demanded truculently, and sent over such an engaging grin that the words did not smart. "Now, like I said, I'm only curing a symptom. What you have to get through your thick head is that the disease doesn't exist. All that stuff about your sister Anna, and Joey, that doesn't exist because it happened and it's finished and it's years ago and doesn't matter any more. Lutie, Barnes . . . well, they bother you mostly because they won't listen to you. *They'll listen to you now.* So that botherment is over with, too; finished, done with, nonexistent. For all practical purposes yesterday is as far beyond recall as twenty years ago; just as finished, just as dead. So the little boy who got punished by his big sister until he thought he deserved being punished—*he* doesn't exist. The man with the guilty feeling killing a kid called Joey, he doesn't exist either any more, and by the way he wasn't guilty in the first place. The copy man who lets a pipsqueak sadist prick him with petty sarcasms—he's gone too, because now there's a man who won't swallow what he wants to say, what he knows is right. He'll say it, just because *people will listen.* A beer stein is pretty useless to anyone until you put beer in it. The gadget I'm going to give you won't do you a bit of good unless you put yourself, your real self into it." He had finished with the keys while he spoke, had turned and was holding Joe absolutely paralyzed with his strange light eyes.

Inanely, Joe said, "G-gadget?"

"Listen." Zeitgeist hit the master switch and Joe's voice again came from the speaker. "We only advertise in trade magazines. The engineer'll come to me with something he wants to promote and—"

And the voice was his voice, but it was something else, too. Its pitch was the same, inflection, accent; but there was a forceful resonance in it somewhere, somehow. It was a compelling voice, a rich voice; above all it was assertive and sure. (And when the 'I means' came, and the scalding light flashed, it wasn't laughable or embarrassing; it was simply unnecessary.)

"That isn't me."

"You're quite right. It isn't. But it's the way the world will hear you. It's behind the way the world will treat you. And the way the world treats a man is the way the man grows, if he wants to and he's got any growing left in him. Whatever is in that voice you can *be* because I will help and the world will help. But you've got to help, too."

"I'll help," Joe whispered.

118

"Sometimes I make speeches," said Zeitgeist, and grinned shyly. The next second he was deeply immersed in work.

He drew out a piece of paper with mimeographed rulings on it, and here and there in the ruled squares he jotted down symbols, referring to the keyboard in front of him. He seemed then to be totaling columns; once he reset two or three keys, turned on the audio and listened intently, then erased figures and put down others. At last he nodded approvingly, rose, stretched till his spine cracked, picked up the paper and went over to the third bench.

From drawers and cubbyholes he withdrew components—springs, pads, plugs, rods. He moved with precision and swift familiarity. He rolled out what looked like a file drawer, but instead of papers it contained ranks and rows of black plastic elements, about the size and shape of miniature match boxes, each with two bright brass contacts at top and bottom.

"We're living in a wonderful age, Joe," said Zeitgeist as he worked. "Before long I'll turn the old soldering iron out to stud and let it father waffles. Printed circuits, sub-mini tubes, transistors. These things here are electrets, which I won't attempt to explain to you." He bolted and clipped, bent and formed, and every once in a while, referring to his list, he selected another of the black boxes from the file and added it to his project. When there were four rows of components, each row about one and a half by six inches, he made some connections with test clips and thrust a jack into a receptacle in the bench. He glanced up at the 'scope, grunted, unclipped one of the black rectangles and substituted another from the files.

"These days, Joe, when they can pack a whole radar set—transmitter, receiver, timing and arming mechanisms and a power supply into the nose of a shell, a package no bigger than your fist—these days you can do anything with a machine. Anything, Joe. You just have to figure out how. Most of the parts exist, they make 'em in job lots. You just have to plug 'em together." He plugged in the jack, as if to demonstrate, and glanced up at the 'scope. "Good. The rest won't take long." Working with tin-snips, then with a small sheet-metal brake, he said, "Some day you're going to ask me what I'm doing, what all this is for, and I'll just grin at you. I'm going to tell you now and if you don't remember what I say, well, then forget it.

"They say our technology has surpassed, or by-passed, our souls, Joe. They say if we don't turn from science to the spirit, we're doomed. I agree that we're uncomfortably close to damnation, but I don't think we'll appease any great powers by throwing our gears and gimmicks over the cliff as a sacrifice, a propitiation. Science didn't get us into this mess; we *used* science to get us in.

"So I'm just a guy who's convinced we can use science to get us out. In other words, I'm not for hanging the gunsmith every time someone gets shot. Take off your shirt."

"What?" said Joe, back from a thousand miles. "Oh." Bemused, he took off his jacket and shirt and stood shyly clutching his thin ribs.

Zeitgeist picked up his project from the bench and put it over Joe's head. A flat band of spring steel passed over each shoulder, snugly. The four long flat casings, each filled with components, rested against his collar-bones, pressing upward in the small hollow just below the bones, and against his shoulder blades. Zeitgeist bent and manipulated the bands until they were tight but comfortable. Then he hooked the back pieces to the

120

front pieces with soft strong elastic bands passing under Joe's arms. "O.K.? O.K. Now—say something."

"Say what?" said Joe stupidly, and immediately clapped his hand to his chest. *"Uh!"*

"What happened?"

"It . . . I mean, it buzzed!"

Zeitgeist laughed. "Let me tell you what you've got there. In front, two little speakers, an amplifier to drive them, and a contact microphone that picks up your chest tones. In back, on this side, a band-pass arrangement that suppresses all those dominating high-frequency whimperings of yours and feeds the rest, the stuff you're weak in, up front to be amplified. And over here, in back—that's where the power supply goes. Go over there where you were and record something. And remember what I told you—you have to help this thing. Talk a little slower and you won't have to say 'I mean' while you think of what comes next. You *know* what comes next, anyway. You don't have to be afraid to say it."

Dazed, Joe stepped back to where he had been when the first recording was made, glanced for help up at the green line of the oscilloscope, closed his eyes and said, falteringly at first, then stronger and steadier, " 'Four score and seven years ago, our fathers brought forth upon this contin—' "

"Cut!" cried Zeitgeist. "Joe, see that tone-generator over there? It's big as a spinet piano. I can do a lot but believe me, you haven't got one of those strapped on you. Your amplifier can only blow up what it gets. You don't have much, but for Pete's sake give it what you have. Try talking with your lungs full instead of empty. Push your voice a little, don't just let it fall out of you."

"Nothing happens, though. I sound the same to myself. Is it working? Maybe it doesn't work."

"Like I told you before," said Zeitgeist with exaggerated patience, "people who are talking aren't listening. It's working all right. Don't go looking for failures, Joe. Plenty'll come along that you didn't ask for. Now go ahead and do as I said."

Joe wet his lips, took a deep breath. Zeitgeist barked, "Now slowly!" and he began: " 'Four score and seven years—' " The sonorous words rolled out, his chest vibrated from the buzzing, synchronized to his syllables. And though he was almost totally immersed in his performance, a part of him leaped excitedly, realizing that never in his whole life before had he listened, really listened to that majestic language. When he was finished he opened his eyes and found Zeitgeist standing very near him, his eyes alight.

"Good," the man breathed. "Ah, but . . . good."

"Was it? Was it really?"

In answer, Zeitgeist went to the controls, rewound the tape, and hit the playback button.

And afterwards, he said gently to Joe, "You *can* cry—see?"

"Damn foolishness," said Joe.

"No it isn't," Zeitgeist told him.

Outside, it was morning—what a morning, with all the gold and green, thrust and rustle of a new morning in a new summer. He hadn't been out all night; he had died and was born again! He stood tall, walked tall, he carried his shining new voice sheathed like Excalibur, but for all its concealment, he was armed!

He had tried to thank Zeitgeist, and that strange man had shaken his head soberly and said, "Don't, Joe. You're going to pay me for it."

"Well I will, of course I will! Anything you say . . . how much, anyhow?"

Zeitgeist had shaken his head slightly. "We'll talk

about it later. Go on—get in the car. I'll drive you to work." And, silently, he had.

Downtown, he reached across Joe and opened the door. For him, the door worked. "Come see me day after tomorrow. After dinner—nine."

"O.K. Why? Got another . . . treatment?"

"Not for you," said Zeitgeist, and his smile made it a fine compliment for both of them. "But no power plant lasts forever. Luck." And before Joe could answer the door was closed and the big car had swung out into traffic. Joe watched it go, grinning and shaking his head.

The corner clock said five minutes to nine. Just time, if he hurried.

He didn't hurry. He went to Harry's and got shaved, while they pressed his suit and sponged his collar in the back room. He kept the bathrobe they gave him pulled snugly over his amplifier, and under a hot towel he reached almost the euphoric state he had been in last night. He thought of Barnes, and the anger stirred in him. With some new internal motion he peeled away its skin of fear and set it free. Nothing happened, except that it lived in him instead of just lying there. It didn't make him tremble. It made him smile.

Clean, pressed, and smelling sweet, he walked into his building at eight minutes before ten. He went down to the express elevator and stepped into the one open door. Then he said, "Wait," and stepped out again. The operator goggled at him.

Joe walked up to the starter, a bushy character in faded brown and raveled gold braid. "Hey . . . you."

The starter pursed a pair of liver-colored lips and glowered at him. "Whaddayeh want?"

Joe filled his lungs and said evenly, "Day before yesterday you took hold of me and shoved me into an elevator like I was a burlap sack."

The starter's eyes flickered. "Not me."

"You calling me a liar, too?"

Suddenly the man's defenses caved. There was a swift pucker which came and went on his chin, and he said, "Look, I got a job to do, mister, rush hours, if I don't get these cars out of here it's *my* neck, I didn't mean nothing by it, I——"

"Don't tell me your troubles," said Joe. He glared at the man for a second. "All right, do your job, but don't do it on me like that again."

He turned his back, knowing he was mimicking Zeitgeist with the gesture and enjoying the knowledge. He went back to the elevator and got in. Through the closing gate he saw the starter, right where he had left him, gaping. The kid running the elevator was gaping, too.

"Eleven," said Joe.

"Yes, *sir*," said the boy. He started the car. "You told *him*."

"Bout time," said Joe modestly.

"Past time," said the kid.

Joe got out on the eleventh floor, feeling wonderful. He walked down the hall thumped a door open, and ambled in. Eleanor Bulmer, the receptionist, looked up. He saw her eyes flick to the clock and back to his face. "Well!"

"Morning," he said expansively, from his inflated lungs. She blinked as if he had fired a cap pistol, then looked confusedly down at her typewriter.

He took a step toward his corner desk when there was a flurry, a botherment up from the left, then an apparition of thinning hair and exophthalmic blue eyes. Barnes, moving at a half-trot as usual, jacket off, suspenders, arm-bands pulling immaculate cuffs high and away from rust-fuzzed scrawny wrists. "Eleanor, get me

Apex on the phone. Get me Apex on the—" And then he saw Joe. He stopped. He smiled. He had gleaming pale-yellow incisors like a rodent. He, too, flicked a glance at the clock.

Joe knew exactly what he was going to say, exactly how he was going to say it. He took a deep breath, and if old ghosts were about to rise in him, the friendly pressure of the amplifier just under his collar-bones turned them to mist. *Why, Miss Terr Fritch,* Barnes would say with exaggerated and dramatic politeness, *how ki-i-ind of you to drop in today.* Then the smile would snap off and the long series of not-to-be-answered questions would begin. Didn't he know this was a place of business? Was he aware of the customary starting time? Did it not seem that among fourteen punctual people, he alone—and so on. During it, seven typewriters would stop, a grinning stock boy would stick his head over a filing cabinet to listen, and Miss Bulmer, over whose nape the monologue would stream, would sit with her head bowed waiting for it to pass. Already the typewriters had stopped. And yes, sure enough: behind Barnes he could see the stock boy's head.

"Why, Miss Terr Fritch!" said Barnes happily.

Joe immediately filled his lungs, turned his back on Barnes, and said into the stunned silence, "Better get him Apex on the phone, Eleanor. He has the whole place at a stand-still." He then walked around Barnes as if the man were a pillar and went to his desk and sat down.

Barnes stood with his bony head lowered and his shoulders humped as if he had been bitten on the neck by a fire-ant. Slowly he turned and glared up the office. There was an immediate explosion of typewriter noise, shuffling feet, shuffling papers. "I'll take it in my office," Barnes said to the girl.

He had to pass Joe to get there, and to Joe's great

delight he could see how reluctant Barnes was to do it. "I'll see you later," Barnes hissed as he went by, and Joe called cheerfully after him, "You just betcha." Out in the office, somebody whistled appreciatively; somebody snickered. Joe knew Barnes had heard it. He smiled, and picked up the phone. "Outside, Eleanor. Personal."

Eleanor Bulmer knew Barnes didn't allow personal calls except in emergencies, and then preferred to give his permission first. Joe could hear her breathing, hesitating. Then, "Yes, Mr. Fritch." And the dial tone crooned in his ear. *Mr. Fritch*, he thought. *That's the first time she ever called me Mr. Fritch. What do you know. Why . . . why, she never called me anything before! Just "Mr. Barnes wants to see you," or "Cohen of Electrical Marketing on the line."*

Mr. Fritch dialed his home. "Hello—Lutie?"

"Joe! Where were you all night?" The voice was waspish, harrying; he could see her gathering her forces, he could see her mountain of complaints about to be shoveled into the telephone as if it were a hopper.

"I called up to tell you I'm all right because I thought it was a good idea. Maybe it was a bad idea."

"What?" There was a pause, and then in quite a different tone she said, "Joe? Is this . . . Joe, is that you?"

"Sure," he said heartily. "I'm at work and I'm all right and I'll be home for dinner. Hungry," he added.

"You expect me to cook you a dinner after—" she began, but without quite her accustomed vigor.

"All right, then I won't be home for dinner," he said reasonably.

She didn't say anything for a long time, but he knew she was still there. He sat and waited. At last she said faintly, "Will veal cutlets be all right?"

* * *

On the second night after this fledging, Mr. Joseph Fritch strode into the porte-cochère and bounded up the steps. He ground the bell-push with his thumb until it hurt, and then knocked. He stood very straight until the door opened.

"Joe, boy! Come on in." Zeitgeist left the door and opened another. Joe had the choice of following or of standing where he was and shouting. He followed. He found himself in a room new to him, low-ceilinged like the others, but with books from floor to ceiling. In a massive fieldstone fireplace flames leaped cheerfully, yet the room was quite cool. Air-conditioned. Well, he guessed Zeitgeist just *liked* a fire. "Look," he said abruptly.

"Sit down. Drink?"

"No. Listen, you've made a mistake."

"I know, I know. The bill. Got it with you?"

"I have."

Zeitgeist nodded approvingly. Joe caught himself wondering why. Zeitgeist glided across to him and pressed a tall glass into his hand. It was frosty, beaded, sparkling. "What's in it?" he snapped.

Zeitgeist burst out laughing, and in Joe fury passed, and shame passed, and he found himself laughing, too. He held out his glass and Zeitgeist clinked with him. "You're a . . . a—Luck."

"Luck," said Zeitgeist. They drank. It was whisky, the old gentle muscular whisky that lines the throat with velvet and instantly heats the ear lobes. "How did you make out?"

Joe drank again and smiled. "I walked into that office almost an hour late," he began, and told what had happened. Then, "And all day it was like that. I didn't know a job . . . people . . . I didn't know things could be like that. Look, I told you I'd pay you. I said I'd pay you anything you—"

"Never mind that just now. What else happened? The suit and all?"

"That. Oh, I guess I was kind of—" Joe looked into the friendly amber in his glass, "well, intoxicated. Lunch time I just walked into King's and got the suit. Two suits. I haven't had a new suit for four years, and then it didn't come from King's. I just signed for 'em," he added, a reflective wonderment creeping into his voice. "They didn't mind. Shirts," he said, closing his eyes.

"It'll pay off."

"It did pay off," said Joe, bouncing on his soft chair to sit upright on the edge, shoulders back, head up. His voice drummed and his eyes were bright. He set his glass down on the carpet and swatted his hands gleefully together. "There was this liaison meeting, they call it, this morning. I don't know what got into me. Well, I do; but anyway, like every other copywriter I have a project tucked away; you know—I like it but maybe no one else will. I had it in my own roughs, up to yesterday. So I got this bee in my bonnet and went in to the Art Department and started in on them, and you know, they caught fire, they worked almost all *night?* And at the meeting this morning, the usual once-a-month kind of thing, the brass from the main office looking over us step-children and wondering why they don' fold us up and go to an outside agency. It was so easy!" he chortled.

"I just sat there, shy like always, and there was old Barnes as usual trying to head off product advertising and go into institutionals, because he likes to write that stuff himself. Thinks it makes the brass think he loves the company. So soon as he said 'institutionals' I jumped up and agreed with him and said let me show you one of Mr. Barnes' ideas. Yeah! I went and got it and you should *see* that presentation; you could eat it! So here's two

VP's and a board secretary with their eyes bugging out and old Barnes not daring to deny anything, and everybody in the place knew I was lying and thought what a nice fellow I was to do it that way. And there sat that brass, looking at my haircut and my tie and my suit and me, and *buying* it piece by piece, and Barnes, old Barnes sweating it out."

"What did they offer you?"

"They haven't exactly. I'm supposed to go see the chairman Monday."

"What are you going to do?"

"Say no. Whatever it is, I'll say no. I have lots of ideas piled up—nobody would *listen* before! Word'll get around soon enough; I'll get my big raise the only smart way a man can get a really big one—just before he goes to work for a new company. Meanwhile I'll stay and work hard and be nice to Barnes, who'll die a thousand deaths."

Zeitgeist chuckled. "You're a stinker. What happened when you went home?"

Joe sank back into his chair and turned toward the flames; whatever his thoughts were, they suffused him with firelight and old amber, strength through curing, through waiting. His voice was just that mellow as he murmured, "That wasn't you at all. That was me."

"Oh, sorry. I wasn't prying."

"Don't get me wrong!" said Joe. "I want to tell you." He laughed softly. "We had veal cutlets."

A log fell and Joe watched the sparks shooting upward while Zeitgeist waited. Suddenly Joe looked across at him with a most peculiar expression on his face. "The one thing I never thought of till the time came. I couldn't wear that thing all night, could I now? I don't want her to know. I'll be . . . you said I'd grow to . . .

that if I put my back into it, maybe some day I wouldn't need it." He touched his collarbone.

"That's right," said Zeitgeist.

"So I couldn't wear it. And then I couldn't talk. Not a word." Again, the soft laugh. "She wouldn't sleep, not for the longest time. 'Joe?' she'd say, and I'd know she was going to ask where I'd been that night. I'd say, '*Shh.*' and put my hand on her face. She'd hold on to it. Funny. Funny, how you know the difference," he said in a near whisper, looking at the fire again. "She said, 'Joe?' just like before, and I knew she was going to say she was sorry for being . . . well, all the trouble we've had. But I said '*Shh.*' " He watched the fire silently, and Zeitgeist seemed to know that he was finished.

"I'm glad," said Zeitgeist.

"Yeah."

They shared some quiet. Then Zeitgeist said, waving his glass at the mantel, "Still think the bill's out of line?"

Joe looked at it, at the man. "It's not a question of how much it's worth," he said with some difficulty. "It's how much I can pay. When I left here I wanted to pay you whatever you asked—five dollars or five hundred, I didn't care what I had to sacrifice. But I never thought it would be five *thousand!*" He sat up. "I'll level with you; I don't have that kind of money. I never did have. Maybe I never will have."

"What do you think I fixed you up for?" Zeitgeist's voice cracked like a target-gun. "What do you think I'm in business for? I don't gamble."

Joe stood up slowly. "I guess I just don't understand you," he said coldly. "Well, at those prices I guess I can ask you to service this thing so I can get out of here."

"Sure." Zeitgeist rose and led the way out of the room and down the hall to the laboratory. His face was absolutely expressionless, but not fixed; only relaxed.

Joe shucked out of his jacket, unbuttoned his shirt and took it off. He unclipped the elastics and pulled the amplifier off over his head. Zeitgeist took it and tossed it on the bench. "All right," he said, "get dressed."

Joe went white. "What, you want to haggle? Three thousand then, when I get it," he said shrilly.

Zeitgeist sighed. "Get dressed."

Joe turned and snatched at his shirt. "Blackmail. Lousy blackmail."

Zeitgeist said, "You know better than that."

There is a quality of permanence about the phrase that precedes a silence. It bridges the gap between speech and speech, hanging in midair to be stared at. Joe pulled on his shirt, glaring defiantly at the other man. He buttoned it up, he tucked in the tails, he put on his tie and knotted it, and replaced his tie-clasp. He picked up his coat. And all the while the words hung there.

He said, miserably, "I want to know better than that."

Zeitgeist's breath hissed out; Joe wondered how long he had been holding it. "Come here, Joe," he said gently.

Joe went to the bench. Zeitgeist pulled the amplifier front and center. "Remember what I told you about this thing—a mike here to pick up the chest tones, band-passes to cut down on what you have too much of, and the amplifier here to blow up those low resonances? And this?" he pointed.

"The power supply."

"The power supply," Zeitgeist nodded. "Well, look; there's nothing wrong with the theory. Some day someone will design a rig this compact that will do the job, and it'll work just as I said." His pale gaze flicked across Joe's perplexed face and he laughed. "You're sort of impressed with all this, aren't you?" He indicated the whole lab and its contents.

"Who wouldn't be?"

"That's the mythos of science, Joe. The layman is as willing to believe in the super-powers of science as he once did in witches. Now, I told you once that I believe in the ability of science to save our souls . . . our *selves,* if you like that any better. I believe that it's legitimate to use any and all parts of science for this purpose. And I believe the mythos of science is as much one of its parts as Avogadro's Law or the conservation of energy. Any layman who's seen the size of a modern hearing-aid, who knows what it can do, will accept with ease the idea of a band-passing amplifier with five watts output powered by a couple of penlite cells. Well, we just can't do it. We will, but we haven't yet."

"Then what's this thing? What's all this gobbledegook you've been feeding me? You give me something, you take it away. You make it work, you tell me it can't work. I mean, what are you trying to pull?"

"You're squeaking. And you're saying 'I mean,'" said Zeitgeist.

"Cut it out," Joe said desperately.

The pale eyes twinkled at him, but Zeitgeist made a large effort and went back to his subject. "All this is, this thing you've been wearing, is the mike here, which triggers these two diaphragm vibrators here, powered by these little dry cells. No amplifier, no speaker, no nothing but this junk and the mythos."

"But it worked; I heard it right here on your tape machine!"

"With the help of half a ton of components."

"But at the office, the liaison meeting, I . . . I— Oh—"

"For the first time in your life you walked around with your chest out. You faced people with your shoulders back and you looked 'em smack in the eye. You dredged up what resonance you had in that flattened-out chest of yours and flung it in people's faces. I didn't lie to you when I said they *had* to listen to you. They had to as long as you believed they had to."

"Did you have to drag out all this junk to make me believe that?"

"I most certainly did! Just picture it: you come to me here all covered with bruises and guilt, suicidal, cowed, and without any realizable ambition. I tell you all you need to do is stand up straight and spit in their eye. How much good would that have done you?"

Joe laughed shakily. "I feel like one of those characters in the old animated cartoons. They'd walk off the edge of a cliff and hang there in midair, and there they'd stay, grinning and twirling their canes, until they looked down. Then—boom!" He tried another laugh, and failed with it. "I just looked down," he said hoarsely.

"You've got it a little backwards," said Zeitgeist. "Remember how you looked forward to graduating—to the time when you could discard that monkey-puzzle and stand on your own feet? Well, son, you just made it. Come on; this calls for a drink!"

Joe jammed his arms into his jacket. "Thanks, but I just found out I can talk to my wife."

They started up the hall. "What do you do this for, Zeitgeist?"

"It's a living."

"Is that streamlined mousetrap out there the only bait you use?"

Zeitgeist smiled and shook his head.

For the second time in fifteen minutes Joe said, "I guess I just don't understand you," but there was a world of difference. Suddenly he broke away from the old man and went into the room with the fireplace. He came back, jamming the envelope into his pocket. "I can handle this," he said. He went out.

Zeitgeist leaned in the doorway, watching him go. He'd have offered him a ride, but he wanted to see him walk like that, with his head up.

TALENT

Mrs. Brent and Precious were sitting on the farmhouse porch when little Jokey sidled out from behind the barn and came catfooting up to them. Precious, who had ringlets and was seven years old and very clean, stopped swinging on the glider and watched him. Mrs. Brent was reading a magazine. Jokey stopped at the foot of the steps.

"MOM!" he rasped.

Mrs. Brent started violently, rocked too far back, bumped her knobby hairdo against the clapboards, and said, "Good heavens, you little br— darling, you frightened me!"

Jokey smiled.

Precious said, "Snaggletooth."

"If you want your mother," said Mrs. Brent reasonably, "why don't you go inside and speak to her?"

Disgustedly, Jokey vetoed the suggestion with "Ah-h-h . . ." He faced the house. "MOM!" he shrieked, in a tone that spoke of death and disaster.

There was a crash from the kitchen, and light footsteps. Jokey's mother, whose name was Mrs. Purney, came out, pushing back a wisp of hair from frightened eyes.

"Oh, the sweet," she cooed. She flew out and fell on her knees beside Jokey. "Did it hurt its little, then? Aw, did it was . . ."

Jokey said, "Gimme a nickel!"

"Please," suggested Precious.

"Of course, darling," fluttered Mrs. Purney. "My word, yes. Just as soon as ever we go into town, you shall have a nickel. Two, if you're good."

"Gimme a nickel," said Jokey ominously.

"But, darling, what for? What will you do with a nickel out here?"

Jokey thrust out his hand. "I'll hold my breath."

Mrs. Purney rose, panicked. "Oh, dear, don't. Oh, please don't. Where's my reticule?"

"On top of the bookcase, out of my reach," said Precious, without rancor.

"Oh, yes, so it is. Now, Jokey, you wait right here and I'll just . . ." and her twittering faded into the house.

Mrs. Brent cast her eyes upward and said nothing.

"You're a little stinker," said Precious.

Jokey looked at her with dignity. "Mom," he called imperiously.

Mrs. Purney came to heel on the instant, bearing a nickel.

Jokey, pointing with the same movement with which he acquired the coin, reported, "She called me a little stinker."

"Really!" breathed Mrs. Purney, bridling. "I think, Mrs. Brent, that your child could have better manners."

"She has, Mrs. Purney, and uses them when they seem called for."

Mrs. Purney looked at her curiously, decided, apparently, that Mrs. Brent meant nothing by the statement (in which she was wrong) and turned to her son, who was walking briskly back to the barn.

"Don't hurt yourself, Puddles," she called.

She elicited no response whatever, and, smiling vaguely at Mrs. Brent and daughter, went back to her kitchen.

"Puddles," said Precious ruminatively. "I bet I know why she calls him that. Remember Gladys's puppy that—"

"Precious," said Mrs. Brent, "you shouldn't have called Joachim a word like that."

"I s'pose not," Precious agreed thoughtfully. "He's really a—"

Mrs. Brent, watching the carven pink lips, said warningly, "Precious!" She shook her head. "I've asked you not to say that."

"Daddy—"

"Daddy caught his thumb in the hinge of the car trunk. That was different."

"Oh, no," corrected Precious. "You're thinking of the time he opened on'y the bottom half of the Dutch door in the dark. When he pinched his thumb, he said—"

"Would you like to see my magazine?"

Precious rose and stretched delicately. "No, thank you, Mummy. I'm going out to the barn to see what Jokey's going to do with that nickel."

"Precious . . ."

"Yes, Mummy."

"Oh—nothing. I suppose it's all right. Don't quarrel with Jokey, now."

"Not 'less he quarrels with me," she replied, smiling charmingly.

Precious had new patent leather shoes with hard heels and broad ankle-straps. They looked neat and very shiny against her yellow socks. She walked carefully in the path, avoiding the moist grasses that nodded over the edges, stepping sedately over a small muddy patch.

Jokey was not in the barn. Precious walked through, smelling with pleasure the mixed, warm smells of chaff-dust, dry hay and manure. Just outside, by the wagon door, was the pigpen. Jokey was standing by the rail fence. At his feet was a small pile of green apples. He picked one up and hurled it with all his might at the brown sow. It went *putt!* on her withers, and she went *ergh!*

"Hey!" said Precious.

Putt-ergh! Then he looked up at Precious, snarled silently, and picked up another apple. *Putt-ergh!*

"Why are you doing that for?"

Putt-ergh!

"Hear that? My mom done just like that when I hit her in the stummick."

"She did?"

"Now this," said Jokey, holding up an apple, "is a stone. Listen." He hurled it. *Thunk-e-e-e-ergh!*

Precious was impressed. Her eyes widened, and she stepped back a pace.

"Hey, look out where you're goin', stoopid!"

He ran to her and grasped her left biceps roughly, throwing her up against the railings. She yelped and stood rubbing her arm—rubbing off grime, and far deeper in indignation than she was in fright.

Jokey paid her no attention. "You an' your shiny feet," he growled. He was down on one knee, feeling for two twigs stuck in the ground about eight inches apart. "Y'might've squashed 'em!

Precious, her attention brought to her new shoes, stood turning one of them, glancing light from the toe-caps, from the burnished sides, while complacency flowed back into her.

"What?"

With the sticks, Jokey scratched aside the loose earth and, one by one, uncovered the five tiny, naked, blind creatures which lay buried there. They were only about three-quarters of an inch long, with little withered limbs

140

and twitching noses. They writhed. There were ants, too. Very busy ants.

"What are they?"

"Mice, stoopid," said Jokey. "Baby mice. I found 'em in the barn."

"How did they get there?"

"I put 'em there."

"How long have they been there?"

" 'Bout four days," said Jokey, covering them up again. "They last a long time."

"Does your mother know those mice are out here?"

"No, and you better not say nothin', ya hear?"

"Would your mother whip you?"

"Her?" The syllable came out as an incredulous jeer.

"What about your father?"

"Aw, I guess he'd like to lick me. But he ain't got a chance. Mom'd have a fit."

"You mean she'd get mad at him?"

"No, stoopid. A fit. You know, scrabbles at the air and get suds on her mouth, and all. Falls down and twitches." He chuckled.

"But—why?"

"Well, it's about the on'y way she can handle Pop, I guess. He's always wanting to do something about me. She won't let 'um, so I c'n do anything I want."

"What do you do?"

"I'm talunted. Mom says so."

"Well, what do you do?"

"You're sorta nosy."

"I don't believe you can do anything, stinky."

"Oh, I can't?" Jokey's face was reddening.

"No, you can't! You talk a lot, but you can't really do anything."

Jokey walked up close to her and breathed in her face the way the man with the grizzly beard does to the clean-cut cowboy who is tied up to the dynamite kegs in the movies on Saturday.

"I can't, huh?"

She stood her ground. "All right, if you're so smart, let's see what you were going to do with that nickel!"

Surprisingly, he looked abashed. "You'd laugh," he said.

"No, I wouldn't," she said guilelessly. She stepped forward, opened her eyes very wide, shook her head so that her gold ringlets swayed, and said very gently, "Truly I wouldn't, Jokey . . ."

"Well—" he said, and turned to the pigpen. The brindled sow was rubbing her shoulder against the railing, grunting softly to herself. She vouchsafed them one small red-rimmed glance, and returned to her thoughts.

Jokey and Precious stood up on the lower rail and looked down on the pig's broad back.

"You're not goin' to tell anybody?" he asked.

" 'Course not."

"Well, awright. Now lookit. You ever see a china piggy bank?"

"Sure I have," said Precious.

"How big?"

"Well, I got one about this big."

"Aw, that's nothin'."

"And my girl-friend Gladys has one *this* big."

"Phooey."

"Well," said Precious, "in town, in a big drugstore, I saw one THIS big," and she put out her hands about thirty inches apart.

"That's pretty big," admitted Jokey. "Now I'll show you *something*." To the brindled sow, he said sternly, "You are a piggy bank."

The sow stopped rubbing herself against the rails.

142

She stood quite still. Her bristles merged into her hide. She was hard and shiny—as shiny as the little girl's hard shoes. In the middle of the broad back, a slot appeared—or had been there all along, as far as Precious could tell. Jokey produced a warm sweaty nickel and dropped it into the slot.

There was a distant, vitreous, hollow bouncing click from inside the sow.

Mrs. Purney came out on the porch and creaked into a wicker chair with a tired sigh.

"They are a handful, aren't they?" said Mrs. Brent.

"You just don't know," moaned Mrs. Purney.

Mrs. Brent's eyebrows went up. "Precious is a model. Her teacher says so. That wasn't too easy to do."

"Yes, she's a very good little girl. But my Joachim is—talented, you know. That makes it very hard."

"How is he talented? What can he do?"

"He can do anything," said Mrs. Purney after a slight hesitation.

Mrs. Brent glanced at her, saw that her tired eyes were closed, and shrugged. It made her feel better. Why must mothers always insist that their children are better than all others?

"Now, my Precious," she said, "—and mind you, I'm not saying this because she's my child—my Precious plays the piano very well for a child her age. Why, she's already in her third book and she's not eight yet."

Mrs. Purney said, without opening her eyes, "Jokey doesn't play. I'm sure he could if he wanted to."

Mrs. Brent saw what an inclusive boast this might be, and wisely refrained from further itemization. She took another tack. "Don't you find, Mrs. Purney, that it is easy to make a child obedient and polite by being firm?"

Mrs. Purney opened her eyes at last, and looked troubledly at Mrs. Brent. "A child should love its parents."

"Oh, of course!" smiled Mrs. Brent. "But these modern ideas of surrounding a child with love and freedom to an extent where it becomes a little tyrant—well! I just can't see that! Of course I don't mean Joachim," she added quickly, sweetly. "He's a *dear* child, really . . ."

"He's got to be given everything he wants," murmured Mrs. Purney in a strange tone. It was fierce and it was by rote. "He's *got* to be kept happy."

"You must love him very much," snapped Mrs. Brent viciously, suddenly determined to get some reaction out of this weak, indulgent creature. She got it.

"I hate him," said Mrs. Purney.

Her eyes were closed again, and now she almost smiled, as if the release of those words had been a yearned-for thing. Then she sat abruptly erect, her pale eyes round, and she grasped her lower lip and pulled it absurdly down and to the side.

"I didn't mean that," she gasped. She flung herself down before Mrs. Brent, and gabbled. "I didn't mean it! Don't tell him! He'll do things to us. He'll loosen the house-beams when we're sleeping. He'll turn the breakfast to snakes and frogs, and make that big toothy mouth again out of the oven door. Don't tell him! Don't tell him!"

Mrs. Brent, profoundly shocked, and not comprehending a word of this, instinctively put out her arms and gathered the other woman close.

"I can do lots of things," Jokey said. "I can do anything."

"Gee," breathed Precious, looking at the china pig. "What are you going to do with it now?"

144

"I dunno. I'll let it be a pig again, I guess."

"Can you change it back into a pig?"

"I don't hafta, stoopid. It'll be a pig by itself. Soon's I forget about it."

"Does that always happen?"

"No. If I busted that ol' china pig, it'd take longer, an' the pig would be all busted up when it changed back. All guts and blood," he added, sniggering. "I done that with a calf once."

"Gee," said Precious, still wide-eyed. "When you grow up you'll be able to do anything you want."

"Yeah." Jokey looked pleased. "But I can do anything I want now." He frowned. "I just sometimes don't know what to do next."

"You'll know when you grow up," she said confidently.

"Oh, sure. I'll live in a big house in town and look out of the windows, and bust up people and change 'em to ducks and snakes and things. I'll make flies as big as chickenhawks, or maybe as big as horses, and put 'em in the schools. I'll knock down the big buildings an' squash people."

He picked up a green apple and hurled it accurately at the brown sow.

"Gosh, and you won't have to practice piano, or listen to any old teachers," said Precious, warming to the possibilities. "Why, you won't even have to—*oh!*"

"What'sa matter?"

"That beetle. I hate them."

"Thass just a stag beetle," said Jokey with superiority. "Lookit here. I'll show you something."

He took out a book of matches and struck one. He held the beetle down with a dirty forefinger, and put the flame in its head. Precious watched attentively until the creature stopped scrabbling.

"Those things scare me," she said when he stood up.

"You're a sissy."

"I am not."

"Yes you are. *All* girls are sissies."

"You're dirty and you're a stinker," said Precious.

He promptly went to the pigpen and, from beside the trough, scooped up a heavy handful of filth. From his crouch, Jokey hurled it at her with a wide overhand sweep, so that it splattered her from the shoulder down, across the front of her dress, with a great wet gob for the toe of her left shiny shoe.

"Now who's dirty? Now who stinks?" he sang.

Precious lifted her skirt and looked at it in horror and loathing. Her eyes filled with angry tears. Sobbing, she rushed at him. She slapped him with little-girl clumsiness, hand-over-shoulder fashion. She slapped him again.

"Hey! Who are you hitting?" he cried in amazement. He backed off and suddenly grinned. "I'll fix you," he said, and disappeared without another word.

Whimpering with fury and revulsion, Precious pulled a handful of grass and began wiping her shoe.

Something moved into her field of vision. She glanced at it, squealed, and moved back. It was an enormous stag beetle, three times life-size, and it was scuttling toward her.

Another beetle—or the same one—met her at the corner.

With her hard black shiny shoes, she stepped on this one, so hard that the calf of her leg ached and tingled for the next half-hour.

The men were back when she returned to the house. Mr. Brent had been surveying Mr. Purney's fence-lines. Jokey was not missed before they left. Mrs. Purney looked drawn and frightened, and seemed glad that

146

Mrs. Brent was leaving before Jokey came in for his supper.

Precious said nothing when asked about the dirt on her dress, and, under the circumstances, Mrs. Brent thought better of questioning her too closely.

In the car, Mrs. Brent told her husband that she thought Jokey was driving Mrs. Purney crazy.

It was her turn to be driven very nearly mad, the next morning, when Jokey turned up. Most of him.

Surprising, really, how much beetle had stuck to the hard black shoe, and, when it was time, turned into what they found under their daughter's bed.

ONE FOOT
AND THE GRAVE

I was out in Fulgey Wood trying to find out what had happened to my foot, and I all but walked on her. Claire, I mean. Not Luana. You wouldn't catch Luana rolled up in a nylon sleeping bag, a moonbeam bright on her face.

Her face gleamed up like a jewel sunk deep in a crystal spring. I stood looking at it, not moving, not even breathing, hoping that she would not wake. I'd found that horror of a skull ten minutes ago and I'd much rather she didn't see it.

She stirred. I stepped back and sideward into a bear-trap. The steel jaws were cushioned by my heavy boot; they sliced through from instep to heel, but did not quite meet. All the same, it was a noise in the soughing silences of the wood, and Claire's eyes opened. She studied the moon wonderingly for a moment because, I presume, her face was turned to it. Then she seemed to recall where she was. She sat up and glanced about. Her gaze swept over me twice as I stood there stiff and straight, trying to look like a beech. Or a birch. I must be of the wrong family. She saw me.

"Thad . . ." She sat up and knuckled her eyes. Claire has a deep voice, and meticulous. She peered. "It—*is* Thad?"

"Most of me. Hi."

"Hi." She moved her mouth, chewing, apparently,

151

the end of sleepiness. She swallowed it and said, "You've been looking for me."

"For years," I said gallantly. That might have been true. At the moment, however, I was in pursuit of my foot, and possibly some peace and quiet. I hadn't counted on this at all.

"Well, Lochinvar, why don't you sweep me into your arms?"

"I've told you before. You're everything in the world I need, but you don't strike sparks. Go on back to bed."

She shook her hair, forward, out and down, and then breathtakingly back. She had masses of it. In the moonlight it was blue-gray, and obedient cloud. "You don't seem surprised to find me out here."

"I'm not. The last thing I said to you in town was to sit tight, stay where you were, and let me handle this. The fact that you are here therefore does not surprise me."

"You know," she said, putting one elbow on one knee, one chin in one palm, and twinkling, "you say 'therefore' prettier than anyone else I ever met. Why don't you come over here and talk to me? Are you standing in a bear-trap?"

She was wearing a one-piece sunsuit. It was backless and sideless and the summer flying suit, hanging on the bush at her head, plus the light nylon sleeping bag, were obviously everything in the world she had with her. About the bear-trap I said, "Well, yes."

She laughed gaily, and lay back. Her hair spread and spilled; she burrowed into it with the back of her head. She pulled the sleeping bag tight up around her throat and said, "All right, silly. Stand there if you want to. It's a big boudoir."

I said nothing. I tugged cautiously at the trap, moving just my leg. The boot all but parted; the moon gleamed on the steel jaws, now only an inch apart and closing slowly. I stopped pulling. I hoped she would go back to sleep. I hoped the trap wouldn't clank together when it finally went all the way through. I stood still. There was sweat on my mouth.

"You still there?"

"Yup," I said.

She sat up again. "Thad, this is stupid! *Do* something! Go away, or talk to me or something, but don't just *stand* there!"

"Why don't you just go on to sleep and let me worry about what I do? I'm not in your way. I won't touch you."

"That I don't doubt," she said acidly. "Go away." She thumped down, turned away, turned back and sat up, peering. "I just thought . . . maybe you *can't* . . ." She flung out of the bag and stood up, slim in the moonlight. I could see her toenails gleam as she stepped on the fabric. Her right toenails, I mean. Her left foot wasn't a foot. It was a cloven hoof, hairy-fetlocked, sharp and heavy. She was as unselfconscious about it as she was of the casual coverage her sunsuit afforded her. She came to me, limping slightly.

"Go on back to—let me al—oh for Pete's sake, Claire, I'm perfectly—"

She breathed a wordless, sighing syllable, all horror and pity. "Thad," she cried, "Your—your *foot!*"

"I didn't want you to know."

"How could you just *stand* there with that—that— Oh!" She knelt, reached toward my trapped foot, recoiled before she touched it and stayed there looking up at me with her eyes bright in the silver light, silver tear-streaks on her face like lode-veinings. "What shall I *do?*"

I sighed. "Keep your fingers away from the trap." I leaned back and pulled. The macerated leather of my high-laced hunting boot held, gave, held—and then the

153

jaws whanged together, close-meshed. I fell back against a birch-trunk, banging my head painfully. Claire, seeing almost the entire foot dangling under the arch of the trap's jaws, started a shriek, then jammed it back into her mouth with her whole hand. I grunted.

"Oh," she said, "you poor *darling!* Does it hurt?" she added inanely.

"No," I said, rubbing my skull. "It was just my head. . . ."

"But your foot! Your poor foot!"

I began unlacing what was left of the boot. "Don't bother your pretty little head about it," I said. I pulled the boot-wings aside and slipped my leg out of boot and woolen stocking together. She looked, and sat down plump! before me, her jaw swinging slackly. "Shut it," I said conversationally. "You really looked beautiful a while back. Now you look silly."

She pointed to my hoof. It was larger than hers, and shaggier. "Oh, Thad! I didn't know . . . how long?"

"About three weeks. Damn it, Claire, I didn't want you to know."

"You should have told me. You should have told me the second it started."

"Why? You had enough on your mind. You'd already been through all the treatment that anyone could figure out, and I was in on all of it. So when it happened to me, I didn't see the sense in making a federal case out of it." I shrugged. "If Dr. Ponder can't cure this no one can. And he can't. Therefore—"

Through her shock, she giggled.

"Therefore," I continued, "there was nothing left for me to do but try to find out what had happened, by myself." I saw her lower lip push out before she dropped her face and hid it. "What's the matter?" I asked.

"I—kind of thought you were trying to help just me."

154

Claire can switch from giggles to tears, from shock to laughter to horror to fright, faster than anyone I ever met. It goes all the way down too. I said, "Don't kid yourself. I don't do things for people."

"Well," she said in a very small voice, "that's what I thought, for a while anyway."

"You better get back in that sleeping bag. You'll catch cold," I said.

She rose and crept obediently back to the sleeping bag. Once into it, she said, "Well, you'll care if I catch cold."

I went and hunkered down beside her. "Well sure. I might catch it."

"You wouldn't get that close!"

"Oh, I don't know. I read somewhere that a sneeze can travel thirty feet."

"I hate you."

"Because I sneaked out behind your back and got a fancy foot just like yours?"

"Oh, Thad! How can you joke about it?"

I sat back and lifted my hoof, regarding it thoughtfully. I had found it possible to spread the two halves and relax suddenly. They made a nice loud click. I did this a couple of times. "I'd rather joke about it. How frantic can you get?"

"Thad, Thad . . . It's my fault, it is, it is!"

"Uh-huh. That's what I get for playing footsie with you in roadhouses. You're contagious, that's what."

"You're no comfort."

"I don't comfort stupid people. This isn't your fault, and you're being stupid when you talk like that. Does yours itch?"

"Not any more."

"Mine does." I clicked my hoof some more. It felt good. "What gave you the idea of coming out here?"

"Well," she said shyly, "after you said you'd track

155

this thing down for me, but wouldn't say how, I thought it all out from the very beginning. This crazy trouble, whatever it is, started out here; I mean, it developed after I came out here that time. So I figured that this is where you'd be."

"But why come?"

"I didn't know what you'd get into here. I thought you might—might need me."

"Like a hole in the head," I said bluntly.

"And I thought you were doing it just for me. I didn't know you had a foot like that too." Her voice was very small.

"So now you know. And you're sorry you came. And first thing in the morning you'll hightail it straight back to town where you belong."

"Oh no! Not now. Not when I know we're in this together. I like being in something together with you, Thad."

I sighed. "Why does my luck run like this? If I got all hog-wild and feverish about you, you'd turn around and get short of breath over some other joker. Everybody loves somebody—else."

"You're thinking about Luana," she said with accuracy. Luana was Dr. Ponder's typist. She had taut coral pneumatic lips, a cleft chin, and a tear-stained voice like that of an English horn in the lower register. She had other assets and I was quite taken with both of them.

"If I were as honest about my feelings as you are about yours," I said, "and as loud-mouthed, I'd only hurt your feelings. Let's talk about our feet."

"All right," she said submissively. "Thad. . . ."

"Mm?"

"What did you mean when you said you'd seen me be beautiful?"

"Oh, for Pete's sake! Skip it, will you? What has that to do with feet?"

"Well. . . . Nothing, I guess." She sounded so forlorn that, before I could check myself, I reached out and patted her shoulder. "I'm sorry, Claire. I shouldn't brutalize you, I guess. But it's better than stringing you along."

She held my hand for a moment against her cheek. "I s'pose it is," she said softly. "You're so good . . . so good, and—and so sensible."

"So tired. Give me back my hand. Now; let's put all this fantastic business together and see what comes out. You start. Right from the beginning, now; somewhere, somehow, there's got to be an answer to all this. I know we've been over it and over it, but maybe this time something will make sense. You start."

She lay back, put her hands behind her head, and looked at the moon. She had to turn her head for this, because the moon was sinking, and there were knife-edges of light among the cords of her throat. "I still say it was the night I met you. Oh, don't worry; I won't get off on that again . . . but it was. You were just a face among faces to me then. A nice face, but—anyway, it was the Medusa Club meeting, the night we got talking about magic."

"I'll never forget that night," I said. "What a collection of neurotics! Saving your presence, ma'am."

"That's the only purpose of the club—to find those things which frighten neurotics and stare them down, and to keep on doing it until somebody drops dead. Score to date: umpteen-odd dead boogie-men, no dead people. Hence the discussion of magic that night."

"That makes sense. And I remember Ponder's point that we are not as far removed from the days of the witches and wizards as we like to think. We knock on wood; we slip bits of wedding-cake under our pillows; we hook fingers with each other when we suddenly say the same thing together, and so on and on. And he said

157

that perhaps this subconscious clinging to ritual was not because of a lingering childishness, but because the original magic forces were still in operation!"

"That was it," said Claire. "And a fine flurry of snorts he got for that!"

"Yup. Especially from you. I still don't understand why you got so steamed up."

"I *hate* that kind of talk!" she said vociferously. "But I hated it especially hearing it from Dr. Ponder. Ever since I've known him he's been so reasonable, so logical, so—well, so wonderful—"

I grinned. "I'm jealous."

"Are you, Thad? Are you really?" she said eagerly; then, "No. You're laughing at me, you heel . . . anyway, I couldn't stand hearing that kind of poppycock from him."

I put out my cloven hoof and snapped it in front of her nose. "What do you think now?"

"I don't know what to think . . ." she whispered, and then, with one of her startling switches of mood, continued in a normal voice, "so the next day I decided to track down some of the old superstitions for myself. Heaven knows this part of the country is full of them. The Indians left a lot, and then the Dutch and the French and the Spanish. There's something about these hills that breeds such things."

I laughed. "Sounds like Lovecraft."

"Sounds like Charles Fort, too!" she snapped. "Some day you'll learn that you can't laugh at one and admire the other. Where was I?"

"In the woods."

"Oh. Well, the most persistent superstition in these parts is the old legend of the Camel's Grave. I came out here to find it."

I scrabbled up some of the soft earth to make a pit for my elbow and a hummock for my armpit. I lay on my side, propped up my head with my hand, and was comfortable. "Just run off that legend again, once over lightly."

She closed her eyes. "Somewhere in this no-good country—no one's ever been able to farm it, and there's too much jimson weed and nightshade for grazing—there's supposed to be a little hollow called Forbidden Valley. At the north end of it they say there's a grave with something funny about it. There's no headstone. Just a skull. Some say a man was buried there up to his neck and left to die."

"The Amazon Indians have a stunt like that. But they pick an anthill for the job. Cut off the feller's eyelids first. After that, the potato race, ducking for apples and ice cream is served in the main tent."

"A picnic," she agreed, shuddering. "But there was never anything like that among the local Indians here. Besides, we don't run to that kind of ant either. Anyway, this skull is chained, so the story goes, with a link through the edge of the eye-socket. It's supposed to be a magician buried there. Thing is, the legend is that he isn't dead. He'll live forever and be chained forever. Nothing can help him. But he doesn't know it. So if anyone wanders too close, he'll capture whoever it is and put 'em to work trying to dig him out. The old tales keep coming out—kids who had wandered out here and disappeared, the old woman who went out of her head after she got back to town, the half-witted boy who mumbled something about the skull that talked to him out of the ground. You know."

"Why do they call it the Camel's Grave?"

"*I* don't know. Some say the magician was an Egyptian who used to ride a camel around. Some say it comes from some Indian name. The nearest I can find in the library to 'Camel' is 'ko-mai' which means the green stick they used to spit meat over a fire. But that's

Winnebago, and there were no Winnebagos around here."

"Wait. You mean there were Indian legends about this?"

"Oh, sure. I dug those out. There are all sorts of stories. Some of them are shocking—I mean in a nice way." She giggled. "But they all have one thing in common—the imprisoned magician, who, by the way, was old, old as the hills. He wasn't an Indian either. They made that quite clear. And always Camel, or 'Grave of the Camel.' Just to mix that up even more for you, I looked up 'camel' in the dictionary and found out that the word is derived from 'Djemal,' which is Arabic, or 'Gamal,' which is Hebrew."

"Fine," I said bitterly. "Much progress. So go on with your little trip out here."

"That first time? Oh, nothing happened. I brought some chow and stayed out here about four days at the full moon, which is supposed to be the time when the Forbidden Valley can be found. I didn't see a soul but old Goo-goo running his traps. No one pays attention to Goo-goo."

"Not even people who step into one of his bear-traps? You're lucky you didn't bed down in it."

"Oh, don't blame him, Thad! He's a sweet old man, really. He's deaf and dumb, you know. He keeps out of people's way as much as he can. Comes in with a few skins every now and then and lives off the land. He could tell us a thing or two about Forbidden Valley if he could talk. But he can't even write. They say he doesn't mind the haunted hills because no one ever found a way to tell him about them. What he doesn't know can't hurt him. As for the trap, he put it where he thought it might do him some good, among the birches where bears sometimes come to hunt for bugs under the

160

bark. Practically no one ever comes out here. When they do, it's their lookout, not Goo-goo's."

"Hey." I straightened up. "How can you be so casual about bunking out here with a wildcat or two and an occasional bear wandering around? There are copperheads too, to say nothing of a trapper who must be lonesome, to put it mildly."

"Why I—" She paused, wonderingly. "I never thought about it, I guess. Thad—nothing ever hurt me. I mean it. No dog ever bit me, no cat ever scratched me. I don't seem to be very tempting to mosquitos. Once when I was a little girl a bull gored a hired man who was walking across a field with me. The bull bellowed and jumped and capered all around me, but he didn't touch me. I've never even been stung by a bee."

"You don't say." I considered her thoughtfully. "I begin to see why I asked you out for a beer the night of the meeting."

"Why, Thad?"

"Now don't get ideas. I just pegged you as being— different, that's all. Not better—different. You puzzled me. I've been a lot of places, Claire. Tropics. At sea. Construction jobs. I've met a lot of people, but no one like you."

"That again," she snorted. "People are always telling me that, one way or another. And what's it get me? The very first time I fall for a big dead-pan stranger, he doesn't know I'm alive. All large muscles and bad taste."

"What do you mean bad taste?"

"Luana."

"Now look. I won't bandy her about. Stay off the subject, see?"

Surprisingly, she laughed. "Temper—temper," she cautioned. "My, you roar purty. But back to the subject at hand. I was out here four days and nights, wandering around, trying to find the Forbidden Valley. Once I thought I had it. It was about midnight. The moon was bright, like tonight. I was near here somewhere. There was a little swag in the ground with a high bluff at one end. I went up to it. I tripped over something. I don't know what it was. I almost *never* fall over things but I sure did that time. I fell right on top of some little animal. I hope I didn't hurt it. I don't know what it was. It wriggled out from under me and whizzed away fast as a deerfly. I never saw anything move so fast; a blur and it was gone. It was about as big as a chipmunk, but longer—oh, three times as long. I got a vague impression of pointed ears and the funniest broad, flat tail. It was like nothing I've ever seen."

"I thought nothing happened in those four days."

"Well—that couldn't be important. Oh; I see what you mean. *Anything* might be important. All right. Now —what else?"

"Goo-goo."

"Oh. I saw him once. Twice. The first time he was setting a whip-snare in a clearing in the woods. I waved at him and smiled and he nodded and gurgled the way he does and smiled back. The second time I don't think he saw me. He was out in the open. Early morning. He was tramping round and round in a circle in the grass. Then he stopped and faced the sun. He did something with his knife. Held it out, sort of, and touched himself on the shoulders and chin with it. I don't remember very clearly. It didn't last long. And that's all."

"Hmp." I plucked some grass and skinned it with my front teeth, to get the juice. "Then you came back to town and your foot went haywire."

"Yes. It only took about six days to get the way it is. It was awful at first. The toes gathered, and the whole foot began to get pointed. It was longer at first. I mean, my foot straightened out like a ballet dancer's, and I

162

couldn't get my heel down. Then the whole thing thickened up and grew shorter, and the tip turned black and hardened and—"

I interrupted, "I know, I know. Had one once myself. Now, how many people did you tell about it?"

"Oh, nobody. I mean, Dr. Ponder, of course, and then you. Dr. Ponder was so—so—"

"Wonderful," I submitted.

"Shut up. So *understanding,* I mean."

"That's an odd word to use."

"Is it? Anyway, he said I had a—a—"

"Chitinous podomorphia."

"Yes. How did you know?"

"You told me, right after he told you. Only *I* remembered it. Mine began shortly afterward, and I remembered it again." I spit out my grass and selected another stem. "A brilliant diagnosis."

"Thad . . . you—sometimes you say things in a way I don't understand."

"Do I?" In the growing predawn darkness, I could feel her sharp swift gaze on me. I said, "Go on. He treated the foot?"

"He bound it. It was very clever. As the foot changed shape from day to day he changed the bandages, so that it never looked any worse than a slightly sprained ankle. He seemed to know all about the trouble. He predicted the course of the trouble as it developed, and told me that it would go just so far and stop, and he kept me from getting frightened, and explained why I should keep it a secret."

"What did he say?"

"He harked back to the meeting, and the things that had been said. Especially about the readiness of people to believe in so-called mystical events. He said there was enough residual superstition in town to make life

163

miserable for a girl with a cloven hoof. Especially for me."

"Why you especially?"

"Didn't I ever tell you? I thought I had. . . . See, my mother and father . . . they were engaged. I mean, they were each engaged to someone else. Dad came from Scoville way. That's eight miles or more on the other side of these woods. He didn't know Mother at all. He took to coming out here at night. He didn't know why. He couldn't help it. And Mother—she was about eighteen at the time—Mother jumped up from the dinner table one night and ran. She just *ran* out here. It's a long way. Granddad tried to follow her, but she ran like a deer. When he finally came huffing and puffing into the wood—it was a white night like tonight—and stopped to get his breath back, he heard a man calling, 'Jessica! Jessica!' That was Mother's name. Granddad followed the sound. It was out here in the open somewhere. Granddad climbed a rise and looked down and saw this young man standing with his arms out, calling and calling, turning every which way as he called. Granddad was going to yell at him but then he saw Mother. She was going down the slope ahead of him, walking slowly—he used to say 'as if the meadow was a grand marble stair, and she in a gold dress, for all she was tattered with thorns.'

"The two of them stopped two yards apart and stood there staring at one another for longer than it took Granddad to get to them. He had to yell twice or three times before she even knew he was there. She kept her eyes on the young man's face and just said, 'Yes, Father.' And Granddad bellowed at her to come home. She stepped to the young man—that was my dad—and she put a hand on his arm and said, 'He'll come too.' Granddad said, 'The hell he will!' He wouldn't talk to my dad, he was so upset and angry. 'I don't even know his name!' and Mother said quietly, 'No more do I. You'd better ask him, Father.' And that was how it was."

I sat up and crossed my legs, entranced. "You mean that was the first time they saw each other?"

She nodded, though by now I could barely see her, for the moon was gone and only its cold loom stood in the sky over the western hills. "The very first time," she said. "And they were together every minute they could be after that. They were married right away."

"How?"

She shifted uncomfortably as I asked it, and said, "By a judge. It wasn't a church wedding. It was quicker. People talked. They still talk. They have lots of ideas about what went on out here, but what I'm telling you is the truth. Anyway, Granddad got used to the idea very soon, though he was against it at first. Even the talk didn't bother him; those two lived in a world of their own. Nothing touched them. Dad made wood-carvings—clock cases and newel-figurines and so on, and Mother was with him almost every minute. Granddad used to say if you pinched the one, the other'd say 'Ouch.' He said nobody could stay mad in that house; he knew because he tried. So . . . it didn't matter what people said." She paused, and I just waited. Later, questions.

Presently she said sleepily, "And it *doesn't* matter. My mother and dad are like that now. They always will be. Nothing can change what you remember."

I waited again. This was a long time. Finally I asked, gently, "Where are they?"

"They died."

She slept. Somehow the moon had moved around to the east again. No: it wasn't the moon. It was a cloudless dawn, a dilution; light staining the hem of the sky. I sank back with my elbow in the hole I had dug and my armpit on the me-shaped hummock, and looked at the sleeping girl. I knew now what the single thing was that made her different. She was as changeable as bubble-colors; she felt, immediately and noticeably, all the emotions except one. And that was her difference. She was absolutely fearless.

That story . . . so simply told, and then, "They died."

Cloven hooves.

"They died." People like that . . . for a time I was angrier at such a death than I was, even, at the ugly excrescence that was once a foot. Dr. Ponder seemed to know a lot about these things. "Chitinous podomorphia." Oh, fine. That meant "Change of a foot into chitin—hoof, horn, and fingernail material." I hadn't gone to Ponder. I couldn't really say why. Maybe Luana was the reason for that. Somehow I couldn't take the idea of Luana writing up my case history on her neat file cards. And there was no other doctor in town. Here was Claire with the same trouble, and I'd been in on that from the word go. I just did for my foot what Ponder had done for Claire's, and hoped that Luana would never hear about it. What girl would give a tumble to a man with a cloven hoof?

The sun poked a flaming forehead over the wall of hills. By its light I studied Claire's relaxed face. She was not beautiful, by any means. She had a round, pleasant face. When she laughed, a transverse crease appeared under her nose; she was the only human being with that particular upper lip that I had ever liked. Her lashes were thick but not long, and now, with her eyes closed, half the beauty she had was cloaked, for she had the most brilliant eyes I had ever seen. Her jaw was round and small, slightly cleft. She missed being square and stocky by fractional proportions.

166

"I must be out of my mind," I muttered. Claire was a wonderful person . . . a wonderful person. Genuine, honest, full of high humor, and, for me, no fireworks.

But Luana, the beautiful secretary of Dr. Ponder, now, that was a different story. She had an odd, triangular face and a skin that seemed lit softly from underneath. Her cheeks were a brighter rose than the sides of her neck but you couldn't tell just where the gradations began. Her hair was the extremely dark but vivid red of black-iron in a forge just beginning to heat. Her hands were so delicate and smooth you'd think they'd break on a typewriter, and her canine teeth were a shade too long, so that her head looked like a flower with fangs. She had one expression—complete composure. Her unshakable poise made me grind my teeth; some way, somehow, I wanted it broken. I don't think she had brain-one and I didn't care; it wasn't her brains I was after. Her face floated before me on the flames of the fireworks she generated in me, and there wasn't a thing in the world I could do about it. When I was in town I'd date her, when I could. On the dates we didn't talk. She danced sedately and watched movies attentively and ate pineapple frappés with delicacy and thoroughness, and I'd just sit there and bask, and count the seconds until, after I walked her to her gate, she closed it between us and leaned across for a demure kiss. Her lips were cool, smooth, and taut. Pneumatic. Then I'd stride away snarling at myself. "You're a bumpkin," I'd say. "You're all feet and Adam's apple." I'd tell myself I had a hole in the head. I called myself forty kinds of a fool. "There's no future in it," I'd say. I'd tell myself, "You know that ten years from now, when the bloom is off, she'll look like something the cat dragged in, her and her teeth." And thinking about the teeth would make me visualize those lips again, and—so cool!

Often, those nights, I'd run into Claire, who just happened to be in Callow's Friendly Drug and Meat Market buying a whodunit, and we'd get a soda or something and talk. Those were the talks where everything came out. I never got so thick with anyone so fast. Talking to Claire is like talking to yourself. And she told me, somehow or other, about the foot, right from the first. She didn't tell anyone else. Except Dr. Ponder, of course. . . .

What a strange person she was! It was inconceivable that she should not have questioned Dr. Ponder more about her foot—yet she had not. His prognosis was that the condition would stop at her ankle, and may or may not be permanent, and, for her, that was that. In the same situation anyone else on earth would be scrambling around from specialist to specialist between trips to a wailing wall. Not Claire. She accepted it and was not afraid.

A patch of sun the size of a kitten crept up the edge of her sleeping bag and nestled in her hair. After a pause to warm and brighten itself, it thrust a golden pseudopod around the curve of her cheek and touched her eyelid. She stirred, smiled briefly at what must have been a most tender dream, and woke.

"Good morning."

She looked at me mistily, and smiled a different smile. "I fell asleep."

"You did. Come on—stir your stumps. I want to show you something that I've discovered."

She stretched and yawned. "I was talking to you and I fell asleep right in the middle of it. I'm sorry."

"I'm glad. You got your beauty sleep." Her face softened, so I added. "You need it."

"You're so sweet, Thad," she said. "Much sweeter than gall. 'Bout like vinegar, when you try hard." She slid out of the sleeping bag and idly scratched her hairy ankle. "If I had to choose between this thing with you, and my ordinary old foot without you, I think I'd keep the hoof. How do you make that noise with it?"

I showed her. She tried it. All she could get was a muffled pop, like fingers snapping with gloves on. She laughed and said I was a genius, and rose and climbed into her flying suit. She had half-length boots, padded inside to support her hoof. Once they were on, no one could have guessed. While she was about these small chores, and others concerning folding and stowing the sleeping bag and breaking out some C and K rations, I rescued my amputated shoe from the beartrap and, by cutting and piecing the leather straps, made a sort of stirrup that would hold it together once it was on.

When that was done, Claire, looking shapeless and tousled in the loose-fitting coverall, handed me one of the sticky-rich candy bars from the rations. "Thad," she said with her mouth full, "you just *wouldn't* go to see Dr. Ponder. Why not? Don't you trust him?"

"Sure I trust him," I said shortly. Why mention that I was keeping away from him because of Luana? "Come on," I said.

We crossed through a neck of the forest to the rolling scrub meadow on the other side, and down and across the first little valley.

"This is where I was last night. There's something just over the next rise that I want you to see. Last night I was afraid you'd see it."

"What's so different about today, then?"

"I found out last night you're not afraid of anything."

She did not answer. I looked back at her. She was grinning. "You said something nice about me," she half-sang.

"Not necessarily. Sometimes fearlessness is nothing more than rank stupidity."

She swallowed that silently. As we climbed the rise

169

she asked, "Will you tell me about the time you saw me be beautiful?"

"Later," I said.

Abruptly she clutched my arm. *"Look!"*

"Where? What?"

"There!" She pointed. "No—there—there, see?" She pointed rapidly to the ground, to a rock, to a spot in midair to our left. "See?"

"What is it, Claire? A deer-fly? or spots in the eyes?"

"Just watch," she said with exaggerated patience. "The little animal I fell on that time—remember? It's all around here, and moving so *fast!*"

There are certain optical illusions where a missing object becomes vividly clear as soon as you know what to look for. I focused my mind's eye on what she had described as a tapering, fan-tailed monstrosity with two front legs and a blue-black hide, and suddenly, fleetingly, there it was, crouching against the sheer side of the bluff. It blinked at me, and then disappeared, only to pop into sight for a fraction of a second right in front of us. We moved back with alacrity as if pulled by the same string.

"I want out!" I gasped. "That's the thing that gave you the fancy boot!"

Somehow we were twenty feet back and still backing. Claire laughed. "I thought that was your specialty."

"You pick the dog-gonnedest times . . . get back, Claire! Heaven knows what will happen to you if it gets to you again!"

She stood still, peering. The thing, whatever it was, appeared twice, once a little to the right, once—and this time, for a full two or three seconds—over against the side-hill. It balanced on two forelegs, its head thrust out, its wide fluked tail curled up over its back, and it blinked rapidly. Its eyes were the same color as its skin, but shiny. It disappeared. Claire said, "It can't hurt us.

Dr. Ponder said the condition would be arrested where it is."

I snorted. "That's like saying you're immunized against being bumped by a truck because one ran over you once. Let's get out of here."

She laughed at me again. "Why, Thad! I've never seen you like this! You're pale as milk!"

"You have so seen me like this," I quavered. "The last time you called me sensible. Remember?"

The blue-black thing appeared again almost under my feet. I squeaked and jumped. Then it was by Claire, inches away. She bent toward it, hand outstretched, but it vanished.

"Thad, it seems terribly excited. I think it wants something."

"That I don't doubt," I said through clenched teeth. "Claire. Listen to me. Either you will hightail with me out of this imp-ridden corner of hell, or you and that monstrosity can stay here and watch me dwindle."

"Oh, *Thad!* stop blithering. The poor little thing is probably ten times as frightened as you are."

"Oh no it isn't," I said with authority. "It's alive, isn't it?"

She snorted and squatted down in the grass, her hands out and close together. Simultaneously with my warning cry, the creature appeared between her hands. Very slowly she moved them together. I stood petrified, babbling. "Claire, don't, please don't, just this once how do you know what that thing might do, Claire. . . . Okay—it's small, Claire. So is a *fer de lance*. So is a forty-five slug. Please, Claire—"

"*Will* you stop that infernal chattering!" she snapped. And just before her closing hands could touch the beast it was gone, to reappear six inches to the left.

She rose and stepped forward gently, stooping. The poised animal—if it was an animal—waited until she

171

was a fraction of an inch away and again bounded out of visibility and in again, this time a yard away, where it waited, blinking violently.

"I think it wants us to follow it," said Claire. "Come on, Thad!"

It moved again, farther away, and bounced up and down.

"Oh, Claire," I said at last, "I give up. We're in this together and we've got to depend on each other. Maybe you're right after all."

Surprisingly, there were tears in her eyes as she said, "I feel as if you had been away a long time and just got back."

I thumped her shoulder, and we went on. We followed the strange creature up the slope to its crest, where the creature disappeared again, this time, apparently for good.

Claire had been right, we found a moment later. Distantly, sunlight flashed on the windshield of Ponder's parked convertible, which was parked where the wood road skirted the desolate flatland. Nearing the foothills where we stood were two plodding figures, and it was easy to spot Ponder, for no one else in the area had his stooped height and breadth. He was so perfectly in proportion that he made normal people look underdone. The other, I noticed with a gulp, was Luana, with her contained, erect posture, and the sunlight, after its cold journey through space, reveling in the heat of her hair.

We went to meet them. I looked once at Claire, catching her at the woman's trick of swift comparative appraisal of Luana's trim plaid skirt and snug windbreaker, and I smiled. Claire's coverall was not a company garment.

"Thad!" the doctor boomed. He had an organ voice; in conversation it always seemed to be throttled down, and his shout was a relaxation rather than an effort. "And Claire . . . we were worried."

"Why?" asked Claire. We reached them. I buzzed right on past the doctor—"Hi, Doc"—and took both Luana's hands. "Lu."

She looked up at me and smiled. Those lips, so taut, so filled with what strange honey . . . when they smiled they grew still fuller. She said Hello, and I thought, what's language for? what's poetry for? when two small syllables can mean so much . . . I held her hands so hard and so long that it may have been embarrassing. It was for me, anyway, when Claire's voice broke into my ardent scansion of Luana's eyes with "Hey! Svengali! Got her hypnotized yet?"

I released Luana, who looked Claire's rumpled flying suit up and down. "Hello, Claire," she purred. "Hunting?"

"Just walking the dog," said Claire through her teeth.

I met the doctor's eyes and he grinned. "Good of you to take all this trouble over Claire's trouble," he said. "She just told me you knew about it. Does anyone else?"

I shook my head, but said, "Why all the mystery, Doctor?"

"I certainly don't have to tell you that this is not an ordinary medical matter."

Claire said, "Let's go on up to the Wood and sit down and talk. It's getting hot."

"I'll tote that if it's heavy," I offered, indicating Ponder's black bag.

"Oh no. Just a couple of things I brought with me, just in case."

He and Claire started back up toward the Wood. I put my hand on Luana's forearm and checked her.

"What is it, Thad?"

"I just want them to get a little way ahead. Luana,

173

this is wonderful. What on earth made him come out here? And with you?"

"I don't know. He's a strange man, Thad. Sometimes I think he knows everything. Nothing surprises him." We began to walk. "We were working this morning—he was dictating some letters—and he all of a sudden stopped as if he was listening to something. Next thing I knew we were on our way."

"Does he really know what's the matter with Claire's foot?"

She looked at me. Her eyes were auburn and most disturbing. "I'm not supposed to talk about it."

"She told me. It turned into a cloven hoof. I've seen it."

"Oh. Then why ask?"

I hadn't expected this kind of resistance. "I mean, does he know *why* it happened?"

"Of course he does."

"Well, why?" I asked impatiently.

"Why not ask him?" She shrugged. "He's the doctor. I'm not."

"Sorry I asked," I said glumly. I was annoyed—I think at myself. I don't know why, subconsciously, I always expected this vision to melt into my arms, and was always sticking my neck out. But that's the way it is when you get fireworks.

We walked on in silence. Claire and the doctor had disappeared into the Wood when we entered the edge of it. We stopped for a moment to look about. There was, of course, no path, and the windless growth muffled and absorbed sounds, so it was difficult to know which way they had gone. I started in, but Luana held me back. "I don't think they're that way."

"I'll yell," I said, but she put a hand to her mouth. "Oh, *no!*"

"Why not, Lu?"

174

"I'm—I don't know. You shouldn't, in here." She looked about the silent halls of the forest. "Please, Thad. Go look for them. I'll wait. But don't shout, please."

Completely puzzled, I said, "Well, sure, honey. But I don't get it. Is something the matter?"

"No. Nothing." Her arched nostrils twitched. "Go look for them, Thad. I'll wait here, in case they come back for us."

"You're sure you'll be all right?"

"Go on. Go on," she said urgently. I suddenly thought that for certain reasons I might be behaving tactlessly. I must have blushed like a schoolgirl. "Well, sure. I'll be right back. I mean, I'll find 'em and call you." I flapped a good-bye self-consciously and blundered off through the woods. That girl really threw me for a loss.

I followed the level ground until I emerged from the Wood at the other side of its narrow neck—just what I should have done in the first place. Doctor Ponder and Claire were out in the open fifty yards away, apparently waiting for us. I went to them. "We lost you," I said. "Luana's waiting back there. She didn't want to thrash around in the woods hunting for you. Hold on and I'll get her."

Ponder's big head went up, and his eyes seemed to focus on something I couldn't see for a moment. Then, "Don't bother," he said. "She's all right. I wanted to talk to you two anyway. Let's go in the shade and sit down.

"But—will she be all right?"

"She'll be all right," he grinned. He had good teeth.

I shrugged. "Everybody seems to know what's right around here but me," I said petulantly. "All right." I led the way to a thicket at the edge of the wood and plumped down with my back against a tree. Claire and

175

the doctor joined me, Ponder setting his bag carefully within his reach.

"Now for heaven's sake tell us," said Claire, who had kept an amused silence during my jitterings about Luana. She turned to me. "He wouldn't say a thing until you got here."

"Tell us about what? Who knows anything?" I said resignedly.

"You know about her foot," said Dr. Ponder. He looked down. "What, speaking of feet, has happened to your boot?"

I happened to be looking at Claire, and microscopically shook my head. "Oh," I said casually, "I left it on a railroad track while I was frog hunting in a culvert. Go on about Claire." Claire's eyes widened in astonishment at this continued deception, but she said nothing. I was pleased.

Ponder leaned back. He had a long head and a big jaw. The touch of gray at his temples and the stretched smoothness of his skin told lies about each other. He said, "First, I want to thank you both—you, Claire, because you have trusted me in this matter, when I had every reason to expect nothing but hysteria from you, and you, Thad, for having kept your own counsel. Now I'll tell you what I know. Please don't mind if I seem to wander a bit. I want you to get this straight in your minds." He closed his eyes for a moment, his brow furrowed. Then he wet his lips and continued.

"Imagine a man walking up to a door which stands firmly locked. He raises his hand and makes a certain motion. The door opens. He enters, picks up a wand. He waves it; it suddenly glows with light. He says two words, and a fire appears in the fireplace. Now: could you duplicate that?"

"I've seen doors open for people in a railroad station," said Claire. "They had a beam of light in front of them. When you walked into it, a photoelectric cell made the door open."

"About that wand," I put in. "If it was made of glass, it could have been a fluorescent tube. If there was a radio frequency generator in the room, it could make a tube glow, even without wire connections."

"I once saw a gadget connected to a toy electric train," Claire said. "You say 'Go!' into a speaker and the train would go. You say 'Now back up' and it would back up. It worked by the number of syllables you spoke. One would make the train go forward; three would make it stop and back up. That fire you mentioned, that could be controlled by a gadget like that."

"Right. Quite right," said the doctor. "Now, suppose you fixed up all that gadgetry and took it back in time a couple of centuries. What would the performance look like to a person of the time—even an intelligent, reasonable one?"

I said, "Witchcraft." Claire said, "Why, magic."

Ponder nodded. "But they'd understand a kitchen match. But take a kitchen match back a couple more centuries, and you'd get burned at the stake. What I'm driving at is that given the equipment, you can get the results, whether those results can be understood by the observer or not. The only sane attitude to take about such things is to conclude that they are caused by some natural, logically explained agency—and that we haven't the knowledge to explain it any more than the most erudite scholar could have explained radar two centuries ago."

"I follow that," I said, and Claire nodded.

"However," said Ponder, "most people don't seem to accept such things that easily. Something happens that you can't understand, and either you refuse to believe it happened at all—even if you saw it with your own eyes—or you attribute it to supernatural forces, with all

177

their associated claptrap of good and evil, rituals and exorcisms. What I'm putting to you is that everything that's happened to you is perfectly logical and believable in its own terms—but it's much larger than you think. I'm asking you to accept something much more mysterious than a r-f generator would be to a Puritan settler. You just have to take my word for it that it's as reasonable a thing as an r-f generator."

"I don't understand an r-f generator, as it is," smiled Claire. I heard the soft sound of her hoof clicking. "Go ahead, Doctor. At this point I'm ready to believe anything."

"Fine," applauded the doctor. "It's a pleasure to talk to you. Now, I'm going to use 'good' and 'evil' in this explanation because they're handy. Bear in mind that they are loose terms, partial ones: external evidences of forces that extend forward and back and to either side in time and space." He laughed. "Don't try to follow that. Just listen.

"A long time ago there were two opposed forces—call them intelligences. One was good and one was evil. It turned out to be quite a battle, and it went on for some time. There were gains and losses on each side, until one was captured by the other. Now, these intelligences were not living creatures in the ordinary sense, and in the ordinary sense they could not be killed. There are legends of such captures—the bound Prometheus, for example, and the monster under Yggdrasil. The only way to keep such forces imprisoned is to lock them up and set a watch over them. But, just as in our civilization, it may take profound intelligence and a great deal of hard work to capture a criminal, but far less intelligence and effort to keep him in jail.

"And that's the situation we have here. Not far from where we sit, one of those things is imprisoned, and he—I say 'he' for convenience—has his jailer.

178

"That's the thing known as 'The Camel's Grave.' The Camel is a living intelligence, captured and held here and, if right has its way, doomed to spend the rest of eternity here."

"That's a long time," I put in. "The earth won't last that long."

"He'll be moved in time," said Ponder complacently; and that was when I began to realize how big this thing was. There was that about Doctor Ponder which made it impossible to disbelieve him. I stared at Claire, who stared back. Finally she turned to him and asked in a small voice, "And—what about my foot?"

"That was a piece of tough luck," said Ponder. "You are a sort of—uh—innocent bystander. You see, the Camel is surrounded by . . . damn it, it's hard to find words that make sense! Fields. Look: if I call them 'spells,' will you understand that I'm not talking mumbo-jumbo? If I call them 'fields,' it presupposes coils and generators and circuits and so on. In this way 'spells' is more accurate."

"I'm with you so far," I said. Claire nodded.

"Well, the Camel is conscious. He wants out. Like any other prisoner, he looks through the bars from time to time and talks with his jailer—and with anyone else he can reach. What you stumbled into, though, wasn't the Camel: he's pretty well sealed away from that. You hit one of the spells—one of the small warning devices set there in case he should begin to escape. If it had hit him, it would have stung him a little, perhaps like an electric fence. But when you walked into it, you got that hoof. Why the result was exactly that I can't say. It's the nature of the thing. It's happened before, as mythology will tell you."

"I've thought of that," I said. "Pan and the satyrs, and so on. They all had cloven hooves. And isn't the Devil supposed to have one too?"

"One of the marks of the beast." Ponder nodded. "Now, as to what can be done about it, I'm here to do the best I can. Claire, exactly where was it that you walked into—whatever it was, and fell down on that little animal?"

"I don't know," she said calmly. "I haven't been able to locate it. I should be able to—ever since I was a child I've had dream compulsions to come out here, and I know this country like my own house."

"I wish you could find it. It would help." Ponder twiddled the catch on his black bag thoughtfully. "We have to try to get through to the Camel and let him know what has happened to you. He could counteract it. Well, anyway, we might be able to do something, We'll see."

"Doc," I said, "about that hoof. You're sure it was from contact with something out here. I mean, couldn't it have been something in town that caused it?"

"Positively not," he said. And I said to myself, now that is damned interesting, because I have a hoof too and I was never out here before last night.

Ponder turned to Claire. "Exactly why did you come out here that time you saw the little animal?"

"In a way it was your doing, Doctor. It was that Medusa Club meeting. You made me so mad with your intimations that there were still magical forces at work, and that superstitions served to guard humanity against them." She laughed diffidently. "I don't feel the same way now, so much. . . . Anyway, I know this part of the country well. I made up my mind to go to the most magical part of it at the most magical time—the full moon—and stick my neck out. Well, I did."

"Uh-huh," said the doctor. "And why did you come out yesterday?"

"To find Thad."

"Well, Thad? What were you after?"

"I wanted to see what it was Claire had walked into."

"Didn't trust my diagnosis?"

"Oh, it wasn't that. If I'd found anything at all, I probably would have told you about it. I was just curious about the cause and cure of cloven hooves."

"Well, I could have told you that you wouldn't find anything. Claire might, but you wouldn't."

"How so?"

"Hasn't it dawned on you yet that Claire is something special? In a sense she's a product of this very ground. Her parents—"

"I told him that story," said Claire.

"Oh. Well, that was the Camel at work. The only conceivable way for him to break out of his prison is through a human agency; for there is that in human nature that not even forces such as the one which imprisoned him can predict. They can be controlled, but not predicted. And if the Camel should ever be freed—"

"Well?" I asked, after a pause.

"I can't tell you. Not 'won't.' 'Can't.' It's big, though. Bigger than you can dream. But as I was saying, Claire's very presence on earth is his doing."

"My parents were murdered," said Claire.

I turned to her, shocked. She nodded soberly. "When I was six."

"I think you're right," said Ponder. "Their marriage was a thing that could cancel many of the—the devices that imprison the Camel. The very existence of a union like that threatened the—what we can call the prison walls. It had to be stopped."

"What happened?"

"They died," said Claire. "No one knew why. They were found sitting on a rock by the road. He had his arm around her and her head was on his shoulder and they were dead. I always felt that they were killed on purpose, but I never knew why."

"The Camel's fault," said Ponder, shrugging.

I asked. "But why didn't they—he—kill Claire too while he was about it?"

"She was no menace. The thing that was dangerous was the—the radiation from the union that her parents had. It was an unusual marriage."

"My God!" I cried. "You mean to say that Camel creature, whatever it is, can sit out here and push people's lives around like that?"

"That's small fry, Thad. What he could do if he were free is inconceivable."

I rubbed my head. "I dunno, Doc. This is getting to be too much. Can I ask some questions now?"

"Certainly."

"How come you know so much about all this?"

"I am a student of such things. I stumbled on this whole story in some old documents. As a matter of fact, I took the medical practice out here just so I could be near it. It's the biggest thing of its kind I've ever run across."

"Hm. Yet you don't know where the Camel's Grave is, exactly."

"Wrong," said the doctor. "I do. I wanted to know if Claire been able to find it. If she had been able to, it would mean that the Camel had established some sort of contact with her. Since he hasn't, I'll have to do what I can."

"Oh. Anyone who can find the Grave is in contact with the Camel, then."

"That's right. It takes a special kind of person."

I very consciously did not meet Claire's gaze. There was something very fishy going on here, and I began to feel frightened. This thing that could shrivel a foot into a hoof, it could kill too. I asked, "What about this 'jailer' you mentioned. Sort of a low-grade variety of the Camel himself?"

motionless except for the irregular flick-
strils, which quivered in a way reminiscent
vift, seeking tongue. Slowly she began to
hen I could no longer see her face I came

d see. I shall never forget it. That was
orks went out . . . and a terrible truth
e.

of a little bush was a bare spot, brushed
oose leaves, doubtless by the struggles of
as a large brown-brindle rabbit caught in
which had fouled in the bush. The snare
e animal around the barrel, just behind
obably having been set in a runway. The
much alive and frightened.

t slowly and put out her hands. She
it up. I said to myself, the darling! She's
t! . . . and I said, down deeper, but a
enderly at the thing she is about to help,
ace, now, whatever it was, it wasn't

e rabbit and bit into it as if it were an

what I did. Not exactly. I remember a
and dim green. I think I heard Luana
a sigh, perhaps—even a low laugh. I
d I must have run. Once I hit something
ler. Anyway, when I reached Claire and
as panting hoarsely. They looked up at
panting, not speaking. Then without a
ot up and ran back the way I had come.
Thad—what is it?"

beside her and shook my head.

something happen to Luana, Thad?"
," I whispered. Something trickled down

"Something like that."

"That little animal—would that be it?"

A peculiar expression crossed the doctor's face, as if he had remembered something, dragged it out, glanced at it, found it satisfactory, and put it away again. "No," he said. "Did you ever hear of a familiar?"

"A familiar?" asked Claire. "Isn't that the sort of pet that a witch or a wizard has—black cats and so on?"

"Yes. Depending on the degree of 'wizard' we're dealing with, the familiar may be a real animal or something more—the concretion, perhaps, of a certain kind of thought-matrix. That little animal you described to me is undoubtedly the Camel's familiar."

"Then where's the jailer?" And as I asked, I snapped my fingers. "Goo-goo!"

"Not Goo-goo!" Claire cried. "Why, he's perfectly harmless. Besides—he isn't all there, Thad."

"He wouldn't have to be," said the doctor, and smiled. "It doesn't take much brains to be a turnkey."

"I'll be darned," I said. "Well, now, what have we got? A cloven hoof and an imprisoned *something* that must stay imprisoned or else. A couple of nice people murdered, and their pixilated daughter. All right, Doctor—how do you go about curing cloven hooves?"

"Locate the Camel's Grave," said Doctor Ponder. "and then make a rather simple incantation. Sound foolish?" He looked at both of us. "Well, it isn't. It's as simple and foolish as pressing a button—or pulling a trigger. The important thing is who does it to which control on what equipment. In this case Claire is the one indicated, because she's—what was it Thad said?— pixilated. That's it. Because of the nature of her parents' meeting, because of what they had together, because she is of such a character as to have been affected by the Camel to the extent of the thing that happened to her foot—it all adds up. She's the one to do it."

"Then anyone who's subject to this particular kind of falling arches could do it?" I asked innocently.

" 'Anyone'—yes. But that can't happen to just anyone."

I asked another question, quickly, to cover up what I was thinking. "About familiars," I said. "Don't I recall something about their feeding on blood?"

"Traditionally, yes. They do."

"Uh-huh. The blood of the witch, as I recall. Well how in time can the Camel character supply any blood to his familiar if he's been buried here for—how long is it?"

"Longer than you think . . . Well, in a case like that the familiar gets along on whatever blood it can find. It isn't as good, but it serves. Unless, of course, the familiar makes a side trip just for variety. Occasionally one does. That's where the vampire legends come from."

"How do you like that?" I breathed. "I'll bet a cookie that the animals Goo-goo traps are supplying blood to the Camel's familiar—and Goo-goo supposed to be guarding the jail!"

"It's very likely—and not very important. The familiar can do very little by itself," said the doctor. He turned to Claire. "Did you ever see anything like a familiar taking blood? Think, now."

Claire considered. "No. Should I have?"

"Not necessarily. You could though," he indicated her foot, "being what you are."

She shuddered slightly. "So I'm privileged. I'd as soon not, thank you."

I sprang to my feet. "I just thought . . . Luana. What could have happened to her?"

"Oh, she's all right. Sit down, Thad."

"No," I said. "I'd better go look for her."

Claire leaned back, caught her knee in her hands,

and made a soft and
wolf-howl. "Drop de
Doctor Ponder, "Th
tell 'em to drop dead

It took only a few
had left Luana. She

I stood still, my br
iars . . . people w
blood, and people
cloven hoof than the
theory that such a t
thing out here, when
mine in town . . .
her to do and anoth
bursting with some

I moved into the
cause of caution fo
reason, and peering
with my eyes fixed
into a nest of paper
started violently an
swarmed out and a
after me as I sidled
bled against my mc
one stung me. I rer
clear of them, tha
bees . . . but befc
saw Luana.

If it had not beer
bly have seen her.
little glade, her he
struggled on the gr
see her face; and, se
have to call out to h
round-eyed, with cu

was comple te
ering of her n
of a snake's s
bend down. V
closer.

Then I co
when the fire
took their pla

At the foo
clean now of
the rabbit. It
a whip-snare
had caught t
the forelegs,
rabbit was ve

Luana kne
picked the ra
going to help
woman looks
and Luana's
tender.

She lifted
apple.

I don't kno
blur of trunks
make a soun
don't know. A
with my shou
the doctor I
me as I stoo
word, Ponder

"Thad! Oh,
I sank dow
"Luana? D
"I'll tell yo

the outside of my nose. Sweat, I suppose. "I'll tell you, but not now."

She pushed my hair back. "All right, Thad," she said. And that was all, until I got my breath back.

She began to talk then, softly and in a matter-of-fact tone, so that I had to follow what she said; and the sharp crooked edges of horror blunted themselves on new thoughts. She said, "I'm beginning to understand it now, Thad. Some of it is hard to believe, and some of it I just don't *like* to believe. Doctor Ponder knows a lot, Thad, a whole lot. . . . Look." She reached into the doctor's bag, now open, and brought out a limp black book. On its cover, glittering boldly in a sunbeam, was a gilt cross. "You see, Thad? Good and evil . . . Doctor Ponder's using this. Could that be evil? And look. Here—read it yourself." She opened the book at a mark and gave it to me.

I wiped my eyes with my knuckles and took the book. It was the Bible, the New Testament, open to the sixth chapter of Matthew. The thirteenth verse was circled: It was the familiar formula of praise:

"Thine is the Kingdom, the Power, and the Glory, for ever and ever. Amen."

"Look at the bottom margin," she urged.

I looked at the neat block lettering penciled there. *"Ah-tay mahlkuth vé-G'boorah vé-Gédula lé o'lam, om,"* I read haltingly. "What on earth is that?"

"It's the Hebrew translation of the thirteenth verse. And—it's the trigger, the incantation Doctor Ponder told us about."

"Just that? That little bit?"

"Yes. And I'm supposed to go to the Camel's Grave and face the east and say it. Then the Camel will know that I have been affected and will fix the trouble. Doctor Ponder says that although he is evil—a 'black' magician—he can have no reason to leave me in this state."

187

She leaned forward and lowered her voice. "Nor you either. You'll go with me and we'll both be cured."

"Claire—why haven't you told him I've got a hoof too?"

She looked frightened. "I—can't," she whispered. "I tried, and I can't. There's something that stops me."

I looked at the book, reading over the strange, musical sounds of the formula. They had a rhythm, a lilt. Claire said, "Doctor Ponder said I must recite that in a slow monotone, all the while thinking 'Camel, be buried forever, and never show yourself to mankind.' "

"Be buried forever? What about your foot? Aren't you supposed to say something about your foot?"

"Well, didn't I?"

"You did not." I leaned forward and looked close into her eyes. "Say it again."

" 'Camel, be buried forever, and never show yourself to mankind.' "

"Where's the part about the foot?"

She looked at me, puzzled. "Thad—didn't you hear me? I distinctly said that the Camel was to restore my foot and yours and then lie down and rest."

"Did you, now? Say it again, just once more, the way you're supposed to."

Obediently she said, " 'Camel, be buried forever, and never show yourself to mankind.' There. Was that clear enough? About the foot, and all?"

Suddenly I understood. She didn't know what she was saying! I patted her knee. "That was fine," I said. I stood up.

"Where are you going?"

"I have to think," I said. "Mind, Claire? I think better when I walk. Doctor Ponder'll be back soon. Wait here, will you?"

She called to me, but I went on into the Wood. Once out of her sight, I circled back and downgrade, emerging on the rim of what I now knew was the Forbidden Valley. From this point I could easily see the bluff at the far end. There was no sign of the skull. I began to walk down to where it should be. I knew now that it was there, whether it could be seen or not. I wished I could be sure of a few dozen other things. Inside, I was still deeply shaken by what I had seen Luana doing, and by what it meant—by what it made of me, of Claire, of Ponder. . . .

Behind me there was a horrible gargling sound. It was not a growl or a gurgle; it was exactly the hollow, fluid sound that emerges from bathrooms in the laryngitis season. I spun, stared.

Staring back at me was one of the most unprepossessing human being I have ever seen. He had matted hair and a scraggly beard. His eyes were out of line horizontally, and in disagreement with each other as to what they wanted to look at. One ear was pointed and the other was a mere clump of serrated flesh.

I backed off a pace. "You're Goo-goo."

He gabbled at me, waving his arms. It was a disgusting sound. I said, "Don't try to stop me, Mister America. I know what I'm doing and I mean to do it. If you get too near me I'll butter these rocks with you."

He gargled and bubbled away like mad, but kept his distance. Warily I turned and went on down the slope. I thought I heard Claire calling. I strode on, my mind awhirl. Luana. Ponder. Claire. Goo-goo. The chained skull, and the blue beast. The rabbit. Luana, Luana and those lips . . . *Ah-tay mahlkuth* . . . and a cloven hoof. I shook my head to clear my brain . . . *vé-G'boorah*. . . .

I was on level ground, approaching the bluff. "Get up, Camel!" I barked hoarsely. "Here I come, ready or not!"

Shocking, the skull, the famous mark of the Camel's

Grave, appeared on the ground. It was a worn, weather-beaten skull, worn far past the brilliant bleaching of bones merely desiccated and clean. It was yellowed, paper-brittle. The eyebrow ridges were not very prominent, and the lower jaw, what I could see of it, was long, firm. Its most shocking feature was part of it, but not naturally part of it. It was a chain of some black metal, its lower link disappearing into the ground, its upper one entering the eye socket and coming out through the temple. The chain had a hand-wrought appearance, and although it was probably as thick as the day it was made, unrusted and strong, I knew instinctively that it was old, old. It seemed to be—it *must* be—watching me through its empty sockets. I thought I heard the chain clink once. The bleached horror seemed to be waiting.

There was a small scuffling sound right at my heels. It was Goo-goo. I wheeled, snarling at him. He retreated, mouthing. I ground out, "Keep out of my reach, rosebud, or I'll flatten you!" and moved around to the left of the skull where I could face the east.

"*Ah-tay mahlkuth vé*—" I began; and something ran across my foot. It was the blue beast, the familiar. It balanced by the skull, blinking, and disappeared. I looked up to see Goo-goo approaching again. His face was working; he was babbling and drooling.

"Keep clear," I warned him.

He stopped. His clawlike hand went to his belt. He drew a horn-handled sheath knife. It was blue and keen. I had some difficulty in separating my tongue from the roof of my mouth. I stood stiffly, trying to brace myself the way an alerted cat does, ready to leap in any direction, or up, or flat down.

Goo-goo watched me. He was terrifying because he did not seem particularly tense, and I did not know what he was going to do. What was he, anyway? Surely more than a crazy deaf-mute, mad with loneliness. Was he really the jailer of a great Power? Or was he, in some way, in league with that disappearing bad-dream of a familiar?

I began again: "*Ah-tay Mahlkuth vé-G'boor—*" and again was distracted by the madman. For instead of threatening me with his glittering blade, he was performing some strange manual of arms with it, moving it from shoulder to shoulder as I spoke, extending it outward, upward . . . and he stopped when I stopped, looking at me anxiously.

At last there seemed to be some pattern, some purpose, to what he was trying to do. When I spoke a certain phrase, he made a certain motion with the knife. "*Ah-tay . . .*" I said experimentally. He touched his forehead with the knife. I tried it again; he did it again. Slowly, then, without chanting, I recited the whole rigmarole. Following me attentively, he touched his forehead, his chest, his right shoulder, his left, and on the final "*om*" he clasped his hands together with the point of the knife upward.

"Okay, chum," I said. "Now what?"

He immediately extended the knife to me, hilt first. Amazed, I took it. He nodded encouragingly and babbled. He also smiled, though the same grimace a few minutes earlier, before I was convinced of his honest intentions, would have looked like a yellow-fanged snarl to me. And upon me descended the weight of my appalling ignorance. How much difference did the knife make to the ritual? Was it the difference between blanks and slugs in a gun? Or was it the difference between pointing it at myself or up in the air?

Ponder would know. Ponder, it developed, did, and he told me, and I think he did it in spite of himself. As I stood there staring from the steel to the gibbering Goo-

goo, Ponder's great voice rolled down to me from the Wood end of the vale. *"Thad! Not with the knife!"*

I glanced up. Ponder was coming down as fast as he could, helping Claire with one hand and all but dragging Luana with the other. Goo-goo began to dance with impatience, guggling away like an excited ape, pointing at me, at his mouth, at the knife, the staring skull. The blue beast flickered into sight between his legs, beside him, on his shoulder, and for a brief moment on his head, teetering there like some surrealistic plume. I took all this in and felt nothing but utter confusion.

Claire called, "Put down the knife, Thad!"

Something—some strange impulse from deep inside me, made me turn and grin at them as they scurried down toward me. I bellowed, "Why, Doc! I don't qualify, do I?"

Ponder's face purpled. "Come out of there!" he roared. "Let Claire do it!"

I reached down and yanked the makeshift stirrup from my boot, laughing like a maniac. I kicked off the toe of the boot with its padding, and hauled the rest up my leg. "What's she got that I haven't got?" I yelled.

Ponder, still urging the girls forward, turned on Luana. "You see? He saw you feeding! He could *see* you! You should have known!" and he released her and backhanded her viciously. She rolled with the blow deftly, but a lot of it connected. It was not she, however, but Claire who gasped. Luana's face was as impassive as ever. I grunted and turned to face the skull, raising the knife. "How's it go, little man?" I asked Goo-goo. I put the point of the knife on my forehead. "That it?"

He nodded vociferously, and I began to chant.

"Ah-tay . . ." I shifted the knife downward to my chest. Ponder was bellowing something. Claire screamed my name.

192

"Mahlkuth. . . ." With part of my mind I heard, now, what Ponder was yelling. "You'll free him! Stop it, you fool, you'll free him!" And Claire's voice again: "A gun. . . ." I thought, down deep inside, *Free him!* I put the knife-point on my right shoulder.

"Vé-G'boorah!" There was the sharp bark of a shot. Something hit the small of my back. The blue beast stumbled from between my feet, and as I shifted the knife to my left shoulder, I saw it bow down and, with its mouth, lay something at my feet. It teetered there for a split second, its eyes winking like fan blades in bright light, and I'll swear the little devil grinned at me. Then it was gone, leaving behind a bullet on the grass.

"Vé-Gédula . . ." I chanted, conscious that so far I had not broken the compelling rhythm of the ancient syllables, nor missed a motion with the knife. Twice more the gun yapped, and with each explosion I was struck, once in the face, once on the neck. Not by bullets, however, but by the cold rubbery hide of the swift familiar, which dropped in front of me with its little cheeks bulging out like those of a chipmunk at acorn time. It put the two bullets down by the first and vanished. I clasped my hands on the knife hilt, pressing it to my chest, point upward the way Goo-goo had done.

"Lé o'lam. . . ." From the corner of my eye I saw Ponder hurling himself at me, and the ragged figure of little Goo-goo rising up between us. Ponder struck the little man aside with one bear-like clubbing of his forearm, and was suddenly assaulted either by fifty of the blue familiars or by one moving fifty miles as fast as a living thing ought to. It was in his ears, fluttering on his face, nipping the back of his neck, clawing at his nostrils, all at once. Ponder lost one precious second in trying to bat the thing away, and then apparently decided to ignore it. He launched himself at me with a roar, just as I came out with the final syllable of the incantation: *"OM!"*

It isn't easy to tell what happened then. They say The Egg hit Hiroshima with "a soundless flash." It was like that. I stood where I was, my head turned away from the place where the skull had been, my eyes all but closed against that terrible cold radiance. Filtering my vision through my lashes, I saw Ponder still in midair, still coming toward me. But as he moved, he—changed. For a second he must have been hot, for his clothes charred. But he was cold when he hit me, cold as death. His clothes were a flurry of chilled soot; his skin was brittle, frigid eggshell through which his bones burst and powdered. I stood, braced for a solid impact that never came, showered with the scorched and frozen detritus of what had been a man.

Still I stood, holding the knife, for hardly a full second had passed; and my vision went out with that blinding light. I saw Claire thirty yards away on her knees, her face in her hands; and whether she had fallen or was praying I could not know. Goo-goo was on the ground where Ponder had stretched him, and near his body was the familiar, still at last. Beyond stood Luana, still on her feet, her auburn eyes blindly open to the great light, her face composed. She stepped forward slowly, hanging her arms, but with her head erect, her heated hair flung back. The cruel, steady light made sharp-edged shadows on the hinges of her jaw, for all they were sunlit. For a brief moment she was beautiful, and then she seemed to be walking down a staircase, for she grew shorter as she walked. Her taut skin billowed suddenly like a pillow-slip on a clothesline, and her hair slipped down and drifted off in a writhing cloud. She opened her mouth, and it made a triangle, and she began to bleat.

They were wordless sounds, each one higher in pitch than the one before. Up and up they went, growing fainter as they grew higher, turning to rat-squeaks, mouse-squeaks, bat-squeaks, and at last a high thin whistle that was not a sound at all but a pressure on the eardrums. Suddenly there was nothing moving there at all; there was only a plaid skirt and a windbreaker tumbled together with blood on them. And a naked, lizard-like thing nosed out of the pathetic pile, raised itself up on skinny forelimbs, sniffed with its pointed snout at the light, and fell dead.

Claire drew a long, gasping breath. The sound said nothing for Claire, but much for the vale. It said how utterly quiet it was. I looked again at the plaid skirt lying tumbled on the grass, and I felt a deep pain. I did not mourn Luana, for Luana never was a woman; and I knew now that had I never seen her again after our last kiss over the gate, I would not have remembered her as a woman. But she had been beauty; she had been cool lips and infernal hair, and skin of many subtle sorts of rose; I mourned these things, in the face of which her lack of humanity was completely unimportant.

The light dimmed. I dropped the knife and went to Claire. I sank down beside her and put my arms around her. She let her hands slide off her face and turned it into my shoulder. She was not crying. I patted her hair, and we rested there until I was moved to say, "We can look at him now," and for a moment longer while we enjoyed the awe of knowing that all the while he had been standing there, released.

Then, together, we turned our heads and looked at him.

He had dimmed his pent-up light, but still he blazed. I will not say what he looked like, because he looked like only himself. I will not say he looked like a man, because no man could look like him. He said, "Claire, take off your boot."

She bent to do it, and when she had, something flowed from him to us. I had my hoof under me. I felt it writhe and swell. There was an instant of pain. I grasped the hairy ankle as the coarse hair fell out, and then my foot was whole again. Claire laughed, patting and stroking her restored foot. I had never seen her face like that before.

Then *he* laughed. I will not say what that was like either. "Thad, Thad, you've done it. You've bungled and stumbled, but you've done it." I'll say how he spoke, though. He spoke like a man.

"What have I done?" I asked. "I have been pushed and pulled; I've thought some things out, and I've been both right and wrong—what have I done?"

"You have done right—finally," he chuckled. "You have set me free. You have broken walls and melted bars that are inconceivable to you . . . I'll tell you as much as I can, though.

"You see, for some hundreds of thousands of years I have had a—call it a jailer. He did not capture me: that was done by a far greater one than he. But the jailer's name was Korm. And sometimes he lived as a bird and sometimes as an animal or a man. You knew him as Ponder. He was a minor wizard, and Luana was his familiar. I too have a familiar—Tiltol there." He indicated the blue beast, stretched quietly out at his feet.

"Imprisoned, I could do very little. Korm used to amuse himself by watching my struggles, and occasionally he would set up a spell to block me even further. Sometimes he would leave me alone, to get my hopes up, to let me begin to free myself, so that he could step in and check me again, and laugh. . . .

"One thing I managed to do during one of those periods was to bring Claire's parents together. Korm thought that the magic thing they had between them was the tool I was developing, and when it began to look like a strong magic, he killed them. He did not know until much later that Claire was my magic; and when he found it out, he made a new and irritating spell around me, and induced Claire to come out here and walk into it. It was supposed to kill her, but she was protected; all it did was to touch her with the mark of the beast—a cloven hoof. And it immobilized me completely for some hours.

"When I could, I sent Tiltol after her with a new protection; without it she would be in real danger from Korm, for he was bound to find out how very special she was. Tiltol tried to weave the new protection around her—and found that he could not. Her aura was no longer completely her own. She had fallen in love; she had given part of herself away to you, Thad. Now, since the new spell would work only on one in Claire's particular condition, and since he could not change that, Tiltol found a very logical solution: He gave you a cloven hoof too, and then cast the protection over both of you. That's why the bear-trap did not hurt you, and why the wasps couldn't sting you."

"I'm beginning to see," I said. "But—what's this about the ritual? How did it set you free?"

"I can't explain that. Roughly, though, I might say that if you regard my prison as locked, and your presence as the key in the lock, then the ritual was the turning of the key, and the use of the knife was the direction in which the key was turned. If you—or Claire, which was Korm's intention—had used the ritual without the knife, I would have been more firmly imprisoned than ever, and you two would have lived out your lives with those hooves."

"What about Goo-goo? I thought for a while that he was the jailer."

He chuckled. "Bless you, no. He is what he seems to be—a harmless, half-demented old man, keeping himself out of people's way. He isn't dead, by the way. When he wakes, he'll have no recollection of all this. I practiced on him, to see if I could get a human being to perform the ritual, and he has been a good friend. He won't lose by it. Speaking of the ritual, though, I'd like you to know that, spectacular as it might have been, it wasn't the biggest part of the battle. That happened before—when you and Claire were talking to Ponder. Remember when Claire recited the spell and didn't know what she was saying?"

"I certainly do. That was when I suddenly decided there was something funny about Ponder's story. He had hypnotized her, hadn't he?"

"Something very like it . . . he was in her mind and I, by the way, was in yours. That's what made you leap up and go to Luana."

I shuddered. "That was bad . . . evil. What about this 'good and evil' theory of Ponder's, incidentally? How could he have worked evil on you with a spell from the Bible?"

There was a trace of irritation in his voice. "You'll have to get rid of this 'black and white magic' misconception," he said. "Is a force like electricity 'white' or 'black'? You use it for the iron lung. You use it also for the electric chair. You can't define magic by its methods and its materials, but only in terms of its purpose. Regard it, not as 'black' and 'white' but as High and Low magic. As to the Testament, why, that ritual is older than the Bible or it couldn't have been recorded there. Believe me, Ponder was using it well out of its context. Ah well, it's all over with now. You two are blessed—do you realize that? You both will keep your special immunity, and Claire shall have what she most wants, besides."

"What about you?"

"I must go. I have work to do. The world was not ordained to be without me.

"For there is reason in the world, and all the world is

free to use it. But there has been no will to use it. There's wilfulness aplenty, in individuals and in groups, but no great encompassing will to work with reason. Almost no one reads a Communist newspaper but Communists, and only prohibitionists attend a dry convention. Humanity is split up into tiny groups, each clinging to some single segment of Truth, and earnestly keeping itself unaware of the other Truths that make up the great mosaic. And even when humans are aware of the fact that others share the same truth, they allow themselves to be kept apart from each other. The farmer here knows that the farmer there does not want to fight a war against him, yet they fight. I am that Will. I am the brother of Reason, who came here with me. My brother has done well, but he needs me, and you have set me free."

"Who are you?" I asked.

"The earliest men called me Kamäel."

"The Camel . . . in every language," murmured Claire. Suddenly her eyes widened. "You are—an . . . an *archangel*, Kamäel! I've read . . ."

He smiled, and we looked down, blinded.

"Tiltol!"

The tiny familiar twitched and was suddenly balancing on its two legs. It moved abruptly, impossibly fast, zoomed up to Kamäel, where it nestled in the crook of his arm. And suddenly it began to grow and change. Great golden feathers sprouted from its naked hide, and a noble crest. It spread wide wings. Its plumage was an incredible purple under its golden crest and gold-tipped wings. We stared, filling our minds with a sight no human being alive had seen—of all birds, the noblest.

"Good-bye," said Kamäel. "Perhaps one day you will know the size of the thing you have done. The One who imprisoned me will come back, one day, and we will be ready for him."

"Satan?"

"Some call him that."

"Did he leave earth?"

"Bless you, yes! Mankind has had no devil but himself these last twenty thousand years! But we'll be ready for the Old One, now."

There was more sun, there were more colors in the world as we walked back to town.

"It was the Phoenix!" breathed Claire for the twentieth time. "What a thing to tell our children."

"Whose children?"

"Ours."

"Now look," I said, but she interrupted me. "Didn't he say I was to have what I wanted most?"

I looked down at her, trying hard not to smile. "Oh, all right," I said.

THE TOUCH
OF YOUR HAND

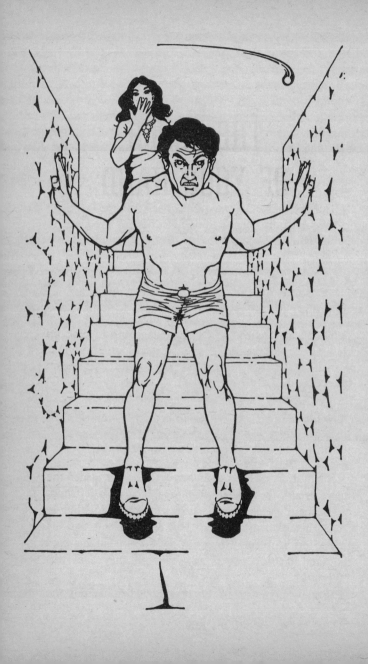

"Dig there," said Osser, pointing.

The black-browed man pulled back. "Why?"

"We must dig deep to build high, and we are going to build high."

"Why?" the man asked again.

"To keep the enemy out."

"There are no enemies."

Osser laughed bitterly. "I'll have enemies."

"Why?"

Osser came to him. "Because I'm going to pick up this village and shake it until it wakes up. And if it won't wake up, I'll keep shaking until I break its back and it dies. Dig."

"I don't see why," said the man doggedly.

Osser looked at the golden backs of his hands, turned them over, watched them closing. He raised his eyes to the other.

"This is why," he said.

His right fist tore the man's cheek. His left turned the man's breath to a bullet which exploded as it left him. He huddled on the ground, unable to exhale, inhaling in small, heavy, tearing sobs. His eyes opened and he looked up at Osser. He could not speak, but his eyes did; and through shock and pain all they said was "Why?"

"You want reasons," Osser said, when he felt the

man could hear him. "You want reasons—all of you. You see both sides of every question and you weigh and balance and cancel yourselves out. I want an end to reason. I want things done."

He bent to lift the bearded man to his feet. Osser stood half a head taller and his shoulders were as full and smooth as the bottoms of bowls. Golden hairs shifted and glinted on his forearms as he moved his fingers and the great cords tensed and valleyed. He lifted the man clear of the ground and set him easily on his feet and held him until he was sure of his balance.

"You don't understand me, do you?"

The man shook his head weakly.

"Don't try. You'll dig more if you don't try." He clapped the handle of the shovel into the man's hand and picked up a mattock. "Dig," he said, and the man began to dig.

Osser smiled when the man turned to work, arched his nostrils and drew the warm clean air into his lungs. He liked the sunlight now, the morning smell of the turned soil, the work he had to do and the idea itself of working.

Standing so, with his head raised, he saw a flash of bright yellow, the turn of a tanned face. Just a glimpse, and she was gone.

For a moment he tensed, frowning. If she had seen him she would be off to clatter the story of it to the whole village. Then he smiled. Let her. Let them all know. They must, sooner or later. Let them try to stop him.

He laughed, gripped his mattock, and the sod flew. So Jubilith saw fit to watch him, did she?

He laughed again. Work now, Juby later. In time he would have everything.

Everything.

* * *

The village street wound and wandered and from time to time divided and rejoined itself, for each house was built on a man's whim—near, far, high, small, separate, turned to or away. What did not harmonize contrasted well, and over all it was a pleasing place to walk.

Before a shop a wood-cobbler sat, gouging out sabots; and he was next door to the old leatherworker who cunningly wove immortal belts of square-knotted rawhide. Then a house, and another, and a cabin; a space of green where children played; and the skeleton of a new building where a man, his apron pockets full of hardwood pegs, worked knowledgeably with a heavy mallet.

The cobbler, the leatherworker, the children and the builder all stopped to watch Jubilith because she was beautiful and because she ran. When she was by, they each saw the others watching, and each smiled and waved and laughed a little, though nothing was said.

A puppy lolloped along after her, three legs deft, the fourth in the way. Had it been frightened, it would not have run, and had Jubilith spoken to it, it would have followed wherever she went. But she ignored it, even when it barked its small soprano bark, so it curved away from her, pretending it had been going somewhere else anyway, and then it sat and puffed and looked after her sadly.

Past the smithy with its shadowed, glowing heart she ran; past the gristmill with its wonderful wheel, taking and yielding with its heavy cupped hands. A boy struck his hoop and it rolled across her path. Without breaking stride, she leaped high over it and ran on, and the glassblower's lips burst away from his pipe, for a man can smile or blow glass, but not both at the same time.

When at last she reached Wrenn's house, she was breathing deeply, but with no difficulty, in the way possible only to those who run beautifully. She stopped by the open door and waited politely, not looking in until Oyva came out and touched her shoulder.

Jubilith faced her, keeping her eyes closed for a long moment, for Oyva was not only very old, she was Wrenn's wife.

"Is it Jubilith?" asked Oyva, smiling.

"It is," said the girl. She opened her eyes.

Oyva, seeing their taut corners, said shrewdly, "A troubled Jubilith as well. I'll not keep you. He's just inside."

Juby found a swift flash of smile to give her and went into the house, leaving the old woman to wonder where, where in her long life she had seen such a brief flash of such great loveliness. A firebird's wing? A green meteor? She put it away in her mind next to the memory of a burst of laughter—Wrenn's, just after he had kissed her first—and sat down on a three-legged stool by the side of the house.

A heavy fiber screen had been set up inside the doorway, to form a sort of meander, and at the third turn it was very dark. Juby paused to let the sunlight drain away from her vision. Somewhere in the dark before her there was music, the hay-clean smell of flower petals dried and freshly rubbed, and a voice humming. The voice and the music were open and free, but choked a listener's throat like the sudden appearance of a field of daffodils.

The voice and the music stopped short, and someone breathed quietly in the darkness.

"Is . . . is it Wrenn?" she faltered.

"It is," said the voice.

"Jubilith here."

"Move the screen," said the voice. "I'd like the light, talking to you, Jubilith."

She felt behind her, touched the screen. It had many hinges and swung easily away to the doorside. Wrenn sat

206

crosslegged in the corner behind a frame which held a glittering complex of stones.

He brushed petal-dust from his hands. "Sit there, child, and tell me what it is you do not understand."

She sat down before him and lowered her eyes, and his widened, as if someone had taken away a great light.

When she had nothing to say, he prompted her gently: "See if you can put it all into a single world, Jubilith."

She said immediately, "Osser."

"Ah," said Wrenn.

"I followed him this morning, out to the foothills beyond the Sky-tree Grove. He—"

Wrenn waited.

Jubilith put up her small hands, clenched, and talked in a rush. "Sussten, with the black brows, he was with Osser. They stopped and Osser shouted at him, and, when I came to where I could look down and see them, Osser took his fists and hammered Sussten, knocked him down. He laughed and picked him up. Sussten was sick; he was shaken and there was blood on his face. Osser told him to dig, and Sussten dug, Osser laughed again, he laughed . . . I think he saw me. I came here."

Slowly she put her fists down. Wrenn said nothing.

Jubilith said, in a voice like a puzzled sigh, "I understand this: when a man hammers something, iron or clay or wood, it is to change what he hammers from what it is to what he wishes it to be." She raised one hand, made a fist, and put it down again. She shook her head slightly and her heavy soft hair moved on her back. "To hammer a man is to change nothing. Sussten remains Sussten."

"It was good to tell me of this," said Wrenn when he was sure she had finished.

"Not good," Jubilith disclaimed. "I want to understand."

Wrenn shook his head. Juby cocked her head on one side like a wondering bright bird. When she realized that his gesture was a refusal, a small paired crease came and went between her brows.

"May I not understand this?"

"You *must* not understand it," Wrenn corrected. "Not yet, anyway. Perhaps after a time. Perhaps never."

"Ah," she said. "I—I didn't know."

"How could you know?" he asked kindly. "Don't follow Osser again, Jubilith."

She parted her lips, then again gave the small headshake. She rose and went out.

Oyva came to her. "Better now, Jubilith?"

Juby turned her head away; then, realizing that this was ill-mannered, met Oyva's gaze. The girl's eyes were full of tears. She closed them respectfully. Oyva touched her shoulder and let her go.

Watching the slim, bright figure trudge away, bowed with thought, drag-footed, unseeing, Oyva grunted and stumped into the house.

"Did she have to be hurt?" she demanded.

"She did," said Wrenn gently. "Osser," he added.

"Oh," she said, in just the tone he had used when Jubilith first mentioned the name. "What has he done now?"

Wrenn told her. Oyva sucked her lips in thoughtfully. "Why was the girl following him?"

"I didn't ask her. But don't you know?"

"I suppose I do," said Oyva, and sighed. "That mustn't happen, Wrenn."

"It won't. I told her not to follow him again."

She looked at him fondly. "I suppose even you can act like a fool once in a while."

He was startled. "Fool?"

"She loves him. You won't keep her from him by a word of advice."

"You judge her by yourself," he said, just as fondly. "She's only a child. In a day, a week, she'll wrap someone else up in her dreams."

"Suppose she doesn't?"

"Don't even think about it." A shudder touched his voice.

"I shall, though," said Oyva with determination. "And you'd do well to think about it, too." When his eyes grew troubled, she touched his cheek gently, "Now play some more for me."

He sat down before the instrument, his hands poised. Then into the tiny bins his fingers went, rubbing this dried-petal powder and that, and the stones glowed, changing the flower-scents into music and shifting colors.

He began to sing softly to the music.

They dug deep, day by day, and they built. Osser did the work of three men, and sometimes six or eight others worked with him, and sometimes one or two. Once he had twelve. But never did he work alone.

When the stone was three tiers above ground level, Osser climbed the nearest rise and stood looking down at it proudly, at the thickness and strength of the growing walls, at the toiling workers who lifted and strained to make them grow.

"Is it Osser?"

The voice was as faint and shy as a fern uncurling, as promising as spring itself.

He turned.

"Jubilith," she told him.

"What are you doing here?"

"I come here every day," she said. She indicated the copse which crowned the hill. "I hide here and watch you."

"What do you want?"

She laced her fingers. "I would like to dig there and lift stones."

"No," he said, and turned to study the work again.

"Why not?"

"Never ask me why. 'Because I say so'—that's all the answer you'll get from me—you or anyone."

She came to stand beside him. "You build fast."

He nodded. "Faster than any village house was ever built." He could sense the 'why' rising within her, and could feel it being checked.

"I want to build it, too," she pleaded.

"No," he said. His eyes widened as he watched the work. Suddenly he was gone, leaping down the slope in great springy strides. He turned the corner of the new wall and stood, saying nothing. The man who had been idling turned quickly and lifted a stone. Osser smiled a quick, taut smile and went to work beside him. Jubilith stood on the slope, watching, wondering.

She came almost every day as the tower grew. Osser never spoke to her. She watched the sunlight on him, the lithe strength, the rippling gold. He stood like a great tree, squatted like a rock, moved like a thundercloud. His voice was a whip, a bugle, the roar of a bull.

She saw him less and less in the village. Once it was a fearsome thing to see. Early in the morning he appeared suddenly, overtook a man, lifted him and threw him flat on the ground.

"I told you to be out there yesterday," he growled, and strode away.

Friends came and picked the man up, held him softly while he coughed, took him away to be healed.

No one went to Wrenn about it; the word had gone around that Osser and his affairs were not to be understood by anyone. Wrenn's function was to explain those few things which could not be understood. But certain of these few were not to be understood at all. So Osser

210

was left alone to do as he wished—which was a liberty, after all, that was enjoyed by everyone else.

Twilight came when Jubilith waited past her usual time. She waited until by ones and twos the workers left the tower, until Osser himself had climbed the hill, until he had paused to look back and be proud and think of tomorrow's work, until he, too, had turned his face to the town. Then she slipped down to the tower and around it, and carefully climbed the scaffolding on the far side. She looked about her.

The tower was now four stories high and seemed to be shaping toward a roof. Circular in cross-section, the tower had two rooms on each floor, an east-west wall between them on the ground floor, a north-south wall on the next, and so on up.

There was a central well into which was built a spiral staircase—a double spiral, as if one helix had been screwed into the other. This made possible two exits to stairs on each floor at the same level, though they were walled off one from the other. Each of the two rooms on every floor had one connecting doorway. Each room had three windows in it, wide on the inside, tapering through the thick stone wall to form the barest slit outside.

A portion of the castellated roof was already built. It overhung the entrance, and had slots in the overhang through which the whole entrance face of the tower could be covered by one man lying unseen on the roof, looking straight down.

Stones lay in a trough ready for placing, and there was some leftover mortar in the box. Jubilith picked up a trowel and worked it experimentally in the stuff, then lifted some out and tipped it down on the unfinished top of the wall, just as she had seen Osser do so many times. She put down the trowel and chose a stone. It

211

was heavy—much heavier than she had expected—but she made it move, made it lift, made it seat itself to suit her on the fresh mortar. She ticked off the excess from the join and stepped back to admire it in the fading light.

Two great clamps, hard as teeth, strong as a hurricane, caught her right thigh and her left armpit. She was swung into the air and held helpless over the unfinished parapet.

She was utterly silent, shocked past the ability even to gasp.

"I told you you were not to work here," said Osser between his teeth. So tall he was, so long were his arms as he held her high over his head, that it seemed almost as far to the parapet as it was to the ground below.

He leaned close to the edge and shook her. "I'll throw you off. This tower is mine to build, you hear?"

If she had been able to breathe, she might have screamed or pleaded with him. If she had screamed or pleaded, he might have dropped her. But her silence apparently surprised him. He grunted and set her roughly on her feet. She caught at his shoulder to keep her balance, then quickly transferred her hold to the edge of the parapet. She dropped her head between her upper arms. Her long soft hair fell forward over her face, and she moaned.

"I told you," he said, really seeing her at last. His voice shook. He stepped toward her and put out his hand. She screamed. "Be *quiet!*" he roared. A moan shut off in mid-breath. "Ah, I told you, Juby. You shouldn't have tried to build here."

He ran his great hands over the edge of the stonework, found the one she had laid, the one that had cost her such effort to lift. With one hand, he plucked it up and threw it far out into the shadows below.

"I wanted to help you with it," she whispered.

212

"Don't you understand?" he cried. "No one builds here who *wants* to help!"

She simply shook her head.

She tried to breathe deeply and a long shudder possessed her. When it passed, she turned weakly and stood, her back partly arched over the edge of the parapet, her hands behind her to cushion the stone. She shook the hair out of her face; it fell away on either side like a dawnlit bow-wave. She looked up at him with an expression of such piteous confusion that his dwindling rage vanished altogether.

He dropped his eyes and shuffled one foot like a guilty child. "Juby, leave me alone."

Something almost like a smile touched her lips. She brushed her bruised arm, then walked past him to the place where the scaffolding projected above the parapet.

"Not that way," he called. "Come here."

He took her hand and led her to the spiral staircase at the center of the tower. It was almost totally dark inside. It seemed like an age to her as they descended; she was alone in a black universe consisting of a rhythmic drop and turn, and a warm hard hand in hers, holding and leading her.

When they emerged, he stopped in the strange twilight, a darkness for all the world but a dazzle to them, so soaked with blackness were their eyes. She tugged gently, but he would not release her hand. She moved close to see his face. His eyes were wide and turned unseeing to the far slopes; he was frowning, yet his mouth was not fierce, but irresolute. Whatever his inward struggle was, it left his face gradually and transferred itself to his hand. Its pressure on hers became firm, hard, intense, painful.

"Osser!"

He dropped the hand and stepped back, shamed.

"Juby, I will take you to . . . Juby, do you want to understand?" He waved at the tower.

She said, "Oh, yes!"

He looked at her closely, and the angry, troubled diffidence came and went. "Half a day there, half a day back again," he said.

She recognized that this was as near as this feral, unhappy man could come to asking a permission. "I'd like to understand," she said.

"If you don't, I'm going to kill you," he blurted. He turned to the west and strode off, not looking back.

Jubilith watched him go, and suddenly there was a sparkle in her wide eyes. She slipped out of her sandals, caught them up in her hand, and ran lightly and silently after him. He planted his feet strongly, like the sure, powerful teeth of the millwheel gears, and he would not look back. She sensed how immensely important it was to him not to look back. She knew that right-handed men look back over their left shoulders, so she drifted along close to him, a little behind him, a little to his right. How long, how long, until he looked to see if she was coming?

Up and up the slope, to its crest, over . . . down . . . ah! Just here, just at the last second where he could turn and look without stopping and still catch a glimpse of the tower's base, where they had stood. So he turned, and she passed around him like a windblown feather, unseen.

And he stopped, looking back, craning. His shoulders slumped, and slowly he turned to his path again—and there was Jubilith before him.

She laughed.

His jaw dropped, and then his lips came together in a thin, angry seal. For a moment he stared at her; and suddenly, quite against his will, there burst from him a single harsh bark of laughter. She put out her hand and he came to her, took it, and they went their way together.

They came to a village when it was very late and very dark; and Osser circled it. They came to another, and Jubilith thought he would do the same, for he turned south; but when they came abreast of it, he struck north again.

"We'll be seen," he explained gruffly, "but we'll be seen coming from the south and leaving northward."

She would not ask where he was taking her, or why he was making these elaborate arrangements, but already she had an idea. What lay to the west was—not forbidden, exactly, but, say discouraged. It was felt that there was nothing in that country that could be of value. Anyone traveling that way would surely be remembered.

So through the village they went, and they dined quickly at an inn, and went northward, and once in the darkness, veered west again. In a wood so dark that she had taken his hand again, he stopped and built a fire. He threw down springy boughs and a thick heap of ferns, and this was her bed. He slept sitting up, his back to a tree trunk, with Jubilith between him and the fire.

Jubilith awoke twice during the long night, once to see him with his eyes closed, but feeling that he was not asleep; and once to see him with his eyes open and the dying flames flickering in the pupils, and she thought then that he was asleep, or at least not with her, but lost in the pictures the flames painted.

In the morning they moved on, gathering berries for breakfast, washing in a humorous brook. And during this whole journey, nothing passed between them but the small necessary phrases: "You go first here." "Look out—it drops." "Tired yet?"

For there was that about Jubilith which made explanations unnecessary. Though she did not know where they were going, or why, she understood what must be done to get them there within the framework of his desire: to go immediately, as quickly as possible, undetected by anyone else.

She did only what she could to help and did not plague him with questions which would certainly be answered in good time. So: "Here are berries." "Look, a red bird!" "Can we get through there, or shall we go around?" And nothing more.

They did well, the weather was fine, and by midmorning they had reached the tumbled country of the Crooked Hills. Jubilith had seen them from afar—great broken mounds and masses against the western sky—but no one ever went there, and she knew nothing about them.

They were in open land now, and Jubilith regretted leaving the color and aliveness of the forest. The grasses here were strange, like yet unlike those near her village. They were taller, sickly, and some had odd ugly flowers. There were bald places, scored with ancient rain-gullies, as if some mighty hand had dashed acid against the soil. There were few insects and no animals that she could see, and no birds sang. It was a place of great sadness rather than terror; there was little to fear, but much to grieve for.

By noon, they faced a huge curved ridge, covered with broken stones. It looked as if the land itself had reared up and pressed back from a hidden something on the other side—something which it would not touch. Osser quickened their pace as they began to climb, although the going was hard. Jubilith realized that they were near the end of their journey, and uncomplainingly struggled along at the cruel pace he set.

At the top, they paused, giving their first attention to their wind, and gradually to the scene before them.

The ridge on which they stood was nearly circular, and perhaps a mile and a half in diameter. In its center was a small round lake with unnaturally bare shores. Mounds of rubble sloped down toward it on all sides, and farther back was broken stone.

But it was the next zone which caught and held the eye. The weed-grown wreckage there was beyond description. Great twisted webs and ribs of gleaming metal wove in and out of the slumped heaps of soil and masonry. Nearby, a half-acre of laminated stone stood on the edge like a dinner plate in a clay bank. What could have been a building taller than any Jubilith had ever heard about lay on its side, smashed and bulging.

Gradually she began to realize the peculiarity of this place—All the larger wreckage lay in lines directly to and from the lake in a monstrous radiation of ruin.

"What is this place?" she asked at last.

"Don't know," he grunted, and went over the edge to slip down the steep slope. When she caught up with him near the bottom, he said, "There's miles of this, west and north of here, much bigger. But this is the one we came to see. Come."

He looked to right and left as if to get his bearings, then plunged into the tough and scrubby underbrush that vainly tried to cover those tortured metal bones. She followed as closely as she could, beating at the branches which he carelessly let whip back.

Just in front of her, he turned the corner of a sharp block of stone, and when she turned it no more than a second later, he was gone.

She stopped, turned, again. Dust, weeds, lonely and sorrowful ruins. No Osser. She shrank back against the stone, her eyes wide.

The bushes nearby trembled, then lashed. Osser's

head emerged. "What's the matter? Come on!" he said gruffly.

She checked an impulse to cry out and run to him, and came silently forward. Osser held the bushes briefly, and beside him she saw a black hole with broken steps leading downward.

She hesitated, but he moved his head impatiently, and she passed him and led the way downward. When he followed, his wide flat body blocked out the light. The darkness was so heavy, her eyes ached.

He prodded her in the small of the back. "Go on, go on!"

The foot of the steps came sooner than she expected and her knees buckled as she took the downward step that was not there. She tripped, almost fell, then somehow got to the side wall and braced herself there, trembling.

"Wait," he said, and the irrepressible smile quirked the corners of her mouth. As if she would go anywhere!

She heard him fumbling about somewhere, and then there was a sudden aching blaze of light that made her cry out and clap her hands over her face.

"Look," he said. "I want you to look at this. Hold it."

Into her hands he pressed a cylinder about half the length of her forearm. At one end was a lens from which the blue-white light was streaming.

"See this little thing here," he said, and touched a stud at the side of the cylinder. The light disappeared, came on again.

She laughed delightedly, took the cylinder and played its light around, switching it on and off. "It's wonderful!" she cried. "Oh, wonderful!"

"You take this one," he said, pleased. He handed her another torch and took the first from her. "It isn't as good, but it will help. I'll go first."

She took the second torch and tried it. It worked the same way, but the light was orange and feeble. Osser strode ahead down a slanting passageway. At first there was a great deal of rubble underfoot, but soon the way was clear as they went farther and deeper. Osser walked with confidence, and she knew he had been here before, probably many times.

"Here," he said, stopping to wait for her. His voice echoed strangely, vibrant with controlled excitement.

He turned his torch ahead, swept it back and forth.

They were at the entrance to a room. It was three times the height of a man, and as big as their village green. She stared around, awed.

"Come," Osser said again, and went to the far corner.

A massive, boxlike object stood there. One panel, about eye-level, was of a milky smooth substance, the rest of black metal. Projecting from the floor in front of it was a lever. Osser grasped it confidently and pulled. It yielded sluggishly, and returned to its original position. Osser tugged again. There was a low growling sound from the box. Osser pulled, released, pulled, released, each time a little faster. The sound rose in pitch, higher and higher.

"Turn off your light," he said.

She did so and blackness snapped in around them. As the dazzle faded from her eyes, she detected a flicker of silver light before her, and realized that it came from the milky pane in the box. As Osser pulled at the lever and the whine rose and rose in pitch, the square got bright enough for her to see her hands when she looked down at them.

And then—the pictures.

Jubilith had never seen pictures like these. They moved, for one thing; for another, they had no color.

Everything in them was black and white and shades of gray. Yet everything they showed seemed very real.

Not at first, for there was flickering and stopped motion, and then slow motion as Osser's lever moved faster and faster. But at last the picture steadied, and Osser kept the lever going at the same speed, flicking it with apparent ease about twice a second, while the whine inside the box settled to a steady, soft moan.

The picture showed a ball spinning against a black, light-flecked curtain. It rushed close until it filled the screen, and still closer, and Jubilith suddenly had the feeling that she was falling at tremendous velocity from an unthinkable height. Down and down the scene went, until at last the surface began to take on the qualities of a bird's-eye view. She saw a river and lakes, and a great range of hills—

And, at last, the city.

It was a city beyond fantasy, greater and more elaborate than imagination could cope with. Its towers stretched skyward to pierce the clouds themselves—some actually did. It had wide ramps on which traffic crawled, great bridges across the river, parks over which the buildings hung like mighty cliffs. Closer still the silver eye came to the scene, and she realized that the traffic was not crawling, but moving faster than a bird, faster than the wind. The vehicles were low and sleek and efficient.

And on the walks were people, and the scene wheeled and slowed and showed them. They were elaborately clothed and well-fed; they were hurried and orderly at the same time. There was a square in which perhaps a thousand of them, all dressed alike, were drawn up in lines as straight as stretched string. Even as she watched, they all began to move together, a thousand left legs coming forward, a thousand right arms swinging back.

Higher, then, and more of the city—more and more of it, until the sense of wonder filled her lungs and she hardly breathed; and still more of it, miles of it. And at last a great open space with what looked like sections of road crossing on it—but such unthinkable roads! Each was as wide as her whole village and miles long. And on these roads, great birdlike machines tilted down and touched and rolled, and swung and ran and took the air, dozens of them every minute. The scene swept close again, and it was as if she were in such a machine herself; but it did not land. It raced past the huge busy crossroads and out to a coastline.

And there were ships, ships as long as the tallest buildings were high, and clusters, dozens, hundreds of other vessels working and smoking and milling about in the gray water. Huge machines crouched over ships and lifted out cargoes; small, agile machines scurried about the docks and warehouses.

Then at last the scene dwindled as the magic eye rose higher and higher, faster and faster. Details disappeared, and clouds raced past and downward, and at last the scene was a disc and then a ball floating in starlit space.

Osser let the lever go and it snapped back to its original position. The moan descended quickly in pitch, and the motion on the screen slowed, flickered, faded and went out.

Jubilith let the darkness come. Her mind spun and shook with the impact of what she had seen. Slowly she recovered herself. She became conscious of Osser's hard breathing. She turned on her dim orange torch and looked at him. He was watching her.

"What was it?" she breathed.

"What I came to show you."

She thought hard. She thought about his tower, about

221

his refusal to let her work on it, about his cruelty to those who had. She looked at him, at the blank screen. And this was to supply the reason.

She shook her head.

He lowered himself slowly and squatted like an animal, hunched up tight, his knees in his armpits. This lifted and crooked his heavy arms. He rested their knuckles on the floor. He glowered at her and said nothing. He was waiting.

On the way here, he had said, "I'll kill you if you don't understand." But he wouldn't really, would he? Would he?

If he had towered over her, ranted and shouted, she would not have been afraid. But squatting there, waiting, silent, with his great arms bowed out like that, he was like some patient, preying beast.

She turned off the light to blot out the sight of him, and immediately became speechless with terror at the idea of his sitting there in the dark so close, waiting. She might run; she was so swift . . . but no; crouched like that, he could spring and catch her before she could tense a muscle.

Again she looked at the dead screen. "Will you . . . tell me something?" she quavered.

"I might."

"Tell me, then: When you first saw that picture, did you understand? The very first time?"

His expression did not change. But slowly he relaxed. He rocked sidewise, sat down, extended his legs. He was man again, not monster. She shuddered, then controlled it.

He said, "It took me a long time and many visits. I should not have asked you to understand at once."

She again accepted the timid half-step toward an apology, and was grateful.

He said, "Those were men and women just like us. Did you see that? Just like us."

"Their clothes—"

"Just like us," he insisted. "Of course they dressed differently, lived differently! In a world like that, why not? Ah, how they built, how they built!"

"Yes," she whispered. Those towers, the shining, swift vehicles, the thousand who moved like one . . . "Who were they?" she asked him.

"Don't you know? Think—think!"

"Osser, I want to understand. I truly want to!"

She hunted frantically for the right thing to say, the right way to catch at this elusive thing which was so frighteningly important to him. All her life she had had the answers to the questions she wanted to understand. All she ever had to do was to close her eyes and think of the problem, and the answers soon came.

But not this problem.

"Osser," she pleaded, "where is it, the city, the great complicated city?"

"Say, 'Where was it?' " he growled.

She caught his thought and gasped. "This? These ruins, Osser?"

"Ah," he said approvingly. "It comes slowly, doesn't it? No, Juby. Not here. What was here was an outpost, a village, compared with the big city. North and west, I told you, didn't I? Miles of it. So big that . . . so big—" He extended his arms, dropped them helplessly. Suddenly he leaned close to her, began to talk fast, feverishly. "Juby, that city—that world—was built by *people*. Why did they build and why do we not? What is the difference between those people and ours?"

"They must have had . . ."

"They had nothing we don't have. They're the same kind of people; they *used* something we haven't been

223

using. Juby, I've got that something. I can build. I can make others build."

A mental picture of the tower glimmered before her. "You built it with hate," she said wonderingly. "Is that what they had—cruelty, brutality, hatred?"

"Yes!"

"I don't believe it! I don't believe anyone could live with that much hate!"

"Perhaps not. Perhaps they didn't. But they *built* with it. They built because some men could flog others into building for them, building higher and faster than all the good neighbors would ever do helping one another."

"They'd hate the man who made them build like that."

Osser's hands crackled as he pressed them together. He laughed, and the echoes took everything that was unpleasant about that laughter and filled the far reaches of the dark room with it.

"They'd hate him," he agreed. "But he's strong, you see. He was strong in the first place, to make them build, and he's stronger afterward with what they built for him. Do you know the only way they can express their hatred, once they find he's too strong for them?"

Jubilith shook her head.

"They'd build," he chuckled. "They'd build higher and faster than he did. They would find the strongest man among them and *ask* him to flog them into it. That's the way a great city goes up. A strong man builds, and strong men follow, and soon the man who's strongest of all makes all the other strong ones do his work. Do you see?"

"And the . . . the others, the weak?"

"What of them?" he asked scornfully. "There are more of them than strong ones—so there are more hands to do the strong man's work. And why shouldn't

224

they? Don't they get the city to live in when it's built? Don't they ride about in swift shining carriers and fly through the air in the bird-machines?"

"Would they be—happy?" she asked.

He looked at her in genuine puzzlement. "Happy?" He smashed a heavy fist into his palm. "They'd have a *city!*" Again the words tumbled from him. "How do you live, you and the rest of the village? What do you do when you want a—well, a garden, food from the ground?"

"I dig up the soil," she said. "I plant and water and weed."

"Suppose you want a plow?"

"I make one. Or I do work for someone who has one."

"Uh," he grunted. "And there you are, hundreds of you in the village, each one planting a little, smithing a little, thatching and cutting and building a little. Everyone does everything except for how many—four, five?—the leatherworker, old Griak who makes wooden pegs for house beams, one or two others."

"They like to do just one work. But anyone can do any of the work. Those few, we take care of. Someone has to keep the skills alive."

He snorted. "Put a strong man in the village and give him strong men to do what he wants. Get ten villagers at once and make them all plant at once. You'll have food then for fifty, not ten!"

"But it would go to waste!"

"It would not, because it would all belong to the head man. He would give it away as he saw fit—a lot to those who obeyed him, nothing to those who didn't. What was left over he could keep for himself, and barter it out to keep building. Soon he would have the biggest house and the best animals and the finest women, and the more he got, the stronger he would be.

225

And a city would grow—a *city!* And the strong man would give everyone better things if they worked hard, and protect them."

"Protect them? Against what?"

"Against the other strong ones. There would be others."

"And you—"

"I shall be the strongest of all," he said proudly. He waved at the box. "We were a great people once. We're ants now—less than ants, for at least the ants work together for a common purpose. I'll make us great again." His head sank onto his hand and he looked somberly into the shadows. "Something happened to this world. Something smashed the cities and the people and drove them down to what they are today. Something was broken within them, and they no longer dared to be great. Well, they will be. *I* have the extra something that was smashed out of them."

"What smashed them, Osser?"

"Who can know? I don't. I don't care, either." He tapped her with a long forefinger to emphasize. "All I care about is this: They were smashed because they were not strong enough. I shall be so strong I can't be smashed."

She said, "A stomach can hold only so much. A man asleep takes just so much space. So much and no more clothing makes one comfortable. Why do you want more than these things, Osser?"

She knew he was annoyed, and knew, too, that he was considering the question as honestly as he could.

"It's because I . . . I want to be strong," he said in a strained voice.

"You *are* strong."

"Who knows that?" he raged, and the echoes giggled and whispered.

"I do. Wrenn. Sussten. The whole village."

226

"The whole world will know. They will all do things for me."

She thought, But everyone does everything for himself, all over the world. Except, she added, those who aren't able . . .

With that in mind, she looked at him, his oaken shoulders, his powerful, bitter mouth. She touched the bruises his hands had left, and the beginnings of the understanding she had been groping for left her completely.

She said dully, "Your tower . . . you'd better get back there."

"Work goes on," he said, smiling tightly, "whether I'm there or not, as long as they don't know my plans. They are afraid. But—yes, we can go now."

Rising, he flicked the stud of his torch. It flared blue-white, faded to the weak orange of Jubilith's, then died.

"The light . . ."

"It's all right," said Jubilith. "I have mine."

"When they get like that, so dim, you can't tell when they'll go out. Come—hurry! This place is full of corridors; without light, we could be lost here for days."

She glanced around at the crowding shadows. "Make it work again," she suggested.

He looked at the dead torch in his hand. "You," he said flatly. He tossed it. She caught it in her free hand, put her torch on the floor, and held the broken one down so she could see it in the waning orange glow. She turned it over twice, her sensitive hands feeling with every part rather than with fingertips alone. She held it still and closed her eyes; and then it came to her, and she grasped one end with her right hand and the other with her left, and twisted.

There was a faint click and the outer shell of the torch separated. She drew off the butt end of it; it was

227

just a hollow shell. The entire mechanism was attached to the lens end and was now exposed.

She turned it over carefully, keeping her fingers away from the workings. Again she closed her eyes and thought, and at last she bent close and peered. She nodded, fumbled in her hair, and detached a copper clasp. She bent and broke off a narrow strip of it and inserted it carefully into the light mechanism. Very carefully, she pried apart two small strands of wire, dipped a little deeper, hooked onto a tiny white sphere, and drew it out.

"Poor thing," she murmured under her breath.

"Poor what?"

"Spider's egg," she said ruefully. "They fight so to save them; and this one will never hatch out now. It's been burned."

She picked up the butt-end housing, slipped the two parts together, and twisted them until they clicked. She handed the torch to Osser.

"You've wasted time," he complained, surly.

"No, I haven't," she said. "We'll have light now."

He touched the stud on the torch. The brilliant, comforting white light poured from it.

"Yes," he admitted quietly.

Watching his face as he handled the torch, she knew that if she could read what was in his mind in that second, she would have the answer to everything about him. She could not, however, and he said nothing, but led across the room to the dark corridor.

He was silent all the way back to the broken steps.

They stood halfway up, letting their eyes adjust to the daylight which poured down on them, and he said, "You didn't even try the torch to see if it would work, after you took out that egg."

"I knew it would work." She looked at him, amazed. "You're angry."

"Yes," he said.

He took her torch and his and put them away in a niche in the ruined stair-well, and they climbed up into the noon light. It was all but intolerable, as the two suns were all but in syzygy, the blue-white midget shining through the great pale gaseous mass of the giant, so that together they cast only a single shadow.

"It will be hot this afternoon," she said, but he was silent, steeped in some bitterness of his own, so she followed him quietly without attempting conversation.

Old Oyva stirred sleepily in her basking chair, and suddenly sat upright.

Jubilith approached her, pale and straight. "Is it Oyva?"

"It is, Jubilith," said the old woman. "I knew you would be back, my dear. I'm sore in my heart with you."

"Is he here?"

"He is. He has been on a journey. You'll find him tired."

"He should have been here, with all that has happened," said Jubilith.

"He should have done exactly as he has done," Oyva stated bluntly.

Jubilith recognized the enormity of her rudeness, and the taste of it was bad in her mouth. One did not criticize Wrenn's comings and goings.

She faced Oyva and closed her eyes humbly.

Oyva touched her. "It's all right, child. You are distressed. Wrenn!" she called. "She is here!"

"Come, Jubilith," Wrenn's voice called from the house.

"He knows? *No* one knew I was coming here!"

"He knows," said Oyva. "Go to him, child."

Jubilith entered the house. Wrenn sat in his corner.

229

The musical instrument was nowhere in sight. Aside from his cushions, there was nothing in the room.

Wrenn gave her his wise, sweet smile. "Jubilith," he said. "Come close." He looked drawn and pale, but quite untroubled. He put a cushion by him and she crossed slowly and sank down on it.

He was quiet, and when she was sure it was because he waited for her to speak, she said, "Some things may not be understood."

"True," he agreed.

She kneaded her hands. "Is there never a change?"

"Always," he said, "when it's time."

"Osser—"

"Everyone will understand Osser very soon now."

She screwed up her courage. "Soon is not soon enough. I must know him now."

"Before anyone else?" he inquired mildly.

"Let everyone know now," she suggested.

He shook his head and there was no appeal in it.

"Then let me. I shall be a part of you and speak of it only to you."

"Why must you understand?"

She shuddered. It was not cold, or fear, but simply the surgings of a great emotion.

"I love him," she said. "And to love is to guard and protect. He needs me."

"Go to him then." But she sat where she was, her long eyes cast down, weeping. Wrenn said, "There is more, then?"

"I love . . ." She threw out an arm in a gesture which enfolded Wrenn, the house, the village. "I love the people, too, the gardens, the little houses; the way we go and come, and sing, and make music, and make our own tools and clothes. To love is to guard and protect . . . and I love these things, and I love Osser. I can destroy Osser, because he would not expect it of me; and, if I did, I would protect all of you. But if I protect him, he will destroy you. There is no answer to such a problem, Wrenn; it is a road," she cried, "with a precipice at each end, and no standing still!"

"And understanding him would be an answer?"

"There's no other!" She turned her face up to him, imploring. "Osser is strong, Wrenn, with a—new thing about him, a thing none of the rest of us have. He has told me of it. It is a thing that can change us, make us part of him. He will build cities with our hands, on our broken bodies if we resist him. He wants us to be a great people again—he says we were, once, and have lost it all."

"And do you regard that as greatness, Jubilith—the towers, the bird-machines?"

"How did you know of them? . . . Greatness? I don't know, I don't know," she said, and wept. "I love him, and he wants to build a city with a wanting greater than anything I have ever known or heard of before. Could he do it, Wrenn? Could he?"

"He might," said Wrenn calmly.

"He is in the village now. He has about him the ones who built his tower for him. They cringe around him, hating to be near and afraid to leave. He sent them one by one to tell all the people to come out to the foothills tomorrow, to begin work on his city. He wants enough building done in one hundred days to shelter everyone, because then, he says, he is going to burn this village to the ground. Why, Wrenn—why?"

"Perhaps," said Wrenn, "so that we may all face his strength and yield to it. A man who could move a whole village in a hundred days just to show his strength would be a strong man indeed."

"What shall we do?"

"I think we shall go out to the foothills in the morning and begin to build."

She rose and went to the door.

"I know what to do now," she whispered. "I won't try to understand any more. I shall just go and help him."

"Yes, go," said Wrenn. "He will need you."

Jubilith stood with Osser on the parapet, and with him stared into the dappled dawn. The whole sky flamed with the loom of the red sun's light, but the white one preceded it up in the sky, laying sharp shadows in the soft blunt ones. Birds called and chattered in the Sky-tree Grove, and deep in the thickets the seven-foot bats grunted as they settled in to sleep.

"Suppose they don't come?" she asked.

"They'll come," he said grimly. "Jubilith, why are you here?"

She said, "I don't know what you are doing. Osser. I don't know whether it's right or whether you will keep on succeeding. I do know there will be pain and difficulty and I—I came to keep you safe, if I could . . . I love you."

He looked down at her, as thick and dark over her as his tower was over the foothills. One side of his mouth twitched.

"Little butterfly," he said softly, "do you think *you* can guard *me?*"

Everything beautiful about her poured out to him through her beautiful face, and for a moment his world had three suns instead of two. He put his arms around her. Then his great voice exploded with two syllables of a mighty laugh. He lifted her and swung her behind him, and leaped to the parapet.

Deeply shaken, she came to follow his gaze.

The red sun's foggy limb was above the townward horizon, and silhouetted against it came the van of a procession. On they came and on, the young men of the village, the fathers. Women were with them, too, and everything on wheels that the village possessed—flatbed wagons, two-wheeled rickshaw carts, children's and vendors' and pleasure vehicles. A snorting team of four tiger oxen clawed along before a heavily laden stone-boat, and men shared packs that swung in the center of long poles.

Osser curled his lip. "You see them," he said, as if to himself, "doing the only thing they can think of. Push them, they yield. The clods!" he spat. "Well, one day, one will push back. And when he does, I'll break him, and after that I'll use him. Meantime—I have a thousand hands and a single mind. We'll see building now," he crooned. "When they've built, they'll know what they don't know now—that they're men."

"They're all come," breathed Jubilith. "All of them. Osser—"

"Be quiet," he said, leaning into the wind to watch, floating. With the feel of his hard hands still on her back, she discovered with a crushing impact that there was no room in his heart for her when he thought of his building. And she knew that there never would be, except perhaps for a stolen moment, a touch in passing. With the pain of that realization came the certainty that she would stay with him always, even for so little.

The procession dipped out of sight, then slowly rose over and down the near hill and approached the tower. It spread and thickened at the foot of the slope, as men cast about, testing the ground with their picks, eyeing the land for its color and vegetation and drainage . . . or was that what they were doing?

Osser leaned his elbows on the parapet and shook his head pityingly at their inefficiency. Look at the way they went about laying out houses! And their own houses. Well, he'd let them mill about until they were completely confused, and then he'd go down and make

233

them do it his way. Confused men are soft men; men working against their inner selves are easy to divert from outside.

Beside him, Jubilith gasped.

"What is it?"

She pointed. "There—sending the men to this side, that side. See, by the stone boat? It's Wrenn!"

"Nonsense!" said Osser. "He'd never leave his house. Not to walk around among people who are sweating. He deals only with people who tell him he's right before he speaks."

"It's Wrenn, it is, it is!" cried Jubilith. She clutched his arm. "Osser, I'm afraid!"

"Afraid? Afraid of what? . . . By the dying Red One, it *is* Wrenn, telling men what to do as if this was *his* city." He laughed. "There are few enough here who are strong, Juby, but he's the strongest there is. And look at him scurry around for me!"

"I'm afraid," Jubilith whimpered.

"They jump when he tells them," said Osser reflectively, shading his eyes. "Perhaps I was wrong to let them tire themselves out before I help them do things right. With a man like him to push them . . . Hm. I think we'll get it done right the first time."

He pushed himself away from the parapet and swung to the stairway.

"Osser, don't, please don't!" she begged.

He stopped just long enough to give her a glance like a stone thrown. "You'll never change my mind, Juby, and you'll be hurt if you try too often." He dropped into the opening, went down three steps, five steps . . .

He grunted, stopped.

Jubilith came slowly over to the stairwell. Osser stood on the sixth step, on tiptoe. Impossibly on tiptoe: the points of his sandals barely touched the step at all.

He set his jaw and placed his massive hands one on

234

each side of the curved wall. He pressed them out and up, forcing himself downward. His sandals touched more firmly; his toes bent, his heels made contact. His face became deep red, and the cords at the sides of his neck ridged like a weathered fallow field.

A strained crackle came from his shoulders, and then the pent breath burst from him. His hands slipped, and he came up again just the height of the single stair-riser, to bob ludicrously like a boat at anchor, his pointed toe touching and lifting from the sixth step.

He gave an inarticulate roar, bent double, and plunged his hands downward as if to dive headfirst down the stairs. His wrists turned under and he yelped with the pain. More cautiously he felt around and down, from wall to wall. It was as if the air in the stairway had solidified, become at once viscous and resilient. Whatever was there was invisible and completely impassable.

He backed slowly up the steps. On his face there was fury and frustration, hurt and a shaking reaction.

Jubilith wrung her hands. "Please, please, Osser, be care—"

The sound of her voice gave him something to strike out at, and he spun about, raising his great bludgeon of a fist. Jubilith stood frozen, too shocked to dodge the blow.

"Osser!"

Osser stopped, tensed high, fist up, like some terrifying monument to vengeance. The voice had been Wrenn's—Wrenn speaking quietly, even conversationally, but magnified beyond belief. The echoes of it rolled off and were lost in the hills.

"Come watch men building, Osser!"

Dazed, Osser lowered his arm and went to the parapet.

Far below, near the base of the hill, Wrenn stood,

looking up at the tower. When Osser appeared, Wrenn turned his back and signaled the men by the stone-boat. They twitched away the tarpaulin that covered its load.

Osser's hands gripped the stone as if they would powder it. His eyes slowly widened and his jaw slowly dropped.

At first it seemed like a mound of silver on the rude platform of the ox-drawn stone-boat. Gradually he perceived that it was a machine, a machine so finished, so clean-lined and so businesslike that the pictures he had shown Jubilith were clumsy toys in comparison.

It was Sussten, a man Osser had crushed to the ground with two heavy blows, who sprang lightly up on the machine and settled into it. It backed off the platform, and Osser could hear the faintest of whines from it. The machine rolled and yet it stepped; it kept itself horizon-level as it ran, its long endless treads dipping and rising with the terrain, its sleek body moving smooth as a swan. It stopped and then went forward, out to the first of a field of stakes that a crew had been driving.

The flat, gleaming sides of the machine opened away and forward and locked, and became a single blade twice the width of the machine. It dropped until its sharp lower edge just touched the ground, checked for a moment, and then sank into the soil.

Dirt mounded up before it until flakes fell back over the wide moldboard. The machine slid ahead, and dirt ran off the sides of the blade to make two straight windrows. And behind the machine as it labored, the ground was flat and smooth; and it was done as easily as a smoothing hand in a sandbox. Here it was cut and there it was filled, but everywhere the swath was like planed wood, all done just as fast as a man can run.

Osser made a sick noise far back in his tight throat. Guided by the stakes, the machine wheeled and returned, one end of the blade now curved forward to catch up the windrow and carry it across the new parallel cut. And now the planed soil was twice as wide.

As it worked, men worked, and Osser saw that, shockingly, they moved with no less efficiency and certainty than the machine. For Osser, these men had plodded and sweated, drudged, each a single, obstinate unit to be flogged and pressed. But now they sprinted, sprang; they held, drove, measured, and carried as if to swift and intricate music.

A cart clattered up and from it men took metal spikes, as thick as a leg, twice as tall as a man. Four men to a spike, they ran with them to staked positions on the new-cut ground, set them upright. A man flung a metal clamp around the spike. Two men, one on each side, drove down on the clamp with heavy sledges until the spike would stand alone. And already those four were back with another spike.

Twenty-six such spikes were set, but long before they were all out of the wagon, Sussten spun the machine in its own length and stopped. The moldboard rose, hinged, folded back to become the silver sides of the machine again. Sussten drove forward, nosed the machine into the first of the spikes, which fitted into a slot at the front of the machine. There was the sound of a frantic giant ringing a metal triangle, and the spike sank as if the ground had turned to bread.

Leaving perhaps two hands'-breadths of the spike showing, the machine slid to the next and the next, sinking the spikes so quickly that it had almost a whole minute to wait while the spike crew set the very last one. At that a sound rolled out of the crowd, a sound utterly unlike any that had ever been heard during the building of the tower—a friendly, jeering roar of laughter at the crew who had made the machine wait.

Men unrolled heavy cable along the lines of spikes;

others followed right behind them, one with a tool which stretched the cable taut, two with a tool that in two swift motions connected the cable to the tops of the sunken spikes. And by the time the cable was connected, two flatbeds, a buckboard and a hay wagon had unloaded a cluster of glistening machine parts. Men and women swarmed over them, wrenches, pliers and special tools in hand, bolting, fitting, clamping, connecting. Three heavy leads from the great ground cable were connected; a great parabolic wire basket was raised and guyed.

Wrenn ran to the structure and pulled a lever. A high-pitched scream of force dropped sickeningly in pitch to a jarring subsonic, and rose immediately high out of the audible range.

A rosy haze enveloped the end of the new machine, opposite the ground array and under the basket. It thickened, shimmered, and steadied, until it was a stable glowing sphere with an off-focus muzziness barely showing all around its profile.

The crowd—not a group now, but a line—cheered and the line moved forward. Every conceivable village conveyance moved in single file toward the shining sphere, and, as each stopped, heavy metal was unloaded. Cast-iron stove legs could be recognized, and long strips of tinning solder, a bell, a kettle, the framing of a bench. The blacksmith's anvil was there, and parts of his forge. Pots and skillets. A ratchet and pawl from the gristmill. The weights and pendulum from the big village clock.

As each scrap was unloaded, exactly the number of hands demanded by its weight were waiting to catch it, swing it from its conveyance into the strange sphere. They went in without resistance and without sound, and they did not come out. Wagon after wagon, pack after handsack were unloaded, and still the sphere took and took.

It took heavy metal and more mass than its own dimensions. Had the metal been melted down into a sphere, it would have been a third again, half again, twice as large as the sphere, and still it took.

But its color was changing. The orange went to burned sienna and then to a strident brown. Imperceptibly this darkened until at last it was black. For a moment, it was a black of impossible glossiness, but this softened. Blacker and blacker it became, and at length it was not a good thing to look into—the blackness seemed to be hungry for something more intimate than metal. And still the metals came and the sphere took.

A great roar came from the crowd; men fell back to look upward. High in the west was a glowing golden spark which showed a long blue tail. It raced across the sky and was gone, and moments later the human roar was answered by thunder from above.

If the work had been swift before, it now became a blur. Men no longer waited for the line of wagons to move, but ran back along it to snatch metal and stagger forward again to the sphere. Women ripped off bracelets and hammered earrings and threw them to the implacable melanosphere. Men threw in their knives, even their buttons. A rain of metal was sucked silently into the dazzling black.

Another cry from the crowd, and now there was hurried anguish in it; again the craning necks, the quick gasp. The golden spark was a speed-blurred ovoid now, the blue tail a banner half a horizon long. The roar, when it came, was a smashing thunder, and the blue band hung where it was long after the thing had gone.

A moan of urgency, caught and maintained by one exhausted throat after another, rose and fell and would not leave. Then it was a happy shout as Sussten drove in, shouldering the beautiful cutting machine through the scattering crowd. Its blade unfolded as it ran, latched high and stayed there like a shining forearm flung across the machine's silver face.

As the last scrambling people dove for safety, Sussten brought the huge blade slashing downward and at the same time threw the machine into its highest speed. It leaped forward as Sussten leaped back. Unmanned, it rushed at the sphere as if to sweep it away, crash the structure that contained it. But at the last microsecond, the blade struck the ground; the nose of the machine snapped upward, and the whole gleaming thing literally vaulted into the sphere.

No words exist for such a black. Some people fell to their knees, their faces covered. Some turned blindly away, unsteady on their feet. Some stood trembling, fixed on it, until friendly hands took and turned them and coaxed them back to reality.

And at last a man staggered close, squinting, and threw in the heavy wrought-iron support for an inn sign—

And the sphere refused it.

Such a cry of joy rose from the village that the sleeping bats in the thickets of Sky-tree Grove, two miles away, stirred and added their porcine grunting to the noise.

A woman ran to Wrenn, screaming, elbowing, unnoticed and unheard in the bedlam. She caught his shoulder roughly, spun him half around, pointed. Pointed up at the tower, at Osser.

Wrenn thumbed a small disc out of a socket in his belt and held it near his lips.

"Osser!" The great voice rang and echoed, crushing the ecstatic noises of the people by its sheer weight. *"Osser, come down or you're a dead man!"*

The people, suddenly silent, all stared at the tower. One or two cried, "Yes, come down, come down . . ." but the puniness of their voices was ludicrous after Wrenn's magnified tones, and few tried again.

Osser stood holding the parapet, legs wide apart, eyes wide—too wide—open. His hands curled over the edge, and blood dripped slowly from under the cuticles.

"Come down, come down . . ."

He did not move. His eyeballs were nearly dry, and unnoticed saliva lay in a drying streak from one corner of his mouth.

"Jubilith, bring him down!"

She was whimpering, begging, murmuring little urgencies to him. His biceps were as hard as the parapet, his face as changeless as the stone.

"Jubilith, leave him! Leave him and come!" Wrenn, wise Wrenn, sure, unshakable, imperturbable Wrenn had a sob in his voice; and under such amplification the sob was almost big enough to be voice for the sobs that twisted through Jubilith's tight throat.

She dropped to one knee and put one slim firm shoulder under Osser's wrist. She drove upward against it with all the lithe strength of her panicked body. It came free, leaving a clot of fingertip on the stone. Down she went again, and up again at the other wrist; but this was suddenly flaccid, and her tremendous effort turned to a leap. She clutched at Osser, who tottered forward.

For one endless second they hung there, while their mutual center of gravity made a slow deliberation, and then Jubilith kicked frantically at the parapet, abrading her legs, mingling her blood with his on the masonry. They went together back to the roof. Jubilith twisted like a falling cat and got her feet down, holding Osser's great weight up.

They spun across the roof in an insane staggering

dance; then there was the stairway (with its invisible barrier gone) and darkness (with his hand in hers now, holding and leading) and a sprint into daylight and the shattering roar of Wrenn's giant voice: *"Everybody down, down flat!"*

And there was a time of running, pulling Osser after her, and Osser pounding along behind her, docile and wide-eyed as a cat-ox. And then the rebellion and failure of her legs, and the will that refused to let them fail, and the failure of that will; the stunning agony of a cracked patella as she went down on the rocks, and the swift sense of infinite loss as Osser's hand pulled free of hers and he went lumbering blindly along, the only man on his feet in the wide meadow of the fallen.

Jubilith screamed and someone stood up—she thought it was old Oyva—and cried out.

Then the mighty voice again, *"Osser! Down, man!"* Blearily, then, she saw Osser stagger to a halt and peer around him.

"Osser, lie down!"

And then Osser, mad, drooling, turning toward her. His eyes protruded and he slashed about with his heavy fists. He came closer, unseeing, battling some horror he believed in with great cuts and slashes that threatened elbow and shoulder joints by the wrenching of their unimpeded force.

His voice—but not his, rather the voice of an old, wretched crone—squeaking out in a shrill falsetto, "Not down, never down, but up. I'll build, build, build, break to build, kill to build, and all the ones who can do everything, anything, everything, they will build everything for me. I'm strong!" he shrieked, soprano. "All the people who can do anything are less than one strong man . . ."

He jabbered and fought, and suddenly Wrenn rose, quite close by, his left hand enclosed in a round flat box. He moved something on its surface and then waved it at Osser, in a gesture precisely like the command to a guest to be seated.

Down went Osser, close to Jubilith, with his face in the dirt and his eyes open, uncaring. On him and on Jubilith lay the invisible weight of the force that had awaited him in the stairway.

The breath hissed out of Jubilith. Had she not been lying on her side with her face turned skyward in a single convulsive effort toward air, she would never have seen what happened. The golden shape appeared in the west, seen a fraction of a second, but blazoned forever in tangled memories of this day. And simultaneously the earth-shaking cough of the machine as its sphere disappeared.

She could not see it move, but such a blackness is indelible, and she sensed it when it appeared in the high distances as its trajectory and that of the golden flyer intersected.

Then there was —*Nothing*.

The broad blue trail swept from the western horizon to the zenith, and sharply ended. There was no sound, no concussion, no blaze of light. The sphere met the ship and both ceased to exist.

Then there was the wind, from nowhere, from everywhere, all the wind that ever was, tearing in agony from everywhere in the world to the place where the sphere had been, trying to fill the strange space that had contained exactly as much matter as the dead golden ship. Wagons, oxen, trees and stones scraped and flew and crashed together in the center of that monstrous implosion.

The weight Wrenn had laid on Jubilith disappeared, but her sucking lungs could find nothing to draw in. There was air aplenty, but none of it would serve her.

243

Finally she realized there was unconsciousness waiting for her if she wanted it. She embraced it, sank into it, and left the world to its wailing winds.

Ages later, there was weeping.

She stirred and raised her head.

The sphere machine was gone. There was a heap of something down there, but it supported such a tall and heavy pillar of roiling dust that she could not see what it was. There, and there, and over yonder, in twos and threes, silent, shaken people sat up, some staring about them, some just sitting, waiting for the shock-stopped currents of life to flow back in.

But the weeping . . .

She put her palm on the ground and inched it, heel first, in a weak series of little hops, until she was half sitting.

Osser was weeping.

He sat upright, his feet together and his knees wide apart, like a little child. He rocked. He lifted his hands and let them fall, lifted them and punctuated his crying with weak poundings on the ground. His mouth was an O, his eyes were single squeezed lines, his face was wet, and his crying was the most heartrending sound she had ever heard.

She thought to speak to him, but knew he would not hear. She thought to go to him, but the first shift of weight sent such agony through her broken kneecap that she almost fainted.

Osser wept.

She turned away from him—suppose, later, he should remember that she had seen this?—and then she knew why he was crying. He was crying because his tower was gone. Tower of strength, tower of defiance, tower of hope, tower of rebellion and hatred and an ambition big enough for a whole race of city-builders, gone without a fight, gone without the triumph of taking him with it, gone in an instant, literally in a puff of wind.

"Where does it hurt?"

It was Wrenn, who had approached unseen through the blinding, sick compassion that filled her.

"It hurts there." She pointed briefly at Osser.

"I know," said Wrenn gently. He checked what she was about to say with a gesture. "No, we won't stop him. When he was a little boy, he never cried. He has been hurt more than most people, and nothing ever made him cry, ever. We all have a cup for tears and a reservoir. No childhood is finished until all the tears flow from the reservoir into the cup. Let him cry; perhaps he is going to be a man. It's your knee, isn't it?"

"Yes. Oh, but I can't stand to hear it, my heart will burst!" she cried.

"Hear him out," said Wrenn softly, taking medication from a flat box at his waist. He ran feather-fingers over her knee and nodded. "You have taken Osser as your own. Keep this weeping with you, all of it. It will fit you to him better through the healing time."

"May I understand now?"

"Yes, oh yes . . . and since he has taught you about hate, you will hate me for it."

"I couldn't hate you, Wrenn."

Something stirred within his placid eyes—a smile, a pointed shard of knowledge—she was not sure. "Perhaps you could."

He kept his eyes on his careful bandaging, and as he worked, he spoke.

"Stop a man in his work to tell him that each of his fingers bears a pattern of loops and whorls, and you waste his time. It is a thing he knows, a thing he has seen for himself, a thing which can be checked on the instant—in short, an obvious, unremarkable thing. Yet, if his attention is not called to it, it is impossible to

245

teach him that these patterns are exclusive, original with him, unduplicated anywhere. Sparing him the truism may cost him the fact.

"It is that kind of truism through which I shall pass to reach the things you must understand. So be patient with me through the familiar paths; I promise you a most remarkable turning.

"We are an ancient and resourceful species, and among the many things we have—our happiness, our simplicity, our harmony with each other and with ourselves—some are the products of intelligence, per se, but most of the good things spring from a quality which we possess in greater degree than any other species yet known. That is—logic.

"Now, there is the obvious logic: you may never have broken your knee before, but you knew, in advance, that if you did it would cause you pain. If I hold this pebble so, you may correctly predict that it will drop when I release it, though you have never seen this stone before. This obvious logic strikes deeper levels as well; for example, if I release the stone and it does not fall, logic tells you not only that some unpredicted force is now acting on it, but a great many things about that force: that it equals gravity in the case of this particular pebble; that it is in stasis; that it is phenomenal, since it is out of the statistical order of things.

"The quality of logic, which we (so far as is known) uniquely possess, is this: any of us can do literally anything that anyone else can do. You need ask no one to solve the problems that you face every day, providing they are problems common to all. To cut material so that a sleeve will fit a shoulder, you pause, you close your eyes; the way to cut material then comes to you, and you proceed. You never need do anything twice, because the first way is the most logical. You may finish the garment and put it away without trying it on for fit, because you know you have done it right and it is perfect.

"If I put you before a machine which you had never seen before, which had a function unknown to you, and which operated on principles you had never heard of, and if I told you it was broken and needed repairing, you would look at it carefully, inside, outside, top and bottom, and you would close your eyes, and suddenly you would understand the principles. With these and the machine, function would explain itself. The step from that point to the location of a faulty part is self-evident.

"Now I lay before you parts which are identical in appearance, and ask you to install the correct one. Since you thoroughly understand the requirements now, the specifications for the correct part are self-evident. Logic dictates the correct tests for the parts. You will rapidly reject the tight one, the heavy one, the too soft one, and the too resilient one, and you will repair my machine. And you will walk away without testing it, since you now know it will operate."

Wrenn continued, "You—all of us—live in this way. We build no cities because we don't need cities. We stay in groups because some things need more than two hands, more than one head, or voice, or mood. We eat exactly what we require, we use only what we need.

"And that is the end of the truism, wherein I so meticulously describe to you what you know about how you live. The turning: Whence this familiar phenomenon, this closing of the eyes and mysterious appearance of the answer? There have been many engrossing theories about it, but the truth is the most fascinating of all.

"We have all spoken of telepathy, and many of us have experienced it. We cannot explain it, as yet. But most of us insist on a limited consideration of it; that is, we judge its success or failure by the amount of detail

247

sent and received. We expect *facts* to be transmitted, *words,* idea sequences—or perhaps pictures; the clearer the picture, the better the telepathy.

"Perhaps one day we will learn to do this; it would be diverting. But what we actually *do* is infinitely more useful.

"You see, we *are* telepathic, not in the way of conveying details, but in the much more useful way of conveying a *manner of thinking*.

"Let us try to envisage a man who lacks this quality. Faced with your broken machine, he would be utterly at a loss, unless he had been specially trained in this particular field. Do not overlook the fact that he lacks the conditioning of a whole life of the kind of sequence thinking which is possible to us. He would probably bumble through the whole chore in an interminable time, trying one thing and then another and going forward from whatever seems to work. You can see the tragic series of pitfalls possible for him in a situation in which an alternate three or four or five consecutive steps are possible, forcing step six, which is wrong in terms of the problem.

"Now, take the same man and train him in this one job. Add a talent, so that he learns quickly and well. Add years of experience—terrible, drudging thought! —to his skill. Face him with the repair problem and it is obvious that he will repair it with a minimum of motion.

"Finally, take this skilled man and equip him with a device which constantly sends out the habit-patterns of his thinking. Long practice has made him efficient in the matter; in terms of machine function he knows better than to question whether a part turns this way or that, whether a rod or tube larger than x diameter is to be considered. Furthermore, imagine a receiving device which absorbs these sendings whenever the receiver is faced with an identical problem. The skilled sender controls the unskilled receiver as long as the receiver is engaged in the problem. Anything the receiver does which is counter to the basic patterns of the sender is automatically rejected as illogical.

"And now I have described our species. We have an unmatchable unitary existence. Each of us with a natural bent—the poets, the musicians, the mechanics, the philosophers—each gives of his basic thinking method every time anyone has an application for it. The expert is unaware of being tapped—which is why it has taken hundreds of centuries to recognize the method. Yet, in spite of what amounts to a veritable race intellect, we are all very much individuals. Because each field has many experts, and each of those experts has his individual approach, only that which is closest both to the receiver *and* his problem comes in. The ones without special talents live fully and richly with all the skills of the gifted. The creative ones share with others in their field as soon as it occurs to any expert to review what he knows; the one step forward then instantly presents itself.

"So much for the bulk of our kind. There remain a few specializing *non*-specialists. When you are faced with a problem to which no logical solution presents itself, you come to one of these few for help. The reason no solution presents itself is that this is a new line of thinking, or (which is very likely) the last expert in it has died. The non-specialist hears your problem and applies simple logic to it. Immediately, others of his kind do the same. But, since they come from widely divergent backgrounds and use a vast variety of methods, one of them is almost certain to find the logical solution. This is your answer—and through you, it is available to anyone who ever faces this particular problem.

"In exceptional cases, the non-specializing specialist

encounters a problem which, for good reason, is better left out of the racial 'pool'—as, for example, a physical or psychological experiment within the culture, of long duration, which general knowledge might alter. In such cases, a highly specialized hypnotic technique is used on the investigators, which has the effect of cloaking thought on this particular matter.

"And if you began to fear that I was never coming to Osser's unhappy history, you must understand, my dear, I have just given it to you. Osser was just such an experiment.

"It became desirable to study the probable habit patterns of a species like us in every respect except for our unique attribute. The problem was attacked from many angles, but I must confess that using a live specimen was my idea.

"By deep hypnosis, the telepathic receptors in Osser were severed from the rest of his mind. He was then allowed to grow up among us in real and complete freedom.

"You saw the result. Since few people recognize the nature of this unique talent, and even fewer regard it as worth discussion, this strong, proud, highly intelligent boy grew up feeling a hopeless inferior, and never knowing exactly why. Others did things, made things, solved problems, as easily as thinking about them, while Osser had to study and sweat and piece and try out. He had to assert his superiority in some way. He did, but in as slipshod a fashion as he did everything else.

"So he was led to the pictures you saw. He was permitted to make what conclusions he wished—they were that we are a backward people, incapable of building a city. He suddenly saw in the dreams of a mechanized, star-reaching species a justification of himself. He could not understand our lack of desire for possessions, not knowing that our whole cultural existence is based on

250

sharing—that it is not only undesirable, but impossible for us to hoard an advanced idea, a new comfort. He would master us through strength.

"He was just starting when you came to me about him. You could get no key to his problem because we know nothing about sick minds, and there was no expert you could tap. I couldn't help you—you, of all people—because you loved him, and because we dared not risk having him know what he was, especially when he was just about to take action.

"Why he chose this particular site for his tower I do not know. And why he chose the method of the tower I don't know either, though I can deduce an excellent reason. First, he had to use his strength once he became convinced that in it lay his superiority. Second, he had to *try out* this build-with-hate idea—the bugaboo of all other man-species, the trial-and-error, the inability to *know* what will work and what will not.

"And so we learned through Osser precisely what we had learned in other approaches—that a man without our particular ability must not live among us, for, if he does, he will destroy us.

"It is a small step from that to a conclusion about a whole race of them coexisting with us. And now you know what happened here this afternoon."

Jubilith raised her head slowly. "A whole ship full of . . . of what Osser was?"

"Yes. We did the only thing we could. Quick, quite painless. We have been watching them for a long time—years. We saw them start. We computed their orbit—even to the deceleration spiral. We chose a spot to launch our interceptor." He glanced at Osser, who was almost quiet, quite exhausted. "What sheer hell he must have gone through, to see us build like that. How could he know that not one of us needed training, explanation, or any but the simplest orders? How could he ra-

251

tionalize to himself our possession of machines and devices surpassing the wildest dreams of the god-like men he admired so? How could he understand that, having such things, we use them only when we must, and that otherwise we live in ways which will not violate the walking, working animal we are?"

She turned to him a mask so cold, so beautiful, he forgot for a moment to breathe. "Why did you do it? You had other logics, other approaches. Did you have to do *that* to him?"

He studiously avoided a glance at Osser. "I said you might hate me," he murmured. "Jubilith, the men in that ship were so like Osser that the experiment could not be passed by. We had astronomical data, historical, cultural—as far as our observations could go—and ethnological. But only by analogy could we get such a psychological study. And it checked too well. As for having him see this thing, today . . . building, Jubilith, is sometimes begun by tearing down."

He looked at her with deep compassion. "This was not the site chosen for the launching of the interceptor. We uprooted the whole installation, brought it here, rebuilt it, just for Osser; just so that he could stand on his tower and see it happen. He had to be broken, leveled to the earth. Ah-h-h . . ." he breathed painfully, "Osser has earned what he will have from now on."

"He can be—well again?"

"With your help."

"So very right, you are," she snarled suddenly. "So sure that this or that species is fit to associate with superiors like us." She leaned toward him and shook a finger in his startled face. The courtly awe habitual to all when speaking to such as Wrenn had completely left her.

"So fine we are, so mighty. And didn't we build cities? Didn't we have giant bird-machines and shiny carts

252

on our streets? Didn't we let our cities be smashed—haven't you seen the ruins in the west? Tell me," she sparked, "did we ruin them ourselves, because one superior city insisted on proving its superiority over another superior city?"

She stopped abruptly to keep herself from growling like an animal, for he was smiling blandly, and his smile got wider as she spoke. She turned furiously, half away from him, cursing the broken knee that held her so helpless.

"Jubilith."

His voice was so warm, so kind and so startling in these surroundings, held such a bubbling overtone of laughter that she couldn't resist it. She turned grudgingly.

In his hand he held a pebble. When her eye fell to it he rolled it, held it between thumb and forefinger, and let it go.

It stayed motionless in mid-air. "Another factor, Jubilith."

She almost smiled. She looked down at his other hand, and saw it aiming the disc-shaped force-field projector at low power.

He lifted it and, with the field, tossed the pebble into the air and batted it away. "We have no written history, Jubilith. We don't need one, but once in a while it would be useful.

"Jubilith, our culture is one of the oldest in the Galaxy. If we ever had such cities, there are not even legends about it."

"But I saw—"

"A ship came here once. We had never seen a humanoid race. We welcomed them and helped them. We gave them land and seeds. Then they called a flotilla, and the ships came by the hundreds.

"They built cities and, at that, we moved away and

left them alone, because we don't *need* cities. Then they began to hate us. They couldn't hate us until they had tall buildings to do it in. They hated our quiet; they hated our understanding. They sent missionaries to change our ways. We welcomed the missionaries, fed them and laughed with them, but when they left us glittering tools and humble machines to amuse us, we let them lie where they were until they rotted.

"In time they sent no more missionaries. They joked about us and forgot us. And then they built a city on land we had not given them, and another, and another. They bred well, and their cities became infernally big. And finally they began to build that one city too many, and we turned a river and drowned it. They were pleased. They could now rid themselves of the backward natives."

Jubilith closed her eyes, and saw the tumbled agony of the mounds, radiating outward from a lake with its shores too bare. "All of them?" she asked.

Wrenn nodded. "Even one might be enough to destroy us." He nodded toward Osser, who had begun to cry again.

"They seemed . . . good," she said, reflectively. "Too fast, too big . . . and it must have been noisy, but—"

"Wait," he said. "You mean the people in the picture Osser showed you?"

"Of course. They were the city-builders you—we—destroyed, weren't they?"

"They were not! The ones who built here were thin, hairy, with backward-slanting faces and webs between their fingers. Beautiful, but they hated us . . . The pictures, Jubilith, were made on the third planet of a pale star out near the Rim; a world with one Moon; a world of humans like Osser . . . the world where that golden ship came from."

"How?" she gasped.

"If logic is good enough," Wrenn said, "it need not be checked. Once we were so treated by humanoids, we built the investigators. They are not manned. They draw their power from anything that radiates, and they home on any planet which could conceivably rear humans. They are, as far as we know, indetectible. We've never lost one. They launch tiny flyers to make close searches—one of them made the pictures you saw. The pictures and other data are coded and sent out into space and, where distances warrant it, other investigators catch the signal and add power and send them on.

"Whenever a human or humanoid species builds a ship, we watch it. When they send their ships to this sector, we watch their planet *and* their ship. Unless we are sure that those people have the ability we have, to share all expertness and all creative thinking with all who want it—they don't land here. And no such species ever will land here."

"You're so sure."

"We explore no planets, Jubilith. We like it here. If others like us exist—why should they visit us?"

She thought about it, and slowly she nodded. "I like it here," she breathed.

Wrenn knelt and looked out across the rolling ground. It was late, and most of the villagers had gone home. A few picked at the mounds of splinters at the implosion center. Their limbs were straight and their faces clear. They owned little and they shared their souls.

He rose and went to Osser, and sat down beside him, facing him, his back to Jubilith. "M-m-mum, mum, mum, mum, mum-mum-mum," he intoned.

Osser blinked at him. Wrenn lifted his hand and his ring, green and gold and a shimmering oval of purple,

255

caught the late light. Osser looked at the ring. He reached for it. Wrenn moved it slightly. Osser's hand passed it and hit the ground and lay there neglected. Osser gaped at the ring, his jaws working, his teeth not meeting.

"Mum, mum, *mummy,* where's your mummy, Osser?"

"In the house," said Osser, looking at the ring.

Wrenn said, "You're a good little boy. When we say the word, you won't be able to do anything but what *you* can do. When we say the key, you'll be able to do anything *anybody* can do."

"All right," Osser said.

"Before I give the word, tell me the key. You must remember the key."

"That ring. And 'last 'n' lost.' "

"Good, Osser. Now listen to me. Can you hear me?"

"Sure." He grabbed at the ring.

"I'm going to change the key. It isn't 'last 'n' lost' any more. 'Last 'n' lost' is no good now. Forget it."

"No good?"

"Forget it. What's the key?"

"I—forgot."

"The key," said Wrenn patiently, "is this." He leaned close and whispered rapidly.

Jubilith was peering out past the implosion center to the townward path. Someone was coming, a tiny figure.

"Jubilith," Wrenn said. She looked up at him. "You must understand something." His voice was grave. His hair reached for an awed little twist of wind, come miles to see this place. The wind escaped and ran away down the hill.

Wrenn said, "He's very happy now. He was a happy child when first I heard of him, and how like a space-bound human he could be. Well, he's that child again. He always will be, until the day he dies. I'll see he's

256

cared for. He'll chase the sunbeams, a velvet red one and a needle of blue-white; he'll eat and he'll love and be loved just as is right for him."

They looked at Osser. There was a blue insect on his wrist. He raised it slowly, slowly, close to his eyes, and through its gauze wings he saw the flame-and-silver sunset. He laughed.

"All his life?"

"All his life," said Wrenn. "With the bitterness and the trouble wiped away, and no chance to mature again into the unfinished thing that fought the world with the conviction it had something extra."

Then he dropped the ring into Jubilith's hand. "But if you care to," he said, watching her face, the responsive motion of her sensitive nostrils, the most delicate index of her lower lip, "if you care to, you can give him back everything I took away. In a moment, you can give him more than he has now; but how long would it take you to make him as happy?"

She made no attempt to answer him. He was Wrenn, he was old and wise; he was a member of a unique species whose resources were incalculable; and yet he was asking her to do something he could not do himself. Perhaps he was asking her to correct a wrong. She would never know that.

"Just the ring," he said, "and the touch of your hand."

He went away, straight and tall, quickening his pace as, far away, the patient figure she had been watching earlier rose and came to meet him. It was Oyva.

Jubilith thought, "He needs her."

Jubilith had never been needed by anyone.

She looked at her hand and in it she saw all she was, all she could ever be in her own right; and with it, the music of ages; never the words, but all of the pressures of poetry. And she saw the extraordinary privacy of love in a world which looked out through her eyes, placed all of its skills in her hands, to do with as she alone wished.

With a touch of her hand . . . what a flood of sensation, what a bursting in of voices and knowledge, for a child!

How long a child?

She closed her eyes, and quietly the answer came, full of pictures; the lute picked up and played; the instant familiarity with the most intricate machine; the stars seen otherwise, and yet again otherwise, and every seeing an honest beauty. A thousand discoveries, and manhood with a rush.

She slipped the ring on her finger, and dragged herself over to him. She put her arms around him and his cheek came down to the hollow of her throat and burrowed there.

He said, sleepily, "Is it nighttime, Mummy?"

"For just a little while," said Jubilith.

THE TRAVELING CRAG

"I know agents who can get work out of their clients," said the telephone acidly.

"Yes, Nick, but—"

"Matter of fact, I know agents who would be willing to drop everything and go out to that one-shot genius's home town and—"

"I did!"

"I know you did! And what came of it?"

"I got a new story. It came in this morning."

"You just don't know how to handle a real writer. All you have to do is—you what?"

"I got a new story. I have it right here."

A pause. "A new Sig Weiss story? No kidding?"

"No kidding."

The telephone paused a moment again, as if to lick its lips. "I was saying to Joe just yesterday that if there's an agent in town who can pry work out of a primadonna like Weiss, it's good old Crisley Post. Yes, sir. Joe thinks a lot of you, Cris. Says you can take a joke better than—how long is the story?"

"Nine thousand."

"Nine thousand. I've got just the spot for it. By the way, did I tell you I can pay an extra cent a word now? For Weiss, maybe a cent and a half."

"You hadn't told me. Last time we talked rates you were overstocked. You wouldn't pay more than—"

"Aw, now, Cris, I was just—"

"Goodbye, Nick."

"Wait! When will you send—"

"Goodbye, Nick."

It was quiet in the office of Crisley Post, Articles, Fiction, Photographs. Then Naome snickered.

"What's funny?"

"Nothing's funny. You're wonderful. I've been waiting four years to hear you tell an editor off. Particularly that one. Are you going to give him the story?"

"I am not."

"Good! Who gets it? The slicks? What are you going to do: sell it to the highest bidder?"

"Naome, have you read it?"

"No. I gave it to you as soon as it came in. I knew you'd want to—"

"Read it."

"Wh—now?"

"Right now."

She took the manuscript and carried it to her desk by the window. "Corny title," she said.

"Corny title," he agreed.

He sat glumly, watching her. She was too small to be so perfectly proportioned, and her hair was as soft as it looked, which was astonishing. She habitually kept him at arm's length, but her arms were short. She was loyal, arbitrary, and underpaid, and she ran the business, though neither of them would admit it aloud. He thought about Sig Weiss.

Every agent has a Sig Weiss—as a rosy dream. You sit there day after day paddling through oceans of slush, hoping one day to run across a manuscript that means something—sincerity, integrity, high word rates—things like that. You try to understand what editors want in spite of what they say they want, and then you try to tell it to writers who never listen unless they're talking. You lend them money and psychoanalyze them and agree with them when they lie to themselves. When they write stories that don't make it, it's your fault. When they write stories that do make it, they did it by themselves. And when they hit the big time, they get themselves another agent. In the meantime, nobody likes you.

"Real stiff opening," said Naome.

"Real stiff," Cris nodded.

And then it happens. In comes a manuscript with a humble little covering note that says, "This is my first story, so it's probably full of mistakes that I don't know anything about. If you think it has anything in it, I'll be glad to fix it up any way you say." And you start reading it, and the story grabs you by the throat, shakes your bones, puts a heartbeat into your lymph ducts and finally slams you down gasping, weak and oh so happy.

So you send it out and it sells on sight, and the editor calls up to say thanks in an awed voice, and tells an anthologist, who buys reprint rights even before the yarn is published, and rumors get around, and you sell radio rights and TV rights and Portuguese translation rights. And the author writes you another note that claims volubly that if it weren't for you he'd never have been able to do it.

That's the agent's dream, and that was Cris Post's boy Sig Weiss and *The Traveling Crag*. But, like all dream plots, this one contained a sleeper. A rude awakening.

Offers came in and Cris made promises, and waited. He wrote letters. He sent telegrams. He got on the long distance phone (to a neighbor's house, Weiss had no phone).

No more stories.

So he went to see Weiss. He lost six days on the project. It was Naome's idea. "He's in trouble," she announced, as if she knew for sure. "Anyone who can write like that is sensitive. He's humble and he's generous and he's probably real shy and real good-looking. Someone's victimized him, that's what. Someone's taken advantage of him. Cris, go on out there and find out what's the matter."

"All the way out to Turnville? My God, woman, do you know where that is? Besides, who's going to run things around here?" As if he didn't know.

"I'll try, Cris. But you've got to see what's the matter with Sig Weiss. He's the—the greatest thing that ever happened around here."

"I'm jealous," he said, because he was jealous.

"Don't be silly," she said, because he wasn't being silly.

So out he went. He missed connections and spent one night in a depot and had his portable type-writer stolen and found he'd forgotten to pack the brown shoes that went with the brown suit. He brushed his teeth once with shaving cream and took the wrong creaking rural bus and had to creak in to an impossibly authentic small town and creak out again on another bus. Turnville was a general store with gasoline pumps outside and an abandoned milk shed across the road, and Cris wasn't happy when he got there. He went into the general store to ask questions.

The proprietor was a triumph of type-casting. "Whut c'n I dew f'r you, young feller? Shay—yer f'm the city, ain't cha? Heh!"

Cris fumbled vaguely with his lapels, wondering if someone had pinned a sign on him. "I'm looking for someone called Sig Weiss. Know him?"

"Sure dew. Meanest bastard ever lived. Wouldn't have nought to dew with him, I was you."

"You're not," said Cris, annoyed. "Where does he live?"

"What you want with him?"

"I'm conducting a nation-wide survey of mean bastards," Cris said. "Where does he live?"

"You're on the way to the right place, then. Heh! You show me a man's friends, I'll tell you what he is."

"What about his friends?" Cris asked, startled.

"He ain't got any friends."

Cris closed his eyes and breathed deeply. "Where does he live?"

"Up the road a piece. Two mile, a bit over. That way."

"Thanks."

"He'll shoot you," said the proprietor complacently, "but don't let it worry you none. He loads his shells with rock salt."

Cris walked the two miles and a bit, every uphill inch. He was tired, and his shoes were designed only to carry a high shine and make small smudges on desk tops. It was hot until he reached the top of the mountain, and then the cool wind from the other side made him feel as if he was carrying sacks of crushed ice in his armpits. There was a galvanized tin mailbox on a post by the road with S. WEISS and advanced erosion showing on its ancient sides. In the cutbank near it were some shallow footholds. Cris sighed and started up.

There was a faint path writhing its way through heavy growth. Through the trees he could see a canted shingle roof. He had gone about forty feet when there was a thunderous explosion and shredded greenery settled about his head and shoulders. Sinking his teeth into his tongue, he turned and dove head first into a tree-bole, and the lights went out.

A fabulous headache was fully conscious before Cris was. He saw it clearly before it moved around behind his eyes. He was lying where he had fallen. A rangy

265

youth with long narrow eyes was squatting ten feet away. He held a ready shotgun under his arm and on his wrist, while he deftly went through Cris's wallet.

"Hey," said Cris.

The man closed the wallet and threw it on the ground by Cris's throbbing head. "So you're Crisley Post," said the man, in a disgusted tone of voice.

Cris sat up and groaned. "You're—you're not Sig Weiss?"

"I'm not?" asked the man pugnaciously.

"Okay, okay," said Cris tiredly. He picked up his wallet and put it away and, with the aid of the tree trunk, got to his feet. Weiss made no move to help him, but watchfully rose with him. Cris asked, "Why the artillery?"

"I got a permit," said Weiss. "This is my land. Why not? Don't go blaming me because you ran into a tree. What do you want?"

"I just wanted to talk to you. I came a long way to do it. If I'd known you'd welcome me like this, I wouldn't've come."

"I didn't ask you to come."

"I'm not going to talk sense if I get sore," said Cris quietly. "Can't we go inside? My head hurts."

Weiss seemed to ponder this for a moment. Then he turned on his heel, grunted, "Come," and strode toward the house. Cris followed painfully.

A gray cat slid across the path and crouched in the long grass. Weiss appeared to ignore it, but as he stepped by, his right leg lashed out sidewise and lifted the yowling animal into the air. It struck a tree trunk and fell, to lie dazed. Cris let out an indignant shout and went to it. The cat cowered away from him, gained its feet and fled into the woods, terrified.

"Your cat?" asked Weiss coldly.

"No, but damn if—"

"If it isn't you cat, why worry?" Weiss walked steadily on toward the house.

Cris stood a moment, shock and fury roiling in and about his headache, and then followed. Standing there or going away would accomplish nothing.

The house was old, small, and solid. It was built of fieldstone, and the ceilings were low and heavy beamed. Overlooking the mountainside was an enormous window, bringing in a breathtaking view of row after row of distant hills. The furniture was rustic and built to be used. There was a fireplace with a crane, also more than ornamental. There were no drapes, no couch covers or flamboyant upholstery. There was comfort, but austerity was the keynote.

"May I sit down?" Cris asked caustically.

"Go ahead," said Weiss. "You can breathe, too, if you want to."

Cris sat in a large split-twig chair that was infinitely more comfortable than it looked. "What's the matter with you, Weiss?"

"Nothing the matter with me."

"What makes you like this? Why the chip on your shoulder? Why this shoot-first-ask-questions-afterward attitude? What's it get you?"

"Gets me a life of my own. Nobody bothers me but once. They don't come back. You won't."

"That's for sure," said Cris fervently. "but I wish I knew what's eating you. No normal human being acts like you do."

"That's enough," said Weiss very gently, and Cris knew how very seriously he meant it. "What I do and why is none of your business. What do you want here, anyhow?"

"I came to find out why you're not writing. That's my business. You're my client, remember?"

"You're my agent," he said. "I like the sound of it better that way."

Cris made an olympian effort and ignored the remark. *The Traveling Crag* churned up quite a stir. You made yourself a nice piece of change. Write more, you'll make more. Don't you like money?"

"Who doesn't? You got no complaints out of me."

"Fine. Then what about some more copy?"

"You'll get it when I'm good and ready."

"Which is how soon?"

"How do I know?" Weiss barked. "When I feel like it, whenever that is."

Cris talked, then, at some length. He told Weiss some of the ins and outs of publishing. He explained how phenomenal it was that a pulp sale should have created such a turmoil, and pointed out what could be expected in the slicks and Hollywood. "I don't know how you've done it, but you've found a short line to the heavy sugar. But the only way you'll ever touch it is to write more."

"All right, all right," Weiss said at last. "You've sold me. You'll get your story. Is that what you wanted?"

"Not quite." Cris rose. He felt better, and he could allow himself to be angry now that the business was taken care of. "I still want to know how a guy like you could have written a story like *The Traveling Crag* in a place like this."

"Why not?"

Cris looked out at the rolling blue distance. "That story had more sheer humanity in it than anything I've ever read. It was sensitive and—damn it—it was a *kind* story. I can usually visualize who writes the stuff I read; I spend all my time with writing and writers. That story wasn't written in a place like this. And it wasn't written by a man like you."

268

"Where was it written?" asked Weiss in his very quite voice. "And who wrote it?"

"Aw, put your dukes down," said Cris tiredly, and with such contempt that he apparently astonished Weiss. "If you're going to jump salty over every little thing that happens, what are you going to do when something big comes along and you've already shot your bolt?"

Weiss did not answer, and Cris went on: "I'm not saying you didn't write it. All I'm saying is that it reads like something dreamed up in some quiet place that smelled like flowers and good clean sweat . . . Some place where everything was right and nothing was sick or off balance. And whoever wrote it suited that kind of a place. It was probably you, but you sure have changed since."

"You know a hell of a lot, don't you?" The soft growl was not completely insulting, and Cris felt that in some obscure way he had scored. Then Weiss said, "Now get the hell out."

"Real glad to," said Cris. At the door, he said, "Thanks for the drink."

When he reached the cutbank, he looked back. Weiss was standing by the corner of the house, staring after him.

Cris trudged back to the crossroads called Turnville and stopped in at the general store. "Shay," said the proprietor. "Looks like a tree reached down and whopped ye. Heh!"

"Heh!" said Cris. "One did. I called it a son of a beech."

The proprietor slapped his knee and wheezed. "Shay, thet's a good 'un. Come out back, young feller, while I put some snake oil on your head. Like some cold beer?"

269

Cris blessed him noisily. The snake oil turned out to be a benzocaine ointment that took the pain out instantly, and the beer was a transfusion. He looked at the old man with new respect.

"Had a bad time up on the hill?" asked the oldster.

"No worse'n sharing an undershirt with a black widow spider," said Cris. "What's the matter with that character?"

"Nobuddy rightly knows," said the proprietor. "Came up here about eight years ago. Always been thet way. Some say the war did it to him, but I knew him before he went overseas and he was the same. He jest don't like people, is all. Old Tom Sackett, drives the RFD wagon, he says Weiss was weaned off a gallbladder to a bottle of vinegar. Heh!"

"Heh!" said Cris. "How's he live?"

"Gits a check every month. Some trust company. I cash 'em. Not much, but enough. He don't dew nahthin. Hunts a bit, roams these hills a hull lot. Reads. Heh! He's no trouble, though. Stays on his own reservation. Just don't want folks barrelin' in on him. Here comes yer bus."

"My God!" said Naome.

"You're addressing me?" he asked.

She ignored him. "Listen to this:

Jets blasting, Bat Durston came screeching down through the atmosphere of Bbllzznaj, a tiny planet seven billion light years from Sol. He cut out his super-hyper-drive for the landing . . . and at that point a tall, lean spaceman stepped out of the tail assembly, proton gun-blaster in a space-tanned hand.

'Get back from those controls, Bat Durston,' the tall stranger lipped thinly. 'You don't know it, but this is your last space trip.'"

She looked up at him dazedly. "That's Sig Weiss?"

"That's Sig Weiss."

"The same Sig Weiss?"

"The very same. Leaf through that thing, Naome. Nine bloody thousand words of it, and it's all like that. Go on—read it."

"No," she said. It was not a refusal, but an exclamation. "Are you going to send it out?"

"Yes. To Sig Weiss. I'm going to tell him to roll it and stuff it up his shotgun. Honey, we have a one-shot on our hands."

"That is—it's impossible!" she blazed. "Cris, you can't give him up just like that. Maybe the next one . . . maybe you can . . . maybe you're right at that," she finished, glancing back at the manuscript.

He said tiredly, "Let's go eat."

"No. You have a lunch."

"I have?"

"With a Miss Tillie Moroney. You're quite safe. She's the Average American Miss. I mean it. She was picked out as such by pollsters last year. She's five-five, has had 2.3 years of college, is 24 years old, brown hair, blue eyes, and so on."

"How much does she weigh?"

"34B," said Naome, with instant understanding, "and presents a united front like a Victorian."

He laughed. "And what have I to do with Miss Tillie Moroney?"

"She's got money. I told you about her—that personals ad in the *Saturday Review*—remember? 'Does basic character ever change? $1000 for authentic case of devil into saint.'"

"Oh my gosh yes. You had this bright idea of calling her in after I told you about getting the Weiss treatment in Turnville." He waved at the manuscript. "Doesn't

271

that change your plans any? You might take a case out of *The Traveling Crag* versus the cat-kicking of Mr. Weiss, if you use that old man's testimony that he's been kicking cats and people for some years. But from my experience," he touched his forehead, which was almost healed, "I'd say it was saint into devil."

"Her ad didn't mention temporary or permanent changes," Naome pointed out. "There may be a buck in it. You can handle her."

"Thanks just the same, but let me see what she looks like before I do any such thing. Personally, I think she's a crank. A mystic maybe. Do you know her?"

"Spoke to her on the phone. Saw her picture last year. The Average American Miss is permitted to be a screwball. That's what makes this country great."

"You and your Machiavellian syndrome. Can't I get out of it?"

"You cannot. What are you making such a fuss about? You've wined and dined uglier chicks than this."

"I know it. Do you think I'd have a chance to see her if I acted eager?"

"I despise you," said Naome. "Straighten your tie and go comb your hair. Oh, Cris, I know it sounds wacky. But what doesn't, in this business? What'll you lose? The price of a lunch!"

"I might lose my honor."

"Authors' agents have no honor."

"As my friend in the general store is wont to remark: Heh! What protects you, little one?"

"My honor," replied Naome.

The brown hair was neat and so was the tailored brown suit that matched it so well. The blue eyes were extremely dark. The rest well befit her Average Miss title, except for her voice, which had the pitch of a husky one

272

while being clear as tropical shoals. Her general air was one of poised shyness. Cris pulled out a restaurant chair for her, which was a tribute; he felt impelled to do that about one time in seven.

"You think I'm a crank," she said when they were settled with a drink.

"Do I?"

"You do," she said positively. He did, too.

"Well," he said, "your ad did make it a little difficult to suspend judgement."

She smiled with him. She had good teeth. "I can't blame you, or the eight hundred-odd other people who answered. Why is it a thousand dollars is so much more appealing than such an incredible thought as a change from basic character?"

"I guess because most people would rather see the change from a thousand dollars."

He was pleased to find she had the rare quality of being able to talk coherently while she laughed. She said, "You are right. One of them wanted to marry me so I could change his character. He assured me that he was a regular devil. But—tell me about this case of yours."

He did, in detail: Sig Weiss's incredible short story, its wide impact, its deep call on everything that is fine and generous in everyone who read it. And then he described the man who had written it.

"In this business, you run into all kinds of flukes," he said. "A superficial, tone-deaf, materialistic character will sit down and write something that positively sings. You read the story, you know the guy, and you say he couldn't have written it. But you know he did. I've seen that time after time, and all it proves is that there are more facets to a man than you see at first—not that there's any real change in him. But Weiss—I'll admit

273

that in his case the theory has got to be stretched to explain it. I'll swear a man like him simply could not contain the emotions and convictions that made *The Traveling Crag* what it is."

"I've read it," she said. He hadn't noticed her lower lip was so full. Perhaps it hadn't been, a moment ago. "It was a beautiful thing."

"Now, tell me about this ad of yours. Have you found such a basic change—devil into saint? Or do you just hope to?"

"I don't know of any such case," she admitted. "But I know it can happen."

"How?"

She paused. She seemed to be listening. Then she said, "I can't tell you. I . . . know something that can have that effect, that's all. I'm trying to find out where it is."

"I don't understand that. You don't think Sig Weiss was under such a influence, do you?"

"I'd like to ask him. I'd like to know if the effect was at all lasting."

"Not so you'd notice it," he said glumly. "He gave me that bouncing around after he wrote *The Traveling Crag,* not before. Not only that . . ." He told her about the latest story.

"Do you suppose he wrote that under the same circumstances as *The Traveling Crag?*"

"I don't see why not. He's a man of pretty regular habits. He probably—wait a minute! Just before I left, I said something to him . . . something about . . ." He drummed on his temples. ". . . Something about the *Crag* reading as if it had been written in a different place, by a different person. And he didn't get sore. He looked at me as if I were a swami. Seems I hit the nail right on the thumb."

The listening expression crossed her smooth face again. She looked up, startled. "Has he got any . . ." She closed her eyes, straining for something. "Has he a radio? I mean—a shortwave set—a transmitter—diathermy—a fever cabinet—any . . . uh . . . RF generator of any kind?"

"What in time made you ask that?"

She opened her eyes and smiled shyly at him. "It just came to me."

"Saving your presence, Miss Moroney, but there are moments when you give me the creeps," he blurted. "I'm sorry. I guess I shouldn't have said that, but—"

"It's all right," she said warmly.

"You hear voices?" he asked.

She smiled. "What about the RF generator?"

"I don't know." He thought hard. "He has electricity. I imagine he has a receiver. About the rest, I really can't say. He didn't take me on a grand tour. Will you tell me what made you ask that?"

"No."

He opened his mouth to protest, but when he saw her expression he closed it again. She asked, "What are you going to do about Weiss?"

"Drop him. What else?"

"Oh, please don't!" she cried. She put a hand on his sleeve. "Please!"

"What else do you expect me to do?" he asked in some annoyance. "A writer who sends in a piece of junk like that as a followup to something like the *Crag* is more than foolish. He's stupid. I can't use a client like that. I'm busy. I got troubles."

"Also, he gave you a bad time."

"That hasn't anyth—well, you're right. If he behaved like a human being, maybe I would take a lot of trouble and analyze his trash and guide and urge and wipe his nose for him. But a guy like that—nah!"

275

"He has another story like the *Crag* in him."

"You think he has?"

"I know he has."

"You're very positive. Your . . . voices tell you that?"

She nodded, with a small secret smile.

"I have the feeling you're playing with me. You know this Weiss?"

"Oh, no! And I'm not playing with you. Truly. You've got to believe me!" She looked genuinely distressed.

"I don't see why I should. This begins to look real haywire, Tillie Moroney. I think maybe we'd better get down to basics here." She immediately looked so worried that he recognized an advantage. Not knowing exactly what she wanted of him, he knew she wanted something, and now he was prepared to use that to the hilt. "Tell me about it. What's your interest in Weiss? What's this personality-alteration gimmick? What are you after and what gave you your lead? And what do you expect me to do about it? That last question reads, 'What's in it for me?' "

"Y-you're not always very nice, are you?"

He said, more gently, "That last wasn't thrown in to be mean. It was an appeal to your good sense to appeal to my sincerity. You can always judge sincerity—your own or anyone else's—by finding out what's in it for the interested party. Altruism and real sincerity are mutually exclusive. Now, talk. I mean, talk, please."

Again that extraordinary harking expression. Then she drew a deep breath. "I've had an awful time," she said. "Awful. You can't know. I've answered letters and phone calls. I've met cranks and wolves and religious fanatics who have neat little dialectical capsules all packed and ready to make saints out of devils. They all

276

yap about proof—sometimes it's themselves and sometimes it's someone they know—and the proof always turns out to be a reformed drunk or a man who turned to Krishna and no longer beats his wife, not since Tuesday . . ." She stopped for breath and half-smiled at him and, angrily, he felt a warm surge of liking for her. She went on, "And this is the first hint I've had that what I'm looking for really exists."

She leaned forward suddenly. "I need you. You already have a solid contact with Sig Weiss and the way he works. If I had to seek him out myself, I—well, I just wouldn't know how to start. And this is urgent, can't you understand—urgent!"

He looked deep into the dark blue eyes and said, "I understand fine."

She said, "If I tell you a . . . story, will you promise not to ask me any questions about it?"

He fiddled about with his fork for a moment and then said, "I once heard tell of a one-legged man who was pestered by all the kids in the neighborhood about how he lost his leg. They followed him and yelled at him and tagged along after him and made no end of a nuisance of themselves. So one day he stopped and gathered them all around him and asked if they really wanted to know how he lost his leg, and they all chorused YES! And he wanted to know if he told them, would they stop asking him, and they all promised faithfully that they would stop. 'All right,' he said. 'It was bit off.' And he turned and stumped away. As to the promise you want—no."

She laughed ruefully. "All right. I'll tell you the story anyway. But you've got to understand that it isn't the whole story, and that I'm not at liberty to tell the whole sorry. So please don't pry too hard."

He smiled. He had, he noticed in her eyes, a pretty nice smile. "I'll be good."

"All right. You have a lot of clients who write science fiction, don't you?"

"Not a lot. Just the best," he said modestly.

She smiled again. Two curved dimples put her smile in parenthesis. He liked that. She said, "Let's say this is a science fiction plot. How to begin . . ."

"Once upon a time . . ." he prompted.

She laughed like a child. "Once upon a time," she nodded, "there was a very advanced humanoid race in another galaxy. They had had wars—lots of them. They learned how to control them, but every once in a while things would get out of hand and another, and worse, war would happen. They developed weapon after weapon—things which make the H-bomb like a campfire in comparison. They had planet-smashers. They could explode a sun. They could do things we can only dimly understand. They could put a local warp in time itself, or unify the polarity in the gravitomagnetic field of an entire solar system."

"Does this gobbledegook come easy to you?" he asked.

"It does just now," she answered shyly. "Anyway, they developed the ultimate weapon—one which made all the others obsolete. It was enormously difficult to make, and only a few were manufactured. The secret of making it died out, and the available stocks were used at one time or another. The time to use them is coming again—and I don't mean on Earth. The little fuses we have are flea-hops. This is important business.

"Now, a cargo ship was travelling between galaxies on hyperspatial drive. In a crazy, billion-to-one odds accident, it emerged into normal space smack in the middle of a planetoid. It wasn't a big one; the ship wasn't atomized—just wrecked. It was carrying one of these super-weapons. It took thousands of years to trace

278

it, but it has been traced. The chances are strong that it came down on a planet. It's wanted.

"It gives out no detectible radiation. But in its shielded state, it has a peculiar effect on living tissues which come near it."

"Devils into saints?"

"The effect is . . . peculiar. Now . . ." She held up fingers. "If the nature of this object were known, and if it fell into the wrong hands, the effect here on Earth could be dreadful. There are megalomaniacs on earth so unbalanced that they would threaten even their own destruction unless their demands were met. Point two: If the weapon were used on Earth, not only would Earth as we know it cease to exist, but the weapon would be unavailable to those who need it importantly."

Cris sat staring at her, waiting for more. There was no more. Finally he licked his lips and said, "You're telling me that Sig Weiss has stumbled across this thing."

"I'm telling you a science fiction plot."

"Where did you get your . . . information?"

"It's a science fiction story."

He grinned suddenly, widely. "I'll be good," he said again. "What do you want me to do?"

Her eyes became very bright. "You aren't like most agents," she said.

"When I was in a British Colony, the English used to say to me, every once in a while, 'You aren't like most Americans.' I always found it slightly insulting. All right; what do you want me to do?"

She patted his hand. "See if you can make Weiss write another *Traveling Crag*. If he can, then find out exactly how and where he wrote it. And let me know."

They rose. He helped her with her light coat. He said, "Know something?" When she smiled up at him he said, "You don't strike me as Miss Average."

"Oh, but I was," she answered softly. "I was."

TELEGRAM

PLEASE UNDERSTAND THAT WHAT FOLLOWS HAS
NOTHING WHATEVER TO DO WITH YOUR GROSS
LACK OF HOSPITALITY. I REALIZE THAT YOUR WAY
OF LIFE ON YOUR OWN PROPERTY IS JUSTIFIED IN
TERMS OF ME, AN INTRUDER. I AM FORGETTING
THE EPISODE. I ASSUME YOU ALREADY HAVE. NOW
TO BUSINESS: YOUR LAST MANUSCRIPT IS THE
MOST UTTERLY INSULTING DOCUMENT I HAVE
SEEN IN FOURTEEN PROFESSIONAL YEARS. TO IN-
SULT ONE'S AGENT IS STANDARD OPERATING PRO-
CEDURE: TO INSULT ONESELF IS INEXCUSABLE
AND BROTHER YOU'VE DONE IT. SIT DOWN AND
READ THE STORY THROUGH, IF YOU CAN, AND
THEN REREAD THE TRAVELING CRAG. YOU WILL
NOT NEED MY CRITICISM. MY ONLY SUGGESTION
TO YOU IS TO DUPLICATE EXACTLY THE CIRCUM-
STANCES UNDER WHICH YOU WROTE YOUR FIRST
STORY. UNLESS AND UNTIL YOU DO THIS WE NEED
HAVE NO FURTHER CORRESPONDENCE. I ACCEPT
YOUR SINCERE THANKS FOR NOT SUBMITTING YOUR
SECOND STORY ANYWHERE.

                                        CRISLEY POST

Naome whistled. "Really—a straight telegram? What about a night letter?"

Cris smiled at the place where the wall met the ceiling. "Straight rate."

"Yes, master." She wielded a busy pencil. "That's costing us $13.75, sir," she said at length, "plus tax. Grand total, $17.46. Cris, you have a hole in your head!"

"If you know of a better 'ole, go to it," he quoted dreamily. She glared at him, reached for the phone, and continued to glare as she put the telegram on the wire.

In the next two weeks Cris had lunch three times with Tillie Moroney, and dinner once. Naome asked for a raise. She got it, and was therefore frightened.

Cris returned from the third of these lunches (which was the day after the dinner) whistling. He found Naome in tears.

"Hey . . . what's happening here? You don't do that kind of thing, remember?"

He leaned over her desk. She buried her face in her arms and boohooed lustily. He knelt beside her and put an arm around her shoulders. "There," he said, patting the nape of her neck. "Take a deep breath and tell me about it."

She took a long, quavering breath, tried to speak, and burst into tears again. "F-f-fi-fi . . ."

"What?"

"F—" She swallowed with difficulty, then said, *"Fire of Heaven!"* and wailed.

"What?" he yelled. "I thought you said *'Fire of Heaven.'*"

She blew her nose and nodded. "I did," she whispered. "H-here." She dumped a pile of manuscript in front of him and buried her face in her arms again. "L-leave me alone."

In complete bewilderment, he gathered up the typewritten sheets and took them to his desk.

There was a covering letter.

Dear Mr. Post: There will never be a way for me to express my thanks to you, nor my apologies for the way I treated you when you visited me. I am willing to do anything in my power to make amends.

Knowing what I do of you, I think you would be most pleased by another story written the way I did the Crag. Here it is. I hope it measures up. If it doesn't, I earnestly welcome any suggestions you may have to fix it up.

I am looking forward very much indeed to meeting you again under better circumstances. My house is yours when you can find time to come out, and I do hope it will be soon. Sincerely, S. W.

With feelings of awe well mixed with astonishment, Cris turned to the manuscript. *Fire of Heaven,* by Sig Weiss, it was headed. He began to read. For a moment, he was conscious of Naome's difficult and diminishing sniffs, and then he became completely immersed in the story.

Twenty minutes later, his eyes, blurred and smarting, encountered "The End." He propped his forehead on one palm and rummaged clumsily for his handkerchief. Having thoroughly mopped and blown, he looked across at Naome. Her eyes were red-rimmed and still wet. "Yes?" she said.

"Oh my God yes," he answered.

They stared at each other for a breathless moment. Then she said in a soprano near-whisper: "*Fire of . . .*" and began to cry again.

"Cut it out," he said hoarsely.

When he could, he got up and opened the window. Naome came and stood beside him. "You don't read that," he said after a time. "It . . . happens to you."

She said, "What a tragedy. What a beautiful, beautiful tragedy."

"He said in his letter," Cris managed, "that if I had any suggestions to fix it up . . ."

282

"Fix it up," she said in shaken scorn. "There hasn't been anything like him since—"

"There hasn't been anything like him period." Cris snapped his fingers. "Get on your phone. Call the airlines. Two tickets to the nearest feederfield to Turnville. Call the Drive-Ur-Self service. Have a car waiting at the field. I'm not asking any woman to climb that mountain on foot. Send this telegram to Weiss: Taking up your very kind offer immediately. Bringing a friend. Will wire arrival time. Profound thanks for the privilege of reading *Fire of Heaven*. From a case hardened ten percenter those words come hard and are well earned. Post."

"Two tickets," said Naome breathlessly. "Oh! Who's going to handle the office?"

He thumped her shoulder. "You can do it, kid. You're wonderful. Indispensable. I love you. Get me Tillie Moroney's number, will you?"

She stood frozen, her lips parted, her nostrils slightly distended. He looked at her, looked again. He was aware that she had stopped breathing. "Naome!"

She came to life slowly and turned, not to him, but on him. "You're taking that—that Moron-y creature—"

"Moroney. What's the matter with you?"

"Oh Cris, how could you?"

"What have I done? What's wrong? Listen, this is business. I'm not romancing the girl! Why—"

She curled her lip. "Business! Then it's the first business that's gone on around here that I haven't known about."

"Oh, it isn't office business, Naome. Honestly."

"Then there's only one thing it could be!"

Cris threw up his hands. "Trust me this once. Say! Why should it eat you so much, even if it was monkey-business, which it isn't?"

"I can't bear to see you throw yourself away!"

283

"You—I didn't know you felt—"

"Shut up!" she roared. "Don't flatter yourself. It's just that she's . . . average. And so are you. And when you add an average to an average, you've produced NOTHING!"

He sat down at his desk with a thump and reached for the phone, very purposefully. But his mind was in such a tangle at the moment, that he didn't know what to do with the phone once it was in his hands, until Naome stormed over and furiously dropped a paper in front of him. It had Tillie's number on it. He grinned at her stupidly and sheepishly and dialled. By this time, Naome was speaking to the airlines office, but he knew perfectly well that she could talk and listen at the same time.

"Hello?" said the phone.

"Ull-ull," he said, watching Naome's back stiffen. He spun around in his swivel chair so he could talk facing the wall.

"Hello?" said the phone again.

"Tillie, Weiss found it he wrote another story it's a dream he invited me down and I'm going and you're coming with me," he blurted.

"I beg your—Cris, is anything the matter? You sound so strange."

"Never mind that," he said. He repeated the news more coherently, acutely conscious of Naome's attention to every syllable. Tillie uttered a cry of joy and promised to be right over. He asked her to hang on and forced himself to get the plane departure from Naome. Pleading packing and business odds and ends, he asked her to meet him at the airport. She agreed, for which he was very thankful. The idea of her walking into the office just now was more than he could take.

Naome had done her phoning and was in a flurry of

effort involving her files, which had always been a mystery to Cris. She kept bringing things over to him. "Sign these." "You promised to drop Rogers a note about this." "What do you want done about Borilla's scripts?" Until he was snowed under. "Hold it! These things can wait!"

"No they can't," she said icily. "I wouldn't want them on my conscience. You see, this is my last day here."

"Your—Naome! You can't quit! You can't!"

"I can and I am and I do. Check this list."

"Naome, I—"

"I won't listen. My mind's made up."

"All right then. I'll manage. But it's a shame about *Fire of Heaven*. Such a beautiful job. And here it must sit until I get back. I did want you to market it."

"You'd trust me to market that story?" Her eyes were huge.

"No one else. There isn't anyone who knows the market better, or who would make a better deal. I trust you with it absolutely. After you've done that one last big thing for me—go, then, if you'll be happier somewhere else."

"Crisley Post, I hate you and despise you. You're a fiend and a spider. Th-thank you. I'll never forget you for this. I'll type up four originals and sneak them around. Movies, of course. What a TV script! And radio . . . let's see; two, no—three British outfits can bid against each other . . . you're doing this on purpose to keep me from leaving!"

"Sure," he said jovially. "I'm real cute. I wrote the story myself just because I couldn't get anyone to replace you."

At last, she laughed. "There's one thing I'm damn sure you didn't do. An editor is a writer who can't write, and an agent is a writer who can't write as well as an editor."

He laughed with her. He bled too, but it was worth it, to see her laughing again.

The plane trip was pleasant. It lasted a long time. The ship sat down every 45 minutes or so all the way across the country. Cris figured it was the best Naome could do on short notice. But it gave them lots of time to talk. And talking to Tillie was a pleasure. She was intelligent and articulate, and had read just as many of his favorite books as he had of hers. He told her enough about *Fire of Heaven* to intrigue her a lot and make her cry a little, without spoiling the plot for her. They found music to disagree about, and shared a view of a wonderful lake down through the clouds, and all in all it was a good trip. Occasionally, Cris glanced at her—most often when she was asleep—with a touch of surmise, like a little curl of smoke, thinking of Naome's suspicions about him and Tillie. He wasn't romancing Tillie. He wasn't. Was he?

They landed at last, and again he blessed Naome; the Drive-Ur-Self car was at the airfield. They got a road map from a field attendant and drove off through the darkest morning hours. Again Cris found himself glancing at the relaxed girl beside him, half asleep in the cold glow of the dash lights. A phrase occurred to him: "undivided front like a Victorian"—Naome's remark. He flushed. It was true. An affectation of Tillie's, probably; but everything she wore was highnecked and full-cut.

The sky had turned from grey to pale pink when they pulled up at the Turnville store. Cris honked, and in due course the screen door slammed and the old proprietor ambled down the wooden steps and came to peer into his face.

"Heh! If 'taint that city feller. How're ya, son? Didn't know you folks ever got up and about this early."

286

"We're up late, dad. Got some gas for us?"

"Reckon there's a drop left."

Cris got out and went back with the old man to unlock the gas tank. "Seen Weiss recently?" he asked.

"Same as usual. Put through some big orders. Seen him do that before. Usually means he's holing up for five, six months. Though why he bought so much liquor an' drape material and that, I can't figure."

"How'd he behave?"

"Same as ever. Friendly as a wet wildcat with fleas."

Cris thanked him and paid him and they turned up the rocky hill road. As they reached the crest, they gasped together at the sun-flood valley that lay before them. "Memories are the only thing you ever have that you always keep," said Tillie softly, "and this is one for both of us. I'm . . . glad you're in it for me, Cris."

"I love you, too," he said in the current idiom, and found himself, hot-faced, looking into a face as suffused as his. They recoiled from each other and started to chatter about the weather—stopped and roared together with laughter. He took her hand and helped her up the cutbank. They paused at the top. "Listen," he said in a low voice. "That old character in the store has seen Weiss recently. And he says there's no change. I think we'd better be just a little careful."

He looked at her and again caught that listening expression. "No," she said at length, "it's all right. The store's outside the . . . the influence he's under. He's bound to revert when it's gone. But he'll be all right now. You'll see."

"Will you tell me how you know these things?" he demanded, almost angry.

"Of course," she smiled. Then the smile vanished. "But not now."

"That's more than I've gotten so far," he grumbled. "Well, let's get to it."

Hand in hand, they went up the path. The house seemed the same, and yet . . . there was a difference, an intensification. The leaves were greener, the early sun warmer.

There were three grey kittens on the porch.

"Ahoy the house!" Cris called self-consciously.

The door opened, and Weiss stood there, peering. He looked for a moment exactly as he had when he watched Cris stride off on the earlier visit. Then he moved out into the sun. He scooped up one of the kittens and came swiftly to meet them. "Mr. Post! I got your wire. How very good of you to come."

He was dressed in a soft sport shirt and grey slacks— a startling difference from his grizzled boots-and-khaki appearance before. The kitten snuggled into the crook of his elbow, made a wild grab at his pocket-button, caught its tail instead. He put it down, and it fawned and purred and rubbed against his shoe.

Weiss straightened up and smiled at Tillie. "Hello."

"Tillie, this is Sig Weiss. Miss Moroney."

"Tillie," she said, and gave him her hand.

"Welcome home," Weiss said. He turned to Cris. "This is your home, for as long as you want it, whenever you can come."

Cris stood slack-jawed. "I ought to be more tactful," he said at length, "but I just can't believe it. I should have more sense than to mention my last visit, but this— this—"

Weiss put a hand on his shoulder. "I'm glad you mentioned it. I've been thinking about it, too. Hell—if you'd forgotten all about it, how could you appreciate all this? Come on in. I have some surprises for you."

Tillie held Cris back a moment. "It's here," she whispered. "Here in the house!"

The weapon—here? Somehow, he had visualized it as huge—a great horned mine or a tremendous torpedo shape. He glanced around apprehensively. The ultimate weapon—invented after the planet-smasher, the sun-burster—what incredible thing could it be?

Weiss stood by the door. Tillie stepped through, then Cris.

The straight drapes, the solid sheet of plate glass that replaced the huge sashed window; the heavy skins that softened the wide-planked floor, the gleaming andirons and the copper pots on the fieldstone wall; the record-player and racks of albums—all the other soothing, comforting finishes of the once-bleak room—all these Cris noticed later. His big surprise was not quite a hundred pounds, not quite five feet tall—

"Cris . . ."

"Naome's here," he said inanely, and sat down to goggle at her.

Weiss laughed richly. "Why do you suppose you and Tillie got that pogo-plane cross country, stopping at every ball-park and cornfield? Naome got a non-stop flight to within fifty miles of here, and air-taxi to the bottom of the mountain, and came up by cab."

"I had to," said Naome. "I had to see what you were getting into. You're so—impetuous." She came smiling to Tillie. "I am glad to see you."

"Why, you idiot!" said Cris to Naome. "What could you have done if he—if—"

"I'm prettier than you are, darling," laughed Naome.

"She came pussyfooting up to the house like a kid playing Indian," said Weiss. "I circled through the woods and pussyfooted right along with her. When she was peeping into the side window, I reached out and put a hand on her shoulder."

"You might have scared her into a conniption!"

"Not here," said Weiss gravely.

Surprisingly, Tillie nodded. "You can't be afraid here, Cris. You're saying all those things about what might have happened, but they're not frightening to think about now, are they?"

"No," Cris said thoughtfully. "No." He gazed around him. "This is—crazy. Everybody should be this crazy."

"It would help," said Weiss. "How do you like the place now, Cris?"

"It's—it's grand," said Cris. Naome laughed. She said, "Listen to the vocabulary kid there. 'Grand.' You meant 'Peachy,' didn't you?"

Cris didn't laugh with the others. "Fear," he said. "You can't eliminate fear. Fear is a survival emotion. If you didn't know fear, you'd fall out of windows, cut yourself on rocks, get hunted and killed by mountain lions."

"If I open the window," Weiss asked, "would you be afraid to jump out? Come over here and look."

Cris stepped to the great window. He had not known that the house was built so close to the edge. Crag on crag, fold after billow, the land fell down and away to the distant throat of the valley. Cris stepped back respectfully. "Open it if you like," he said, and swallowed, "and somebody else can jump. Not me, kiddies."

Sig Weiss smiled. "Q.E.D. Survival fear is still with us. What we've lost here is fear of anything that is not so. When you came here before, you saw a very frightened man. Most of my fears were 'might-be' fears. I was afraid people might attack me, so I attacked first. I was afraid of seeming different from people, so I stayed where my imagined difference would not show. I was afraid of being the same as people, so I tried to be different."

"What does it?" Cris asked.

"What makes us all what we are now? Something I found. I won't tell you what it is or where it is. I call it an amulet, a true magic amulet, knowing that it's no more or less magic than flame springing to the end of a wooden stick." He took a kitchen match from his pocket and ran his thumbnail across it. It flared up, and he flipped it into the fireplace. "I won't tell you where or what it is because, although I've lost my fear, I haven't lost my stubbornness. I've lived miserably, a partial, hunted, hunting existence, and now I'm alive. And I mean to stay this way."

"Where did you find it?" Tillie asked. "Mind telling us that?"

"Not at all. A half mile down the mountain there was a tremendous rockfall a couple of years ago. No one owns that land; no one noticed. I climbed down there once looking for hawks' eggs. I found a place . . .

"How can I tell you what that place was like, or what it was like to find it? It was a brush-grown, rocky hillside near the gaping scar of the slide, where the crust of years had sloughed away. Maybe the mountain moved its shoulder in its sleep. There were flowers—ordinary wildflowers—but perfect, vivid, vital. They lived long and hardily, and they were beautiful. The bushes had an extraordinary green and a fine healthy gloss, and it was a place where the birds came close to me as I sat and watched them. It was the birds who taught me that fear never walked in that place.

"How can I tell you—what can I say about the meaning of that place to me? I'd been a psychic cripple all my life, hobbling through the rough country of my own ideas, spending myself in battle against ghosts I had invented to justify my fears, for fear was there first. And when I found that place, my inner self threw away its crutches. More than that—it could fly!

"How can I tell you what it meant to me to leave that place? To walk away from it was to buckle on the braces, pick up the crutches again, to feel my new wings moult and fall away.

291

"I went there more and more. Once I took my typewriter and worked there, and that was *The Traveling Crag*. Cris never knew how offended I was, how invaded, to find that he had divined the existence of that place through the story. That was why I turned out that other abortion, out of stubbornness—a desire to prove to Cris and to myself that my writing came from me and not from the magic of that place. I know better now. I don't know what another writer would do here. Better than anything he could conceivably do anywhere else. But it wouldn't be the *Crag* or *Fire,* because they could only have been mine."

Cris asked, "Would you let another writer work here?"

"I'd love it! Do you mean to ask if I want to monopolize this place, and the wonders it works? Of course not. One or another fear or combinations of fear are at the base of any monopoly, whether it's in industry, or in politics, or in the area of religious thought. And there's no fear here."

"There should be some sort of a—a shrine here," murmured Naome.

"There is. There will be, as long as I can keep the amulet. I found it, you see. It was lying right out in the sun. I took it and brought it here. The birds wouldn't forgive me for a while, but I've made them happy here since. And here it is and here it will stay, and there's your shrine."

Fear walked in then. It closed gently on Cris's heart, and he turned to look at Tillie. Her eyes were closed. She was listening.

A hell of an agent I turned out to be, he thought. How much I was willing to do for Weiss, how much for all the world through his work! By himself he found himself, the greatest of human achievements. And I have done the one thing that will take that away from

292

him and from us all, leaving only the dwindling memory of this life without fear—and two great short stories.

He looked at Tillie again. His gaze caught hers, and she rose. Her features were rigidly controlled, but through his mounting fear Cris could recognize the thing she was fighting. She surely understood what was about to happen to Weiss and to the world if she succeeded. Her understanding versus her . . . orders, was it?

Cris had sat in that incredible aura, listening to the joyous expression of Sig Weiss's delivery from fear, and he had thought of killing. Now, he realized that part of her already thought as he did, and perhaps . . . perhaps . . .

"Sig, can we look around outside?" Cris had stepped over to Tillie almost before he knew he wanted to.

"You own the place," said Weiss cheerfully. "Naome and I'll stir up some food. You've had a nice leisurely trip. I wonder if you realize that Naome spent fourteen hours on a typewriter before she took that long hop? *Fire of Heaven*'s well launched now, thanks to her. Anyway, she deserves food."

"And a golden crown, which I shall include in the next pay envelope. Thank you, Naome. You're out of your mind."

"Thank you," she twinkled.

Cris led Tillie out, and they walked rapidly away from the house. "Not too far," she cautioned. "Let's stay where we can think. We're in a magic circle, you know, and outside we'll be afraid of each other, and of ourselves and of all our ghosts."

He asked her, "What are you going to do?"

"I shouldn't have got you into this. I should have come by myself."

"I'd have stopped you then. Don't you see? Sig would

have told me. Even with whatever help you have, you couldn't have succeeded in getting the weapon on the first try. He's too alert, too alive, far too jealous of what the 'amulet' has given him. He'd have told me, and I'd have stopped you, to save him and his work. You made me an ally, and that prevented me."

"Cris, Cris, I didn't think that out!"

"I know you didn't. It was done for you. Who is it, Tillie? Who?"

"A ship," she whispered. "A space ship."

"You've seen it?"

"Oh, yes."

"Where is it?"

"Here."

"Here, in Turnville?"

She nodded.

"And it—they—communicate with you?"

"Yes."

He asked her again. "What are you going to do?"

"If I tell you I'll get the weapon, you'll kill me to save Weiss, and his work, and his birds, and his shrine, and all they can mean to the world. Won't you, Cris?"

"I will certainly try."

"And if I refuse to get it for them—"

"Would they kill you?"

"They could."

"If they did, could they then get the weapon?"

"I don't know. I don't think so. They've never forced me, Cris, never. They've always appealed to my reason. I think if they could control me or anyone else, they'd have done it. They'd have to find another human ally, and start the persuading process all over again. By which time Weiss and everyone else would be warned, and it would be much more difficult for them."

"Nothing's difficult for them," he said suddenly. "They can smash planets."

"Cris, we don't think as well as they do, but we don't think the way they do, either. And from what I can get, I'm sure that they're good—that they will do anything they can to spare this planet and the life on it. That seems to be one of the big reasons for their wanting to get that weapon away from here."

"And what of their other aims, then? Can we take all this away from humanity in favor of some cosmic civilization that we don't know and have never seen, which regards us as a dust-fleck in a minor galaxy? Let's face it, Tilly: they'll get it sooner or later. They're strong enough. But let's keep it while we can. A minute, a day of this aura is a minute or a day in which a human being can know what it's like to live without fear. Look at what it's done for Weiss; think what it can do for others. What are you going to do?"

"I— Kiss me, Cris."

His lips had just touched hers when there was a small giggle behind them. Cris whirled.

"Bless you, my children."

"Naome!"

"I didn't mean to bust anything up. I mean that." She skipped up to them. "You can go right back to it after I've finished interrupting. But I've just got to tell you. You know the fright Sig tried to throw into me when I got here last night? I'm getting even. I found his amulet. I really did. It was stuck to the underside of a shelf in the linen closet. You'd have to be my size to see it. I swiped it."

Tillie's breath hissed in. "Where is it? What did you do with it?"

"Oh, don't worry, it's safe enough. I hid it good, this time. Now we'll make him wonder where it is."

"Where is it?" asked Cris.

"Promise not to tell him?"

"Of course."

"Well, it's smack in the innards of one of his pet new possessions. You haven't been in the west room—the ell he calls a library—have you?"

They shook their heads.

"Well, he's got himself a great big radio. I lifted the lid, see, and down inside among the tubes and condensers and all that macaroni are some wire hoops, sort of. This amulet, it's a tiny thing—maybe four inches long and as wide as my two thumbs. It's sort of—blurry around the edges. Anyway, I stuck it inside one set of those hoops. Cris—you're green! What's the matter?"

"Tillie—the coil—the RF coil! If he turns that set on—"

"Oh, dear God . . ." Tillie breathed.

"What's the matter with you two? I didn't do anything wrong, did I?"

They raced into the house, through the living room. "In here!" bellowed Cris. They pounded to the west room, getting into each other's way as they went in.

Sig Weiss was there, smiling. "Just in time. I want to show you the best damn transceiver in—"

"Don't! Don't touch it—"

"Oh, a little hamming won't hurt," said Sig.

He threw the switch.

There was a loud click and a shower of dust.

And silence.

Naome came all the way in, went like a sleepwalker to the radio and opened the lid. There was a hole in the grey crinkle-finished steel, roughly rectangular. Weiss looked at it curiously, touched it, looked up. There was a similar hole in the ceiling. He bent over the chassis. "Now how do you like that! A coil torn all to hell. Something came down through the roof—see?—and smashed right through my new transmitter."

"It didn't go down," said Cris hoarsely. "It went up."

Naome began to cry.

"What the hell's the matter with you people?" Sig demanded.

Cris suddenly clutched Tillie's arm. "The ship! The space ship! They wouldn't let it go off while they're here!"

"They did," said Tillie in a flat voice.

"Will somebody please tell me what gives here?" asked Sig plaintively.

Through a thick silence, Tillie said, "I'll tell it." She sank down on her knees, slowly sat on the rug. "Cris knows most of this," she said. "Don't stop to wonder if it's all true. It is." She told about the races, the wars, the weapons of greater and greater destructiveness and, finally, the ultimate weapon, and its strange effect on living tissue. "Eight months ago, the ship contacted me. There was a connection made with my nerve-endings. I don't understand it. It wasn't telepathy; they were artificial neural currents. They talked to me. They've been talking ever since."

"My amulet!" Sig suddenly cried. "Sit down," said Tillie flatly. He sat.

Cris said, "I thought you required some physical contact for them to communicate with you. But I've been with you while you were communicating, and you had no contact."

"I hadn't?" She began to unbutton her blouse at the throat. She stopped with the fourth button, and gently drew out a metal object shaped somewhat like a bulbous spearhead with a blunt point. It glittered strangely with a color not quite that of gold and not quite of polished brass. It seemed to be glazed with a thin layer of clear crystal.

"Oh-h-h," breathed Naome, in a revelatory tone.

Tillie smiled suddenly at her. "You minx. You always wondered why I never wore a V-neck. Come here, all of you. Down on the rug."

Mystified, they gathered around. "Put your hands on it." They did so, and stared at each other and at their hands, waiting like old maids over a Ouija board. "It hurts a tiny bit at first as the probes go in, but it passes quickly. Be very still."

A strange, not unpleasant prickling sensation came and went. There was a slight shock, another; more prickling.

Testing. Testing. Naome Cris Sig Tillie . . .

"Everybody get that?" asked Tillie calmly.

Naome squeaked. "It's like someone talking inside my sinuses!"

"It said our names," said Sig tautly. Cris nodded, fascinated.

The silent voice spoke: *Sig, your amulet is gone and you have lost nothing.*

Tillie, you have been faithful to your own.

Naome, you have been used, and you have done no wrong.

Cris, we have observed that it takes superhuman understanding to guide and direct work you cannot do yourself.

Reorient your thinking, all of you. You insist that what is lethal or cosmically important must be huge. You insist that anything which transcends a horror must be greater horror.

The amulet was indeed the ultimate weapon. Its effect is not to destroy, but to stop useless conflict. At this moment there is a chain reaction occurring throughout this planet's atmosphere affecting only one rare isotope of nitrogen. In times to come, your people will understand its radiochemistry; it is enough for you now to know that its most significant effect is to turn on the full analytical powers of the mind whenever fear is experi-

enced. Panic occurs when analysis is shut off. Embarrassment occurs when fear is not analyzed. Hereafter, no truck-driver will fear to use the word 'exquisite', no propagandist will create the semblance of truth by repeating falsehoods, no human group will be able to instill fears about any other human group which are not common to the respective individuals of the groups. There will be no fear-ridden movements of securities, and no lovers will be with each other and afraid to state their love. In large issues and in small ones, the greater the emergency the greater will be the stimulation of the analytical powers.

That is the meaning and purpose and constitution of the ultimate weapon. To you it is a gift. There are few races in cosmic history with a higher potential than yours, or with a more miserable expression of it. The gift is yours because of this phenomenon.

As for us, our quest is as stated to you. We were to seek out the weapon and bring it back with us. We gave it to you instead, by manipulation of your impulses, Naome, and yours, Sig, with the radio. Earth needs it more than we do.

But we have not failed. The radio-chemistry of the nitrogen-isotope reaction and its catalyses are now widely available to us. It will be simplicity itself for us to recreate the weapon, and the time it will take us is as nothing . . .

. . . For we are a race which commands the fluxes of time, and we can braid a distance about our fingers, and hold Alpha and Omega together in the palms of our hands.

"The probes are gone," said Tillie, after a long silence.

Reluctantly, they removed their hands from the communicator, and flexed them.

Cris said, "Tillie, where is the ship?"

299

She smiled. "Remember? 'You insist that what is cosmically important must be huge.'" She pointed. "That is the ship."

They stared at the bulbous arrowhead. It rose and drifted toward the door. It paused there, tilted toward them in an obvious salute, and then, like a light extinguished, it was gone.

Naome sprang to her feet. "Is it all true, about the propaganda, the panic, the—the lovers who can speak their minds?"

"All true," smiled Tillie.

Naome said, "Testing. Testing. Sig Weiss, I love you."

Sig picked her up and hugged her. "Come on, all of you. I want to talk clear down to the corners and have a beer with the old man. I want to tell him something I've never said before—that he's my neighbor."

Cris helped Tillie up. "I think he stocks some real V-type halters."

Outside, it was a greener world, and all over it the birds sang.

The Latest Science Fiction And Fantasy From Dell

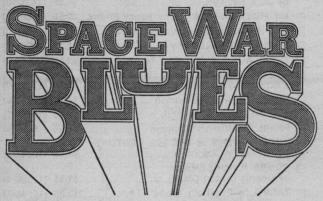

Dell Bestsellers

HOW TO
BUY A CAR

"A comprehensive, detailed, and down-to-earth guide to the art of buying a new or used car. The author exposes secret sales techniques, tricks, and games used by salespeople and tells how to avoid them...Extremely well-written."

—*Library Journal*

"The book is filled with dozens of hints on how to increase your negotiating edge and bargaining power."

—*Christian Science Monitor*

"How to avoid gimmicks, compute prices, inspect a car, negotiate, close a deal. Detailed and straightforward advice by an expert."

—*Denver Post*

HOW TO BUY A CAR

A Former Car Salesman Tells All

JAMES R. ROSS

ST. MARTIN'S PAPERBACKS

HOW TO BUY A CAR

Copyright © 1980, 1983, 1988, 1992 by James R. Ross.

All rights reserved. No part of this book may be used or reproduced in any manner whatsoever without written permission except in the case of brief quotations embodied in critical articles or reviews. For information address St. Martin's Press, 175 Fifth Avenue, New York, N.Y. 10010.

Library of Congress Catalog Card Number: 92-146

ISBN: 0-312-95151-5

Printed in the United States of America

First St. Martin's Press trade paperback edition published 1980
Second St. Martin's Press trade paperback edition published 1983
St. Martin's Paperbacks edition/April 1986
Third St. Martin's Press trade paperback edition/May 1988
Second St. Martin's Paperbacks edition/January 1989
Fourth St. Martin's Press trade paperback edition/June 1992
Third St. Martin's Paperbacks edition/July 1993

10 9 8 7 6 5 4 3 2 1

To Shirley for her encouragement and moral support;
and to Linda for her patience and understanding.

Contents

Introduction

EACH YEAR approximately 5 percent of the nation's populace (roughly 10 million people) do battle with new-car salesmen and eventually buy a new car. Another 8 percent (about 17 million) lock horns with used-car salesmen and eventually buy a used car. Less than 10 percent of these people know exactly what they are doing and how to do it. The remaining 90 percent lose approximately $4 billion on the negotiated purchase price of the cars they buy and waste another $500 to $700 million dollars for something they usually do not receive anyway—dealer preparation. And, as if this were not bad enough, the new-car buyer/owner must sometimes live with shoddy workmanship, poor quality control, and a too-busy dealership service department that just cannot seem to find the time to correctly fix his or her car.

The used-car buyer is at the mercy of someone. Perhaps he is only at the mercy of his own set of circumstances—he cannot afford to buy a new car, or when he buys a used car he is not quite sure what to check and how to negotiate the deal. Perhaps, too, he is at the mercy of the system—a system of apathy in which no one cares whether he gets a lemon or has mechanical problems with the car—a system designed to bleed every dollar possible from his purchase.

This book was written to take you inside dealership thinking and balance the gap between what the salesman knows and uses against you, and what you know about car buying based on your own past experiences—good or bad.

The very first thing you must realize, both as the reader and as the consumer, is that there are few inflexible rules to follow when learning to buy a car. As you read, learn, and practice, you will notice similarities among all dealers and salesmen, and upon those similarities you build your car shopping and buying foundation. But aside from the truisms of the business, there are myriad variables surrounding the situation. You may scour seven different dealers and talk to as many salesmen, each with his own approach and technique. And each with his own individual bag of tricks. Strategies you successfully employ on one salesman may not work on another. So, flexibility should be your key watchword.

Author's Note. The fact that I have used the word *salesman* rather than *salesperson* throughout the book is not intended as a slight to those women who sell cars. The word *salesman* is used simply as a matter of convenience, and as a way to make this a shorter, more compact book.

HOW TO BUY A CAR

1
Choosing the Car
and the Dealer

CHOOSING THE BASICS

CHOOSING MEANS selecting one from among several choices. The problems inherent in choosing are knowing what is best for you, and avoiding the myriad myths presented by salesmen anxious only for a sale. You must rely heavily on a salesman for product knowledge and advice, but you need not be completely at his mercy. Do not accept everything he says without question, for *you* are making the selection, and *you* must live with the consequences of a poor choice.

The process of choosing can be reduced to a single question: Does the function satisfy my needs? Whenever your process of selection reaches an impasse, ask this basic question: "Will it do what I need done?"

It is easy to become confused about exactly which car, with which engine in it, will be the right car for you. The best rule of thumb for the average family putting average mileage (12,000 miles per year) on its car is to avoid the smallest and the largest engines available in a given series or a given model. Make a selection from the engine(s) in the middle, provided there is a midsize offering. If you drive fewer than 12,000 miles per year, the smaller engine offers both economy and performance. If you drive more than 12,000 miles per year, the larger engine offers performance and durability.

Your personal driving habits and the use to which you put the car determine the size that is best for you. Explain to your salesman just how you plan to use the car, what economy and performance you expect, the miles you plan to drive each year, and how long you plan to keep the car. Individual needs are different and require individual consideration.

1

Knowing your intended use, the salesman can better counsel you according to his knowledge of the individual capabilities of the models within his product lineup. However, sometimes there is a catch. Salesmen are trained to sell what they have in stock, rather than factory order what you want or lose the sale to another dealer. Immediate sale equals immediate cash flow. When a salesman's advice seems contrary to what you ask for, test him. Does he have what you want in stock? Is he trying to sell you something only because it is all he has to offer? Will he factory order what you want? If he doesn't have what you want and is not willing to factory order it, his advice and motives are to be questioned.

Some people have preferences that will not change regardless of the arguments and logic used to dissuade them. Past experience, good or bad, will dictate their preference and choice of engine and transmission. You must avoid all myths and misconceptions based on hearsay or product misuse. Talk to people who own what you are considering and decide for yourself what is best for your needs. A car must be chosen and driven according to its limitations and capabilities.

Four Versus Six Versus Eight Cylinders. The sub-compact six-cylinder engines pose a four-cylinder problem: too little engine for too much car. There are three basic types of six-cylinder engines: in-line six, slant six, and V-6. Each has beneficial characteristics, but the major comparison consideration is the cubic-inch displacement (CID or C.C. or liter displacement) against the body weight of the vehicle and the rated horsepower, HP. Naturally, in the same weight class, the slightly larger size offers greater longevity and better performance. Your real question is, "Will this engine pull this car for as long as that engine will?" When you have only two engine choices in a given model, take the larger, provided the engines are within 50 CID of each other. If the difference in CID is greater than 50, you should choose the smaller, otherwise you may sacrifice economy for durability that is never used. The same principle applies to four-cylinder and eight-cylinder engines—check the CID against the weight.

Diesel Versus Gasoline Engine. The major considerations here are economic: initial investment, cost of fuel, cost of maintenance, cost of repairs, and depreciated market trade value. A deisel engine is not the ideal car for a weekend backyard mechanic. It requires special tools and special knowledge to repair, which means taking it to a garage or service department after warranty expiration. And there are not that many qualified diesel mechanics around, which means you pay more for labor. The higher initial investment must be weighed against the length of ownership; in other words, will you get extra time and miles for having paid more? The lower cost of fuel and scheduled maintenance items must be brought into perspective, as must diesel durability. The projected life of a diesel is about double the life of a same-size gasoline engine pulling the same load. If you plan to buy the car and drive it until it drops, consider the diesel for longevity, if for nothing else. If you plan to keep the car for 1 or 2 years, consider the gasoline engine.

You must be careful with diesel selection, for there two types: state-of-the-art, and gasoline engine conversions. State-of-the-art is more durable than its weaker, thin-skinned gasoline engine conversions. Finally, you are restricted in model selection, size, and style when considering the diesel. Not everyone makes a diesel.

Automatic Versus Standard Shift Transmission. You gain more economic benefits with the standard shift transmission because it gives a lower initial cost and greater fuel economy. However, some models offer only the automatic transmission, so if you favor the standard, your model selection will be restricted. The greatest advantage to the automatic is that anyone who can drive a car can drive one—no clutch, no shifting of gears. But anyone who has two functional hands and feet can learn the standard, and it only takes about a week. The cost of repairing or replacing an automatic is dramatically higher than the comparable cost for a standard shift. The trade value of the two after four years will not be that much different.

Front- Versus Rear-Wheel Drive. The benefits of pulling a car (front-wheel drive) and those of pushing a car (rear-wheel drive) are the subject of much debate. The front-wheel-drive advantages popularly sold are that front-wheel drive performs better in adverse weather (ice and snow), that there is no transmission hump running the length of the car, and that for service purposes everything is all together, right up front. The truth is that once traction breaks, front wheel drive is no better than rear wheel drive in snow and icy conditions. Front wheel drive is a more complicated drive train system and is more susceptible to malfunction than a rear wheel drive train. Front wheel drive bushings and couplings wear out faster than rear wheel drive component couplings, and are more expensive to repair or replace.

Carburetor Versus Fuel Injection. Fuel injection is more efficient and costs less to maintain and repair than a carburetor. On the same size engine (CID), choose fuel injection when you have such an option.

Other Options. Power-assisted steering is preferred primarily for ease of parking. However, most subcompacts park easily without power assist. The cost of power steering is high enough for you to consider doing without it. Test drive and park both types—with and without power assist—before you make a decision.

Rack-and-pinion steering is preferred to conventional ball-type steering for both durability and handling response. But it is not an optional choice that can be purchased, so you may have to buy a certain brand name to get it.

An overhead cam engine is preferred for longevity and performance. Like rack-and-pinion steering, it is not an option you can buy.

Be wary of component engine parts of dissimilar metals—aluminum heads with a cast-iron engine block or an aluminum engine block with cast-iron heads. Dissimilar metals contract and expand at different rates and tend to warp, crack, and malfunction. Aluminum wears out faster than cast-iron.

The Body Beautiful. Most cars are designed with a specific purpose and a specific consumer market in mind. Once the purpose has been established, the styling must be given consideration to make the car attractive enough to sell to a mass market. The major effort then becomes to design and develop a car that satisfies economy, comfort, function, and style. This is not always possible, and here is where many car shoppers and buyers meet with disappointment. For the most part, you must place your emphasis on function if you expect the greatest value per dollar invested. If the car is also pretty, all the better.

First you must select a category model: subcompact, compact, intermediate, full-size, luxury, import, station wagon, pickup, or van. Once you have selected the category, you should then compare all manufactured offerings within that category. To facilitate comparison, you must realize that there are characteristic similarities among competitive models. A compact is a compact, a full-size car is a full-size car, and so on. Your final decision should then shift emphasis from the manufacturer to function, price, individual dealership, and dealership location.

Even if you plan to keep your new car for only 2 years, project the needs of size and function over a 3-year period. You may not trade the car after 2 years as planned. If your family outgrows the car at the end of 2 years and you are stuck with the car for another year, you and your family will be uncomfortable during that third year.

Are you a one-car family? Is your new car going to be a once-a-week family-get-together car, or an everyday car? If your second car is large enough to hold the whole family, your new car can be smaller. If you are a one-car family and you need large-car roominess, buy a large car and pay extra for it; you cannot afford not to. Better a car a little too big than one too small.

How many miles per year is the car to be driven? One thousand miles per month is considered average, and for that amount of driving, any size will withstand the expected wear and tear, normal maintenance and repairs expected. The higher your mileage, the larger your car needs to be for durability and comfort.

What type of driving will be putting most of the miles on the car? Stop-and-go city driving is rougher than rigid, over-the-road driving. Even if you must sacrifice fuel economy, get the car that will withstand the rougher driving conditions. Less frequent repairs compensate for fuel economy loss.

BUYING A CAR DURING A FUEL SHORTAGE

Regardless of the exact model specification (two-door or four-door) and size best suited to your needs, fuel economy will have an effect on your final decision.

In 1973, an alleged fuel shortage sent many people to the showrooms in search of economy—anything that promised higher gas mileage and fuel savings was bought and a lot of mistakes were made. In 1974, many who impulsively bought economy cars for top dollar (no discount) traded them in on larger cars because the small car did not fit their needs and usage. Any fuel economy realized throughout the year was lost—on the initial purchase by paying full sticker price, and at trade-in time by depreciation. In 1979, another fuel shortage occurred and, again, people panicked, bought economy cars, and were soon sorry for their decision.

To be on the safe side, go back to function and usage and pick the car best suited to you in terms of size, horsepower, and special features.

Profile your "ideal" car against your first choice of economy car—price against price, feature against feature, and MPG against MPG (Miles Per Gallon). (Note: Price is the negotiated purchase price and presumes that very little discount, if any, will be found during periods of supply and demand selling.) Many midsize and full-size cars have standard equipment, such as power steering, power brakes, phonics, and radial tires, which sometimes comes as optional equipment on compacts and for which you pay extra. These costs must be considered before you can accurately analyze economy.

Each car must be compared according to its average rated MPG and according to your estimated fuel costs for 1 year. A car's average MPG is normally found on an Environmental Protection Agency (EPA) sticker found on the car itself or in a full-profile EPA booklet available at the dealership or by writing: Fuel Economy, Consumer Information Center, Pueblo, Colorado 81009. You can compute your annual fuel cost by dividing the estimated EPA rated MPG into the number of miles you expect to drive each year to get the number of gallons needed. Then multiply the quantity (gallons) times the cost per gallon. Now consider:

1. Does the cost difference justify buying a car that may not fit your needs and functional use?

2. Would you normally buy an economy car or has an alleged fuel shortage or illusion of economic crisis influenced your purchase decision?

3. Which car will perform best for you? Which will better fit your family needs and lifestyle? Which will last longest when put to your planned use?

SPECIAL CATEGORIES

Luxury Automobiles. Luxury does not always mean quality. Any luxury car, domestic or import, can have as many bugs and problems as any lower-priced car. A luxury car is built by human hands—sometimes the same hands that put together the cheaper compacts—and, in essence, has more component parts to go bad. This bothers nobody, rich or poor, as long as the car is under warranty. It is after-warranty service that will break your pocketbook if you bought the car on a shoestring. There is little mercy for the luxury car owner who is paying for service and maintenance, parts and labor. It is assumed that if you could afford the car initially, you can now afford the upkeep. Repair parts are more expensive, even though they are compatible with parts costing half as much for non-luxury cars. Tune-ups, oil changes, filters, and other maintenance items also cost more. Before you sign on the dotted line, think of the consequences you may face after the warranty expiration.

Station Wagons and Utility Vehicles. The prime consideration in choosing a station wagon or utility vehicle is function. Will it do the job that you need done? The caution to be observed is that too much power is all right, and not enough is dangerous. If the vehicle you need must haul a ton, it is all right to buy one that can haul a ton and a half; it is a waste of money to buy one designed to haul a half-ton. Pay the extra and buy the capacity you really need.

Pickups and vans at one time were easy to buy. Now you need a slide rule and a degree in engineering. Needless to say, it requires a highly skilled and knowledgeable salesman to help you decide which vehicle is best suited to your needs. Even then, you should obtain multiple opinions from several dealers to be certain the advice is the best to be found.

When considering station wagons, it is easy to get carried away with styles, colors, and amenities and end up with a wagon that does not satisfy function. Making the right choice takes a little willpower and forethought. If sacrifices must be made, always sacrifice the gingerbread items; never sacrifice function.

Imports. Import manufacturers were once the nemesis of American automakers. Economy imports now are not generally good for more than 75,000 miles of use, but then, neither are their domestic subcompact counterparts. What really sets the two apart is the cost of parts and the availability of labor for necessary repairs and maintenance. Many excellent domestic mechanics either do not want to work on imports or lack the knowledge to do so. Some import parts cost double what the comparable domestic parts cost.

Before you buy an import, pick a random service item—say, a brake job—and compare the import and domestic by calling the service departments of each respective dealer. Next, call the parts departments and compare the cost on a random part—say, a master brake cylinder. If you are prepared to live with the higher costs and you really like the import, buy it. But first consider the most common complaints of import owners.

The quality of workmanship is low, and purchase prices have skyrocketed. Critical parts are sometimes not available, and parts cost too much. The metric parts require metric tools, and self-service is often impossible because of the car's design. Trade values are low because nobody but an import dealer wants the used import on his lot; if you want a higher trade allowance you must trade your import for another import.

Brand Name Selection. People buy because other people buy. Brand-name ownership seems to run in and to affect families, coworkers, and neighbors. It is interesting to note that when one family on a given block buys a car, two or three other families on the same block will buy cars within thirty days of the first family's purchase (group contagion). Remember this when you are tempted to rush out and buy and do not know why. Did someone you know just buy a new car?

There is nothing wrong with buying under those circumstances, provided you can afford it. Never buy a car that will squeeze your budget just because someone close to you just bought. Before you take the plunge, stop and think: "Can I afford it? Do I really want it? Do I want the same type car he just bought? Do I really need it? Am I being influenced?"

The real problem with brand-name selection is that a brand name is only that: a brand name. For the most part, you will find similar service, performance, and durability in all brands. If you seriously doubt this, consider that Brand A, Brand B, and Brand C buy and sell component parts from each other. You cannot say that Brand A is better than Brand B if Brand A buys critical parts from Brand B, and vice versa. Consider, too, the industry's personnel turnover. Certain key personnel responsible for the last car that made you so happy may no longer work for the manufacturer. In fact, they may now work for the enemy who is building the car you hesitate to buy.

It is best to approach car selection with an open mind. Forget the name on the fender and let the car speak for itself.

CHOOSING A DEALER

From whom should you buy, a large dealer or a small dealer? If both offer about the same price for the same merchandise, which will take better care of you on after-sale warranty work?

Let's define small and large. A small dealer is not to be confused with a small-town dealer. Most small towns have small dealers and, in some towns, only one dealer of each particular brand name. Here, too, are found multiple-line dealers, two or three dealers who carry most of the major brand names among them. Negotiations are more difficult in a small-town atmosphere because of the element of monopoly. If it is the only movie in town, you go to it; if someone is the only dealer in town who carries the brand name you want to buy, you buy from him—at his price and on his terms.

The two major negotiating tools that may be used against the small-town dealer are time ("I'll wait until next year to buy") and competition ("If you won't give me a better deal, I'll buy Brand B"). It is difficult to shop Brand A against Brand A if the next A dealer is 60 miles away. So you must outwait the small-town dealer on price or threaten to buy Brand B.

The small dealer, by virtue of his size, has a smaller inventory from which to choose, a smaller showroom, fewer salesmen, a smaller service department, fewer mechanics, and, not surprisingly, a lower volume of business than the large dealer.

Small almost always wants to be big. While there are exceptions to the norm, most small dealers want to grow and expand their facilities. They want to increase their sales volume and someday become number one. This is accomplished by developing a clientele of happy, spread-the-good-word, repeat-business customers. Small dealers seem to appreciate your business more than larger dealers; they have not yet acquired the aloofness that often follows success and the status of being the biggest around. They may do more little favors for you than the larger dealer would under the same circumstances. But there is an opposing argument. If a dealer is small and has been small for a good number of years, perhaps there is a reason. It is possible that the small dealer has poor service, sloppy sales-men, and a care-less attitude.

However, large does not always mean better, or even adequate. The large dealer may seem better able to give you the service you need when you need it, but this is not always true. A frequent consumer complaint is that most dealers, especially large dealers, sell more cars than they can possibly service. This means that the large dealer, with a larger sales volume, could be less able to properly service every car sold.

So how do you decide? It is literally impossible to judge quality by size. Choosing a dealer usually boils down to price and reputation, which in-cludes the reputation of the service department.

There is only one way to take the guesswork out of choosing a dealer: Talk to people who have bought from each respective dealer. Most dealers place a bumper sticker or logo label on each car they sell. When you see a car parked somewhere boasting the sticker of one of the dealers you are considering, take a few minutes to meet the owner to ask him a few questions. Do not be bashful about approaching a stranger to ask him what he thinks about his car, and about the dealer from whom he bought.

Do not restrict your investigations to one or two people, and give the small dealer the same consideration you give the large dealer—talk to the same number of people who bought from the large as bought from the small.

Do not ask a car salesman for the names of people who have bought from him. If he does give you a few names they will be those people he is 100 percent certain are happy with him, the dealership, and the car.

Check with the Better Business Bureau in your area. They can tell you much about the dealer, including the number of complaints filed against him. If there is a Consumer Protection Agency in your area, contact it. Even this does not ensure a problem-free purchase. (More on this in chapter 14, "External Recourse.")

The Automobile Broker. An automobile broker will factory order the domestic car of your choice for local delivery through the respective brand-name dealership. The automobile broker's major sales pitch is "dollars saved" (discount). You are told that he has no salesmen to pay and no facilities to maintain, and that he can sell you a new car at a little over dealer cost. Not quite so.

Working as a franchisee, the automobile broker places your order through a buying company (franchisor) who receives a fee per unit ordered. The local dealer who delivers your car receives a courtesy delivery fee of $100 to $125. The automobile broker himself will write as much profit as possible and call it a brokerage fee, a get-ready charge, a buying fee, or any combination of the three. The illusion of savings is simply that—an illusion. There are just too many fingers in the pot.

Buying through an automobile broker has intrinsic disadvantages: You cannot work a trade—you must dispose of your old car on your own; and after-the-purchase service leaves you at the mercy of a dealer who did not make a decent profit on the deal. All disadvantages of factory ordering apply to the automobile broker, for he does not carry an inventory. Inspection of merchandise is severely restricted. Your recourse is limited: the dealer made no representations—he only made the delivery—and the broker only placed an order at your request. That leaves the factory and an elusive factory representative.

2

Decision Making

WHY IS IT SO HARD?

THE HARDEST DECISION to make is the initial one to go out and buy the car. Why, then, do so many people find it so difficult to make the simple decisions about color, style, and options on the car they know they are going to buy? Several reasons seem to be true.

Pride and ego are directly involved. It is important to make the right decision in order to avoid the possibility of criticism. How will it look and how will you feel when you are showing your new car around and someone says, "Why didn't you get body side molding?" Or, "Oh, you got the four-door model; I would have bought the two-door." None of your decisions are any of their business, but some people are insensitive, and whether they mean it or not, they destroy your new-car enthusiasm. There also exists a bit of jealousy—you have a new car and they do not. To these people you need only say, "I bought this car exactly the way I wanted it; nothing more, nothing less," and let it go at that.

Fear of making the wrong decision and subsequently suffering a loss can make it difficult to reach final decisions. It is bad enough that your ego must suffer, but when you err, your pocketbook suffers as well. Any one of a dozen decisions made in error can cost you several hundred dollars. Choose a car with which you are not completely happy and you will trade it sooner than originally planned. Purchase equipment that you seldom use and you will have wasted dollars. Underload or overload the car with optional equipment and you may lose on trade value. The fear of loss can definitely hinder decision making.

If you are making an in-depth analysis of every car on the market, you will eventually become thoroughly confused about what you have seen and read, what you want and do not want, and what you should buy or should not buy. Confusion is dangerous, for it inevitably leads to impulse buying. The sad consequence is that all the research and thought put into your project means nothing if you are too confused to make final decisions. You then buy the car that, for the moment, seems right for you (impulse). It is therefore best to reduce everything to writing. Trust not to memory. Utilize a system.

DECISION MAKING SYSTEMS

Comparative Analysis. To compare anything to anything, you must use the same factors throughout. This requires a firm format if you are to expect reasonably valid results for the effort. Next, your results must be gauged. You may use whatever ranges you prefer, but assigning a number value from one to ten or from one to five seems to produce the most accurate results. Areas of critical importance are measured on a scale of one to ten, and those lesser areas on a scale of one to five. Those areas of major importance will then weigh more heavily in your final average; those of lesser importance will have less effect on the total tally.

Why is it necessary to analyze, check, observe, and nitpick so many small items and so many areas of concern regarding the dealership and the salesman? The major reason is that it slows you down and forces you to think before you leap. Most purchases are emotionally inspired; you do not necessarily use logic and common sense but rather you buy because of what you touch, see, and hear. Because admen, salesmen, and marketing executives know exactly how to inspire impulse purchases, you must force yourself to avoid the influences and to *slow down*. The table on the following page will help.

If the salesman approaches you promptly, engages in polite small talk, relaxes you, and is friendly, give him a 5. If he takes his time getting to you, shows little or no interest, and does not smile, give him a 1; if he is really bad, give him a zero. If he tries to find out just what you are looking for, what you like, and what you do not like, give him a 10. If he says, "Yeh, what are you looking for? Two-door sedan? Yep, I have a few; let's take a look at them," give him a 1 or a 2. And so on down the chart. The only two exceptions will be price and location. If the dealership is 3 miles from your home, subtract 3 from 10 and rate location as 7. If it is more than 10 miles, the rating is zero. To determine a rating for price, you must begin with an arbitrary benchmark figure. It is best

Quality/Feature	Rating	Dealer					
		A	B	C	D	E	F
Approach/small talk	1–5						
Dealer's ability to discover your needs and preferences	1–10						
Presentation of product/demo ride	1–10						
Price/trade allowance	1–10						
Personality/warmth of salesman	1–5						
Total impression of salesman	1–5						
Salesman's ability to communicate	1–5						
Salesman's total product knowledge	1–5						
Dealer reputation	1–10						
Service department reputation	1–10						
Location of dealership	1–10						
Dealer's ability to meet special personal requirements	1–10						
Totals							

to use the gross profit as the benchmark (gross profit is detailed in chapter 5, ''Dealer Cost''). Using a gross profit of $300, subtract 1 point from the high of 10 for each $10 over a $300 gross deal. If a dealer offers you a $330 gross deal, the rating for that deal is 7. If he offers you a $250 gross deal, the rating is 15. This puts price in perspective with all other considerations.

The same principle can be used for model selection, as follows.

Quality/Feature	Rating	Model							
		A	B	C	D	E	F	G	H
Function match to needs	1–10								
Fuel economy (EPA estimate)	1–10								
General reputation of car	1–5								
Performance/engine	1–5								
Handling/steering	1–5								
Total comfort	1–5								
Total roominess	1–5								
Styling/appearance	1–5								
Flaws/blemishes (deductions)	1–10								
Totals									

If the functional match of the car to your personal needs rates extremely high in your opinion, give it a 10. For fuel economy, pick an arbitrary figure, say 30 MPG, and add or subtract 1 point on a base value of 10 for each 1 MPG of variance. Thirty-two MPG would rate as 12; 28 MPG would rate as 8.

If you choose to use comparative analysis to reach a final decision, do not set the results aside just because they are not the results you wanted to see. You might as well save your time and not use the system if you do not abide by the final numbers.

The Balance Sheet. Salesmen use an old technique called the balance sheet to help their customers reach a decision when an impasse occurs. Here is how it works: Form two columns by drawing a line down the middle of a blank sheet of paper. At the top of one column write the word *Advantages*, and top the other column with *Disadvantages*. Then list all the advantages and disadvantages of the decision you are making under the appropriate heading. No matter how trivial or insignificant you may think an item is, list it. On another sheet of paper, make two columns with the headings *Will Use Often* and *Will Not Use Often*. Then list all options under the appropriate headings. This can be done before you begin to shop or when you sit down with a salesman. The balance sheets represent a running record of what your research has uncovered and also can be laid side by side for you to accept or reject options all at the same time. Great for avoiding confusion.

Special problem: How to Get Two or More People to Agree on a Car. Too many couples discover, after the purchase has been made, that what they bought was not really what either of them wanted. This is especially true with impulse purchases, but it applies to the supposedly well-thought-out purchase as well. You will avoid confusion and disappointment if you use a simple system called parallels prior to shopping for your next car.

To best utilize parallels, both parties must begin by keeping their wishes secret. Neither one can know the other's thinking until parallels are finally drawn. This seems to discourage communication, but if you discuss optional preferences, one side may dominate the decisions or one side may yield to the other and not express true feelings. When both can express their desires, in writing, without the intimidation of the other, an accurate picture can be drawn that leads to a final decision both can live with.

You must both follow a preset guideline of exactly what you are deciding. You can choose your color preference, but both will have to choose a color; you can pick the type interior you prefer, but both will need to pick an interior. Everything is directed toward free-will selection, but both must be making selections in the same categories for the system to work. It is therefore necessary to work from two separate lists with all options available on a given model on each list.

You now each have a list and can begin to make your selections in silence. When both lists have been completed, sit down and talk for the first time since you began. This is when you draw parallels. Compare the lists and compose a third list of all options that match on both lists. This third list describes the car with which you will both be happy.

What about items chosen that do not match up on both lists? Compromise. If you can afford everything you both want and also the options you want individually, load the car up, provided a conflict does not exist with equipment that must be one way or the other. It is impossible to have both power brakes and standard (nonpower) brakes on the same car. When you must bring the cost of the car down to an affordable level, delete first those options only one of you wants.

If parallels seems too much bother, consider the consequences: excessive shopping, arguments in front of salesmen, and constant confusion.

RESEARCH GUIDELINE

Research is very important to the decision-making process. The following sources provide information from which you can draw to make final decisions.

1. Literature from the dealer. Handouts and product information pamphlets.
2. Brief, on-the-lot inspection of merchandise before, during, or after business hours to physically acquaint you with models you may like.
3. Newspaper articles regarding particular models you like.
4. Automobile magazines—full profile information or bits and pieces.
5. Conversation with current owners of models you like, friends, neighbors, relatives, various salesmen, and other individuals within the auto industry.
6. Private garage mechanics who service most makes and models. Do not solicit generalities, but ask about a specific model or two.
7. Consumer guides, available in your local library.

If you want technical, in-depth information about a particular automobile, most dealers have product information books that contain everything you could possibly want to know about their model lineup:

specifications of the models, complete with pictures of component parts hidden from the eye—suspension, drive train, weights and measurements, gear ratios, horsepowers and torques.

When you are satisfied that you have seen enough, read enough, looked enough, and tried enough, you are ready to buy the end result of your research. How deeply you investigate and for how long are personal decisions only you can make. There are no guidelines for that.

3
Shopping

WHEN TO SHOP AND BUY

THERE IS NO BEST TIME to buy a car, but there *are* times that are better and easier than others. The consumer finds the greatest negotiating advantage at any time that business is slow. Most dealers will sacrifice more of their gross profit and allow more on trade value when their product is not selling just to do some business and keep the doors open—provided, of course, the consumer asks for the fantastic deal. Even when business is slow, a dealer will still try to make a full gross profit on the deal. When business is slow, the dealer sells fewer units and must make more money per unit just to cover fixed expenses that do not decrease in dollar amount during sales slumps. Although the dealer is more inclined to sell than you are to buy during a slump, you cannot expect a fantastic deal just for walking onto his showroom floor. It will take a little work on your part—but it will be easier.

An indicator of slow sales is the frequency with which a particular dealership runs promotional advertisements. If every day is bargain basement, deal-of-the-century day, the dealer is probably suffering for lack of business.

Your best source of information about the business climate of a particular dealership is the service department personnel. Service personnel are not trained—as the salesman is—to cover up or mislead you about how things are in general and about the dealer's sales volume. As the opportunity offers itself, saunter up to a mechanic and ask him how things are going. "How is the sales department doing? Are they selling a lot of cars?" You may acquire only a tidbit of information, but it all helps.

17

PERIODS

There are two major reasons for the automobile business to slow down: crisis periods and seasonal periods.

The Crisis Period. This is usually economic in nature, and either local or national in scope. When the general economy slumps, people tighten the belt and spend less, and those items they do buy are primarily the necessities of life. So when things are slow, take advantage of it—don't tighten your belt; spend and save.

The Seasonal Period. At certain times of the year, salesmen put forth less effort to sell to a customer and use "the fault of the season" as their excuse. All salesmen experience the seasonal slump at some time during the course of a sales year. The fact that salesmen psyche themselves out like this is a reality, and it works to your definite advantage. The following periods will give you an edge.

1. Around Christmas. This period usually runs from 2 weeks before Christmas to about 3 weeks after. During this period, a salesman's sales enthusiasm slackens as boredom sets in, and he literally becomes rusty standing around waiting for the clock to strike quitting time. To best utilize this period, you must *never* refer to the car as a Christmas present, and you must always convince the salesman that it is not that important that you buy before Christmas Eve. If the salesman suspects the car is a gift, he will hold out for a higher price.

2. Feburary. This is a small slump and most salesmen are waiting for the more active spring market to hit. Your edge is between February and spring.

3. Summer. A slight edge to be found now. It is midyear, between models, and sales are slow. Salesmen think people will be spending their money on vacations and pleasure. Play coy and act as if you can wait for the new cars to hit the market. After all, you would rather take a vacation.

4. Fall. Here there are three periods of significance: before, during, and after new-model introduction (NMI). Before NMI, the salesmen have been driven up a wall by end-of-the-year bargain hunters. The salesmen's resistance has pretty well been worn down, but they can get edgy. During NMI, salesmen become aloof—new product, excitement and enthusiasm, high profits to be made—and hold out for

top dollar on everything. About 1 month after NMI, negotiations begin to loosen up—Christmas is coming.

OTHER PERIODS

Monthly. The better times of the month are at the beginning and at the end. Most dealers project the number of units they want to sell for a given month at the beginning of that month. If they fall short of their goal toward the end of the month, they will sacrifice profit to meet their goal. Also, salesmen on a volume bonus structure will be pushing their sales managers harder to help them meet their quota. All dealers like to kick off the month well—so they write better deals during the first few selling days to get as many sales on the board as possible.

Weekly. The better times of the week follow the same pattern as those of the month—kick off well on Monday and wrap up well on Saturday. Some dealers offer their salesmen a bonus called a "Spiff" for Saturday volume. If a spiff is on, your salesman will eagerly try to see that you get the car you want at the price you want to pay. He wants volume, not profit.

Daily. You could be either too early or too late. The better time of day is from three in the afternoon onward, but not before two hours before dealership closing time. Too early in the day salesmen feel there is still plenty of time to sell someone else for more money. Past two hours before closing time and you will not have the time to employ all your strategies. When the salesman senses you are a tough sale, he will give up the effort of negotiating and appeasing just so he can go home.

Factory Strike. Do not expect to find a bargain during a factory strike. Dealers must make as much profit on their sales as possible, for they have no way of knowing when they will be able to replenish their dwindling inventories.

SHOPPING BY PHONE

A salesman is reluctant to give information by phone because he cannot show you his product, have you sign a contract, or take your money over the telephone. He is also reluctant because as soon as you have the information you need, you no longer need him. If he does not have exactly what you want, there is no reason for you to visit him and give him a chance to sell to you.

If you shop by phone, expect excuses: "I'm very busy right now; give me your name and phone number and I'll call you back in 5 minutes." Or, "I don't have my price sheet with me right now; can I have your name . . ." Be prepared to handle it in your own way. You can simply tell the salesman, that you have an unlisted number that you only give to friends and relatives. If he wants your name, give him one—real or fictitious. Stress the fact that you are indeed in the market for a car, but that you do not plan to waste time and fuel driving to his lot if he does not have what you want or if the price is too high.

To obtain information you must convince the salesman that you already have the information and are only confirming it. Make a statement and follow it with a question to get the information you want.

For example, you want a green two-door sedan. Call and say, "I saw a green two-door sedan on your lot last week and I'm interested in that car. Do you still have it or has it been sold?"

He says, "It's not here now; must have been sold."

"I heard your new pickups are selling for $16,000. Is that true?"

You have an '86 you wish to trade. "I just wrecked my '86, and my insurance company only wants to give me X dollars for it as replacement value. Is that all the car is worth?" If he answers, pause, then ask, "Is that wholesale or retail value?"

You want to buy an '86. "I just wrecked my '86, and my insurance company told me to find a replacement. Do you have something similar? What do you have?"

Many salesmen will still refuse to give information regardless of your tactics, however, and will insist that you drop by for answers.

INFLUENCES ON SHOPPING

Third Party. Third-party influence comes in several assorted shapes and sizes, among which you may find your own children. The predominant third-party influence is affectionately nicknamed "the attorney."

The attorney is a friend, a neighbor, a relative who acts as your car shopping and buying spokesman. According to him, he has all of the answers, knows all about the automobile industry, is sharper than any salesman (or service manager) ever born, and can get you the deal of the century. Naturally, if you get a lousy deal or a lousy car, it will not be his fault, and no money will come from his pocket bailing you out.

You will find, on occasion, a middle-of-the-road attorney who has good intentions but just does not know enough to give excellent advice. What is really important to you is to be able to recognize the nature of the advice, how it is presented, and the individual's motives for helping you.

Bird-Dog. A bird-dog is someone who works with a salesman for a fee (a cut or a kickback) for whatever business he may bring or refer to him. Naturally, under this arrangement, the bird-dog's advice will be biased, for he has a financial interest in the matter, and you do have to buy for him to collect a dime. When you start looking for a car, treat friendly advice lightly, especially if the friend attempts to steer you toward a certain salesman. Definitely suspect his motives if he insists on personally introducing you to the salesman.

There are mechanics who will give bad advice to friends, and even relatives, because a bird-dog fee is involved. Their only concern is money in their pocket. The irony is that if the customer buys the car on the advice of his friendly mechanic and the car develops problems the mechanic should have seen originally, the customer will give him the repair work. Sweet, blind faith.

Children. Children should be seen and not heard. In fact, children should not be taken with you as you shop and negotiate. Salesmen are trained to love and win over to their side the easily influenced minds of your little angels. When the salesman succeeds at this he has a better-than-average chance of selling mom and dad, simply because of the tremendous influence children have on their parents.

Parental. When son or daughter decides to take that first big step toward independence and buy a car, problems inevitably develop. Mom and dad become overprotective, overcautious, and overbearing and want to run the show. However, most young adults know more than their parents about the merchandise and really need only financing and/or contract advice and help. Good advice to parents is this.

1. If your child likes the car, wants the car, and can afford the car, and the car checks out on the inspection and demo ride, let him have the car. It might not be the car you would buy, but it is the car he wants.
2. Do not underestimate the intelligence of your child when it comes to such worldly matters as the purchase of an automobile.
3. If you don't know what you are talking about, keep your mouth shut. You can ask questions, but you need not display your vast

knowledge. Your child knows you are smart—and the salesman couldn't care less.

4. Be an observer, and give advice only when it is solicited, or when you see something obviously amiss and detrimental that your child overlooked.

5. If your child is old enough to pay, he is old enough to play. Do not assume that just because you are cosigning for the loan that you will make all final decisions. You are only cosigning; your child must make all payments. Why should he work and pay for a car that he does not like?

ADVERTISING

Advertising, as such, is designed to draw floor traffic to the showroom where a friendly salesman can transform dreams into reality. Unfortunately, there are tricks in advertising that do more than just get you to come in and look around. Even with strict advertising codes and restrictions, the first thing a would-be offender will do is put all his brainstorm on paper and then clean it up just enough to fall within the letter of the law. Here are some of the pitfalls you should beware of.

1. *Bait and Switch Advertisement.* Bait and switch cannot be recognized by reading the ad. It must be tracked down by a personal visit to determine whether the product exists, and whether it can be bought as advertised. To bait and switch is to run a fantastic bargain-day ad with broad customer appeal. Then, when you arrive at the dealership, you are told, "You didn't respond fast enough to the ad." With bait and switch you are never "fast enough." The plan is to switch you to another car just as nice as the one advertised and, oddly enough, the only choice available. Unfortunately this one cannot be sold for the same low, low price as the one advertised. You are told, "Why not look at it while you are here? No sense making the trip in for nothing." So you look, and maybe you buy.

2. *Leader Advertisement.* A leader ad leads you into the showroom because the price is right and the model is basically what you have been thinking of buying. Unlike the bait and switch model, the car exists and can be bought at the advertised price, but it is usually a stripped-down model. If there is an equipment list in the ad, it will usually consist of standard equipment items; it looks impressive, but you could find that equipment anywhere on the same model series. So you find out that if you want more for your money you must look

at something that will cost you more. Although this is not true bait and switch, caution is advisable to avoid an impulse purchase.

3. *Monthly Payment Advertisement.* This is a direct appeal to those on a very tight budget. Suppose the best monthly payment you have been able to find on the car you want is $300 and you can afford only something around $250 a month. You would fall squarely off your rocking chair if you saw the very car you wanted advertised at a monthly payment of $200, or $50 a month less than the best deal you found thus far, and you shopped them all. Before you jump, read the fine print. A monthly payment depends upon three primary elements: the amount financed, which is derived from the purchase price less your down payment or trade-in equity; the interest rate; and the duration of the loan. If the purchase price is about the same as you found when you shopped, then the monthly payment has been made to appear lower by an increased down payment, a decreased interest rate, an increased duration of loan life, or a combination of the above. If this dealer can do it, any dealer can.

4. *Eye Catchers.* When reading advertising copy and/or literature on cars for sale, scratch out all descriptive adjectives. All words such as super, fantastic, good deal, great buy, beautiful, fully reconditioned, and so on should be removed from the ad before you decide to look at the car. These are superfluous, fill-in eye-catchers and have nothing to do with the actual quality or equipment, or the final price you will pay. The end result of this type of advertising is that you are attracted to good ad copy, rather than to the basic features of the car itself. Do not allow yourself to be influenced. Whenever you suspect advertising fraud or misreresentation, report it to the National Advertising Review Board. (See chapter 14, "External Recourse.")

PROMOTIONALS

General. A promotion (promo) is run for one reason and one reason only—to develop floor traffic. A dealer may run a promo on five to ten cars, moderately equipped, with a special low, low price tag. The special sale price applies only to those few promo cars (limited quantity), is good only through Saturday (limited time), and is a once-in-a-lifetime offering (creates urgency to buy). The merchandise is not stripped down—it has some equipment in it—and the intention is not so much to switch the customer to another car as it is to just sell him something. The two motivating factors are price in dollars and cents, and the bargain stimulus. If these are the only two stimuli you have for going to the dealership, make them the only two conditions under which you will buy; the price must be right and it must be a valid bargain.

Limited Production. Be wary of a factory promo called New Edition, Limited Production. The styling is usually radically different from the factory's normal lineup, and "limited production" means that if it does not sell well it will be discontinued. Think twice about limited production models, for if they die on the vine, trade values die with them. You may have to keep the car until it has classic-car status before you can get a decent price for it.

Midyear Models. Watch the midyear releases. These cars will be around for a while, so you need not worry about their being discontinued. But you lose on depreciation. Even though it may be called a midyear release, in 3 or 4 years when you are ready to trade it, the car will have depreciated back to the beginning of the model year in which it was introduced. Also, since the car is a new release, discounts will be virtually nonexistent: "If you want my new car, you must pay my price for it." You might just as well wait until the next model introduction and buy at that time.

Carryovers. The biggest promo of the year begins about two months before the models come out. "This is the time to buy," you are told. "Fantastic savings are now possible as dealers clean out their showrooms, dealers are at the mercy of the public, and no reasonable offer will be refused"—thus are announced the end-of-the-year campaigns run by dealers coast to coast.

The myth is that you can save a bundle by waiting until the last days of the model year to buy your new car. The truth is that you could have written the same deal on the same car 6 months earlier. However, if a dealer is to sell the almost 1-year-old cars he has in stock, he must make them seem like bargains. He must appeal to natural, instinctive greed. At the end of the year he is not doing you any favors; you are doing him the favor by helping him clean out his inventory.

Until the official new-model introduction (NMI), the gross profit with which a dealer has to work remains unchanged throughout the year. At NMI, his models become last year's models, acquire the name "carryovers," and acquire an extra 5 percent gross profit. This 5 percent is a factory rebate to the dealer for all carryovers delivered to retail customers after the official NMI kickoff. Consider the significance of the numbers on a $20,000 car; the 5 percent rebate adds $1,000 to the available gross profit, which is $1,000 you can save by knowing it is there. Use it when negotiating on a carryover.

Demonstrators. At this time of the year the salesmen demonstrators and factory executive cars also surface to make an appeal for your dollar. The deal that can be worked on a demonstrator (demo) depends on the particular demo plan used by any given dealer, of which there are two basic forms: dealer-supplied demo and salesman-owned demo.

The tipoffs to demonstrators are the type of warranty offered and the wording of the contract placed before you. With rare exceptions, a full-term warranty offered on a salesman's demo means it is a dealer-supplied demo. If the contract to purchase states that "this is not an XYZ Dealer vehicle," it is then a salesman-owned demo, and the dealer will assume no liability whatsoever. With the dealer exempt from the contract, any recourse you need or want must come from the salesman—other than existing warranty coverage, if any.

When you deal on any demo or factory executive car, treat it as a used car as far as condition, inspection, pricing, value, and negotiations go. Dealer-supplied demos are restricted by the dealer cost percentage involved, but you do get a full factory warranty. On a salesman-owned demo, your final deal is restricted only by your ability to talk the salesman down on price. Treat a factory exec demo as you would a dealer-supplied demo, with the exception that there is an extra 5 percent with which to work (total 10 percent rebate to dealer).

When you decide to buy a dealer-supplied demo, be certain the contract to purchase states that you are to have full warranty coverage, beginning from the date of purchase and from the mileage on the car the day you take delivery.

When a dealer has no carryovers or demos in stock, you can negotiate a better deal on a brand-new car. It is no longer necessary for the dealer to create the illusion of a fantastic deal, so he can settle down and sell the new product at his normal discounts, and you can really begin to wheel and deal. With carryovers in stock, dealers go for higher profits and argue, "If you want a fantastic bargain, buy one of these carryovers. I cannot give too much discount on these brand new models." And everyone knows they can.

A few simple facts and rules will put you more in control of the situation. If you plan to win and save money, remember that:

1. The dealer must still make a profit on every car he sells.
2. He must make the carryovers seem like bargains, which mean showing you a $1,000 difference (spread) between last year's model and this year's model (same style and equipment).
3. Holding high gross profits on the new models helps the dealer clear out his old merchandise. Bargain until he comes down to your price.
4. You can work a deal on a brand-new model as good as the end-of-the-year bargains dealers supposedly give. Write your own deal.
5. Determine before you walk onto the showroom whether you are going to ask to see carryover models or brand-new models, for the salesman's course of action is determined by your initial request.
6. While negotiating, treat the car as if it were 6 months into the model year, rather than brand-new. If you pretend you are buying something 6 months old, it will show in your negotiating efforts.

Low-Mileage/As-is Cars. Be wary of the low-mileage car offered for sale with an as-is sticker on it. Chances are it is a repossessed car or a lemon, turned in under lemon laws now in effect in many states. Since the dealer could not or would not fix the car for the previous owner, he will not be able to fix it for the next owner (you?).

If the car is less than one year old and/or has less than 12,000 miles on it, don't buy it until you talk to the previous owner and obtain a written warranty from the dealership. Question the source of the car in no uncertain terms. Ask the salesperson the following questions: Why did the previous owner turn in the car? May I talk with the previous owner? Will you give me his/her phone number? You won't do it? Why not? Then question more directly: Was the car repossessed? Was the car turned in because it is a lemon? Did you buy the car at an auction? Did you buy the car from another dealer?

Regardless of the answers you get, if the car checks out and you really like it, insist that the dealership include the following statement on the purchase agreement: "This is not a repossession vehicle. This vehicle was not turned in as a lemon nor involved in any way with a lemon law. The source of this car was _____."

If the car develops serious problems in or out of warranty, first have the history of the car's ownership traced. Second, have the service records on the vehicle pulled from dealership records. Third, talk to the previous owner. All of this will likely require an attorney's services, but will be well worth the time and effort.

4
Stock Purchase?
Factory Order?
Dealer Trade?

STOCK PURCHASE

SHOULD YOU BUY YOUR CAR from stock or factory order it? To buy from stock is to buy from a dealer's inventory; the car is there and it is yours today if you want it. To factory order is to sit down and literally build the car you want on paper; you pick the color, the interior, and only those options you want.

Dealership upper management place special emphasis and pressure upon their salesmen to get customers to buy from stock instead of factory ordering because it puts immediate profit on the books.

The major advantage to buying from stock is that you know exactly what you are buying—you can see it, feel it, and inspect it. Problems with the car can be discovered during the demonstration ride, which is something you cannot do with a factory-order car. You can delay a stock purchase or switch to another car before firm commitments are made.

Stock purchase disadvantages begin with limitations of choice; the colors, interiors, and options are restricted to what your dealers have in stock. When all dealer inventories are low, for whatever reason, you must be content to take whatever is available and hope that it is close to what you want.

Buying from stock makes you extremely vulnerable to an impulse purchase. You may become charged up emotionally, get carried away, and simply say, "Okay, write it up." A salesman will offer you a today-only deal to help you decide to buy the car: "If you come back tomorrow, it will be too late. I will not be able to give you the same deal. My sales manager wants your business today and he will bend some to get it." Don't be misled; he *will* do it tomorrow.

FACTORY ORDER

The greatest advantage to factory ordering is that you need not take optional equipment you do not want. On a stock purchase, to get the color and interior you want, you must take the equipment on the car as well. It is this preference that costs you extra money, and in this area alone you could save $150 to $500 on a given deal by factory ordering your car. Also, a salesman cannot utilize "Today is the only day" strategy on you. If you are willing to wait 6 weeks for delivery, you are also willing to wait until he can once again give you the price he is offering as a today-only price.

A factory order gives you time to secure a buyer for your present car. Most dealers will go along with a trade-or-sell option on the purchase contract just to make a deal. Basically, the dealer gives you a guaranteed trade-in allowance deal and a contingency deal upon the same purchase contract, which guarantees a straight cash, no-trade discount. If you sell your car, you are guaranteed the no-trade discount. If you do not sell it, the dealer will take your car in trade at a guaranteed trade-in deal price. The trick is to know which set of figures means what. It is easy for the salesman to arrange and juggle figures to make it look like you are receiving both a high trade allowance and a high discount. You must be certain that you understand whether they are collective or separate and be certain that their relationship is spelled out in black and white. How much will the car cost you, cash out of pocket, if you have a trade; and how much will the car cost if you have no trade? The difference between the two cash differences will be your trade-in allowance.

The disadvantages to factory ordering begin with delays. If you place your order and the factory goes on strike, you must wait for strike settlement before you can expect your car to be built. Since a factory strike is not your dealer's fault, the dealer would, in all probability, not be required to refund your deposit.

You cannot drive a factory-order car before you make a commitment to buy. When it arrives from the factory it bears your name, and you must take it as is, good or bad, provided it has every piece of equipment on it as ordered and is the correct color with the correct interior, or you forfeit your deposit.

You may be taken off the market by a dealer who offers you the most fantastic deal you have ever seen. This tactic is the most subtle, most damaging, and most difficult to prove of any trick a dealer might pull on you. In essence, it is a low-ball tactic. The only difference is that the normal low-ball is verbal, whereas this one is presented in writing and approved by the dealership management. You will leave the dealership convinced that you just received the proverbial deal of the century. The more you have shopped, the easier it is to be victimized. Here is how it goes:

You have shopped several dealers and have consistently been offered a deal $250 higher than you want to spend. You enter Dealer B's showroom and the salesman finds out that you want to factory order a car, that you are a shopper, and that you plan to continue to shop until you get the deal you want. He writes the deal exactly the way you want it, goes through the routine of obtaining management approval, and draws a blank. Now the fun starts. He knows he cannot give you the deal you want, so he has two options: to let you leave and take the chance that you will return, or to take you off the market right now. To do the latter, he must give you the deal you want, and so he does. You then give him a healthy deposit and think that your shopping and waiting have paid off. You go home and begin the wait. Four to 5 months later you may still be waiting for your car to arrive.

The salesman has used a twofold strategy. He has taken you off the market and he is now buying time—time for you to cool off and time for your trade-in to depreciate. His purpose is to wait and then rewrite the deal to his benefit. You will not see the car until he decides you are ready for the surprise which will normally be about 3 months later.

After 4 to 6 weeks pass, you begin to wonder where you car is, and you call the dealer. You will at first be inquisitive, then impatient, and finally hostile. You will threaten to cancel the order, ask for a deposit refund, and call the factory, and you will finally resign yourself to patiently waiting for your car. At the time of your personal resignation, progress will be observed. Now the salesman can call you with the good news: Your car is in.

When you arrive to pick up your new car, you will be told, "Prices went up, and your trade is not worth as much now as it was 4 months ago. Had your car arrived from the factory on time, we could honor the deal we originally wrote. Now we must reconstruct the deal, which begins with a fresh appraisal of your trade-in." The dealer rewrites the deal and, oddly enough, it is slightly higher than other deals you had been offered before.

Unfortunately, most victims of this tactic swallow their pride and take the new deal and the car. So what should you do if it happens to you? Refuse the car and demand full refund of all monies involved. Do not give the dealer the satisfaction of making one dime on the deal. However, it won't happen to you if you take a few precautions.

Be certain there is an automatic time-cancellation clause within the factory-order purchase contract. If the car is not delivered to you on or before a certain date, you will automatically have the right to cancel the order with a full refund of your deposit—no questions asked. This protects you against the delaying tactic of an unscrupulous dealer, and against factory workers' strikes delaying delivery. Word the clause informally and allow a reasonable length of time for dealer performance—about 6 to 8 weeks.

One week before the deadline date, find a back-up car to buy if for any reason your factory order deal falls apart. If you have a back-up car located, you will be less tempted to take the factory order if the dealer raises the price.

DEALER TRADE

Dealer trading involves your dealer's (A) contacting another dealer (B) who has a car in stock just the way you want it. Dealer A then either trades one of his cars in stock for the car he wants from Dealer B or he buys the car outright from B to sell to you. Dealer A acquires the car and delivers it to you from his lot. Trading gives you the advantages of a factory-order car without the time delay and avoids the disadvantages of shopping.

How does your dealer know just what is available from every other dealer? He has a coded master book that shows him who has what and when they got it. Some use microfilm and can scan for your car in minutes. The real question is not whether your dealer *can* do it but whether he *will* do it. The two basic reasons he would not are that it is time-consuming—double the paperwork—and that it becomes obligatory to return the favor.

Buy from stock? Factory order? Dealer trade? Give the choices very serious thought before you make a commitment.

5
Dealer Cost

A GOOD DEAL is a state of mind, an attitude. What seems lousy to one seems excellent to another. Some people shop a dozen dealers and never know when enough is enough, and they never recognize a true bargain when they find one. Others shop two dealers, take the lower of the two prices, and consider themselves fortunate. If you are happy with the salesman, the dealership, and the figures you receive, you have found a good deal, even if another dealer might go slightly lower on price and higher on trade value.

A good deal to some is simply a car that their budget can afford. Never feel that a deal is good just because it is affordable.

DEALER COST

Your knowing dealer cost and the way to work a deal does not automatically guarantee performance and cooperation on the part of the salesman and dealership management. What it does do is give you a benchmark from which to begin negotiations. It tells you how much room a salesman has to move on a given deal and eliminates many of the last-moment surprises when the ink hits the paper.

Dealer cost, simply stated, is the cost to the dealer for his merchandise. Cost includes not only the charge for the product, but also all expenses incurred by the dealer before the vehicle is finally sold to the end user, such as the fuel put into the gas tank at the factory, the antifreeze in the cooling system, any advertising charges levied against the dealer by the factory, and the interest paid to a lending institution under floor planning (a system of borrowing and repaying money on a dealer's inventory for a fee).

31

Because of these variables, it is literally impossible to compute pure dealer cost on any given car without having access to the dealer's books. The percent factor is different from model to model, so dealer cost becomes a conditional figure. The best you can ever hope to compute is a practical, functional figure that will permit you to negotiate your deal anywhere. Functional cost percentages are used by salesmen and sales managers alike to do a deal workup, unless they are working an extremely low gross profit deal, at which time they would go to a cost book for a to-the-penny cost on a particular car.

The percent factor used to compute functional dealer cost follows model designation. For domestic automobiles the percent factor is as follows:

- Mini-compacts   6–9 percent
- Subcompacts   10 percent
- Compacts   13 percent
- Intermediates   17 percent
- Full-size   21 percent
- Luxury Full-size   21 percent
- Pick-ups and Vans   20 percent

For import automobiles the percent factor is as follows:

- Mini-compacts   6–9 percent
- Subcompacts   9 percent
- Compacts   10 percent
- Pick-ups   13 percent
- Luxury imports   16 percent

Floor Planning. A floor plan charge is a fixed percentage computed against the dealer's cost on each car he has in stock. This percentage usually follows prime rate and may therefore vary from time to time. For all practical purposes the percentage you use is three-quarters of 1 percent (.0075). When a dealer receives his merchandise he notifies the lendor, the lendor pays the factory, and the floor plan charge begins to accumulate. When the car is sold, the dealer notifies the lendor and either pays the balance on that car or, if the car is financed on dealer paper (see chapter 12, ''Financing''), sends the paper to the lendor to stop the floor plan charge.

Most people believe that the longer a car sits on a dealer's lot the better the deal should be; the dealer should give a larger discount or sacrifice some profit for the sake of getting rid of the car. Quite the contrary is true. The longer the car sits, the more money the dealer has invested, so the higher the price. It is possible to work a $100-better deal between two identically priced cars provided you know about how long they have been in a dealer's inventory.

Most cars have a plate somewhere on the body that gives the month and year of manufacture. The plate will be just inside the doorjamb on the driver's side, or on the firewall or wheel well inside the engine compartment. The lag between date of manufacture and date of delivery is small, for the factory wants the money for the car as soon as possible. If the plate shows November and it is now March, it is safe to assume the car has been on the dealer's lot 4 months. Cost times .0075 per month times 4 months equals floor plan charge.

COST COMPUTATIONS

The percentages you now have can be utilized in two ways: to compute available gross profit, and to compute functional dealer cost (cost). For example, to compute the gross profit on a compact with a sticker price of $13,000, multiply 13 percent by $13,000, which will yield a $1,690 gross profit. From this $1,690 must come the floor plan and dealer's profit. To compute cost on the same car, simply subtract the $1,690 from the sticker price or use a percent multiple. To derive a percent multiple, subtract the 13 percent factor from 100 percent, which yields 87 percent. Multiply 87 percent by the sticker price for a cost of $11,310. A 17 percent gross profit factor will yield an 83 percent cost factor, and so on.

Gross profit and cost computations can be utilized in three ways:

1. Straight, no-trade deal working from dealer cost and adding profit.
2. Straight, no-trade deal using gross profit to discount the sticker price.
3. Trade-involved deal using gross profit to pack the trade.

Various circumstances dictate the use of one method over another, although adding or subtracting will eventually give the same answer.

Dealer cost is generally used on a straight, no-trade deal first computing the actual cost of the car and then negotiating upward. The floor plan charge must be added to cost before you can begin to negotiate.

Gross profit must be used when a trade is involved. It is necessary to know exactly how far down the price can be taken and still have some left for dealer profit. Knowing dealer cost tells you that much but, with a trade, the play money (gross within the car) is used to pack the trade valuation. You must know just how much is available for packing, and how much is left after packing is done. When you are in a situation involving a split deal that uses part of the gross to pack the trade and shows part of it as a discount, it becomes very confusing if you do not know the total gross available.

Here are the dealer cost computations on a $13,000 compact, intermediate, and full-size car set side by side.

Compact	*Intermediate*	*Full-Size*
$13,000 Sticker price	$13,000 Sticker price	$13,000 Sticker
× .87 Factor	× .83 Factor	× .79 Factor
$11,310 Cost	$10,790 Cost	$10,270 Cost

Next, compute and add floor plan if applicable. Assume these cars have been in stock for 3 months. Each would then have .75 percent computed against it per month:

$11,310	Cost	$10,790	Cost	$10,270
× .0075	Floor plan factor	× .0075	Floor plan factor	× .0075
$84.83	Per month	$80.93	Per month	$77.03
× 3	Months	× 3	Months	× 3
$254.48	Floor plan charge	$242.78	Floor plan charge	$231.08

Add the floor plan charge to the cost figure and negotiate up until the dealer says, "Okay, I'll take the deal," or until you have gone as far as you care to go. Once the benchmark has been established, any offer you make over that amount is profit for the dealer. It is then merely a question of how much profit he wants to make and how high you want to go on price.

When you have a trade-in it becomes a bit more difficult. Follow this example using a $13,000 compact as the car you want to buy, and a theoretical wholesale value on your trade-in of $3,000. A salesman may show it like this:

$13,000 Sticker price
−$4,190 Trade allowance

$8,810 Cash difference

How did he get $4,190 for a trade allowance? Your trade is worth only $3,000. Why didn't you receive a discount?

Using a 13 percent factor to compute functional gross, the dealer has $1,690 with which to work. Initially he tries to make a $500 gross profit deal and adds $1,190 of his gross to your trade value to increase it to $4,190. If you negotiate, he will move up in $50 to $75 increments until he has consumed another $200, at which point he will show you a $4,390 trade allowance and a cash difference of $8,610. The only thing that has really changed is the amount of profit he is willing to accept. Your trade is still worth only $3,000.

Suppose that halfway through the negotiations you decide to switch to an intermediate. What then?

The salesman recomputes his opening deal according to the new markup percent. He uses the same trade value—$3,000—but now he has an extra 4 percent to utilize. His available gross is now $2,210; he may offer you $4,710 for your trade, which will yield a cash difference of $8,290, and a profit of $500. Even if you had already negotiated him down to a $200 gross profit deal on the compact, the dealer will use your switch to an intermediate to go back up to a high gross. On a full-size car he can make things look better and make more money. Placed side by side, the deals look like this:

Compact	Intermediate	Full-Size
$13,000 Sticker price	$13,000 Sticker price	$13,000 Sticker price
× .13 Factor	× .17 Factor	× .21 Factor
$ 1,690 Gross profit	$ 2,210 Gross profit	$ 2,730 Gross profit

To hold a $500 profit on each deal written against your trade, the pack is:

$1,190 Compact	$1,710 Intermediate	$2,230 Full-Size

Which gives you a revised trade allowance of:

$3,000 Wholesale	$3,000 Wholesale	$3,000 Wholesale
+ $1,190 Pack	+ $1,710 Pack	+ $2,230 Pack
$4,190 Trade allowance	$4,710 Trade allowance	$5,230 Trade allowance

The cash difference becomes:

$13,000	Sticker price	$13,000	Sticker price	$13,000	Sticker price
− $4,190	Allowance	− $4,710	Allowance	− $5,230	Allowance
$8,810	Cash difference	$8,290	Cash difference	$7,770	Cash difference

Note that the real value of your trade and the profit held did not change during the computations. If the salesman wants to confuse the issue, he can split the deal and show a trade allowance and a discount. This is usually done on cars with high grosses. The trick is to show you what seems to be retail for your trade and still give a discount on top of it all. Retail on your car should be about $3,800 (wholesale plus an $800 spread). Using a $3,000 trade value and a $13,000 full-size car; gross profit to play with is $2,730.

$3,600	Trade allowance	$13,000	Sticker price
+ $ 200	Over allowance	− $1,000	Discount
$3,800	Total allowance	$12,000	Discounted Price
		− $3,800	Total allowance on trade
		$8,200	Cash difference

All of which says the dealer will make a $930 gross profit on this deal if you accept it. Breakdown: The salesman could have shown you a total allowance of $4,800 and derived the same cash difference, but psychologically you would not be as content nor as set up if you saw everything in lump sum. The more he breaks the figures down, the more it seems he is giving. When the salesman offers both a trade figure and a discount, it seems as if you are receiving more than the average customer. Additionally, the dealer has shown you an overallowance on your trade. If you ask for more he will point to the extra $200 and tell you that he has surpassed your car's value as it is; he can go no further. Now it seems the only area left for you to negotiate is the discount. Even there he will fall back upon the fact that nobody gives a discount when a trade is involved. What can you say?

Forget the trade allowance, the overallowance, and the discount and concentrate on the cash difference. Any reference you make to what he has given you thus far is really wasted breath. What is the bottom-line figure? Compute the deal you want based on the gross available and the wholesale value of your car. If the cash differences match, buy the car. If they do not match, then attack the cash difference figure the salesman is quoting.

If one tactic does not work, a salesman will take a different approach. If he cannot grab you by switching or splitting the deal, he will try to nail you on cash difference or monthly payment. In the final analysis it is the bottomline that counts—just how much will the car cost you in dollars and cents?

If a deal does not have enough gross for the salesman to wheel and deal, he may create his own gross. The easiest way is for him to pack (misquote) the sticker price. This is done primarily on factory-order cars and used cars. The salesman may also pack the adding machine, which produces supportive evidence that the price he is quoting is true. A salesman punches the pack (say $200) into the adding machine and, without clearing the machine, tears the tape off. Thereafter, whatever calculations are done on the machine produce a bottom-line figure $200 higher than should be. When a salesman itemizes your options on a tape, you will look at the list and assume that the total is a true and accurate price.

Your best defense is to double-check the prices quoted for options and the base price of the car you plan to buy. These can be checked against the dealer's book and against window stickers on cars already on his lot. Double-check arithmetic personally, either with a pocket calculator or by long-hand addition.

PROFIT LEVELS

Most dealers within a given size hold a certain profit level. There are exceptions, but you do not want to spend 6 months finding an exception. You can go to as few as two dealers and find the deal you want; conversely, you can go to as many as a dozen dealers and not find that much difference between the valid deals you can work and obtain.

Here are the various profit levels held by most dealers:

No discount	Car is sold for full sticker price. If a trade is involved, the wholesale value is allowed; no gross is used for packing.
$500 and higher	Factory order; intermediates and full-size cars; used cars; trucks and vans—new and used.

$400 to $500	Borderline on factory order on intermediates and full-size cars; out-of-stock purchases. Normal, average dealer range.
$350 and up	Guaranteed deal on any car. Dealer may try for more profit, but when he is this close to a deal, he will push very little.
$300 to $350	Negotiating level. Slow market will make dealing easier.
$200 to $300	Strong negotiating necessary; make two or three trips to dealership to obtain acceptance of a $200 gross deal.
$100 to $200	Fleet sales; multiple purchase of three or more; promos.
$ 50 to $100	Dealer promo; demo sales; leader ads; extremely slow market.

These guidelines are not rigid but they do give you an idea of what to expect under certain circumstances. Knowledge is savings.

What May Happen. The easiest way for a salesman to offset your knowledge of dealer cost is to deny that both your knowledge and your figures exist. The logic is that if he says something long enough and loud enough you will begin to believe it, accept it, and act upon it. His story may go like this:

"So many people knew cost that the factory restructured the percentages. We do not have half the money available that we had in the past. The figures you have would have been good last year, but not anymore." With this statement, the salesman confuses you, creates doubt and, for the most part, captures the negotiating advantage. You are not fully certain that he is telling you the truth, and that slight doubt begins to weigh on your mind and has a direct effect on your final decisions. If you ask, "Just how much will the car cost under the new system?" you are nibbling his bait. He then pulls the line by quoting you a best-deal-in-town price. He will begin by assuring you that while your figures are wrong, you are not that far off. "Here is what I can do for you, and it is not far from what you had in mind."

Your best defense against this maneuver is to use the "other dealer approach." Simply tell the salesman that another dealer must still be using the old set of figures (percentages), because he will give you the car you want at the price you want to pay. "If he can do it, why can't you?" Back this up with, "Naturally I would rather buy from your dealership, but price is important."

A salesman may try to convince you that the maximum discount he can give is a fleet discount, which is only 6 percent to 7 percent of sticker price. This, he will assure you, is the discount normally reserved for fleet customers only, and you will be lucky indeed if he can talk his sales manager into giving you that much. Question his discount: "If 7 percent is the best you can do, why can the dealer down the street do better?" Or, "If you give only 7 percent to your fleet accounts, why do they continue to buy from you? Other dealers give much more to the general public, and I am sure they do better for their fleet accounts."

The dealer may advertise copies of so-called factory invoices in the newspapers showing a below-invoice price to you after the discount, or advertise factory invoice disclosure upon personal visit to his showroom and personal request, or show you phony factory invoices prepared by his secretary and passed off as authentic. These phony invoices look real enough, but they generally carry a $200 to $400 pack. No dealer anywhere will sell his product at a loss (below his cost), so do not be misled for a moment. Disregard the ad, and disregard the dealer completely. If he uses this ploy in any form, he is not to be trusted in any other area—service, reliability, or financing. The only way at all that he can sell a new car below invoice without losing money is to sell a used new car, a repossession, a factory exec's car, or a demonstrator—all of which may or may not show the true mileage and carry a full factory warranty.

The real confusion about the cost factor is to be found on compacts that approach intermediate size. Unless the salesman tells you it is a compact, you may become confused by size alone and utilize a 17 percent factor— 4 percent too high for a compact. You will then be negotiating below dealer cost.

If you are in doubt about a cost factor, you will find the answer you need in one of several publications released each year that give dealer cost on any given make and model of new car. These paperbacks can normally be found at most bookstores and at some drugstore book racks. When in doubt, check it out. When you find the dealer cost you need to know, divide that amount by the retail price of the car and you will have your cost factor percentage.

6
Your Old Car Is Worth More Than You Think

GETTING READY

UNLESS YOUR CAR needs body work (it has rust or crash damage), if it has no obvious defects, you can put it in A-1 trade-in shape for less than $75. First and foremost, it must be clean from bumper to bumper—every piece of dirt and dust detracts from its value. The engine compartment is the kicker, for any car will develop dirt on the engine after a few years' use. If your engine is throwing or leaking a little oil, the oil will capture dirt and build a thick layer of goop, making the car look like junkyard material. It costs a lot to have an engine steam-cleaned, but you can do as well at a local spray-jet car wash. Use plastic wrap to completely cover the distributor and alternator before you spray to avoid forcing greasy water into critical electrical parts. Then soap-spray the entire engine and all exposed metal within the engine compartment. Rinse with clear water and you have an engine that looks about the same as when you first bought the car. Clean out the trunk and glove box, leaving the spare tire and jack in the trunk and the owner's manual in the glove box.

Cover, repair, or replace all blemishes on your car. Tape small cuts, tears, or holes in upholstery with matching color rubberized or vinyl tape. Cover blemishes on quarter panels and rocker panels with a quick coat of spray paint (it doesn't have to be a perfect job). Make a vinyl top look new with vinyl spray paint (relatively inexpensive and it comes in colors). You are now psychologically ready to ask top dollar for your car.

When you determine trade value, be fair about it. You must put yourself in the other person's shoes and view the car as he does. As the buyer, would you pay cash-out-of-pocket today what you think your car is worth, or would you try to chop the price by picking the car apart? When you have been to several dealers and all seem to be close on the trade value offered, perhaps an adjustment is necessary in your figures. Be flexible.

You must realize three truisms:

1. Your car is worth only X number of dollars—period.
2. There are only X number of dollars of gross profit available on a given car.
3. A dealer must make a profit on each and every car he sells.

Do not expect full retail allowance for the unused portion of recent repairs and replacement items you have purchased. The dealer does not care how long ago a replacement or repair was made as long as the parts are functional now. He could care less if there are 33 months left on the battery, 30,000 miles left on the tires, and 20 months left on the muffler.

At best, recent repairs and replacement items will give you a little negotiating leverage: "My car will sell for you faster; it will cost you less to fix."

THE APPRAISAL

Dealers use many methods to appraise a car. These methods depend on how the deal is first put together, who makes the intitial move, and who makes the initial dollar offer to whom. The major categories of appraisal are:

1. The salesman inspects the car subject to management approval and does a rough deal workup from his inspection.
2. The sales manager inspects and appraises the car and does a workup offer that the salesman presents to the customer, or the sales manager appraises the car after a workup done by the salesman.
3. A professional appraiser inspects the car, sets a value on it, and gives this figure either to the salesman or to the sales manager to begin a workup. He sets an inflexible value upon your car that nobody (salesman or sales manager) goes above, no matter what. It is always a wholesale figure.

A salesman is taught to inspect your trade-in in silence, while you watch. He will touch blemishes on your trade without saying a word, but he will be sure you see him touch them. This lets you know that he knows the blemish is there without verbally offending you. As he silently lets you know just how much is wrong with your car, your mental value of it diminishes. He is setting you up for final negotiations.

When a salesman says, "Let's take a look at your car," let him go alone. Go over and look at his car again or wander around the lot. If he calls you over to ask you a question, answer the question and wander away again while he continues his visual inspection of your car. If he insists that you stand by while he inspects, tell him you must make a telephone call, or tell him you want to inspect his merchandise, and that there is no real reason that you can see for you to stand around while he looks at a car that you see every day. This ruins his little game and will leave you free to ask for top dollar when you sit down to negotiate the deal.

The inspection is an area in which you can gain a definite advantage over the salesman. He must stand by as you inspect his merchandise, but you need not stand by while he inspects yours. You can do it to him, but he cannot do it to you if you walk away.

Another common ploy to diminish your trade value is to talk your trade down. Since it might offend you to talk about your particular car, most salesmen will third-party your trade by talking about other cars just like yours: how bad they are; what bad luck they have had selling them; how low the value is; and the fact that there is an overabundance of that particular model on all used-car lots just now. Sometimes this is true. Even so, no matter what the story, no matter what the offer to you, you always have the right to negotiate, to make a counteroffer, and to leave and shop elsewhere. Write your own deal, make him an offer, and put the ball in his lap.

After a salesman performs an inspection, he may do a deal workup and make you an offer, or he may try to get you to make a commitment on exactly how much it will take to make you buy. Regardless of who makes the commitment—salesman or customer—final papers must be drawn to bind the deal and make it official. These papers may be called a workup sheet, a specification sheet, an agreement to purchase, or a contract, but the common elements are that the terms are set forth in print, and you must sign on the dotted line. The papers, with deposit, are taken to the sales manager for appraisal and approval or counteroffer. Because the deal is subject to management approval, all the salesman is telling you is that he will try to get the trade allowance on which the two of you have come to terms. There is no commitment on his part, although you must make a commitment to purchase at that price.

The sales manager's appraisal of your car may come after the salesman's inspection and completion of the workup sheet, or it may be used as an entirely different method of handling you. In the first instance, the sales manager will look over the deal as written and then appraise your car and set a trade value from which the final deal will be drawn. The salesman must then reenter the closing room with either an approved deal, as mutually agreed upon, or a counteroffer to present for your approval. In the latter case, when you ask the salesman how much your car is worth, he will have his sales manager perform an appraisal on your car. The sales manager will give the salesman an offer to present to you. The salesman must then sell you the deal his sales manager has written.

For the most part, the advantages of the latter favor the customer; you make no commitment to buy, whether or not the figures are exactly what you want. You have the option to review the deal and accept it or reject it and leave. Why then would a dealer choose this method of appraisal approach?

Even though most of the benefits favor the customer, the dealer gets one major benefit, and it can cost you money. Psychologically, you will feel that this is the best the dealer will do on trade value, and you further believe that since the sales manager did the appraisal, it will do little good to argue with the salesman for a higher allowance. If you do object to the deal the salesman can always stop you from leaving by saying, "Wait a minute. Let me see if my sales manager will go a little higher on your allowance." And so the negotiations begin—offers and counteroffers—until everyone is happy.

Precaution. When a salesman asks for the keys to your car for an appraisal, do not let the keys or the car out of your sight. If the salesman, his sales manager, or a professional appraiser wants to take your car for a ride to check it out—go with him. Any time you are away from your car, have the keys in your pocket. There are three major reasons for this:

1. You want to know where your car is taken. If it is shopped to a wholesaler or a used-car lot, you can expect a very low trade allowance. If the dealer drives it around the block, you know he plans to keep the car for resale.
2. You want to know the dealer or appraiser is not going to hot-rod, sabotage, or otherwise abuse your car while inspecting it.
3. You want to know where your car is finally parked. Some dealers hide the trade-in or keep the keys to coerce the customer to "go ahead and buy" their car. If they feel they are not going to get the sale anyway, they have little to lose by harassing you. It is best to have an expendable set of keys made before you begin to shop. If

someone doesn't want to return your keys, tell him to keep them, get in your car, and leave.

SOURCES OF TRADE VALUE

Even though you will be able to determine trade value by depreciation (computations later in this chapter), it will be worthwhile to average trade value by using one or more of the following sources:

1. Used-car dealer. Direct purchase of your car. Take your car to a used-car dealer and ask him how much he will give you for it today on an outright purchase—no trade, no dickering on price. When he quotes a figure (it will be wholesale), tell him you will think about it and leave.
2. New-car dealer. Same procedure as for the used-car dealer. The figure will be wholesale or less.
3. Used-car ads. New- and used-car dealers and private owners advertising their cars for sale. This will be a retail figure.
4. Wholesale and retail guide books; blue-book value when you have access to the information. You want the wholesale value of your car.
5. Banks, credit unions, loan companies, and insurance companies. They may or may not be willing to give information. You want the wholesale value.

When you have all figures from outside sources, convert the retail to wholesale by subtracting $900 ($1,500 for luxury cars), and add all figures together. Divide that sum by the total number of figures you have added. This gives you an average wholesale profile value based on current market conditions. Add this figure to the depreciated value figure, divide by 2, and you have a sum total average of what your car should bring on the open market.

VALUE BY DEPRECIATION

All cars depreciate at approximately the same rate as their percent of markup. (Refer to dealer cost factors, page 34.) When you buy and drive a new car off the lot, it depreciates down to dealer cost less 10 percent, which is the first-year depreciation. For example, you just bought a new $17,000 sticker-priced full-size car; 79 percent factor (see page 34). It is worth dealer cost ($13,430) less 10 percent ($1,343), or $12,087. To determine true value (wholesale), deduct $900, and the value of your new car is $11,187, or about $11,200. To go into second-year devaluation, take 79 percent of $12,087, which yields $9,548 for the retail valuation of your car in its second year. The 10 percent is deducted only in the first year. Subtract $900 from $9,548 and the wholesale value of your car at age two is $8,648. If you have a 5-year-old model car, you would use the current sticker price of a brand-new model X and depreciate that down 5 years. The following tables will help eliminate confusion about computing value. All figures are rounded off to the nearest dollar.

	Full-Size Car	Intermediate Car	Compact Car	SubCompact Car
Sticker Price	$17,000	$15,000	$13,000	$12,000
Cost Factor	× .79	× .83	× .87	× .90
Dealer Cost	$13,430	$12,450	$11,310	$10,800
Less 10 Percent	× .90	× .90	× .90	× .90
Retail First Year	$12,087	$11,205	$10,179	$9,720
	$12,087	$11,205	$10,179	$9,720
	× .79	× .83	× .87	× .90
Retail Second Year	$9,548	$9,300	$8,855	$8,748
	$9,548	$9,300	$8,855	$8,748
	× .79	× .83	× .87	× .90
Retail Second Year	$7,543	$7,719	$7,703	$7,873

To compute the retail value of your trade-in, run your computations out as above to the age of your car. If it is 4 months into the model year (model year beginning in September), compute the next year (a 5-year-old car would run to the sixth year retail), and subtract the sixth-year figure from the fifth-year figure. This will give you the total depreciation between year 5 and year 6. Divide the difference by 12 to obtain the average depreciation per month for that full year. Multiply that figure by the number of months you are into the model year. Subtract that figure from the retail value fifth year and you will have the current retail value of your car. Progressing the above full-size car example yields:

Retail Fifth Year: $4,706
Retail Sixth Year: $3,718 **$988 depreciation from fifth year to sixth year**

The depreciation per month (rounded off) is $988 divided by 12, or $82. Eighty-two dollars per month times 4 months equals $328 depreciation for

4 months. Retail fifth year, less $328, equals true retail value, current
. . . $4,378. Wholesale fifth (4 months into model year) $4,378 less $900
($1,500 for luxury cars) yields a computed wholesale value of $3,478.
Match this figure against market profile, and with the resulting figure begin
to work your deal.

Note: When the computed retail value of your car reaches $1,500, do not
subtract $900 ($1,500 for luxury cars), but rather divide by 2. This will yield
a more realistic wholesale valuation of your car.

7
Trade It or Sell It?

WHY NOT TRADE?

YOU SHOULD HAVE A GOOD IDEA before you begin to shop whether you want to trade your car or want to sell it yourself. Selling your car represents a savings to you (dollars in pocket), but trading represents convenience. You need not run advertisements in the paper, answer phone calls, show your car to every shopper in town, listen to complaints and criticisms, or negotiate with prospective buyers.

Most people prefer the convenience of driving in with the old car and driving out with the new. It may take several months to sell your car on your own, but it could sell with the first phone call you receive. Because you may not find exactly what you want when your car sells, you may have to accept second best. Also, the sale of your car creates an urgent desire to replace it, which makes you subject to an impulse purchase and vulnerable to a poor deal.

If you can live without your car for a short period of time, at least make the effort to find a buyer. If yours is a one-car family, make the sale of your car contingent upon the purchase of your new car. Put a time limit for performance within the agreement to purchase, take a deposit of good faith from your buyer, and start looking for the car and the deal you want. If a buyer is serious enough about buying your car, he will not mind if the delivery is delayed 2 or 3 days while you consummate your purchase. Naturally, the deposit is returned if your new-car plans fall apart.

SELLING YOUR CAR

It will be necessary to place a realistic price tag on your car if you expect a quick sale. Remember, every dealer in town is in competition

47

with you to sell your potential customer a car just like yours. You must therefore be competitive in both price and quality. Determine what dealers are doing in the marketplace, and make your quotes slightly less to draw customer traffic. From there you can negotiate price right down to whole-sale—something the average dealer will not do. Why sell for wholesale if a dealer will allow you wholesale for your car? Why not just trade it in? Selling your car at any price gives you the negotiating advantage of a straight, no-trade deal.

Set a time limit after which you will stop trying to sell your car. A decent time limit is 7 to 10 days; if the car does not sell by then it may be 6 months before it does. Don't forget, your car continues to depreciate all the while.

Exposure is important to sell anything. Once you set a price for your car, advertise it by every available means with the price right up front. Run short, punchy ads in your local paper emphasizing the car's most desireable features—low mileage, one owner, make and model, AM/FM radio—and include one descriptive adjective, such as *sacrifice, must sell*, or *bargain*. Place notices on bulletin boards at your office or local su-permarkets. And, of course, place a *For Sale* sign in the window of the car itself. List your car with a professional referral service if one is available in your area. The fee for the service is usually based on a percentage of the final selling price. If there is a large flea market in your area, go as a customer, park your car with a *For Sale* sign on it near the activity, and browse around—let the car sell itself. Let all friends, neighbors, and relatives know you want to sell your car, and tell them to spread the word.

A phone number placed in a general public advertisement (such as in a newspaper) may swamp you with calls, but it does allow you to screen the callers before exposing your address to just anyone. This prevents unwanted visitors from appearing at your doorstep at any hour of the day or night. It further prevents your opening your front door to just anyone who may be posing as a buyer. Before you divulge your address to a potential buyer, get contact information on him: "Let me have your phone number and I'll call you right back."

If such precautions are not necessary, you may want to put your address in the ad and omit the phone number. Be specific about the times the car can be seen. This draws only the serious traffic to your home, and draws it when you want it.

An excellent source of prospects is the salesman who will be selling you your new car. If he can pick up an extra $20 by referring a customer to you, he will be more than happy for the opportunity. Even without a bird-dog fee, if he has a sale riding on whether or not you are able to sell your car, he will definitely have you in mind before he pitches someone out on the street unsold. (*Note:* Some states outlaw bird-dog fees.)

CONSUMMATING THE DEAL

If your customer has cash in his hand and you have the title in your hand, there are no complications; you simply trade what you have in your hand for what he has in his. But if you have a balance (such as a lien or encumbrance) with a lendor, and your buyer has a checkbook in hand, assurances are needed on both sides that you will pass clear title and that his check will not bounce. It is best to go to his bank together and have him cash a check (unless it is a loan assumption) or have him draw a certified check on his account made out in your name. Then go to your bank to pay off your loan, cancel the lien (or encumbrance) on your title, and transfer the title to his name. Procedures for transferring title, paying taxes, and obtaining fresh license plates for the car will vary from state to state. If a question comes up, call the AAA, a local new-car dealer, a justice of the peace, your court house, your attorney, a notary public, or a magistrate.

LET CHARLIE DO IT

Another way to sell your car is to put it on the lot of a "we will sell your car for you" dealer. The usual procedure is to pay a nominal registration fee when you place your car on the lot, and then pay a per diem charge until the car sells. When your car is sold by the dealer, you pay him either a flat fixed amount or a percentage of the price for which the car sold. Normally you decide at what price the car will finally be sold. You retain the right of refusal of any negotiating. You usually also retain the right to remove your car at any time with no loss to you other than the original registration fee and the per diem charges already paid.

To use this system successfully, you must get more for your car, after deductions for charges and fees, than you could have received for a trade allowance. The time factor is important; how long will it take to sell your car this way? This is a personal decision. Try it for 1 month, and if the car has not been sold, remove it from the lot and decide either to sell it yourself or to trade it in.

8
Handling the Salesman

THE SALESMAN

NEVER UNDERESTIMATE a salesman. In fact, the first thing you must realize—and appreciate—is just how well-trained most salesmen are. They have books, classes, sales meetings, videotapes, training seminars, and marketing and motivation institutes all designed for one purpose: to teach them how to separate you from your money. A salesman is taught to understand his customer and to make him want to buy, not tomorrow, but today.

In addition to book and classroom training, a salesman has day-to-day practical experience that gives him the opportunity to put his knowledge to use and practice on real people. There are also problem-solving clinics (usually sponsored and directed by the factory) in which salesmen from several dealerships get together and compare notes. Similar to group therapy, these discussions aim at solving mutual problems experienced by the participating salesmen regarding their handling of customers and closing of sales. Even though these salesmen are in direct competition with each other, they openly share their secrets and tactics, because the customer is the enemy.

How do you, the customer, stand a chance when you confront the salesman in a bargaining situation? Begin by approaching the entire situation with an open mind. Realize that everything the salesman does, you, can do; his tactics and maneuvers become your tactics and maneuvers.

While working with a salesman, you should constantly ask yourself, "Am I being controlled and manipulated? Is the salesman interested only in my money? Do I really want what he is suggesting I take? Am I really going to receive what he says I am getting? Is he telling me a story or telling me the truth?'' Take the time and question: "What is happening and why is it happening?''

SYSTEM SELLING

Salesmen are trained to use a system to sell a car: either a canned presentation or a selling cycle. A canned presentation is nothing more than a memorized speech someone else wrote. The salesman commits it to memory and mouths the words to the customer. An experienced salesman can give a canned sales talk and you would bet money he had never used those exact words on anyone else before. Your impression is that everything he says is spontaneous.

A salesman may subsidize a canned talk with a selling cycle or vice versa. A selling cycle is a step-by-step method of selling that allows the salesman to control his customer from start to finish. He will cover one area—one step of his system—and then move on to the next step. When the cycle is finished, it is extremely difficult to say no to his final request for the sale.

Salesmen who are fresh to the business are usually nervous about using a canned talk; they feel that you are aware that it is just that, a canned talk. The timing of a novice salesman is generally poor. He may start to say something entirely out of context to what is happening, stop himself in midsentence, and start off in another direction.

This could also happen to you as you read this book and acquire information and tactics foreign to your natural personality. You will then take them to a showroom and attempt to use them on a salesman. It is only normal for you to be a little nervous about doing so, and to miscue at times. However, like the salesman, with a little practice you will present your talk naturally and easily. It is important to be relaxed, to act as if you know exactly what you are saying, and to say it with confidence.

THE QUESTION PRINCIPLE

A salesman is trained to control his customer by asking questions. He is trained to answer questions by asking questions, and to seek a commitment to purchase by answering a question with a question that asks for the sale. If you are to control the salesman, you must learn to use the question principle.

When you ask, "Can I have the car tomorrow?" the salesman will probably answer you by asking, "Will you buy the car if I can have it ready for you by tomorrow?"

He has not really answered your question but rather set you up. Now you must either answer him or ask another question. If you simply say "yes" or "no," you have not received the answer to your question, but you have answered his question; you either buy or leave the door open to another question from the salesman. A suggested response is, "If I decided to buy the car, yes, I would want delivery within a day. Can you deliver the car within a day if we come to terms?" First, you get yourself off the hook; then you go back to your original question—as yet unanswered—and you have made no commitment.

He who asks the questions, controls the situation. When you ask a question that requires a lengthy response, it gives you a chance to think of your next question and it forces your adversary to stop and think. A question breaks up a salesman's pattern, interrupts his train of thought, and causes him to stop and give you an answer. As long as he is answering, he is not asking. This does not mean you should spend all your time asking questions for the sake of asking, nor does it mean that if a salesman asks you a question, you should refuse to answer him. How you react to a question asked by a salesman depends upon the type of question it is—whether it is a qualifying question or a commitment-seeking question.

There is a fine difference between qualifying you for need, want, and use of what you are looking for, and closing you on a particular car. Qualifying is simply finding out what you want, what is on your mind, and what it will take to make you happy; any good salesman should do this much. Closing is landing you on a particular car and asking purchase commitment questions.

Questions or statements like these are commitment seeking in nature:

"Will you . . . if I can . . . ?" Will you buy, if I can get the price reduced?

"Would you consider this?" Would you consider the blue car instead of the red?

"Would you like to?" Would you like to take it home today?

"Why don't you . . . ?" Why don't you give me a small deposit? Why don't you take it home today?

"Let's do this . . ." As if a group endeavor; watch this one, it's a fooler.

"Let me do this for you." Let me: write up your figures? take another $100 off the price? talk to my boss?

Questions like these are qualifying in nature:

"Do you want . . . ?"

"Have you seen. . . ?"

"What do you have now?"

"Who have you seen thus far?"

"Do you plan to do this?"

"What color, size, style?"

"Do you like this?"

Never hesitate to answer qualifying questions. A salesman must ask them if he is to give you the best he has to offer. If you are not ready to make a commitment, be evasive or simply do not answer commitment-seeking questions. The best way to avoid answering any question is to pretend that you did not hear it; change the subject or ask the salesman an irrelevant question. If the salesman asks too many personal questions, ask him whether you are there to buy a car or to file application for employment.

GAME PLAYING: WHY BOTHER?

It seems obvious that if you know what you want to buy, and what you are able to spend based on the computed cost of the car you want, all you need do is shop from dealer to dealer until you find the salesman willing to sell it to you at your price. Unfortunately, the salesmen you encounter will not know that you know and you cannot tell them that you know. If they are aware that you know, they will stubbornly hold out for a higher price: "This customer is not going to tell me how much profit I'm going to make."

Your task is to go along with the salesman and play the part that has been written for you. You must present the image of average Joe Public who has come in to be sold a car; not to buy, but to be sold. You must play the same games as the salesman, and you must, in the end, justify your position, just as the salesman must justify his offering to you.

There are certain moves that a salesman must make to successfully sell anyone a car. These inflexible moves give you a definite advantage, if for no other reason than that you can leave whenever you so desire; the salesman cannot. He must stay there and play the game.

A salesman will use the following procedure to try to sell a customer:

1. Approach. Butter up, warm up to, and relax the customer.
2. Qualify. Find out what the customer wants and needs.
3. Present and demonstrate. Touch it, see it, drive it.
4. Ask for the sale; write the order. "Will you buy from me today?"
5. Handle objections. Calm fears, close the sale, and ask for the sale.
6. Negotiate. "I will come down a little if you will come up a little."

7. Customer turnover. "I would like for you to meet my sales manager before you leave. Maybe he can give you the deal you want."

None of this means that since you know his next move you are to jump up and say, "I know what you are going to do next, aha! . . . . It means that you can plan your next several moves and that you can be better prepared to handle whatever he might toss in your direction. Whenever you see that you need time to coordinate a counterattack, ask a question that requires a lengthy answer.

JUDGING THE SALESMAN

There is such a thing as gut instinct, which tells you on first meeting whether or not you like someone. There is usually a reason why you may have a first and immediate bad impression of a salesman before a full sentence is spoken. It may be subconscious feedback: the salesman reminds you of someone with whom you once had a bad experience or, for whatever reason, did not like. These are feelings that must be recognized and set aside. Let the salesman prove himself to you before you pass judgment.

The two most important assets of a good salesman are the ability to communicate and product knowledge. If the salesman does not know what he is selling, he is no good to you. Likewise, he is no good if he knows what he is selling but cannot convey that message to you.

A salesman should sell in a relaxed manner, for his job is to make your purchase comfortable, not tense. If the salesman is making you feel uneasy, is not alleviating your fears, and is not relaxing you, he is not doing his job well at all. And it all begins with the approach.

A salesman is taught to be friendly, courteous, and prompt in his approach to you when you walk onto the showroom floor. The two of you are total strangers, so the salesman must become "old friends" with you as quickly as possible. The first few minutes are critical. This is when you decide whether or not you like the salesman and can trust him, and whether or not you want to put your money in his pocket.

While you are deciding about him, he is deciding about you. It is imperative that you realize it is to your advantage to make a favorable impression on the salesman. It will make a definite difference in the deal you are offered when you sit down to negotiate.

Your approach to a salesman should be enthusiastic and friendly. Never be withdrawn, bashful, reticent, or hesitant. The enthusiasm you display can ruin a salesman's timing and throw his procedure completely off track. He will hesitate to do anything which might turn your enthusiasm off. If you want to buy out of procedure and rearrange the normal order of presentation, that is all right with the salesman, provided you continue to display an interest in buying his product. Quite frankly, you can do almost anything you want to do as long as you act as if you are going to buy.

The salesman must find out, as quickly as he can, where you are from, where you were born, where you work, whether you are single or married, and how many children you have. Why is it so important and how does he go about it?

A salesman will usually begin by casually asking, "Are you from this area?" You reply, "No, I am from Hometown." And the dialogue continues, "Oh, were you born there?" "No, I was born in Nextown," you answer. "Where do you work?" "I work for Big Corp, Inc. I am an engineer." "Have you worked for Big Corp very long?" "Well, going on 11 years now, if you consider that a long time." "Are you married?" "Yes, I am." "Do you have any children?" "Yes, we have three." And so on—question after question. A salesman will not machine-gun the questions as above but will space them out and make appropriate comment as he goes along. And all the questions and answers do mean something.

The Serious Customer. Salesmen are trained to be extremely observant. Within the first few minutes after you meet, the salesman looks for indicators that you are a serious buyer worthy of his time. The more positive indicators he finds, the more time he will spend helping you. This is important, for if he does not believe you are serious, he will try to land you on the first car he presents and get you to sit down and sign up, which you will interpret as pushiness.

If you want a salesman to think you are a serious buyer and treat you as such, it will do no harm to set up a few props, a few visible indications that you are a right-now buyer. An older car, worn-out tires, a close-to-expiration safety lane sticker, a cleaned-out trunk or glove box, snow tires not on by November (in northern states), a rough idle, an almost empty fuel tank, a checkbook or title in your shirt pocket—all indicate "ready to buy today."

The Nonserious Customer. If there are indicators that show you to be a serious buyer, there must be indicators that show you as nonserious—just a looker. A classic example is the married person who walks onto a showroom floor alone. If you are married, a salesman may find out by spotting a wedding ring or may acquire a clue from your trade-in: an infant seat, children's clothes, or toys in the back seat. A salesman may ask forthrightly, "Are you married?" You respond that you are. He will then determine whether you have a valid reason for being there alone: "Is your spouse working right now?" You reply, "No, he/she is home with the children." If he/she were working, the salesman would classify you as a serious buyer, for you have a legitimate reason for being there alone. However, if your spouse is home with the kids, you are probably a non-serious customer. If you were a serious buyer you would have your spouse with you.

Another indicator that you are not serious is the little notebook that pops out of your pocket every 5 minutes on which you make notes about price, options, and so on. This is a strong indicator that you are merely shopping. It tells the salesman that you are only compiling information right now and that if he lets you leave he has only a slim chance of ever seeing you again. You may receive a low-ball figure to ensure your return.

Your best move is to bring the notebook to the salesman's attention yourself, rather than have him catch you trying to sneak a few figures down when his back is turned. As you bring the book out for the first time, show it to the salesman (the notebook, not the contents), and say, "I'm going to take a few notes as we go along so that when we sit down for the final paperwork I won't forget anything we have covered." This tells him the notebook is for his benefit as well as your own.

Knowing where you are from gives the salesman an idea of your affluence (or lack of it), social standing, and cultural background. Everything tells the salesman something; if you drive up in a 10-year-old car and live on the wrong side of the tracks, the salesman will quickly determine your degree of sincerity and ability to buy before he wastes his time and effort showing, demonstrating, and trying to sell you a new car. These are all signs that help the salesman decide what he will or will not do for you, what he will or will not show you, and whether or not he will give you a demonstration ride. The more he knows about you, the more he can help you, and the more productive his selling will be. And time is money.

Common Opening Statements. Do not say "I am just looking," or "I am just shopping." Both indicate that you are a nonserious buyer just wasting the salesman's time. His first thought is that you have nothing better to do so you are killing time looking at new cars, or that your only interest is to get another price to add to your long list. Both give him little hope for a sale, and little motivation to be cooperative. Open with, "I am interested in seeing one of your (whatever it is)."

Never say, "I am paying straight cash. This tells the salesman he will not have to worry about the finance profit the dealership makes, which is about 20 percent of the total finance charge. A salesman/dealer will give away more gross profit if he knows from the start he will be making the finance profit. Lead the salesman to believe he will make the finance profit by immediately asking, "Can we finance our purchase here or will we have to go to a bank?"

THE DIRECT APPROACH

There is an approach known as the direct approach that, when used properly, saves everybody a lot of time and effort and eliminates a lot of wear and tear on the nervous system. The direct approach can be used only on a straight, no-trade purchase. It is literally impossible to lay it on the line if a trade is involved, for it is too easy for a salesman to juggle and switch figures around. Never attempt to use the direct approach on a factory-order purchase.

Here's what to do: Walk onto the showroom floor, make a general approach or introduction to the salesman, and tell him, "You have a sale if you will take a $200 gross profit deal. Will you take a two-buck deal?" And then shut up.

The ball is in his lap and he must now say yes, no, or maybe. If he says maybe, continue with, "I know exactly what I want, and I have no trade-in, no tricks, no games. If you will take my deal, fine. If you will not, then say so and I will find someone who will. I'll figure my own deal and I'll compensate for your floor plan charge if necessary. I'll finance it through your dealership, so you will make the finance profit also. Fair enough? Will you do it?"

If he says no, you have the option to leave or try back-up Plan A. Plan A is to find out what kind of deal the salesman will take. "If you will not take a $200 deal, how close will you come?" If the salesman still balks, still does not seem to want to play, then leave. If he does give you a gross profit figure, decide at that time whether it is close enough to satisfy you. You might get lucky and select a car that has just come off the truck, so you will not have to pay a floor plan charge and can afford to give a little on the gross.

If he says yes, he will take a $200 quickie, tell him to check with his sales manager right now, to be sure he will be able to obtain approval on a $200 deal if you write one. Ninety-nine percent of the time a salesman will not be authorized to give a low gross deal to a customer without management approval. You must make it perfectly clear, from the start, that you mean business and that you expect him to also. Then let him show you his stock.

From the nature of your approach, the salesman and his sales manager must assume that you are a sharp trader. They may, however, take the chance that you are bluffing and try to sell you their car at their price. They may go along with you, start to finish, until you prove that you do know what you are doing. At that point they may put pressure on you to see it their way, or flatly refuse to give you the deal, or sigh in resignation and give you the deal exactly as you write it. Their final effort will be something like this: "Look, we simply cannot give you the deal you want; we can give you a $300 deal." From there they will work their way down, $10 at a time, until you finally yield and say, "Okay, I'll take it." For the extra effort made to wear you down, they could make an extra $50. For the sake of a little patience on your part, you can save the fifty and get the deal you want.

Salesmen are cautious of the quickie sale, especially if the person walks in and starts talking buy, buy, buy before he has looked, touched, and driven. The person who tries to move this fast usually does his thinking after the fact. It can therefore be difficult for you to use this direct approach on a salesman, for he will not initially read you as a serious, educated buyer. He will read you as a quickie customer who plans to bluff his way through the sale. You must convince him you are indeed serious, that you are knowledgeable, and that you know what you are doing. How much convincing you must do depends on the individual salesman with whom you are dealing.

THE IMPLIED APPROACH

The most effective approach, with or without a trade-in, is the subtle, implied approach. You lay nothing on the line, make no commitments, and give no ultimatum, yet you set the stage to write the deal you want.

To lay it on the line is to say, "Look, I know you can take $800 off the sticker price. How much better can you do?"

To make a commitment is to say, "If you take $800 off the sticker price, I will buy the car today."

To give an ultimatum is to say, "If you cannot take $800 off the sticker, I do not want to do business with you; I will leave. How about it?"

Any of these approaches will receive a response, but not necessarily the response you expect. To lay it on the line makes the salesman defensive and argumentative. He will say to himself and then to you, "Why should

I take any more off the sticker, even if I want to take the $800 off?" The salesman may then decide that he will give no higher a discount than he absolutely must.

To make a commitment or give an ultimatum kills any chance for negotiating. If the salesman says, "Okay, I can take $800 off the sticker; do you want the car right now or do you want to pick it up in an hour?" you just bought a car. You cannot say, "I just wanted to see if you would take that much off the price." The salesman will physically throw you off the lot.

To use the implied approach is to say, "Are you running a special promotion this week or are you just giving your normal discounts?" (Smile when you ask.) You automatically imply that, promotion or not, the salesman always discounts his merchandise and that it is a fixed (normal) amount. Now, no matter what he says, he loses negotiating strength. If he says, "We do not discount," he will lose you completely; you will go to a dealer who does discount. If he says, "No promotions, just our usual discounts," you may now come back with, "And what is your company policy regarding discounts?" Or, "What are your normal discounts?" and go from there.

Implied approach is implied consent. Any answer to an implied consent question benefits the person asking. Regardless of the answer given, it implies consent, acceptance, and agreement. Implied consent always consists of a choice of two options. "Do you want to take the car home tonight or pick it up tomorrow?" Whichever answer you give, you just bought a car. The salesman implies that you have made the decision to buy, that there is no question about it, and that he just wants to clarify the details of delivery.

Since you will be using implied consent, you must always assume that the answer you want is already there, and that all you are doing is clarifying the details. This principle is particularly effective in the service department, but it can be used anywhere throughout your purchase activities, from approach through negotiations. "Are you going to give me floor mats for the front and back or just for the front?" "Are you going to give me another $100 off or a free rustproofing?" (On a used car: "Are you going to tune up the engine or change the oil?") Use your imagination on this one; it is wide open.

COMMUNICATING

The act of communicating and establishing an understanding is important, both for the customer and for the salesman. Communication that secures an understanding between the two of you will be easier and each of you will feel more comfortable if you seem to be of the same caliber of intelligence. Always attempt to talk on the same level as the salesman, but to a point. If the salesman uses gutter language, you may not want to come down to his level. If, however, he uses simple terms to express himself, then adjust to his level. Always maintain good eye contact with the salesman when communicating. Poor eye contact indicates introversion, or the fact that you have something to hide. Do not look down or to the side when you speak, or walk away trailing a sentence. Be brief, keep points simple, speak clearly and distinctly, and think before you open your mouth.

It is imperative that you have a few select phrases to toss at a salesman to firm up what he is trying to tell you and, when necessary, to bring the conversation down to earth; salesmen are well known for small talk, evasiveness, and double talk. When a salesman says, "You know what I mean?" or, "You do understand, don't you?" simply reply, "No, I do not know what you mean. Could you be a little more specific? Could you explain that in greater detail? Would you mind telling me exactly what you mean by that? What are you trying to tell me?" This will tell the salesman to quit playing games. It also lets him know that you want the whole story, not just part of it, and that he can be specific without being lengthy. If you do not understand something, question it. His intention may be to confuse you by talking around the issue. By remaining silent rather than admitting ignorance of what he is saying, you let the salesman be successful in his effort to sidestep the matter.

STRATEGIES AND PRECAUTIONS

Placing the salesman on the defensive makes him apologetic, makes him explain, makes him give promises, and makes him defend his position—all to your advantage. The more he says, the more he must live up to, not only while you are negotiating the deal, but after the sale as well. It also uncovers hidden information that a salesman would otherwise not offer. Where there is defense there is offense. While the salesman is defending, you are definitely on the offense. As long as he is defending, he is talking, which gives you time to plan your next move and think of your next question, and time to analyze what is happening. It slows the salesman down and interrupts his selling cycle. The technique is simple enough if you follow a few basic rules. First, a question of general interest relative to after-the-purchase service.

"How is your service department?" you ask.

"Our service department is tops in the area," he replies. (Statement)

"People have told me that your service department is not too good, that they have had a few problems and are not all that happy." (Statement, set up).

"Oh no, I cannot imagine who could say that or why they would say it." (Defense) "All my customers are well taken care of when they need service. I personally see to it." (Implied promise)

"Then what you are saying is that if I buy a car from you, I can expect excellent service, and you will personally see to it. Is that right?" (Confirmation)

"Part of getting good service depends upon how well a salesman gets along with the service manager and the service personnel. I get along well with all of them, so you need not worry about the service you are going to get." (Direct promise)

A salesman has been trained to handle problem areas quickly and then to get off the subject or sidestep the issue. If you do not receive the answers, (the promises you desire), you may find it necessary to reopen the issue, so ask again:

"Well, if there is one thing that means a lot to me, it is good service. I don't want to have to argue with a service manager each time I need something done to my car. Can you assure me that I will get good service?"

"Look, buy the car from me and I promise you good service. Is that fair enough?" (Firm promise)

Now the salesman has no choice but to back up his promise. If he does not, you have every right to hold him personally responsible for any bad service you might receive during warranty coverage. A salesman knows whether his service department is good, mediocre, or bad. If it is bad, he will hesitate to make a firm commitment that you will receive good service.

You may prefer third-party evidence to get the answer you need: "People have told me that your service department is not very good." If the salesman says, "Yes, I know our service is not the best in the country, but what can I do about it?" you have the answer you need. If he is evasive and says, "Our service is no worse than that of any other service department in the area," again, you have the answer you need, because he is implying that his service department is not quite up to snuff. If he quickly and strongly defends his service by stating, "It is the best in the area—second to none," chances are that it is.

A statement such as, "I hear you are having trouble with this particular model" brings about interesting conversation. If there are major problems with the model and the salesman knows about them, he will go right along with you and agree; he may even tip you off to exactly what the problems are. If there are no problems that he knows of, he may question you about exactly what problems you have heard about. In that instance, you need only plead ignorant to the facts to get off the hook. "I don't know exactly what the problems are; some friends of mine told me this model is not a very great car," or "They told me that you were having a few problems with this model—a few bugs not yet worked out." That is a relatively safe statement, for every car has at least one bug.

Any statement or question that begins with, "I have heard," "I understand this or that," "Is it true that," or "Is this the model that" requires a response and defense. This weakens a salesman's negotiating strength, for no matter what he does he will never be completely certain how important any fear or objection you express is to you. In the closing room, while he plans what deal to present, he will be thinking of all the negatives you have presented.

When you need honest, sincere advice from a salesman, you do not always know that it will be the best he has to offer, and that it is, in fact, honest. A simple, "Help me make up my mind," is too vague and too open to make a salesman stop and think before he gives you advice.

In this instance, you must play a little dumb ("I do not know that much about cars"), appeal to the salesmam's ego ("I would appreciate it if you would give me your thoughts on this matter"), use a little flattery ("You are in the business, and you should know exactly which car is best for me"), put him on the spot and force him to give you honest advice ("Could you give me your honest opinion on this"), reward him for doing a good job ("I will really appreciate it and it will mean a sale for you"), punish him for a bad job ("Of course if you give me bad advice, I will not be happy, and I will tell you how unhappy I am every day that your doors are open. You will have to listen to me knowing all the time that I will not be buying my next car from you"), and participate and work together toward a common goal ("Do you think we can put our heads together and see what you think will be our best course of action," or "Let's sit down and see what we can come up with").

Be wary of the good-is-good and bad-is-good salesman. As far as he is concerned, whether you like it and want it or do not like it and do not want it, you are smart for your decision. If you comment favorably about disc brakes, the salesman will tell you how wise you are for wanting disc brakes. That same salesman will tell you how wise you are for liking drum-type brakes if you say you do not like disc brakes. Advice from this type of person might as well not have been given, for it is offered only to encourage your purchase and to help you justify what you are doing. Treat the advice lightly, and do not let it influence your final decisions. It will help if you tell the salesman that no one item will destroy your plans to buy his car, and that you are really looking for serious, constructive advice. As always, it is best to solicit multiple opinions rather than one opinion given for the sake of profit.

PAY PLANS

A salesman is paid when you buy a car from him, but he does not necessarily clean up on every sale he makes. Much depends upon how much was made on the deal (gross profit for the dealer) or how many units the salesman sells within a month (sometimes based on weekly production). It is important to be aware of how a salesman is paid, since it can have a definite effect upon the deal you are offered.

There are two major pay plans for car salesmen: the percent-of-gross plan and the per-unit-sold plan.

Under the percent-of-gross plan, the salesman receives a fixed percentage (usually 25 percent) computed against the actual gross profit made on each car he sells. The more profit he makes on the deal, the fatter his paycheck will be. A $400 gross profit deal gives him $100.

Under the per-unit-sold plan, the salesman receives a fixed number of dollars per car sold, regardless of the gross profit made. This amount will vary between dealers and is usually tied to a bonus system to reward high-volume sales production.

Before you can use this information, you must find out how your particular salesman is paid. Needless to say, you cannot bluntly ask, "How are you paid?" You must make the salesman think you are merely interested in the automobile industry in general. Lead into your real question by telling a story or asking a series of small questions. "You know, Mr. Salesman, I thought of being a car salesman at one time. It seems like it could be very lucrative. You work on a commission basis, don't you?" He will answer yes, and you continue, "I am just curious, but how is your commission determined? Do you get so much for each car you sell? Does it make any difference whether I buy a cheap car or an expensive car?" Or, "My brother-in-law told me that car salesmen are paid only when they sell and that they get only a small percentage of the profit. Is that true?" Either approach should yield the information you want.

When you have the information you want, file it for future reference. What you must remember is that the salesman who works on percent of gross will try to get every dollar out of the deal that he can. His income is directly geared to gross profit made. Every dollar he adds to the basic deal is 25¢ in his pocket. Twenty-five cents sounds menial, but a $200 negotiated difference on a deal will put an extra $50 right into his pocket when he convinces you to accept his deal. The credibility of the percent-of-gross salesman is to be questioned at all times, regardless of his sincerity. When he tells you that he is going to try to force his sales manager to accept your terms, can you really believe him? Conversely, the salesman who is paid per unit sold could hardly care less for what price any given car sells. When this salesman tells you that he will do everything he can to get you the deal you want, he usually means it. The per-unit-sold salesman will also be more inclined to make a sincere effort to get you the extras you would like tacked onto the deal as freebies; he will be more inclined to tell his sales manager that the sale hinges upon whether or not you get the freebie. He does not care if his sales manager must give something away to make the sale as long as it does not affect his car count for the month.

BYPASS THE SALESMAN?

Some people think they will get a better deal if they bypass the salesman and deal direct with upper management. They feel that if the dealership does not have to pay a salesman a commission, the savings will be passed on to them. In other words, eliminate the middleman and automatically save money. Quite the contrary. You will pay more when you deal with management than if you deal and negotiate with a salesman.

Most dealerships turn all deals over to the salesman who was "up" on the floor when the deal was written and signed, so if the salesman is going to be paid on these house accounts (deals written by management) anyway there is no savings to be passed on. Even if a dealership retains house accounts and does not pay the salesman, you will still save no money, for the house is going to make as much as possible on each and every deal that is written.

Normal dealership procedure is to turn you over to a salesman with a brief introduction stating who you are and what you plan to buy. This is the same salesman with whom you would have nothing to do a few minutes earlier—the one you chose to ignore. What a small world. What kind of job do you think he is going to do for you? He knows what you tried to do and he knows that you couldn't care less about him. You could consider an appeal for mercy.

By going directly to management you lose negotiating strength, since you can hardly stand there and argue with a manager in the same manner you can argue price, trade allowance, and terms with a salesman. You have approached management because you trust them (friend to friend), and, because you know them and they know you, you trust them to write a fair deal for you. This intrinsic trust gives management an edge in the matter, plus extra profit. You do not question the deal that is offered to you and you assume that the figures quoted are nonnegotiable. If you have bypassed the salesman you cannot use him as a runner and a go-between to management for your negotiations. It is infinitely easier to walk away from a salesman than it is to walk away from that friend you have in management when you decide to "think about it."

The best course of action is to get yourself off the hook from the beginning. Approach the salesman and tell him that you know someone in management, but that you don't want him to lose his commission on your purchase. The salesman will know his dealership's policy regarding house accounts and will either work you or immediately turn you over to management. If he works you and management later chooses not to credit him with the sale, that is a conflict between the salesman and the dealership; you incur no blame for the lost commission. Because you expressed concern for him, the salesman will bend over backward to help you before, during, and after the sale. Keep him on your side.

APATHETIC SALESMEN

Apathetic salesmen are salesmen with an aloof attitude who act as if they are doing you a favor by selling you a car. They are cold and unresponsive to you and your needs. When, by chance, you encounter this type of salesman, you will not want to stay, let alone do business with him There are several ways to handle the bad salesman.

1. Leave the showroom immediately and shop another dealership.
2. Ask to speak to his sales manager. When you meet him, tell him that you are not happy with the salesman and request that another salesman handle you.
3. Leave, and return when the salesman you do not like is not on duty. When all is said and done, advise management of your experience with the first salesman and how close they came to losing your business.

9
Negotiating

BEFORE YOU WHEEL AND DEAL

NEGOTIATING BEGINS WITH your first contact with the salesman. He is beginning to set you up for the close (asking for sale and signature) as early as the initial handshake. Your concern and effort is to set him up, and this begins with the demonstration ride and product inspection. (See page 91 for additional information.)

Even though you are looking at new cars, do not assume that they all drive, handle, and feel alike. Drive at least three of the same model and equipment—all with power steering or without; all with the same size engine and type of transmission. Subject them all to the same roads and conditions. You will notice a slight difference in the handling and feel among the three, but you will get a good idea of how the basic model should perform. One may stand out as the worst of the three and naturally you would reject it.

Driving three or more of the same model also lets you develop a list of objections (small annoyances) that will strengthen your negotiations. There has to be at least one thing wrong with each car—a squeak or a rattle; a steering pull to one side; uncomfortable seats; radio static; a clutch that is spongy or soft or hard; an engine that stalls, hesitates, has a rough idle, or is nonresponsive; or something that is too tight or too loose.

Make comments as you drive, such as: "Do they all pull to one side like this? Do they all idle this rough? I don't like the way this corners. This clutch feels funny. Do they all shift this slowly?" Back on the lot you can continue: "The trunk is too small; the head room and leg room are not quite good enough." And don't forget the standard equipment:

66

"I don't like power brakes, and that's the only way this comes, isn't it? I could do without a vinyl roof. I just can't see paying for something I don't really need. But I do like the car, sort of. Well, if the price is good enough, I guess I can live with it."

When you finally decide on the car you want, meticulously check it out bumper to bumper, and drive it twice—before you negotiate and before you sign anything. Even if the dealer is making half what he would normally make on a new-car deal, you still have the right to demand a blemish-free car. The factory picks up the tab on blemishes anyway. Any flaws you find enhance your negotiating strength. Remember:

1. Check all equipment on the car against the factory label (sticker), to be sure everything is on the car at the time you sign to buy it.

2. Itemize all optional equipment in your notebook and transfer the list onto your purchase contract, including the serial number of the car you are buying. A switch is possible without the serial number.

3. Be prepared to take the car home the same day you buy it. If you leave it overnight, you may find equipment has been switched by the time you take delivery. Steel-belted tires become glass-belted tires; an AM/FM becomes an AM radio.

4. Disregard any extras that are not on the factory label, such as dealer handling charges, equipment additions, road test charges, rustproofing or undercoat, and any switches of equipment that may have been made.

CLOSING THE SALE

The Closing Room. This is where the salesman does his real selling, where you do your real bargaining, where approvals are made and signatures ink the paper, and money changes hands. This is where all hardcore negotiating takes place, where the final deal is given birth. All that preceded was only in preparation for the closing room.

Never fear the closing room. If the salesman is to make the sale that lets you own the car you want, you must sit down together and negotiate, talk it over, work things out. Here are a few common closing approaches and appeals used by salesmen. They are basically simple in design, but the effect and impact they have on your negotiations is not.

1. The sympathy close. There are three types of sympathy close. One is an appeal to your sympathetic nature by the salesman. "Feel sorry for me and buy; sales are down; I have not been making enough money to support my family; I have a wife and three children who

are hungry," and on and on. The salesman who uses the emotionally charged sympathy close does not deserve the sale.

The second-sympathy close involves a factory- or company-sponsored contest or bonus the salesman will receive if he gets just one more sale. Sometimes the contest or bonus is real and sometimes it is not. The key to this close is for the salesman to create a sense of urgency where none exists; you might as well buy the car now and help the salesman win the contest or receive the bonus. This close plays upon your sympathetic nature to "help the salesman out" and is used by salesmen who spot a person with a charitable personality. Do what is convenient for you. If you are not inclined to buy on that very day, tell the salesman he will have to find someone else to help him win his contest or bonus.

The third sympathy close uses reverse sympathy; the salesman wants to make you feel sorry for yourself and to convince you that the only way to ease your sorrow is to buy his product. He may approach this close in a variety of ways but the most frequently used is the "you owe it to yourself" approach.

Just consider what it is that you owe yourself. Do you owe yourself a monthly payment that will burden your budget? Do you owe yourself a car that is not really what you want and need? Think before you leap. Self-indulgence is all right, provided it does not bury you.

2. My boss. A frequently used close is this: "I am mad at my boss today. I do not care if the company makes money on this deal or not. I am going to see that you get the highest discount anyone can get." Just like that. The salesman is mad at his boss, and even though his paycheck depends upon how much he makes on the deal (gross profit), he is going to do special favors for you, a stranger.

Now, unfortunately for you, the price he just quoted is the best that he can obtain; if he could do better, he surely would because he is mad at his boss.

He may turn it around: "My boss is in a good mood today, so we will have no trouble getting the trade allowance you want. Now, the book says that your car is worth $3,000, but I am going to do everything I can to get you the $3,300 you want" (setup). Good mood or bad, his sales manager looks at the numbers with detached emotion. Profit is profit, and he will write as much as he thinks he can get. When the salesman returns, he will begin with, "Well, he is in a better mood than I thought. As I told you, the book value on your car is $3,000. I was able to talk him into giving you an allowance of $3,110'' (look at the difference: $190 less than you want).

3. Oh, brother. The salesman may use the "brother" approach. "Can I talk to you like a brother? If you were my brother, I would give you this advice." Or, "I am going to treat you like my own brother. I will give you the same deal I would give my own brother."

   The "brother" approach is designed to eliminate doubt and close the credibility gap between you and the salesman. When you doubt his sincerity, you need assurances that he is doing nothing different from what he would do with any other customer. Pass over this story as if the salesman had said nothing. His sales manager does not care if he is dealing with a brother, sister, in-law, or whomever; he looks only at profit—"How much are we going to make on this deal?"

4. The green bean. "I am new in this business." Veteran salesmen use this ploy to lower the guard of either a hostile customer or a very quiet customer. If you know you are dealing with a 15-year veteran salesman, you will resist his closing attempts, and you will fear being sold or pressured into making a decision. Conversely, you will feel relaxed and confident around a novice. In the back of your mind your pride and ego whispers, "I can handle this guy." You are therefore relaxed and are not prepared to do battle with an experienced veteran salesman. Be wary of an admission of being new to the business, for most green salesmen will not admit this. They usually want to give the impression of experience.

5. The other customer. To create urgency to buy, a salesman may invent another person who is interested in the car you want. The other person will either be his sales manager or another salesman. The phone will ring and the scenario begins: "Yes, Mr. Jones, I still have that car in stock. In fact, I have a customer sitting here right now who is thinking of buying it. (Pause) No, he hasn't bought it yet. (Pause) Well, how soon can you get here? (Pause) No, I cannot put a hold on the car for you. It is first come, first served. If this gentleman decides to buy it you will just have to buy another one. (Pause) Well, let me check with my sales manager and see what he has to say about holding it for you. But it is really first come, first served."

   Obviously you do not want to lose the car and your first impulse will be to tell the salesman to tell the other customer that you just bought it. Don't do it. Consider that there are other cars on his lot equally as nice. If there is another customer interested in that particular car, let him have it. If the salesman truly had someone else interested, he would not make it first come, first served; he would make it, "Which deal will give me the highest profit?"

Tell the salesman to go ahead and let the other guy have the car. When he hangs up tell him that you are going to sit there until the guy shows up, and that you will not buy anything else until you are sure that car is sold. How long you sit and wait is entirely up to you. Or you can stand up and walk away as if to leave the dealership. When the salesman asks where you are going, simply tell him you are going to another dealer to buy a car at your price.

6. Today only. In a closing or negotiating situation, the salesman may tell you that his sales manager will give you the car you want, the way you want it, for a certain price, but "Only if you buy today. If you come back tomorrow you will not get the same deal." Your first instinct is to say, "If he will sell it to me today for that price, he will sell it to me tomorrow for the same price." To which the salesman will reply, "Look, I've seen him do this before and the customer did not believe he meant it. The next day when he returned, my sales manager refused to give him the car for the same price he had quoted the day before. My sales manager wants your business today, not tomorrow, and he is willing to bend a little to get it. Let's face it; he knows that you may not come back if you leave now. So how about it; let's send you home in your new car today." (Confirmation, appeal to logic, commitment seeking, implied consent.)

It sounds fairly convincing; however, if you leave and return the next day you will be able to get the car at the quoted, lower, today-only price. If the sales manager can sell the car today for a profit, he will not turn that same profit away 24 hours later. To let you walk away is to let you cool off, shop around, change your mind, or ask for a better deal. So he must do everything he can to sign you up today.

7. The sound of silence. When a good salesman asks a closing question (asks for the sale), he will shut up and wait for your answer. If he is a second-class salesman he will ask a closing question and then, before you can answer, butt in with further comment. The logic of silence is that whoever speaks first, loses the battle. If you say yes, he has a sale. If you say no, he will ask, "Why not" which eventually leads to another closing question. If you say nothing, he will sit in silence until you do speak. Your options are:

1. Say yes, no, or maybe.
2. Say anything else—change the subject.
3. Say nothing at all—the sound of silence.
4. Answer his question with a question.

Saying, yes, no, or maybe gives the salesman reentry to the situation and another chance to close you. Saying nothing at all creates enormous tension. The salesman has absolutely no idea what you are thinking, whether you were ready for a closing question or not, or whether or not he has just blown the sale. He thinks you are spending this silent time thinking of *not* buying, and planning how you are going to tell him. The longer the silence, the more he will believe just that. Sooner or later, someone must say something. If you clam up completely you may get a slightly better deal, if it is possible for the salesman to give you one. Changing the subject offers temporary relief and relieves the salesman of the effort of trying to close you for a while. He must handle your subject change and then work himself around to another closing question. Answering his question with a question opens doors for further discussion. The question you ask need not be remotely related to the question he just asked. In fact, if it is unrelated, it directs the course of the conversation away from a close and puts you in control. Strategically, the more questions you ask, the less selling the salesman can do.

8. **An answer to every objection.** Do not think for a moment that you are unique in having reasons for not buying, or in knowing ways to attempt to get away from a salesman. A good salesman has heard them all. And he has an answer to every one of them. The following excuses and stalls show what is commonly used and how the salesman will react.

"We want to think about it. We want to talk it over—we will let you know tomorrow." The salesman's response: "Exactly what do you want to think about? What do you want to talk over? If you need to talk it over, you can do that much right here. I'll leave you two alone and you call me when you are ready."

"I have to go home and talk it over with my wife—I will let you know tomorrow." The salesman's response: "What exactly do you want to talk over? Can't you make the decision without her? Here is a phone; call her right now and talk it over. Is she home right now? Let's take the car to your house and show it to her; it will give you a chance to drive it again."

"The price is too high." The salesman presumes that you do not know how much is too much, so he will ask two questions: "Is it too high because you cannot afford to spend that much?" Or, "Is it too high because you can get a better price from another dealer?" If the price is more than you can afford, he will try to switch you to a less expensive model. If another dealer can give you a better deal, he will attempt to beat the other dealer with amenities—you should pay more to get better service, better salesman, better dealership, and so on.

All excuses are rebutted in a manner that puts the salesman in control. He will ferret out the real reason why you want to leave without buying and force you to give another reason "why not" until you run out of reasons.

When you want to leave, you will find the "sleep on it" excuse very effective. Tell the salesman that you never buy anything without sleeping on it. He can hardly offer to let you sleep at his dealership overnight to reach your final decision.

If you are with someone—spouse, fiancée, or friend—and need to get off the hook, simply start an argument with whomever is with you. This can be fun if you can put on a good act. Few salesmen will dare butt into an argument of this nature. Begin with a simple disagreement: You like blue and she likes red. Then get into the heavy stuff—the major differences of opinion.

If a salesman is persistent, you may have to tell him bluntly, "I do not like pushy salesmen, and I would never buy from a pushy salesman. If you want me to buy your product, we will work at my speed, and my speed is not ready to buy today."

WHEELING AND DEALING

Negotiating. Negotiating is trying to save a few bucks on a purchase that you are going to make anyway. The decision to buy has generally been made when you sit down to work out the price and terms of the purchase. It may, at times, be a conditional decision ("If the price is right, I will buy"), but it is, nevertheless, a decision. Once you have made a decision to buy, your negotiations may be weakened by the fact that you want the car, and that it is difficult to separate the decision to buy from the decision to buy at a specific price. If you want the car badly enough, you will pay almost any price for it; you will not hold out for a $50- better deal if you are led to believe you will lose the car for holding out.

If the dealer is trying to make a killing on the deal, you must consider the fact that there are other cars at other dealers and mentally be prepared to continue to look and shop until you find the price that satisfies you.

Do's & Don'ts. When you decide to go ahead and buy your next new car, wash your old car, mow your lawn, clean out your garage, straighten your house or apartment, and take a cool bath or shower. These actions will help you to carry over the success attitude when you sit down with a salesman to work a deal. As you clear the clutter around you, the mind automatically becomes less cluttered and functions more properly. Things seem to go your way and you pursue what you want with more confidence.

Psychologically, you will negotiate with more confidence if you have the cash in your pocket (a bank account will do as well) when you are firming up a deal. You will have more self-confidence, for you are spending real, cash-out-of-pocket money, not just numbers on paper. You will be more cautious about throwing your money away on an impulse purchase. If you have the money in hand, your attitude toward the salesman will become, "I have the money and you must be very nice to me if you want it. You will have to give me a super deal before I turn my cash over to you." (However, do not tell the salesman you have cash. He must think you plan to give him the finance profit.)

When negotiating, you must always be talking about a specific car. Do not choose a car at random just to have a car with which to test the salesman's figures. Pick the car you would buy provided the salesman and you get together on the terms. His discount, trade allowance, and terms quoted mean nothing if they are for a car that you do not care to buy, and they cannot be used to accurately compare one dealer against another.

Never ask for anything and expect to receive it after you have signed on the dotted line. If the salesman includes something, at your request, after you have signed, it is for appearance's sake alone. His immediate response to you will be, "I will put it right here and do the best I can to get it for you." His first words to his sales manager will be, "He asked for it after he signed the contract, so we can scratch that off right now." When you signed, you bought, and anything after that is forgotten by the salesman and his sales manager.

Never ask a salesman to "try" to do anything for you. Always make it seem as if the entire deal hinges upon his ability to perform; if he does not produce results, you will not buy. "Try to get this for me" tells the salesman that you will buy whether you get it or not. When he returns with the deal, he will tell you he "tried," which is all you asked. "Do you think'' is just as bad. "Do you think your sales manager will give me extra (whatever)?'' This is telling the salesman, "I do not think he will; do you?'' The salesman will say, "I do not think he will, but I will try my best to get it for you. Now, just sign here and I'll see what I can do.''

If you want a freebie added to the deal, by all means ask for it, but keep it short and to the point. "Mr. Salesman, your figures are good, the price is right, the trade allowance is what I had in mind. Now, I will buy the car today if you will include (whatever) as part of the deal.'' Not "thrown in'' and not "give me,'' but "include as part of.'' This throws the ball in his lap, and he must make a response. If he says no, or if he tries to talk you out of the freebie, he may lose the deal. Your job is to make him believe that you will not buy without the freebie.

Never use, "I cannot afford it,'' to get an extra $75 knocked off the price. What you are telling the salesman is that you can afford the first $9,000 of the cost of the car, but that the extra $75 will break your piggy bank. It just is not believable. A salesman who hears this will ignore it and hold out for his figures. Use "I cannot afford'' for the monthly payment only. Approach the topic by telling the salesman that it is not just a few dollars a month, you have already stretched your budget allotment for a car by $25 a month and that is as far as you can possibly go. Most salesmen can talk you into raising $10.00 on a monthly payment, but $50 a month is another matter.

When a salesman writes a deal and makes his presentation (offer) to you, never, ever, ask to use the restroom if you plan to negotiate the deal at all. That simple request will ruin any chance you may have had to work a better deal. If you have just returned from a 1-hour demonstration ride and are ready to sit down and talk business, now is the time to use the restroom. As soon as you sit down and begin to discuss figures, be prepared to sit there until you have the exact deal you want to sign. This may be a little more than difficult for someone with a bladder problem, but as soon as you head for the restroom the salesman will head for his sales manager to tell him to put a deal on the board. Here is why: For the most part, until the time you reach your final decision to buy, most every muscle in your body is tense. When you mentally reach a buy decision the salesman is not aware of it, but your body is. The figures satisfy you and so you relax. When you relax, your body functions go back to normal and what had been suppressed because of tension and anxiety now makes itself known. When you return to the negotiating table you may find the salesman insistent about the deal he is offering you.

BASIC RULES OF NEGOTIATION

Because the final price agreed upon will be somewhere between your opening bid (low) and his opening bid (high), start as close to dealer cost as possible, without going below it. Go too low and the salesman will suspect you are just guessing a deal. Go too high and you automatically lose money.

Whomever you negotiate with, you must remember never to come up on price faster than he comes down on price. If he is yielding in increments of $25 per offer, then you should yield $25 or less for each counteroffer. When a salesman moves only $25 per clip, he is trying to lead you to believe that he is close to his bottom figure; he must be because he can give you only another $25 on discount or trade allowance. His task is to keep the final figures as close to his opening offer as possible. The tactic is also designed to make you come up in leaps and bounds from your opening figure. You must convince the salesman that each offer of $25 you make could be your last offer—end of negotiating.

Never use the same number of dollars twice while making progressive offers; stagger the amounts as you increase your offers. If you consistently make offer after offer using increments of $25 on each increase, the salesman will spot this as a waiting game and simply begin to come down in smaller amounts, if he comes down at all. If he decides that you are using a program of increases, he must assume that there is no limit on the number of times you will come up on price. Use odd numbers for your increases: raise $25, then $32, then back to $25 again. Always go over $50 levels: Rather than an offer of $8250 make an offer of $8255; rather than $8300, make it $8312.

STRATEGIES

At some point in your negotiating the salesman will toss his pen on the desk and say, "Look, we are only $100 apart. Why don't we split the difference; I will come down $50 if you will come up $50." This is the greatest pick-me-up in the business. It usually gives the salesman the deal and an extra $50 more or less.

Normally, when a salesman wants to split the difference, he is just about ready to give you the deal you want and is merely trying to make a little more profit. When he wants to split the difference, get ready to hold to the last offer you made. If he will not come down to your figure, rather than split the difference with him, quarter it. If you are $100 apart, you will come up $25 and make him come down $75. When he sees he will not get the $50 he wants, he will take the $25.

A ploy frequently used by salesmen to gain an extra $50 to $100 on a deal is the break-even plea. The salesman assumes that you do not know dealer cost. The ploy is to convince you that your offer will put him in the hole or at best, give him a break-even deal. Therefore, you must pay a little more for your car. A used-car purchase is especially vulnerable to this tactic, for it is not possible to determine accurately just how much gross is in a particular car. A trade-involved deal is also susceptible because of the elusive true trade value. Caution is advised on a break-even plea. When in doubt, negotiate.

When a salesman writes a trade-involved deal for a new or used car, he must play down the trade-in and play up his car. He will usually itemize every feature of his car upon the face of the contract and will put only the year, model, and mileage of your car down for the trade information. The list on your trade-in will only be the reconditioning necessary to bring your car up to par. Although he originally inspected your car in silence, the salesman can now tear it apart by using the written word as his instrument—the ink on the paper, which has the quality of permanence and gives him the negotiating edge.

To offset this, list all the positive features of your trade-in when he swings the paper around for your signature. If he has listed reconditioning on your car, list whatever you found wrong with his car. If he stops you from itemizing, simply say, "That's all right; you took the time to list all the benefits of your car and I want to take the time to list those of my car."

When the deal is written, those items that are standard equipment from the factory need not be itemized on the contract. However, optional items should be itemized right on the face of the contract for your protection. If they are not on the contract, something may be missing when you take delivery, even if it was on the car when you inspected it and signed to buy it, and even if it was listed on the window sticker. Unless you paid full window-sticker price for the car, the dealer can always say that the discounted price you paid did not include the missing items. If you took delivery of the car, it implies that you accepted the car as equipped at that time.

Reasoning. Reasoning, in a negotiating situation, is nothing more than giving reasons why you feel as you do, why you think as you do, and why the other party should go along with you. Reasoning need not always be logical, valid, true, and accurate. It must make enough sense to convince the other person that unless he accepts what you are saying and makes a change, there will be no deal. As the customer, you must give the salesman reasons (stories, if necessary) that make enough sense to him so that he can go to his sales manager and convince him to make appropriate adjustments. It is not enough to sit there and obstinately demand more allowance or a larger discount; you need reasoning to win.

To talk up your car's trade value, choose from among the following:

1. "My car is a nice clean car that you will have no trouble selling for a nice clean profit."
2. "I could sell it myself for $500 more than you want to give me, but it would be an inconvenience for me to do so."
3. "I could sell my car at an auction for more than you want to give me."
4. "I cannot take that much of a loss on my car. You will have to come up on the trade allowance, which I am certain you can do."
5. "I have already been offered more for my car. I want to do business with your firm but you will have to come up a little before we can get together."
6. "I do not feel this is a fair deal to me. Why don't you sharpen up your pencil and do a little better?"

The salesman has his own set of reasoning tools, which make just enough sense to convince you that if you don't go along with him, there will be no deal. If he uses any of the following, ignore him:

1. "You are moving up 3 years for only X number of dollars. That is a fair deal for you." (Maybe it is and maybe it is not.)
2. "You do like my car (emotional involvement) and I can certainly use your trade-in (to make more profit), but you will have to come up on price."
3. "Here is the reconditioning we must do before we can sell your car for full retail." (The cost of reconditioning is passed on to the next buyer.)
4. "The average book value of your car is $X. (So who wrote the book?)
5. "I can buy the same car at the auction house for less than you want for your trade." (It is not the *same* car. Auction merchandise is always questionable in quality and origin.)
6. "My sales manager has years of experience. He feels your car is only worth $X. (It is only a feeling.)
7. "We are a very reasonable company. If we could do better, we would." (But if they can avoid doing better, they will.)

And so it goes, round for round. "If you must pay more for my product it is because I think my company is worth the extra money." (You are buying the product, not the company.) "We do a better job for you before and after the sale; service has to mean something, doesn't it?" (Why pay more for the same service someone else will get for paying less?) And you counterpropose: "Yes, but if you must allow me more for my trade-in it is because I think it is worth more. And besides, after I buy I will do everything I can to send you business by my personal recommendation. That has to mean something, doesn't it?" "We must get your car ready for our used car lot. Your car is in good shape, but we must take care of a few minor details." "If it is just a question of a few minor details, they can't cost that much to repair. There is nothing wrong with my car, and I have the receipts to show the tender loving care it received."

Disagree By Agreeing. A salesman knows that he must never argue with a customer, for he may win the argument and lose the sale. It is necessary for him to disagree by agreeing, which allows him to argue a point politely without offending the customer. All he must do is preface everything he is about to say with, "I agree with you completely, but I feel this way about it." Simply agree with him and give your side of the story: "I feel exactly the same way. However, I think it is possible that. . . ." "I agree with what you are saying, but here is how I feel about it."

The salesman may say, "My company must make a profit on this deal. You will have to come up to our price before we can deal." To which you counter, "I couldn't agree with you more. I realize your company must make a profit and, personally, I don't care how much profit you make—that's none of my business. But I have already gone over my limit, and I feel that my offer is fair to your company."

The Other Dealer's Price. It is impossible for any salesman to keep abreast of every model on the market, including all features, options, amenities, and changes, let alone sticker prices. What does this mean to you? If you are $100 apart on the deal, you can tell the salesman that you can get the same size car—or the same type of car—from Dealer X for $100 less than the price he proposes. The salesman wants to beat the other deal, if he can, rather than try to prove your credibility. Do not use the same product manufacturer for the comparison. Use a competitive manufacturer's product for price comparison (same basic model size and equipment).

Asking for Your Deal. Confidence in asking for a deal is best developed by lessening the degree of importance you attach to whether or not you get it. The more you want it, the harder it is to play your best hand and employ your best strategies.

Most people know they are to ask, but when the moment of truth arrives they become nervous, squirm in their seats, look down at the floor or up at the ceiling, and meekly ask for the deal. Salesmen know that a customer who asks for a deal meekly really expects to pay more and will oblige him and see that he does, in fact, pay more.

How you ask is very important. The question must be relaxed, as if you had just asked the salesman for a glass of water or a cup of coffee or a light for a cigarette. It must be done with confidence, as though you really expect to receive the deal and will be surprised if you do not. Do not mistake confidence for cockiness. To demand that the salesman give you the car for your price will only create a hostile, stubborn salesman.

Never hesitate to ask for a high trade allowance and discount. The worst that can happen is to be refused, and when you are refused you just give a little and ask again.

Deposits. To the dealership, a purchase agreement is not worth the paper it's written on if there is no deposit of value with it. A deposit can be cash, check, or the title to your trade-in. This indicates that, if the sales manager approves the deal as written and signed by you, you will consummate the purchase.

The question is, how much of a deposit do you need and in what form? A deposit should remain under your control, even though you give it to the salesman at the time you sign. If you give cash or the title to your car, the salesman controls the deposit. However, a salesman cannot cash a personal check immediately, and if necessary you can stop payment on it—therefore you control the deposit.

Your primary goal is to keep the deposit as low as possible. A salesman will ask for a deposit as soon as he thinks he has a deal going. Ask him how much he needs (not how much he wants, but how much he needs) and, regardless of his comments, tell him that you can give him a personal-check deposit for $25. If he asks for more, question his motives: "Why do you need more? What's wrong with twenty-five?" Give a salesman a $200-deposit and you can forget about changing your mind about the deal—you just bought. Always make the check payable to the dealership, never to the salesman.

MANAGEMENT DEAL APPROVAL

Few dealerships allow their salesman to write, negotiate, and finalize their own deals. Ninety-nine percent of the time a deal must be approved by upper management—either a sales manager, a general manager, or an officer of the company. Therefore, whatever a salesman offers or says to you is not binding on the dealership and means literally nothing without management approval. The salesman's job is to write a purchase commitment on your part and take it to management for approval or counteroffer.

Even though you are not dealing directly with the sales manager, your efforts must be just as strong as if you were face-to-face with him. Most salesmen relay your comments and objections to the sales manager just as you have expressed them.

Writing the Deal. When a salesman says, "Here is where I go to work for you," what he really is doing is preconditioning you. To precondition you, the salesman will assure you in the most soothing tones that he has your best interests at heart; that he really wants to see you get that new car; and that he will argue with his sales manager, if necessary, to see that you get a good deal. He will further precondition you to expect the worst possible. The lead-in goes like this: "I do not really think my sales manager will go along with this deal, but I will do my best to get it for you." Now you are set up for the refusal, and it will not be the salesman's fault when it comes.

Never, never tell a salesman your true bottom dollar, even if he is a relative. If his sales production and profit level is low for the month, you will become his high-profit sale for the month, simply because you trust him.

Never discuss your deal with whomever you may be sitting after the salesman leaves, and never divulge your bottom dollar when you think no one is listening. Although it is illegal, some dealers use listening devices, either transmitting bugs or land-line monitors, to listen to your conversation when the salesman is not there. If you want to discuss figures with someone, leave the closing room and talk elsewhere.

While your salesman is gone, you will be thinking, "Maybe I asked for too much. The salesman is probably right; I am a little too low on price. Well, I will go another $100 if his sales manager does not approve my offer. I sure do want that car; I can see it sitting in my driveway now. Wait until my next-door neighbors see this beauty. I wonder what's taking that salesman so long." And now you are ready for the salesman's return.

Even though his sales manager can give him a yes or no in 60 seconds, you will not see your salesman for 15 minutes. If your salesman is to present the illusion of 15 minutes' effort fighting for your deal, he must be gone for 15 minutes. Another reason for his absence is to make you think that each time you make an offer, it will be 15 minutes before you get an answer on the deal. The first 15 minutes bothers no one; it is the second and third and fourth that begin to rattle the nerves. If your salesman takes too long to obtain a rejection, politely tell him that you do not plan to wait around all day each time he must go to management for a conference. "Your sales manager knows whether he can sell me this car for my price or not, so see if you can make it a little quicker this time. I don't have all day to wait for your manager to make up his mind." Now he cannot play his little game, and he will return in 2 minutes with an answer. Your small display of impatience will also prompt them to give you the deal you want. ("He's getting ready to walk. Let's give him the car.")

Here's what normally happens: the salesman takes your offer to his sales manager, quickly presents the deal, gives his opinion of the customer, and estimates how much more money he thinks he can make on the deal. The manager reviews the deal and writes a counteroffer. If the salesman needs advice or help on a specific problem, his manager will offer suggestions. After his manager scratches all over the contract and signs it, the salesman is ready to return and present the counteroffer.

When the salesman finally returns with the magic word, he will hold you in suspense for a moment. You are sitting there eagerly waiting to hear whether or not you own the car, and you want to see the contract. But first, it is story time. The salesman may lead in like this: "Well, I did better than I expected. My sales manager could not give you the full trade value you wanted, but he did give you a fair trade figure (fair deal or good deal) based on current market conditions." (Wow, that's a relief to you and you have not even seen the deal yet.) He may ask, "Do you want to take the car home with you today?" which implies that he got the deal approved. You envision ownership—driving the car home, parking it in your driveway, and displaying it for all to see—all of which lowers your resistance to his counteroffer. Whatever he does say, it will be of a conciliatory nature.

Now he shows you the amended deal and asks for your acceptance. If you do not immediately accept, he will launch into the reasoning behind the counteroffer and again ask for an acceptance. Everything he says will be prefaced with assurances that he is doing the best he can for you.

You may see a lot of red-ink scribbling all over the revised contract that was so neat 15 minutes ago. This represents a red flag to you, for it means changes were made—changes not to your benefit. The purpose of the bright color and the abnormally large size of the figures is to draw your attention away from the deal as originally written and focus your attention on what the true deal is to be. However, do not become alarmed until you hear the salesman's beautifully told story.

If a trade-in is involved, the salesman will make his first reference to the numbers of the deal there. He must justify a lower allowance than you want. "If your car were in perfect condition, my manager could give you the allowance you want. However, as you know, your car needs some reconditioning to make it ready for our used-car lot; we cannot sell it as it sits. So, my manager had to deduct for reconditioning and get-ready charges" (get-ready charges that will be paid by the person who buys your old car). Ignore the deductions and get-ready charges and go back to your basic deal.

CounterOffer. The trade-involved counteroffer begins with a story. "Yes, my car does need some work to make it ready for resale. However, I did find a few things wrong with your car that I had not mentioned earlier. I really didn't want to be as picky as you seem to think you must be. Let's take another look at your car to be sure its condition is not as bad as you seem to think my car's is." (Dealing on a new car: "I did not like the ride; the engine idles rough; the steering pulls to one side. Let's take another drive. I'm not really sure I like it.") This approach is much better than trying to defend your car. You have ruined his procedure, ruined his ability to continue to pick your car apart, and you have put him on the defensive.

Go back to his car and begin your inspection all over again, or repeat the demonstration ride. Now the salesman will start to have second thoughts: maybe he and his sales manager should have taken your initial offer; maybe you will find more wrong with his car; maybe he will lose the deal altogether.

Rather than let you reinspect his car, the salesman may say, "Wait a minute; maybe I can get my sales manager to go along with your original offer." If he returns with his manager you know it is time for customer turnover; the salesman has used all his ammunition. If he returns alone with no deal approval, he has been instructed to continue to try to sell you.

While the salesman is gone, do not sit there and wait for his return. Go out onto the lot and check out his car again. If he obtains deal approval, he can bring it out to you. If it is turnover time, he must call you back to the closing room. If he brings a revised deal that you do not like, you are that much closer to leaving the dealership. The salesman wants you to stay in the closing room. If you wander off every time he leaves you alone, he will be that much quicker about returning and that much more nervous about losing you altogether.

Turnover. At any point, your salesman may elect to turn you over to his sales manager. Known as customer turnover, this technique is usually used only as a last resort effort to sell you. Turning you over to the manager brings fresh ideas to the closing table, as well as the manager's selling experience and expertise. It also brings a fresh, untired mind that will begin the negotiations as if nothing at all had happened thus far. You have become fatigued during the course of your negotiations and your resistance is lower than when you first began. The manager will usually begin at step one and duplicate the salesman's procedure. This ensures that points missed by the salesman are covered and further weakens your resistance to a point where you stop saying *no* and start saying *yes*. Persistence pays.

When you deal with the manager you will feel that when he makes you an offer it is truly the best that he can do. Don't believe it for a minute. The manager's job is to sell you a car, not to chase you out of the dealership. He must win you over, just as the salesman did, but in less time. He cannot take the chance that you will cool off. He may, however, become nasty when he finds out you are not going to buy. So be prepared to leave—quickly.

What works on the salesman works on the sales manager. He is a human being. But do not underestimate his abilities. He is a seasoned veteran in the automobile business. When facing the sales manager or a salesman who has made a counteroffer, you need a final set-up plan. This requires a believable story and a "nothing to lose" attitude.

You might say something like, "Mr. Salesman, I would really like to buy this car from you. You are the first salesman I have met with whom I would like to do business. Your company has a fine reputation, which I am sure will not disappoint me should we ever come to terms. Now, as much as I like the car, as much as I like you, and as much as I like your dealership, I do not feel that you are giving me your best deal possible. I'm quite sure you can do better."

Say nothing more and give the salesman a chance to make an incriminating commitment or statement. When you put it to him this way, there is nothing he can do except take your proposal to management and try for approval. If he returns with his manager for turnover, give him the same story. If he returns without approval of your deal, repeat the steps one more time: you like the car, you want to buy it from him, you have set a limit of how much you can spend, and you have reached your limit. Tell him how to contact you and begin to leave. As you are leaving, drop the hint that you will be buying from another dealer.

"Well, I guess I will have to buy from so-and-so down the street." This can be said to yourself, the salesman, or whomever might be with you—spouse, friend, or relative.

The following morning call the salesman and ask him whether he has had a chance to think about your offer. Repeat what you said the preceding day and tell him to check with his manager for a change of mind. Persistence pays, but there is a point at which it will do no good to ask one more time or a thousand more times. If the salesman still cannot—or will not—give you the deal you want, close with, "I just wanted to give you a chance to sell me a car before I go to another dealer and buy. I really like your car better."

If his response is an emphatic *no*, go elsewhere to buy or consider moving on price yourself. However, if you must spend more than originally planned, make the final decision to do so away from the influence of the dealer or salesman.

Supply and Demand Negotiating. When the supply of certain models is limited, negotiating is more difficult and consumer strategies are restricted. A limited supply can be caused by a popular model selling extremely well; by a factory withholding production to puff demand and restrict supply, or by a fuel shortage such as the ones that occurred in 1973 and 1979 which caused people to over-buy economy cars and created a general shortage. When the supply is low and demand high, dealers obstinately hold out for full window sticker price or very close to it. "If you don't buy it, someone else will," is the general attitude. So, when a dealer offers this lay-it-on-the-line statement, lay it on the line with him:

"Not if they have any sense they won't. Nobody pays full sticker price anymore. How long has that car been sitting on your lot, anyway? I'm offering you a sale right now. When is that someone else going to come along? Are you going to be the salesman who sells it to that someone else or is another salesman going to get the commission? I have the time to wait. There are other economy cars on the market and most other dealers are a little more reasonable than you seem to want to be." Or you might say "The car is four months old and you expect me to pay the full price for it? I'm going to get eight months use for one year's depreciation. No way. You have discounted this model for other people I have talked to, and that was several months ago. And now, when the model is older, you expect me to pay more."

NEGOTIATING SYNOPSIS

1. Someone must make an initial offer. The salesman will normally solicit your bid to him. If you insist that he make you an offer, it will be a token discount to start the negotiations.
2. The salesman's opening offer will be very close to sticker price; so your first offer should be very close to dealer cost.
3. Never come up on price faster than the salesman comes down.
4. The salesman will do as much verbal negotiating as possible. It is easier for him to raise you on price verbally than in writing.
5. The time lag between showing the written figures and getting your signature will be kept minimal by the salesman to decrease the time you have to think about those figures. Take your time before signing, regardless of the salesman's urging.
6. The salesman will seek a commitment to purchase from you each time he makes a lower offer. You must seek a commitment from him to accept your offer each time you raise your offer to him.
7. Everything the salesman does is subject to management approval; everything you do is binding. You must therefore convince the salesman to take an offer to management as soon as possible to discover management thinking about price, discount, and trade allowance.
8. Negotiating with management involves leg work by the salesman, and several rounds of offer and counteroffer. At about the third or fourth round of negotiations, management will have made about its best offer to you. This does not mean you should quit negotiating, but that you are getting close.
9. Continued negotiating is always possible, provided you continue to come up on your price. If you freeze your figure, management may also pick a point and freeze. Raise by some amount, if it is only $5.
10. Don't display excitement; avoid exclamations such as: "We just

have to have that car! I've wanted a car like this for years! I can't wait to show this off to the neighborhood! Wow, what a terrific car!" It is deadly to your deal to show excitement about the car.

OFFER AND COUNTEROFFER PROCEDURE AND DIALOGUE

The salesman's offer to you: "I can sell you this car," or, "You can buy this car for $6,000 and your car in trade. How does that sound?"

Your counteroffer: "Well, I had a different figure in mind. I am thinking of a $5,000 cash difference—$5,000 and my car in trade. How about it?"

His objection or protest: "No, there is no way we can go that low."

Your response: "Is it that you *cannot* meet my price or that you *will* not meet it?" (Wait for an answer.)

"Mr. Customer, at that price we will make no money. My manager would never go along with that deal. Your car in trade, and $6,000 is a fair deal to you. What do you think? Do you want to pick the car up tomorrow or do you want to take it home with you today?"

"Mr. Salesman, if you cannot let me have the car for $5,500 and my car in trade, just how close can you come to my figure?"

"I might be able to come down a little, but I would really be surprised if I could get my manager to go along with it. We are not making much profit at $6,000. Will you buy the car if I can get my manager to go along with a $5,750 cash difference?"

Now you can either counteroffer or take another look at his car.

"Mr. Salesman, before I consider spending a dollar more than $5,500, I will have to take another look at your car. I am already several hundred dollars over my limit, but I do like your car—sort of. Let's go look it over and see if it is really worth the money."

Now reinspect the car entirely, front to back, complete with another demonstration ride. "Can we take it for another ride—there was something about the way it handled the first time I drove it that I didn't like."

Back in the closing room: "Well, Mr. Salesman. To me, $5,500 still seems like a reasonable figure, but if you want more money, I guess I could come up up $5,600. If you will give me the car for $5,600, I'll take it."

"Mr. Customer, I just cannot sell the car for that low a price. Let me write it up for $5,700 and your car and see whether I can get my manager to approve it."

"Since the final approval rests on your sales manager, take him my offer of $5,600 and let him decide."

The salesman may ask you to justify your figure. Now is a good time to tell him about the car you can get for less from another dealer.

"Mr. Customer, if another dealer will sell it to you for less, why don't you buy from him?"

"Well, the price is right, but I prefer the color of your car more than the other. However, I do not plan to spend more than $5,600 for the sake of color. Write it up, and when your manager approves it I can take the car home today. I am ready to do business."

Use time to your advantage: "I am ready to buy today, but I'm not going to throw money away. I can wait to buy the car; there is no hurry."

Be prepared for customer turnover at any time. Relax when it happens.

Let them invest time in you. The more time invested, the less they will want to lose you and the sale. Demonstration rides and inspections are great time consumers.

Let them know that you can find another dealer faster than they can find another customer.

Frequently use the negative notes you took during inspection and demonstration rides.

Frequently use the "sound of silence." Just because the salesman or his manager asks a quick question does not mean you must give a quick answer.

TEN-STEP PROGRAM TO BUY A CAR

1. **Research.** Know what your car is worth, know which cars are on the market, be aware of financing rates and monthly payments.

2. **Know Exactly What You Want.** Sit down and list your wants, needs, preferred model, and desired equipment. Stick to this list except for small items you may have initially overlooked; make no major changes in plans once you begin to look. Determine exactly what you can afford and for how long.

3. **Be Prepared to Shop.** Even though you are knowledgeable about dealer cost and what constitutes a good deal, you may have to shop to find the dealer willing to give you the deal you want.

4. **Do What the Salesman Does.** If he smiles, smile. If he slams the door of your car, slam the door of his car. If he is argumentative, be argumentative. If he asks questions of you, ask them of him. If he is quiet (or loud), be quiet (or loud).

5. **Inspect Your Merchandise.** Always inspect the very same car you plan to buy; never inspect a similar car on the assumption that similar is equal. Inspect methodically and thoroughy; cover

every square inch of the car you plan to buy—new or used.

6. **Negotiate Wisely.** Be emotionally detached from your purchase. When you talk dollars and cents, do not let a pretty color or gingerbread extras influence your final decision.

7. **Write the Deal You Want.** Control the writing of the deal, for this is money out of your pocket. If a salesman will not at least write an offer to submit to upper management, leave the dealership.

8. **Handle the Salesman's Objections.** Be prepared to handle the salesman when he talks higher price or lower trade allowance. Justify your position, present your evidence, utilize your strategies.

9. **Do not exceed Preset Limits.** It does little good to set limits if you can be talked into going over them. Never exceed preset limits without first sleeping on it. Wait one full day before making a final decision.

10. **Double-Check Everything.** Double-check all figures and paperwork—particularly financing papers—and be certain you know exactly what you are receiving and that everything matches what you and the dealer have agreed upon. Reinspect the car you are buying before you take delivery and ownership.

10
Buying a Used Car

THE USED CAR

IF YOU WANT TO BUY a used car, the rules of the game are shop, look, and be patient. You may have to shop twelve to fifteen used-car dealers to get a good car and a good deal. Once you have decided on make, model, year, and price range, you must then go out and find them.

You cannot figure dealer cost on a used car (although there are guidelines to help), so value and cost are elusive. No two cars will be in the same condition, so a careful inspection is mandatory. You will hear unbelievable stories, meet some crazy salesmen, and see tricks that put magicians to shame. But it can be fun.

The statement, "Buying a used car is buying someone else's troubles," is illogical logic, yet the fear of used merchandise persists in the mind of the consumer. If you can believe the fact that not everyone trades in a car just because it is giving him trouble, you will find it easier to make your purchase. Consider, too, that you always have the right to thoroughly inspect the car, drive it, and have it checked out by a mechanic and, when you are certain that it is mechanically fit, you have the right to buy and enjoy it.

Price Tags. There are two major reasons you will not find price tags on most used cars on most lots. The first and most obvious reason is that the tactic forces you to stop and ask a salesman the price of a particular car. The second, and less obvious, reason is that it permits the salesman to juggle his price according to what he sees and hears.

A used-car salesman will rarely start quoting prices until he determines what you have on your mind. He must know the type of buyer you are and what your buying habits are before he begins to make commitments. Are you a trade value buyer, a cash difference buyer, an original purchase price buyer, or a monthly payment buyer? What is important to you? What makes you buy a car? When he has the answers to these questions, he will tailor the deal to best satisfy your buying habits, tell you what you want to hear, and show you what you want to see.

The Monthly Payment Shuffle. By questioning you, a salesman discovers whether he should show you a low purchase price, although it means showing you a low trade allowance, or show you a high trade allowance, although it means puffing the prices of his cars. Ideally, for the salesman, you will give him a monthly payment ceiling. By working backward on his figures, he can compute how much money your monthly payment will buy.

Say you want a monthly payment of $350. He drops back to $300 a month, which will buy about $7,800 spendable cash. He now adds his pack (say, $400) and your trade value ($400), which brings the total to $8,600. He now knows that he will be quoting you $8,600, and that he can allow you up to $800 for your trade-in on any given car and the monthly payment will work out to $300, or $50 less than you said you wanted to spend. He can now show you anything he has in stock in which he has invested no more than $7,800 and make a profit on the sale. He may have only $7,000 invested in a particular car, but he will still quote you $7,800 and allow you $800 trade allowance, because the final figure will be within your affordable monthly payment range.

The Fixed-Dollar Shuffle. Giving a salesman a fixed number of dollars you can spend is just as bad as giving him a monthly payment. Suppose you tell him you can spend $8,000. Naturally, everything he shows you will be priced at about $8,000, because that is what you told him you wanted—an $8,000 price tag. But among the several cars he points out will be one or two that he would normally sell for $7,000 to $7,500. The price goes up when you tip your hand.

When a salesman asks for a price range or how much you want to spend per month, tell him that you are flexible on purchase price and that the monthly payment will depend upon the car you finally choose to buy. Tell him also that what you buy depends in large part upon how good the deal is. If you give him figures, make it a spread: "I am thinking of something between $300 and $350 a month (or $7,800 and $9,100). Naturally, I do not want to go all the way up to a $350 payment, but I will if the car is nice enough and the deal is good enough.'' Now the salesman has a benchmark from which to work, but he has neither a firm commitment nor firm numbers with which to put phony figures together.

Model Selection. Do not request specific brand names; ask for general categories—compact, intermediate, full-size. If you ask for a Brand A compact and he has Brands A, B, and C, the salesman will hold out for a higher price on the Brand A because he knows you want it. ''I could give you the B or C for $8,000, but I have to get at least $9,000 for that Brand A. And it's a great car, popular too. Everybody's looking for a Brand A these days.'' If he has several compacts on his lot, treat the one you want with indifference; use one car against the other.

Even though you may prefer a Brand A, you may find another brand name in the same category at a better price and in better condition. Be flexible and open-minded. The more cars you are willing to look at, the larger your market.

USED-CAR INSPECTION

The inspection of a used car is extremely important, for even if the price is fantastically low it means nothing if you must pay for major repairs or if the car suffers a thousand nickle-and-dime ailments after warranty expiration.

Inspecting a used car is simple—start at the front bumper and check everything from there on back. When you reach the rear bumper you are finished. Some people do it in 5 seconds. These quick inspections create many problems that usually develop after you take ownership.

You need not be a registered mechanic to inspect a car. All it takes is a system to follow so that nothing is overlooked. There are two phases: the physical inspection performed on the lot, and the demonstration ride. During the physical inspection, there are four areas to check: body and attached parts, engine and fluid levels, interior components, and switches that turn on and off. To begin your inspection you must adopt an attitude that leaves nothing to assumption. Just because it is there does not mean it works. The first time you break the rule, it will be on the one item that does not work.

Area One: Body and Attached Parts. Always inspect the body of a car in daylight. Wrinkles, body work, fading and mismatched paint, and small rust spots and scratches are all fairly well hidden or disguised at night regardless of the artificial lighting on the lot. From the front bumper, driver's side, begin a slow walk around the car and let your eyes cover every square inch of the body. When you find a blemish, touch it, but do not comment to the salesman and be certain that he sees you touch it. He knows that you know, but he does not know what you are thinking. When you have finished the walk, stand back 5 to 10 feet and check the car for paint mismatch—one part that is a shade lighter or darker than another part. Do this on both sides, and on the front and back. Mismatch does not automatically spell accident, for even new cars occasionally have mismatched paint, but it is cause for further investigation. Overspray, strong paint mismatch, and/or sanding grooves on doorjambs, inside the hood, and inside the trunk compartment will really tell whether major body work has been done.

Stand at the front and then at the rear of the car and sightline the body. All lines should run together smoothly; a major style line that runs the full length of the car should be straight all the way. Any unusual bulges in the body indicate that patch work has been done. Check suspect areas with a small magnet. The thicker the body putty, the more easily the magnet will slide off. Move the magnet around until you have a feel for what is good metal and what is body putty. This little test will tell you what is under the paint and the size of the repair. The larger the area of body putty, the shoddier the work, and the more likely that problems will develop in the future.

If the car has a vinyl or convertible top, check the top for fit, tears, and slits. Tops shrink, so check to see whether it has pulled loose at the edges. A convertible rear window should be clear and preferably of glass. Bubbles on vinyl tops indicate rusting beneath, which is expensive to remedy.

Bumpers that show signs of rust are on their way out. This situation will get progressively worse as the rust works its way under the good chrome, loosens it, and lifts it off by blistering and peeling. A dented bumper cannot be restored to its original condition without rechroming, which is expensive. All chrome should fit snugly against the body of the car and align properly. Gaps between chrome and body collect dirt and moisture, which will eventually cause rust. A side-view mirror that shows black spots behind the glass is just about shot.

Tires should match by brand name and by tire tread depth. If all four are not the same, they should at least match by pairs (front two or back two). Be sure you can tell the difference between glass-belted, steel-belted, and radial steel-belted tires. A dealer may let some air out of all four tires to give them that flattened, radial look. Read the raised print on the side of the tire. When in doubt, have the kind of tire spelled out on the purchase contract.

Area Two: Engine and Fluid Levels. Inspect the engine compartment from front to rear, beginning with the radiator. Twist the cap off and check the fluid level and color. Sealed and semiclosed cooling systems are exempt from this check. If the coolant is a muddy-looking, rusty color, the engine and radiator need to be flushed and cleaned (relatively inexpensive but a good negotiating point). Run your finger around the inside and underside of the radiator opening. The fluid may look clean only because it was recently changed with fresh water and antifreeze added. A residue is usually left behind at this spot. Be certain that the salesman sees the residue (if any) and remember it when you negotiate.

Next is the fan blade and belt. Grab the top blade and wiggle it back and forth, first toward the engine block and then toward the radiator. There should be a little give when you do this, but too much wiggle indicates that the water pump shaft bearing is bad or is going bad. Caution is advised. (Electric fans are exempt. When you start the engine, the fan will not begin to operate immediately. Most are thermostatically controlled and function only when the engine reaches operating temperature.) Check the fan belt for cracks and wear and tear. Twist it around at various spots and check the underside (the side against the pulleys). A shiny look or deep cracks indicate that replacement is needed.

Twist the oil cap off and inspect. A filthy cap indicates a lack of proper maintenance. Check the oil dipstick for fluid level and color. If it is a quart low, you do not know how many miles made it a quart low (once around the block?). All oil turns a faint brown when exposed to engine heat. However, if the dipstick shows black oil, then the oil and the oil filter need replacement. Rub some oil between thumb and forefinger. If it is gritty with a substance like fine sand, caution is advised. That grit could be fine metal granules, indicating internal engine problems, or dirt from improper maintenance.

Take the cover off the air cleaner (wing nut) and check the air filter. When it is held up to a strong light or direct sunlight, some light should filter through. If it is filthy, it should be replaced. Push open the butterfly (a flat piece of metal within the throat of the carburetor) and look down into the throat. If it is black and sooty, that indicates a lack of proper maintenance, a bad air cleaner, cheap fuel usage, or backfiring through the carburetor. This is a good negotiating point, and a spray can of carburetor cleaner will make it shine like new. (Some dealers bolt the air cleaner on so it cannot be removed. Do not buy the car until you have inspected the carburetor with the air cleaner off.)

Take all caps off the battery and check the fluid levels. (Fully sealed batteries with no caps are exempt.) All cells should be at their proper levels. A cell low on fluid could be a bad cell, indicating that the entire battery is going bad. All cells must be functional for the battery to work it all. Batteries are not cheap.

Optional power equipment gives you more fluid levels to check: power steering fluid, brake fluid, and the air-conditioning system. Small white spots—usually a white, powdery residue—on and around the air-conditioning compressor indicate that Freon (Tm) gas has escaped.

If you notice fresh electrical tape anywhere on the car it indicates recent electrical problems. Check extra carefully; ask questions. The real test of the electrical system is when you check switches that turn on and off.

Check for oil seepage around the engine block. Fresh oil running down the side of the engine block indicates that a gasket must be replaced. The gasket is inexpensive, but the cost of labor is high.

If you have a friend who is a mechanic, have him check the car for you for a small fee, or take it to any private garage and, for a nominal fee, have it inspected. Have the following items checked: the compression, the coolant for antifreeze and degree of protection, battery efficiency, brake linings, and transmission. Do not accept a recent state, county, or city inspection sticker as valid evidence of the car's reliability. The dealer may have a friend who will put a sticker on any car regardless of condition and without a full inspection.

Area Three: Interior Components. If the seats are not missing, the steering wheel is in place, and there are pedals on the floor, all seems to be in order. Not quite. Inspect the full length of the front seat before you sit down. Tears and holes become worse with use and are very costly to repair. Look straight up and inspect the headliner, sunvisors, and dome light for damage. Check the rear seat for damage and/or stains. This is where kids usually sit and do their thing of spilling fluids. The older the car and the lower the price, the less fussy you need be about small stains.

Check all door handles and window crank handles. Crank all windows fully up and down and back up again. If a window catches, sticks, or takes a sudden drop, it may be that there is a bad gear or the window is ready to fall off the track. On power windows, be certain that each individual switch by each window is functional. The master switch by the driver's seat might work on all windows, but an individual switch may be bad—they are expensive.

Check carpeting for tears, holes, and pulling away from edges clamped down. If there are floor mats, lift them up and check the condition of the floor or carpet underneath. No carpet? Check the metal floor for rusting.

Inspect the glove box, open and close it; lock and unlock it. On a remote-control mirror, check to be sure the inside knob is actually connected, and that it works. Check the seat back release on two-door models, and the forward and backward slide of the front seat. Check all locks on all doors, inside with the knob and outside with the key. Seat belts should be functional. If they are of the self-returning reel type they should operate smoothly but, most important, they should operate.

Check the trunk for a spare tire and jack, naturally. If one or the other is missing, insist it be included. Lift the mat or carpet covering the floor of the trunk and check for rusting. Check both side wells for rust and/or body work.

Area Four: Switches That Turn On and Off. Check the mileage first. Twelve thousand miles per year of age is considered normal. It is difficult, even for an expert, to determine whether the odometer has been turned back on any given car. Mileage statement forms are misleading, since many people sign them blank when they trade their car. If there is an oil change sticker on the doorjamb or under the hood, check it against the odometer reading. In the final analysis, it is best to forget the possibility of mileage tampering and concentrate instead on the inspection and your own personal opinion of the condition of the car.

Begin on the driver's side, extreme left, and check everything that pulls, pushes, or switches on and off. Put the emergency brake on and pull the knob to release it. Some models have an automatic emergency brake release that kicks out when the car is placed in gear. Check the headlight switch, bright beam and low beam, dashboard dimmer, and interior dome light switch. With someone standing outside the car, check the left and right turn signals, front and rear; check the horn (the most commonly overlooked item); hit the brakes and be certain the lights work on both sides.

It is best to check windshield wipers from inside. Check that the motor works, the washer fluid squirts, and the wipers clear the windshield properly for a clear field of vision. Bad blades leave wide streaks.

Check heater and air-conditioner during the demonstration ride. A cold engine will throw no heat. In the winter it will be necessary to pull the car indoors to check the air-conditioner. As a precaution, add a conditional clause to your purchase contract: "Air-conditioner will be fixed by dealer, with no charge to customer, if it fails to work when summer arrives."

Check all functions of the radio—AM/FM—to be certain all work. On a tape player, either built in or added on, play a tape all the way through.

Be wary of add-on equipment such as an air-conditioning unit. It might work now, it might work forever, but who knows. Do not assume that just because a clock is present, it works. Car clocks are notorious for not working. Check the cigar lighter and all miscellaneous lights: glove box, ashtray, light groups, and trunk light.

Luxury cars usually have extras such as a tilt steering wheel, speed control, automatic trunk release, power seats, power door locks, and power antenna, all of which should work. Check a power sun roof several times for seal and functional operation. If possible, run the car through a jet-spray car wash to check for leaks everywhere—windows, trunk, sunroof, moonroof.

Put the top of a convertible down and up several times. Many times the motor has the ability to put the top down but cannot quite make it come back up. If the motor is weak or if the hydraulic lines are low on fluid, you will have a problem.

Check the rear window of a station wagon, if it is power operated, to be certain it works both with the switch on the dashboard and with the key in the rear door. Work fold-down seats up and down, and check for looseness and fit. Check the luggage rack for looseness and rattles, rusting and/or pitting. Check woodgrain sidepanels for general condition—discoloration (sun bleaching), and nicks, tears, bubbles, or other damage. Sidepanels cannot be patched and they are expensive to replace.

The effect that rust and blemishes or any other malfunctions on the car have on your final decision depends on the severity of the problems, the price versus the age of the car, and your own personal judgment. The final, bottom-line judgment of value depends upon how one car compares to everything else you have seen. Does the general physical condition justify the price?

If by this time the car checks out and you are interested in it, you are ready for the demonstration ride. The demo ride should follow the physical inspection, never precede it. If the car does not check out, you will have wasted the demo ride and your time. Also, if the engine is operated for several minutes, it disturbs the fluid levels and makes the radiator too hot to check.

Start the engine, put the emergency brake on, and place the transmission in a forward gear. (For Standard shift, place in first gear—clutch pedal depressed.) Give it a little gas (release the clutch pedal slowly) to test the holding power of the emergency brake. (Automatic brake release does not apply here. It will have to be checked on a steep hill with the brake on, the engine off, and the transmission in neutral.) Listen to the muffler system with your door open, preferably between two other cars. Become familiar with all controls and pedal locations and drive away.

Most salesmen have a planned route on which they take their customers, that usually includes hills, city traffic, and highway driving to give them a good profile of what the car can do. You will want a little more from a demo ride than the salesman's route to help you decide. Take the car home and then drive it from there to your place of employment so you will know how it takes the bumps and driving conditions of your normal daily route. If the test drive over that route presents problems, forget that car. If your drive to work does not include hills and highways, find them on your way back to the dealership; check the car under all driving conditions when possible. Utilize all your senses: Listen for any unusual noises; feel for any vibrations in the steering wheel, poor shock absorption on bumps, drift or pull in steering to one side of the road; and keep an eye on all gauges—temp, oil, amp.

When you return to the dealership, check the fluid levels of the power steering unit and the power brakes again. If there is a loss of fluid from your short trip, the unit will have to replaced. The dealer may add fluid as necessary to maintain the fluid level and keep the defective unit working until the car is sold. Thereafter, you will be on your own. Also listen for any hissing noises, such as steam escaping. Some defects do not show up until the engine reaches operating temperature. Check the oil dipstick for oil level, and look under the car for oil leakage.

Inspection Do's and Dont's. Do not slam the doors, trunk lid, or hood of the car unless that is the only way you can get the part to stay closed. This shows a complete lack of concern for something that isn't yours and will not necessarily prove any part to be defective.

Do not redline the engine. This is flooring the accelerator and holding it to the floor while the engine races at full speed, transmission in neutral. Gunning the engine proves nothing more than the ignorance of the person doing it. If you do not blow out the engine, you may cause internal damage that will not appear until months after you buy the car. And you will have to pay for the repairs.

Do not kick the tires as you make your rounds of the car. There is too much weight on each tire for you to be able to tell anything by kicking them. Kicking tires does not harm the car, but it tells the salesman that you are putting on a show as if to say, "I am no dummy when it comes to inspecting a car."

Do not refer to a salesman's merchandise as junk. Customers do this because they think it gives them negotiating leverage—it does not. Never tell a salesman how to run his lot or that he should fix this or that. Do not pick apart every car on his lot, only the one you plan to buy. Criticizing every car will create defensive resistance in the salesman, which will surface when you sit down to negotiate the deal.

Treat the car you inspect as if you owned it, and as you would want someone else to treat your car. Before the day's end it might be your car.

Do take notes on everything as you go along.

Do take your time; be thorough. If the salesman rushes you, slow him down.

Do not hesitate to ask any question—you will not embarrass the salesman.

Inspection Checklist

Rate each block E (Excellent), G(Good), F(Fair), P(Poor)

CAR:	1	2	3	4	5	6	7
Area One: Body and attached parts.							
Wrinkles, body work, and rust							
Sightline for style line continuity							
Vinyl top for tearing and bubbles							
Bumpers for pitting, and general condition							
Tires for match and tread depth							

CAR:	1	2	3	4	5	6	7

Area Two: Engine and Fluid Levels.

Radiator for fluid level and color
Fan blade and belts for wear and fit
Oil dipstick for level and color
Power steering/brake fluid levels
Air cleaner/filter for cleanliness
Air-conditioning system for leaks
Fresh electrical tape
Oil/fluid seepage around engine block

Area Three: Interior Components.

All upholstery, headliner, and carpets
All door handles and window cranks
Glove box, remote-control items
Trunk for spare tire and jack, and for rust

Area Four: Switches That Turn On and Off

Headlights, interior lights
Emergency brake—on and off
Turn signals, brake lights, horn
Windshield wipers and washer fluid
Heater and air-conditioner functions
All functions of radio/tape player

Special Areas.

Add-ons: air-conditioning and tow equipment
Clock, cigar lighter, gauges
Miscellaneous light groups
Tilt steering wheel, speed control
Power seats, windows, and door locks
Top up-and-down on convertible
Rear window and folding seats on station wagon
Luggage rack and woodgrain siding

THE PREVIOUS OWNER

Ever hear of the little old lady who drove her car only 14 miles on Sunday to and from church, and a few miles during the week for shopping and socials? This used to be a good selling point and almost guaranteed a sale when a salesman could prove it was true. Long ago, a low-mileage car was considered a better buy than one with high mileage. It is now known that the worst type of driving you can do is short runs, which actually cause more problems than long-distance driving.

Short runs do not let the engine reach peak operating efficiency. They waste more fuel and, over a period of time, cause carbon build-up that congests the engine. If you are considering two cars—both of the same year, make, and model—and one has higher mileage, the low-mileage car will not necessarily be the better buy. Such information as the previous owner's occupation, the car's major usage, and its maintenance history will tell more than the mileage.

When possible, call the previous owner and get the answers you need (including the kind of gas mileage the car was getting). Also find out what he bought and how he feels about the dealership—whether they have been fair with him, whether he is happy with his new car and the service obtained.

In the final analysis, the car will speak for itself. A good showing on a thorough inspection and good performance during the demo ride are the major criteria. And, of course, the price must be right.

Before you reject a car for having too many small things wrong with it, consider that even though it may have ten (or even twenty) flaws, the balance of the several thousand component parts are good. The real question is: What will it cost to fix the flaws and who will be paying for it? If it is a major component—engine or transmission—the dealer will surely have to make the repair or replacement. The first step is to itemize exactly what is wrong with the car and work from your list, both to reach a buy decision and to negotiate.

If your list contains mostly inexpensive repairs and replacements, consider fixing them yourself for the sake of being able to work a better deal. Ask the salesman how much of your list he will fix and let him obligate himself before the papers are drawn for you to sign. Point out that his car has a long list of flaws but that a good price will offset the small items. "I don't mind if the cigar lighter doesn't work, but the price must be right. Here is what is wrong with the car (go over your list with him). Now, give me the car for this price and fix the radio, and I will take care of the other repairs myself. How about it? Is it a deal?''

The longer the list, the greater your negotiating strength. This is why it is so important to do a thorough job of your initial inspection of the car.

Your guideline: If you plan to take care of the small items, negotiate the major items as part of the original deal and make your offer to the salesman. If you plan to have the dealer take care of your entire list, negotiate the best cash deal possible and then present your list, however long it might be, as a condition of your purchase.

USED-CAR WARRANTY

A warranty, in essence, is a courtesy to the customer and an inducement to buy. It satisfies the psychological fear, ''What if something happens when I drive the car off the lot?''

A warranty must cost someone money, for nothing is free. The longer a warranty runs, and the more areas of the car it covers, the higher the dealer's profit must be. A car that carries a 90-day, 100 percent warranty must cost more than a car that carries a 30-day, 50/50 warranty. The probability of something's going wrong within 90 days is four to five times greater than the probability of its occurring within 30 days. You pay extra for this higher probability, and for this (sometimes illusionary) security and protection. Before you begin to negotiate your deal, decide whether you want a better price or a better warranty.

Instead of a dealer-backed warranty, consider creating your own warranty or repair fund to cover repairs during your first few months of ownership. This gives you negotiating leverage when all other cards have been played. To use this leverage, you must first negotiate the dealer down to his lowest acceptable price and reserve your no-warranty offer until last. You must also determine optimum warranty value—the value of the projected repairs that this particular car will need during normal warranty coverage. You must look at it as the dealer does: ''What could go wrong with this car in a given length of time and how much will it cost to fix or replace it?'' A good rule of thumb is $75 per month of warranty coverage (computed against the dealer's warranty offer) or $75 per year of age of the car you plan to buy. This means that a dealer who offers a 6-month warranty is, in all probability, holding back $500 to pay for necessary warranty repairs. If the car has only a 1-month warranty, use the age of the car to compute optimum warranty value. A 1-year old car will compute to only $75, but it is reasonable to expect that that is all the car needs during your first year of ownership. However, a 4-year-old car will compute to $300 warranty valuation, which is reasonable to expect during the first year of ownership.

When you have negotiated the dealer's bottom-dollar price, make an "as is," no-warranty offer for the car. This is aside from any defects discovered during your inspection that the dealer has agreed to fix. An "as is" offer means that you are willing to take the car as it sits, except for any negotiated repairs. Your "as is" offer will be the salesman's bottom price less the optimum warranty value you have computed. If he will not agree to your offer, ask him how much lower he will go on an "as is" purchase. If it is a reasonable reduction of price, give it consideration. But the value must be there for you to take the chance.

USED-CAR VALUATION

What is the value of a used car? How is value determined?

The value of any car, very simply put, is whatever you, the buyer, are willing to pay for it and whatever price the seller is willing to take for it.

A salesman may call upon evidence to justify value, such as his Blue Book, normal market averages for a particular car, ads in the newspaper, and recent previous sales of the same or very similar merchandise. Point out to him that all this means nothing to you and that you will determine value on the individual merits of the car itself. You then offset his persistence that the value of the car is as he says.

A common sales tactic to justify value is to describe all the work done to the car to make it just the right, problem-free car for you. This is illusion. When the salesman rattles off a list of everything that has been done, consider that it may or may not be true. His dealership might have done the work, as he says, or it might have been done by the previous owner. If the car needed repairs and if the dealer did, in fact, make the repairs, he did not invest his own money on them—he invested the previous owner's money by underallowing for the trade-in.

When the salesman offers a list, say, "The car must have been in pretty poor condition to need all that work. What else is wrong with it that you did not fix?" Or act shocked: "It needed all of that? Maybe I had better look at something a little less abused."

Your benchmark to negotiate a deal on any used car is to start with the wholesale value, or less, and work up from there, since the dealer is going to start from as high as he can and work down. Here are basic guidelines:

1. Compute the depreciated value of the car—wholesale and retail. Assume that the wholesale figure you derive is the maximum amount the dealer allowed the previous owner. More probably it was less.
2. Find out what the previous owner bought; for what new car did he trade?
3. Always assume the dealer has at least a $700 profit built into the price he quotes. From that point adjust your figures according to what the previous owner bought. The following examples help determine at what amount to begin your negotiations.

Example A:	Selling price of car:	$3,500
	Assumed profit level:	−$ 700
	Opening figure to begin negotiating:	$2,800

Example B:	Selling price of car:	$3,500
	Average wholesale price of car:	$3,000
	Customer bought $13,000 full-size car; 21% factor; $2,730 play money (packing). Profit held on new car sale:	$1,000
	Presumed allowance to customer:	$3,500
	$1,730 used to pack trade-in:	−$1,730
	Theoretical cash in trade-in:	$1,770

Here you must second-guess the dealer. Assume first that there is at least the $700 profit level within the car to utilize as negotiating money. Accept as a well-established fact that the dealer will not give a salesman any more of the gross than absolutely necessary to keep him happy. On the higher priced, full-size merchandise, a salesman will usually be content to go along with the dealer and accept a $800 or $1,000 gross on a deal, especially if the dealer insists that he go along with it. So the salesman's loss can be your gain if you know what the prior owner bought. That portion of the available gross that was used to pack the trade brings the dealer's total investment in the trade-in down. In the above examples it would be safe to use a $1,770 to $2,800 opening figure to begin the negotiations, even though the car's wholesale valuation is $3,000. Your concern is not what the car should sell for wholesale or retail, but rather for how much it can be purchased, which is based on how much the dealer has invested.

Example C:	Selling price of car:	$3,900
	Average wholesale price of car:	$3,000
	Customer bought $10,000 mid size car; 17% factor; $1,700	
	play money. Profit held:	$ 700
	Presumed allowance to customer	$3,500
	$ 500 used to pack trade-in:	− $1,000
	Theoretical cash in trade-in:	$2,500

An intermediate car allows the dealer room to negotiate and play with the trade-in figures, but not as much as the full-size car. The dealer will again try to book the car for as little as possible and still keep the salesman happy. A $700 gross pays the salesman $175 (25 percent of gross), which is reasonable.

In the above example you would be safe to use a $2,500 to $3,200 opening neotiating figure. You will fall within the built-in $700 profit level at $3,200. It is safe to assume that the dealer held a profit on the new car sale of about $400, and that the dealer did not allow full retail for the customer's trade, nor was he able to get away with showing him a wholesale figure. The allowance given for the trade had to be somewhere between wholesale and retail; thus $3,500 was the trade allowance.

If the previous owner bought a compact, the gross involved is initially so small that the salesman must work extremely close on the deal. He cannot pack the trade-in nearly as well as he can on a full-size or intermediate purchase. The dealership will look very closely at the trade-in before even allowing wholesale for it. The slightest mistake in judgment could wipe out the entire profit made on the sale. On a compact deal, it is best to assume that the dealer held a $300 to $400 gross profit, and that any overage was used to pack the trade allowance. And there is always the $700 profit level to work with.

THE USED-CAR DEAL

Some salesmen work a deal by trading on terminology—trading retail to retail or wholesale to wholesale. In essence, the salesman is telling you that if you want full retail for your trade-in you must pay full retail for his car. Conversely, if you are to buy his car for wholesale, you must accept wholesale for your car. When a salesman begins to shift his selling efforts to terminology, and the justification of value and price, you are close to paying top dollar for his car (retail) and taking bottom dollar for your trade (wholesale).

Watch the cash differences carefully when involved in terminology trading. If the salesman begins to hop around the contract by quoting you first retail to retail and then wholesale to wholesale, the cash differences should not change, unless the salesman is juggling figures.

Your best course of action is to forget terminology trading. If the salesman begins to sell by terminology, stop him as quickly as possible. Compute each car's value separately, and negotiate from those figures. Concentrate on narrowing the gap between what his car costs and what he will allow for your car in trade.

A very common used-car-deal ploy is splitting the profit. The salesman will tell you, very matter-of-factly, that he has only $300 profit in the car you want to buy. Now, he says, could anything be more fair than his offer to split his profit with you? How could you argue a better deal with him if he has already given you half of his profit? The catch is that you have no way of knowing exactly how much profit *is* in that particular used car. If he tells you his profit is only $300 and offers a discount of $150, it is quite possible he will make a profit of $550 provided his wholesale to retail spread is the usual $700. When confronted with "splitting the profit," ignore the figures and write your own deal according to your own computations.

BEFORE YOU SIGN

Before you sign on the dotted line, be certain that all condition-of-the-purchase replacement parts and/or repairs are spelled out in detail in the contract. Vague, ambiguous terminology could leave you no better off than if nothing at all had been written in the contract.

If it says, "Two new tires installed free of charge"—define "new" tires. Recaps or retreads will do the job as far as the salesman is concerned. Be certain the contract specifies "brand-new tires, not retreads."

If there is a cracked mirror (remote control), and the salesman writes, "Replace mirror at no charge to customer," spell out the type of mirror to be replaced. According to his written word, he could install a regular mirror instead of a remote control one.

"Oil change" does not mean "filter included." The salesman may replace just the oil and save the cost of the filter and one quart of oil.

"Check and inspect" does not mean replace and/or repair anything found wrong or defective. Add "Repair or replace if necessary" to the contract.

Suppose the engine runs rough. "Tune up engine" does not mean the car will receive new points, plugs, condensor, and a scope put on the engine to fine-tune it. The service department may only clean and reset the points and plugs, make minor adjustments on the carburetor and/or timing, and let it go at that. Specify parts replacement.

Used-Car Guideline

1. Acquire as much information as possible about the car in which you are interested before you make a commitment to pay a certain price and monthly payment, and finally, to buy it.

2. Do not be stubbornly silent, but do not give all your information away at once. Allow yourself enough room to move when discussing prices.

3. Do not express a solid, fixed interest in one car only, nor maintain an inflexible price, trade allowance, cash difference, or monthly payment.

4. Inspect the merchandise thoroughly; question the source of the merchandise; call the previous owner.

5. Question service—how good? and warranty—what does it include and for how long?

6. Write your own deal on any given car. Compute your own estimate of the value of your trade-in and the value of the car the salesman is selling.

7. Put everything in writing—leave no loose ends dangling.

8. Read everything word for word; double-check all figures.

9. Always determine beforehand just how much you can afford each month for a payment. (See chapter 12, "Financing.")

10. Realize that most strategies used throughout this book work while buying a used car—in decision making, handling the salesman, and negotiating.

11
Dealer Prep and Other Extras

ADD-ON CHARGES

DEALER PREPARATION. Commonly called dealer prep, dealer preparation is one of the fastest moneymakers in the business, for it is seldom questioned by the customer. It is justified by the dealer as a charge for services rendered, although often the only service performed is to wash the car. For this you may pay from $50 to $250. The dealer must convince you that you are indeed receiving something for your money, and that it is an indisputable charge. "All dealers charge it," you are told. "There are no exceptions and you must pay for the dealer prep. Your new car is inspected bumper-to-bumper by a mechanic prior to delivery." There is a factory checklist that the dealer is supposed to follow in prepping a car for delivery, for this the dealer is reimbursed by the factory. The checklist covers some fifty different areas of the car. Rather than follow the time-consuming checklist, most dealers choose to deliver the car and take their chances that problems will not develop. If problems do not develop, the dealer has been paid but has done nothing for the money. If a problem occurs that should have been caught and corrected by prep, the dealer corrects the problem and tells you that it is covered by the warranty; therefore, there is no charge to you.

There is no guaranteed method to tell whether or not dealer prep has been done. Even when dealer prep is done according to the checklist, problems can still develop. Your best defense is to personally check out the car prior to taking delivery and insist that any bugs found be remedied before you take it.

The charge for dealer prep is always in question. Should you pay for something not received, and should you pay for something already paid for by the factory? In any event, dealer prep, when paid, should never exceed 1 percent of the sticker price of the car you are buying.

Dealer prep may be buffered by the inclusion of one or more miscellaneous extras. The tack-on may read like this: "Dealer prep charge of $200 includes the preparation of this car for delivery, wash and wax, loaner car for warranty service work, first oil change and oil filter, first safety check or state inspection, first front end alignment, etc." This is designed to justify the charge, although if you totaled the real cost of these items, they would probably not exceed $100. In a situation such as this, your best move is to negotiate the dealer prep charge and tell the salesman that you are not interested in receiving an oil change or a free state inspection or a front end alignment, so he can just deduct the $200. You expect the car to be cleaned for delivery and for the factory recommended prep to be done, and you do not plan to pay for it.

Miscellaneous Charges. Handling charges, closing costs, and surcharges are another way of saying extra money for nothing. These charges are usually small in dollar amounts, but they do add up. A $25 handling charge on every car a dealer sells is an extra $2,500 in his pocket if he sells 100 cars in one month. These small charges are presented to you as being insignificant compared to the $10,000 you are spending for your car. As the salesman will point out, "Everybody pays it, and after all, it is only $25."

Ask the salesman exactly what you get for the $25, and if he cannot produce a tangible benefit for the money, do not buy the car until he removes the tack-on charge.

Never announce to the salesman that you do not plan to pay add-on charges until negotiations are completed and you have a signed management-approved deal. If you tell him early in the rounds of negotiating that you do not plan to pay, the salesman will simply hold back enough gross to cover the loss. He will then use the fact that he is not charging you the add-on to hold firm to his price, which will give him the negotiating advantage.

SERVICES RENDERED

Rustproofing. Rustproofing your new car is a paradox. The dealership is telling you that all the technological advances made by the factory mean nothing unless you have your car rustproofed, for it will fall apart within a few years without the rustproofing protection he offers. And maybe he is right.

What about the advertisements you see on television proclaiming deep dip, electrostatic priming, glasslike hardness of the painted surfaces, and so on? Unfortunately, these glorified word pictures do not carry a solid lifetime warranty that ensures problem-free rust protection. It is therefore advisable to have the work done if you plan to keep the car for any length of time, say in excess of 3 years. If you are a 1-to-3-year trader, you probably do not need the protection. There are five options available to you:

1. If the car was rustproofed by the dealer prior to its going into his inventory, the cost was added to the sticker price as a tack-on, and you pay for the service whether you want it or not, and whether you like it or not.
2. If it has not been done to the car, you can elect to pay the dealer for it.
3. Have it done by an outside, independent rustproofing service.
4. Do not have it done and take your chances with the elements.
5. Buy cans of pressure-spray material or a rustproofing kit and do it yourself.

The purpose of option one is to ensure a rustproof profit on every new car sold. Since the dealer is trying to force a profit, you should hold out for the deduction of the rustproofing cost and not buy unless and until it is removed. But save it for last. If the dealer knows this deduction is the only way you will buy, he will remove it.

Option two gives you free choice to take it or do without it. If you decide to have it done, it then becomes a negotiable item. Most dealers offer a bonus to their salesmen—usually $25 to $50—for selling a rust-proofing to the customer. The dealer's cost for labor and material will be about $75, which brings his total investment to $125. For this service you are then charged from $150 to $200, depending on the dealer. To negotiate the rustproof cost, you must convince the salesman and his manager that the entire deal hinges on this one item. However, to succeed, you must also show the dealer a small profit on it. From there, negotiate upward in increments of $5 until you reach acceptance level. If the dealer refuses to negotiate the cost, tell him you will have it done elsewhere.

Option three is the elsewhere. Outside sources usually do a better job and offer a better guarantee than most dealerships who do rustproofing as a sideline.

Whether they are referred to as a guarantee or a warranty, read assurances carefully before you decide who will rustproof your new car. Beware the warranty that only repairs or replaces rust damage up to, but not over, the cost of the rustproofing, If rust problems develop during warranty coverage, you must pay for the excess cost over the rustproof cost.

The fourth option requires a decision: Will you get the use out of the investment for a rustproofing? If you do not plan to keep the car that long, don't have it done. The only benefit is higher resale value, but only if you sell it to a private owner. A dealer will not allow extra on trade value even though he may say he will.

The fifth option is one of convenience, economy, and personal motivation.

Some dealers offer a ScotchGard® service for new cars with cloth interiors. However, you can never be quite certain that the work was done because it is invisible to the eye once it dries on the material. Most automobile upholstery is stain resistant and will give you long life and ease of cleaning without your resorting to a spray-on costing extra money. Definitely refuse to pay for it if you encounter it as a tack-on item. Tell the dealer to prove it was done.

Dealer-Installed Equipment. This is a rip-off, plainly and simply put. With the exception of a vinyl top and other trim and dress-up items, anything installed by a dealer will not be as good as if it were done at the factory. Dealer-installed options are not covered by factory warranty and are usually cheap in design and quality.

If the car you have picked to buy does not have air-conditioning, do not even consider an add-on unit. If air is that important to you, shop until you find the car with factory-installed air-conditioning. If a salesman is desperate enough for a sale, he will tell you that his service department can install air-conditioning ''as good as if it came from the factory.'' Do not believe him. Add-on units almost always spell trouble to the buyer.

Radios, insignia floor mats, body side molding, mud flaps, sport or special chrome mirrors, special wheels and/or tires, and any other miscellaneous add-on items all cost more through a dealership for parts and labor for installation.

If you must have certain add-on equipment, shop department-store automobile centers or discount chain stores before you make final decisions. You may find lower prices and better service after the sale and installation of equipment. Some equipment can be installed by you for additional savings.

12
Financing and Leasing

PAY CASH OR FINANCE?

IF YOU CAN AFFORD to pay cash and still have money in reserve, plan to pay for your purchase in cash. You may want to finance a small balance through the dealer, but only for the purpose of negotiating a better deal. You can always prepay the loan in a month or two. The prepayment penalty is usually nominal enough compared to the leverage it gives you when negotiating your deal.

When you must finance, choose a monthly payment that is comfortable for at least the next 12 months. The payment will be the same for the full term of the loan—usually 36 months—but your income will probably increase during your second and third years of ownership. If the monthly payment is affordable, buy the car. If you must stretch your budget to the point of collapse and sacrifice small luxuries, do not buy the car. Buy a less expensive car.

Never rely upon self-sacrifice to make a monthly payment affordable. It is easy to consider giving up smoking, drinking, or your one night out on the town each week to make up the deficit, but do not count on doing it when you really have to make the sacrifice. If your budget is so tight that you must forfeit part of your life style to buy the car, forfeit the car.

In most instances it is far better to know your limits, how much money you can borrow, and what it will cost you per month to repay it, before you take that first look at an automobile. If you do not know your limits you may waste a great deal of time shopping and haggling price and terms, only to discover that you can afford neither the down payment nor the monthly payment.

111

LENDING INSTITUTIONS

The Loan Officer. Never hesitate to deal directly with a lendor. The loan officer with whom you talk will not bite, will not look down his nose at you, and will try to avoid third-degree interrogation. He will ask no more questions than a dealer, will want no more credit information than a dealer, and will, for the most part, be more involved with the loan approval you need. Bear this in mind: The dealer cannot approve a loan, but the loan officer can.

Call for an appointment and explain that you plan to buy a new or used car. On the appointed day and hour, simply sit down and discuss the entire situation with the loan officer and fill out a credit application (*ap*). Ascertain exactly how much he will lend based on your income and outstanding bills. He can tell you how much you can borrow, a price range to maintain, the monthly payment, the rate of interest, the finance charge, and the cost of insurances and explain, in detail, your specific obligations in the matter, to include default, repossession, and recourse.

A loan officer can tell you exactly how much he will lend on a particular car with a given sticker price. Your down payment will be the difference between what the lendor will lend and the end-result deal you work with a dealer. You will need either X number of dollars (of your own or borrowed from another source), equity in your trade-in, or exceptionally strong credit (no down payment) to make your purchase.

Secondary Financing. Secondary financing generally means borrowing money from a source other than a bank. This money may be used for the full amount you need to buy a car or as a down payment to satisfy a bank's requirements. Most such loans are known as high-risk loans, which means the interest is usually higher, but the credit is more easily obtained. The major sources are finance companies, credit unions, and dealer financing.

Finance companies are called slaughterhouses in the trade. Their interest rates generally run from 15 percent to 23 percent, which is about double that of a bank or a credit union. If you need $500 to fill out a down payment for your new car, they are handy and easy and usually do not place a lien on your car. However, the installment contract you sign lets them pursue everything else you own if you default on the loan. Because of the exorbitant interest rates, use slaughterhouses only as a last resort, and read every word of everything you sign.

Credit unions vary in procedure, but their interest rates are comparable to those of a bank (13 percent to 16 percent). Credit unions offer ease of payment (automatic payroll deduction each week) and are more lenient on credit requirements and approval. They may be used for full or partial financing on your purchase. Caution: most credit unions freeze any savings you might have at the time they grant a loan. If you have $500 accumulated, you may not be able to touch it until the loan is paid off. It is best to transfer your accumulated funds to an outside savings account before you make application to a credit union, if you feel you might need the funds.

There are two types of dealer "paper": that which is written and turned over to a bank (the bank controls the credit and terms), and that which the dealer backs himself—he grants the credit, sets the terms, takes the payments, and takes the car if you do not pay. Dealer-backed financing is usually found on used-car dirt lots and offers little or no money down, easy terms, high interest rates, and quick repossession when you get behind in payments. Generally, the down payment will be about what the dealer has invested in a car—if the price is $500 and he got the car for $100, your down payment will be the $100. Immediately he recaptures his investment, and any payments you make, plus the interest charged, is his profit. If he must repossess the car he keeps all money received and sells the car again. He may sell the same car five times, make a $500 profit, and still have the car on his lot for sale. Avoid this situation. Go to a bank, credit union, or even a slaughterhouse first.

If you have had credit problems or rejections, are a slow payer, or have filed for bankruptcy, tell the person with whom you are dealing; never try to hide anything. Silence about past problems will speak against you when the truth is discovered; your honesty will definitely speak to your benefit. Everything you have ever done with regard to credit is on file somewhere, waiting for a phone call to release the information. Even your application for credit is noted in your credit file. If you have been rejected by several lendors, it will show on a routine credit run and may cause an automatic rejection by the investigating lendor; if others have already rejected you there must be a reason.

When you apply for dealership financing, the information is called in to a lending institution (usually a bank) for credit approval. The lendor has only this phone call and the information he is given to make a loan decision. The lendor has not had a chance to meet you and does not know you. Your personal visit could make the difference between loan approval and rejection if your credit is the least bit shaky. However, some lendors will encourage you to go through the dealer, mostly because a repossession will fall upon the shoulders of the dealer if it is written on dealer paper. If a bank does not want to deal with you personally, shop around a bit. Make a few phone calls to compare interest rates and charges. A 1 percent lower rate on $5000 will save about $150 on a 3-year loan.

Used-Car Financing. All the above financing sources will consider a used-car loan. However, the interest rates are progressively higher and the duration of loan progressively lower according to the car's age. On a used-car loan you must really shop rates and terms to save money because of the wide variance among lendors.

FINANCE INSURANCES

There are three basic types of insurance that can be written into an installment contract: credit life (CL), accident & health (A&H), and comprehensive (comp). In some instances liability insurance can also be included, but CL, A&H, and comp are the most frequently used by lendors and dealers. All three forms can be included in one monthly payment.

Credit life insurance is basically decreasing term insurance. It will pay off the balance owing on your loan if you die. The amount of coverage decreases as you pay down the balance of the loan and has nothing to do with the car's market value when you die. If you double up or triple up on payments, thus reducing the balance of your loan, it will not pay what your balance should have been had you not doubled up on payments. If you prepay the entire loan you will receive a rebate on the cost of any insurances—just as you would on the finance charges—and the coverage stops. If you already have more life insurance than you really need, skip the credit life.

Accident and health insurance is geared to your monthly payment. It becomes active and makes your monthly payment for you when your normal income stops because of illness, accident, or disability. It does not reflect upon your credit standing since you will not miss a payment if you are off work for a few months. *Note:* You must file for the benefits before the payments will be made for you. If the dealer does not have forms, the lendor who holds your note can mail you one. Once you have filed, the payments are made automatically for as long as you are sick or disabled. If you return to work and then are off again, a new claim form must be filed to reactivate the coverage. The customary waiting period before the coverage begins to pay varies from company to company. It is usually 10 days retroactive to the first day you miss work. A&H does not cover strikes, layoffs, being fired, and the like. A&H is nonconflicting insurance and will pay benefits regardless of other health insurance you may have in effect.

Because A&H is more popular than CL, dealers do their best to discourage you from taking it alone—they lose the higher profit on CL. If you want the A&H badly enough, you will take the CL because you will be led to believe that they must be bought as a package. This is not true. Each is an individual protection and can be included in your monthly payment as such. If you want only the A&H, insist upon A&H and tell the dealer, ''If I cannot have the A&H alone, forget about the financing altogether. I will get my own money.'' The dealer will not chance losing the finance charge profit (about 20 percent of the total finance charge) for the sake of holding out for the CL profit.

Comprehensive insurance is generally required by the lendor to protect his investment. If you have a healthy balance on the car and it is smashed up, someone must pick up the pieces, and the lendor does not want it to be him. You have the choice of getting your own coverage or taking a plan through the lendor right along with the other insurances. The advantage to taking it through the lendor is that the rate is usually lower and it is easier than shopping for your own plan. If you have had a few accidents and find it difficult to get your own comprehensive insurance, take the comp offered by the lendor/dealer.

DEALERSHIP FINANCING TACTICS

A dealer sells financing just as he sells a car. Each dealer you encounter is, in essence, his own lending institution and can offer the advantages of one-stop shopping. Financing represents a profit to the dealer, even though the paperwork will be carried on the books of a local lending institution, and you will make your payments to that same lendor. The lendor also handles all facets of pursuing and collecting delinquent accounts. Most dealers work with more than one lendor.

Because of competition, a basic greed for the dollar, and the realization that they were losing the finance profit on three of every four cars they sold, dealers have moved toward using the services of a business manager in ever-increasing numbers each year. The major function of a business manager is to sell financing, on dealer paper, to all customers making a car purchase at the dealership. However, he also advises the dealership on investments, floor planning, and any other incidentals regarding the financial structure of the business. He sells financing with the same enthusiasm the salesman used to sell you your car.

The business manager can work for you or against you depending upon your individual financing plans. If you want to pay cash or finance through your credit union (his biggest competitor for your finance dollar), he will do his best to change your thinking. When he enters the closing room at the request of your salesman, his entire plan is to switch you over to his side and finance through his dealership. If you plan to finance through another source, maintain your position throughout his presentation. If you have no plans, or if your credit rating is the least bit shaky, listen to what he has to say; he may be able to help you. Business managers are well trained in credit requisites, down payments, and alternate finance sources, and most managers have at least one or two favors coming from lendors on border-line cases.

Then there is the other side of the business manager, if you are one of those who plans outside financing. His ploys include misquotes, shuffling of quotes, and overt misrepresentation. He may quote you a higher monthly payment than should be and then say, "Here is where I can save you some money. Instead of $330 a month, I can write the paper on this for $326.50, which will save you $100 over the length of the loan." In reality, the payment should have been $326.50 from the start.

Another method: The business manager can show you in black and white in his time-loan tables that the balance you need to finance will cost you $330 a month. He will then show—in the same set of tables—that $326.50 will save you $100, and he will write the finance papers for $326.50. The evidence is right up front in black and white; however, the $326.50 is without the accident and health and credit life insurances. Your savings is not based on a $100-better deal or interest rate, but rather on deletion of the insurances; the balance due and the finance charges remain the same throughout.

The business manager may intentionally misquote a monthly payment and show you a savings in black and white. But this time it is overt misrepresentation. For this to be successful, you must sign a blank or incompletely filled-in finance contract. The business manager must then see to it that you do not receive a copy of the contract. Since it is blank, but signed, he can fill in whatever figures he desires and ship it off to the lendor to collect the dealer's money.

When you receive your payment book from the lendor and discover the higher monthly payment, you will be given variations of three basic stories by the business manager. He will pacify you and swear that it was nothing more than a simple misunderstanding.

1. You may be told that the lower figure originally quoted did not

include the insurances (CL and A&H). It was assumed that you wanted them since you signed the insurance blocks on the contract. Inclusion of the insurances automatically raised the monthly payment.

Alternate: The lower figure quoted did not include the sales tax. It was assumed that you would be paying it separately, direct to the state. Inclusion of the tax automatically raised the monthly payment.

2. If a trade-in is involved that has a balance due on it, he will tell you that the payoff on your existing loan was higher than expected, which automatically raised the monthly payment.

3. If a story does not fit the situation, the business manager will flatly deny that he quoted you the lower figure and insist that the payment you received from the lendor is the same as quoted from the beginning. It is a simple matter of your memory and your word against his. If you made note of the payment quoted, he will tell you that it is too late now since the paperwork has already been processed through the lendor.

Your best defense is to never, never sign anything that contains blank spaces or incomplete information. Whether the influence to sign a blank contract stems from your pride, ego, or salesman and business manager insistence, be certain there are no loose ends attached to the deal you sign. If you are told that a particular space does not apply to your particular purchase, insert ''N/A'' (not applicable) in the space.

If you do not understand what you are reading or signing, have it explained to you. You have the right to know exactly what everything means within the body of the contract or agreement to purchase. If you sign without understanding and a problem arises, you cannot plead ignorance as your recourse. However, if you sign a blank contract at the insistence of a salesman or manager, you have recourse if he misrepresents verbally and fills in a blank space contrary to agreement.

You have the right to receive a copy of everything you sign, at the time you sign it, not a day later. If you are told that someone who is not immediately available must fill in the blanks, tell him that you will not sign until the blanks are filled in. If it means returning the following day to sign, do it. Any sales manager worth his salt can fill in the necessary information on an installment contract if he has a time-payment book. Whatever the reason given, do not sign blank.

If you are victimized by an unfair contract, your first move is to call the dealership and make the dealer aware of the discrepancy. Tell him that you expect it to be corrected, ignore the excuse for why it happened, and obtain his promise that everything will be handled properly. Then call the lending institution handling the loan and make the installment loan officer aware of the situation. Never tell the dealer that you plan to call the lendor; let him dig his own grave. If he contacts the lendor as promised, all the better for you. If the lendor is aware of a problem and hears nothing from the dealer, it will speak against him. If you receive no satisfaction, call or write the Federal Trade Commission. (See chapter 14, "External Recourse.")

REPOSSESSION

Repossession (repo) need not be a dirty word, nor does it always mean that you lose everything you have put into your car prior to the repo. If you are familiar with a few rules and procedures, it can, at times, work to your benefit.

The two basic forms of repossession are voluntary and aggressive.

Voluntary repo: You realize that you can no longer continue to maintain your monthly payments and, of your own free will, you turn the car over to the dealer or lendor holding the note on it.

Aggressive repo: You are in default of your note or loan and the lendor or the dealer sends someone to collect the car, whether you like it or not.

Of the two, voluntary repo does the least damage to your credit standing. Nobody had to chase you and track you down to get the car. You were responsible enough to realize that you could no longer afford to make payments, and you turned the car in without pressure from the lendor. It is critical that you make the first move and turn the car in. The determining factor of the two repo's is, did you take it back or was it taken?

When you realize that you cannot maintain the payments, call the lendor to see whether something cannot be worked out to make him happy. Usually a lendor will defer a payment or accept an interest-only payment to help you keep the car and get back on your feet. He may also rewrite the loan to give you even more time. But again, you must make the first move.

Deferred payment means that you make no payment for that particular month and pick up your normal payments beginning the following month. You compensate for the deferred month at the end of your loan term.

Interest-only payment means that you pay only the interest portion of your regular monthly payment. This will always be a variable amount, for the total interest due in any given month decreases as the loan becomes older. This gives the lendor his profit on the loan and makes it easier for you to maintain continuity of pay history.

A lendor will usually try for an interest payment first, and if that is impossible he will offer deferred payment. Most lendors will grant a deferred payment or interest-only payment once each year for the life of the loan. If you have already used either the deferred or interest-only solution in a given year, he may suggest, or you may request, a rewrite on the loan.

A rewrite means cancelling the existing loan and writing a fresh loan. This requires a fresh application with a new credit check and credit approval or rejection. A rewrite really depends upon your credit rating, your past payment history, and how the lendor feels about starting all over again.

You will lose a little more money on a rewrite, for you are starting a new loan with fresh interest, but if you can choose between rewriting the loan and turning the car in, take the rewrite. If you back them up, and if the lendor is willing to make two consecutive concessions, you can obtain 75 days between payments—30 for a deferred payment, 45 for a rewrite.

If you have used these options and still find yourself on the verge of a repo, try to sell the car yourself for more than you owe on it. If you sell it, even for break-even money, your credit record is pure and clean, and neither form of repo will show on a future credit check. All that will show is that you prepaid the loan, which is a good reflection on your credit record.

Get a closeout or payoff figure from your lendor, compute a selling price for your car, run an advertisement, and hope for the best. Never, never let a prospective buyer know why you are selling your car. Tell him that you plan to buy a new car and want no trade-in or that you have one too many cars in your family, but never say that you are forced to sell because of financial reasons.

A buyer can assume your loan balance, take over your monthly payments, and pay you the difference between the selling price and the balance due. A loan assumption is subject to lendor approval, and your buyer's credit must be at least as good as your credit, if not better. The major advantage to the buyer is that he saves the large chunk of interest paid at the beginning of a loan's life. Before you run your ad, see whether your lendor will take an assumption.

If you cannot sell your car or find someone to assume your loan, do not play hide-and-seek with the lendor. When you have taken all action possible and still find your back to the wall, turn the car in. If *they* come to *you*, your credit will show a black mark—aggressive repossession.

Once your car goes back to the lendor, you are still not out of the woods. The car must be sold, and you have the first right to purchase (redemption) and save the blemish on your credit. If you do not buy it and it is sold for less than your balance due, you will owe a deficit balance—the difference between what you owed and what the car sold for. If the deficit balance is ridiculously high—the wholesale valuation was $1,800, you owed $1,800, and the car was sold for $1,000—you can appeal the deficit balance. Appeal usually requires legal assistance or arbitration and can be time-consuming and expensive. But it is better to pay several hundred in legal fees than to be stuck with an unfair $800 debt with nothing to show for it. If you are financially destitute, seek help from your local Legal Aid Society.

CAR FINANCING GUIDELINE

Whether you are dealing with a dealership business manager or a lendor, there are certain questions you should ask regarding your loan.

1. What is the annual percentage rate (APR)? Most dealers (and some lendors) will quote an add-on rate of interest that is not the true, simple-interest rate. Six percent add-on is about 11.04 percent, depending on loan duration. There is about 1 percent that can be given away at the discretion of the dealer or lendor to reduce your APR. Shop for the best rate.
2. What is the amount of the loan; total balance due or borrowed?
3. What is the dollar cost of the finance charges and insurances?
4. What is the length of the loan (term or duration in months)?
5. What is the monthly payment? When are the first and last payments due and how much is each?
6. How much is the prepayment penalty; how is it computed?
7. How much are the closing costs and/or any other miscellaneous costs?
8. What is the grace period (time before the loan becomes in default)?
9. What is the charge for a late payment? When is a payment considered late?

DELIVERY

When all the contracts have been signed and approved and the money—whether cash or financed dollars—changes hands, it is time to take delivery of your car. Do not take delivery unless and until all contingencies have been resolved to your complete satisfaction. If the car is missing equipment or still has a malfunction that was to have been corrected, you do not have to take the car. If you desire, you can cancel the deal for breach by nonperformance. Once you take the car, the dealer can take his time satisfying his obligations—the old stall routine. Nothing will make a dealer or salesman move faster than the words: "It does not have what you agreed to furnish. I do not want the car like this. I won't take it." At this point he will either fix it while you wait, ask you to come back for the car a little later in the day, or try to talk you into taking the car on the promise that the work will be done.

This is when it takes tremendous will power to bite the bullet and refuse delivery. If you give in now you may continue to give in until you eventually just quit trying.

When you discover problems that were not remedied or equipment that is missing, make a big deal out of it. To obtain anything from a dealer, you must convince him that it is extremely important to you and that you absolutely will not take the car unless the problem is fixed. The more insistent the salesman is that you take the car, the more you should question his motives. Ask him, "Why is it so important to you that I take the car now? Why are you trying to push me into taking the car? Are you hiding something or is it that you do not plan to fix the car when I bring it back?"

Treat your new car to a used-car inspection—go over every square inch and check out everything that pushes, pulls, or switches on and off. Assume nothing. Everything corrected now is that much less for the future.

All this puts the salesman on the defensive, and his immediate reaction will be to agree with everything you say and begin to expedite solutions. At this point he knows he is very close to losing the sale and the commission he worked so hard to get. If, however, he insists that you take the car, expect the very worst when you return for corrections and promised work.

Most times you will find that dealers take care of the large items and tend to overlook the small items. The logic is that you will create problems for the dealership on a large item but will eventually forget about a small item. If you have something coming, collect it, no matter how small.

LEASE OR FINANCE?

Unless you pay cash, when you buy a car you finance part of the purchase price and pay X dollars for X months. When the last payment is made, you own the car. When you lease a car, you basically rent it on a long-term, month-to-month basis. You pay X dollars for X months and upon lease expiration, you either turn the car in or exercise an option to buy at a predetermined lump-sum price (residual value).

The most common misconception about leasing a car is ease of entry (no down payment, easy terms, low monthly payments) and ease of exit (at the end of the lease, just turn the car in). Well, it's almost that easy. There are different lease types with different terms and various obligations.

The two basic lease types are open end and closed end. Open end gives you the option to buy at residual value or turn the car in. Closed end is an automatic turn in at lease expiration. If you have become attached to the car, you can buy, but at the going market price based on full retail valuation. The difference, then, is that an open end lease guarantees you the right to buy at a preset price regardless of the real value of the car. Say, for example, the residual value was set at $8,000, but at lease expiration the market value of the car is $9,000. Naturally you would exercise your right to buy (open end) at $8,000 and then, if so desired, sell it for $9,000. If, however, market value is $7,000, you would obviously not pay $8,000 to keep the car. Why bother with a closed end lease? The closed end lease is less expensive than the open end; but not always that much. Before you make a commitment, compare the costs of both types. If the monthly payments and terms are close, choose the open end lease to guarantee the right to buy.

Since there are a variety of lease plans available that all fall under open end or closed end, it is wise to shop several dealers and leasing companies before you make a commitment.

When you lease, you will sign a binding contract that details the specific terms—duration, monthly payment, mileage restrictions and allowances, insurance responsibilities, and what happens if you do or don't do this or that. You must understand exactly what you are signing and what your obligations are, and this means *read the contract word for word*. Do not hesitate to ask questions. A lease is usually placed with a local bank and therefore carries an interest rate (just like financing). What is that interest rate? You must maintain insurance; how much and what types?

Not all lease plans require a down payment, but when a down payment is required it is usually the first and last month's payment plus a security deposit. How much is your initial cash outlay? Be aware of hidden costs. How much are they, what are they for, and when must you pay them? A lease generally allows you a certain number of miles per year (10,000 to 15,000). At the end of the lease, you must pay for each mile over the mileage allocation. Who is responsible for maintenance? Some lease plans offer only the factory warranty, which means you are responsible for anything not covered by warranty.

Knowing all this, the big question remains: "Is leasing right for you?" The greatest advantage of leasing is the tax breaks (deductions) it offers—the proverbial write-off. Unless you can take advantage of the tax breaks, you might as well finance your own car, make the payments, and eventually own it free and clear. If you are not self-employed; if the car will not be used for business purposes; if you do not qualify for the tax write offs; leasing is probably not for you.

13
Service Department

THE WARRANTY

MOST PEOPLE THINK that a 12-month, 12,000-mile new-car warranty covers 100 percent of everything on the car for the full 12 and 12. However, most warranties have a 90-day clause that covers everything for 90 days and covers only critical, mechanical drive-train components for the balance of the warranty. What is covered and for how long varies among manufacturers. Some will not cover electrical parts and squeaks and rattles after 90 days. Some offer a fixed time limit and extended mileage—12 months and 50,000 miles, whichever occurs first. Because there are so many different warranties, have the the the salesman explain, in detail, exactly what is covered and when, what is not covered, the required maintenance to keep the warranty in effect, and the maintenance cost. And then read the warranty word for word. Question anything you do not understand.

There are, in some instances, items that are covered but are not advertised as being part of the warranty. For example, the factory may be willing to pay for a front-end alignment or may extend warranty benefits on certain items after warranty expiration. Service managers are aware of these secret warranty items but do not normally hand out the information willingly. When in doubt about something amiss, contact the Federal Trade Commission.

Sale of Extended Warranty Coverage. Most dealers offer an extended warranty you can buy at extra cost. This is really a service contract similar in nature to those sold on major appliances. It does not matter who makes the profit on a service contract—the dealer or the factory or an outside independent. The important question is, do you really need it, and do you really want it.

A service contract generally covers only critical drive-train components and internal engine problems. It is safe to presume that any serious original-manufacture defects in your drive-train are going to develop within the normal warranty 12 and 12 coverage and will be paid for by the factory. It is further safe to presume that if nothing goes seriously wrong in the first 12 and 12, the car will make it at least another 24 months and 24,000 miles, provided you perform prescribed maintenance on schedule and do not abuse the car. The odds of something serious happening between 12 and 12 and 36 and 36 are so slight that it is hardly worth spending several hundred dollars for protection you probably won't use. You can replace a lot of surface equipment for several hundred dollars—alternator, power steering unit, master brake cylinder—things you would have to pay for anyway if you bought the service contract. Money on top of money.

Consider saving the initial investment for a service contract and creating your own warranty repair fund, unless:

1. You plan to keep the car longer than 3 years.
2. You put exceptionally high mileage on a car and will exceed 36,000 to 40,000 miles in 3 years. (Some contracts have a mileage restriction; others do not.)
3. You are notorious for destroying engines and transmissions.

Read the offered service contract word for word and ask these questions:

1. Exactly what is covered for how long and how many miles?
2. Who does the work, and what happens if they are unavailable or cannot fix it?
3. Is the contract renewable upon expiration and what is the cost for renewal?
4. Is there a limit on occurrences and must you pay a deductible each time your car needs work? (Limits and deductibles are no bargain.)
5. Must you continue to pay the high cost of dealership maintenance items—oil changes, filters—or can you do your own?

Factory-Backed Extended Warranty. Be wary of factory-sponsored extended warranties. The main intention of the factory in offering such a warranty is to stimulate sales. Another reason is to push a car that is not selling because of a known defect. In the mid-1970s, a certain compact had a tendency to overheat and lock up the engine. When sales began to drop, the manufacturer, in an effort to diminish public fears of buying, placed a 5-year, 60,000-mile warranty on the car. That may sound good on paper, but what if you are stuck in the middle of nowhere with a car that will not move 1 inch under its own power? If a particular car has a reputation for failing under certain conditions, the extended warranty means literally nothing compared to the headaches that can be created. Do not be lulled into any sense of false security offered by this type of extended warranty. If your instinct says don't buy, then don't buy. Once they have your money, it is a long road back to break even when problems begin to develop.

HANDLING SERVICE PROBLEMS

First, before you become frustrated to the point of tears, find out exactly what is wrong with your car. This requires a visit to the service department. If it is something simple and easily fixed, you will have wasted a lot of time, grief, and anxiety for nothing. Realize that a recurring problem may be caused by more than one part or a cluster of parts. A steering problem may be caused by one of a hundred or more small component parts. It is important to know exactly what was done and what part was bad each time you take your car in.

Be aware that it is not the fault of the service department if you need your car in 1 hour and you don't get it—unless it was promised, and it is not the department's fault if a particular part is not in stock on the very day your car needs it. Realize that dealing with a service department requires a little diplomacy, some politics, and a patient attitude. It never hurts to be polite and considerate. When you run into a grumpy service manager, give him a big smile—win him over.

Reduce It to Writing. Service personnel are always, and notoriously, short of time. You will save their time and your own if your problems are neatly spelled out in black and white. There are three reasons why it is important to keep a copy of your complaint list:

1. It gives you something to double-check against when you retrieve your car.
2. It helps you maintain a running record of your visits to the service department and may itself become the permanent record of your visits.
3. It represents tangible evidence that you can produce when confronting either dealership management or the factory representative.

Bear in mind that several different people may be working on your car—mechanics, bodymen—throughout the day. For mutual convenience, categorize that which you want done. Put all mechanical work in one section and all body work together as best as possible. Categorizing tells the service manager in an instant what needs to be done by whom, so that when you ask, "Can you do all this today?" he can give you a reasonably accurate answer.

Appointments. For best results and cooperation it is always best to make a firm appointment prior to your visit to the service department. Even if you think it is a take-a-quick-look-at-it visit, an appointment is advisable. Before you leave, here are a few dos and don'ts to observe:

1. Set your appointment and *be on time*.
2. Briefly review your list of complaints with the service manager. Explain what your car does and when it does it.
3. Never tell a service manager that he can keep your car for a few days or for as long as it takes to get it done. This is an automatic put-it-off-til-tomorrow clue to do cars with get-it-done-today status.
4. When you arrive for your car and the manager tells you that they could not get it done, immediately schedule another appointment. "Something came up and I don't need the car after all. Can you finish it tomorrow? When can you?"
5. Each time you are unhappy with the service performed on your car, let your salesman know as soon as possible. The first time, tell your salesman only. The second and third times, tell your salesman and his sales manager. The fourth time, tell both of them and the general manager and/or dealership owner. The fifth time, it is time to talk to the factory representative and start writing letters.
6. Whenever possible, have all parties concerned present when complaining. If the service manager defends his position, it is to your advantage to know just what he has to say.

Records. Now is the time to document the visit, to inscribe a permanent record of the situation while everything is fresh in your mind. Your memory is not infallible and the chance of something being forgotten is very high.

Any service department can have a complete record pulled in a few moments that will show everything that was ever done to your car—cost, time, labor, parts, and who did the work. During a dispute, you should be as well prepared to defend your position with names, dates, and items.

A simple but effective system is a small file box that contains index cards. It is easy to use and maintain. There is no need for an elaborate numerical, alphabetical, or cross-indexed system to ensure the best results. Just be faithful to your system and be consistent. It does little good to keep half of any information if you ever plan to use any of it.

Every contact with the dealership should be noted on a card with the date, the names of person(s) talked to or involved, the nature of the problem, what was done and how long it took, the name of the mechanic, the final disposition, and whether or not you were satisfied. Add significant comments as necessary; details help. If you are not certain of terminology, ask questions. "Worked on the brakes" can cover anything from the master cylinder to the caliper clips to a simple adjustment. Specifically what was done? Vague answers will produce vague records. "We fixed the squeak" is not good enough. What was the source of the problem? Always note the car's mileage on your records, both when you dropped it off and when you picked it up. Excessive mileage—more than 5 to 10 miles—means they used your car and your fuel for errands. Expect 1 to 4 miles on the car for road testing; complain about an excess.

Even though you may be receiving beautiful service, maintain records from your very first visit. In most dealerships, the service department gives extra-effort, super-duper service to all fresh customers. This is a staged, lulling tactic designed to make you think that their service is fantastic. After the image is cast and the impression stamped upon your mind, the lullaby stops—not abruptly, but more as a tapering-off of the extra effort. When things start going sour, you lose fighting power if you do not have complete and accurate records. Also, just because something was fixed does not mean it was fixed permanently. If you must eventually go to court, you will need evidence.

HANDLING POOR SERVICE

When you are getting nowhere with your service manager or he tells you that nothing can be done with your car, what then? You can argue with him until you turn blue or until he walks away from you. You can find your salesman and drop your problems in his lap. You can walk away from the situation, firm in the belief that to complain further is futile, and vow never to buy another car from them. Or, you can find out exactly whom you must see and with whom you must talk to obtain results.

At this point you are concerned only with the name of the person who can say, "Fix it and do it right." As long as lower-echelon personnel can solve your problems you need go no higher, but when the lower ranks cease and desist, it is time to appeal to a higher power. When you find out who he is, sit down and lay out your problems. This means that you will need the records you have been faithfully keeping. It also means that you should be prepared to handle the "All-American Runaround."

The All-American Runaround is a pacifier given to a customer to quiet his anger, and it usually boils down to a series of delaying tactics. If, for example, the general manager of the dealership is the only person who can say "Fix it" and if, after listening to your complaint, he does say "Fix it," you may be on your way to resolving your problems. Then again, he may say "Fix it" just to get you off his back. As soon as you leave he may call the service manager and tell him to start delaying tactics.

At some point you will realize you are being put off. Upset, you will return to the general manager, and he will proceed to become upset right along with you. He will assure you that the party responsible for your problems will suffer severely. He may even fake a blasting phone call to the service manager or he may simply promise that everything is just a misunderstanding and will be taken care of, and of course, you have his deepest apologies. You return to the service department, confident that your car will finally be fixed, and again the delaying tactics begin. You may be confronted with a different set of excuses, but the principle and the end result remain the same: Your car is not fixed. By now you are ready either to throw in the towel or to make one last effort to give them a chance to do the right thing. And suppose you do and suppose they don't? What then?

To begin, you must be able to recognize a delaying tactic. A delaying tactic is designed for one purpose: to buy time. If enough time passes, you will either give up the effort or become docile enough to do it their way. If their way means splitting the bill, you will split the bill rather than continue to fight. Anything that consumes time can be considered a delaying tactic. Here are a few of the most common:

1. "Our backlog of scheduled work is 10 days. Call us then."
2. "The mechanic who normally handles that specific problem is in the hospital (is home sick, just quit, is booked solid for the next 2 weeks)."
3. "Bring your car in tomorrow and leave it." (When you return for your car you will be told that they could not get to it and to bring it back tomorrow. This can happen until you tire of bringing your car in and leaving it.)
4. "We will have to order a special part to make the repair." (This is a good one.)
5. "The factory representative will have to look at this before we make

the repair. We will call you on the day that he is to be here." (Don't hold your breath waiting for the call).

When you recognize a delaying tactic, you must go back to the salesman or sales manager for another session. And the sooner the better.

The Attack. "Mr. General Manager, your service manager just told me that he cannot schedule my car to be fixed for 2 weeks."

"Gee, Mr. Customer, that is too bad, but there is nothing I can do about the work load they have. You know, there are other people who have problems also, and if they are first in line I guess you will just have to wait. But I am certain that this will be handled properly just as soon as they can get to your car. In fact, I will call the service manager and tell him to call you immediately if he has a cancellation of an appointment. How does that sound?"

"Mr. General Manager, that sounds terrific, but what about the fact that this is my fourth time in for the same problem? That would really put me first in line, would it not? I think that your service manager can do a better job of scheduling his work than to offer me a 2-week delay, don't you agree? Why don't you give him a call and see whether he can do it sooner, and I will not have to bother you anymore with this." (This implies that you will continue coming to him until your problem is solved.) "Better yet, let's go to the service department together and see if we can't resolve this problem by putting our heads together.

"Mr. General Manager, your service manager just told me that the mechanic who normally handles this type of problem will not be available for some time. You did tell me that this would be handled, and I really believe that it will. To save us both a lot of time and trouble I would like you to call XYZ Garage and authorize them to do the work and let them know they can bill your dealership for the cost."

The general manager will raise stiff objections to this suggestion: "We cannot do that. Just be patient and we will fix your car for you."

To which you reply: "I do not doubt that at all. But I do not plan to wait 6 months until it is done. If your service department cannot handle the problem, you will have to farm the work out to another garage and pay for it, cash out of pocket." *Note:* You can have the work done by another source, but most times a dealership will refuse to pay and you will end up in a small claims court to collect. Good records will help you win your case.

When you are presented with a parts delay, find out exactly what parts are necessary to fix your car and jot down the name of each individual part, complete with the part number when possible. Some dealers will give you a parts slip or a receipt to confirm the fact that the part was indeed ordered. Get an approximate arrival time. If the part is coming from a zone warehouse it should be a matter of a few days. A factory-ordered part could take several weeks, and import parts several months. When the time comes and goes without word of your part's arriving, call to confirm whether it is in or not. If it is not, begin to look for the part needed at other dealers' parts departments or at parts supply outlets. When you have found the parts needed, go to the dealership and give them a chance to quit making excuses and perform. Simply say, "I have found the parts that you say are holding up the work on my car. I am going to give you until (say, 2 days from now) to secure the parts from your own sources, and if you cannot, I want you to buy those parts from my source and fix my car." Or, "Since there will be no problem securing the necessary parts, I would like to schedule my car in for the work to be done." If the dealer cannot—or will not—do so, make a call to someone higher up and lay it on the line.

Here, there are several elements to consider: Are you receiving valid reasons why they cannot fix your car, or excuses? There are few legitimate reasons that cannot be worked out provided the dealer is willing to co-operate and makes a decent effort to satisfy your complaint. Remember that when a service complaint has gone far enough to warrant a visit to the general manager, it has gone far enough so that the dealership may not really plan to fix your car. Therefore, treat all reasons as excuses until proven otherwise. You will hear a lot of excuses from the general manager. His main goal is to get you off his back. Your goal is to get your car fixed. Be prepared to hunt him down, outwait him, and, if necessary, raise a little hell. He will promise anything to get you to leave him alone. But you want results, not promises. Be persistent.

The general manager is playing the numbers. He knows that he will lose X number of customers throughout any given year, for whatever reason, but he also knows that he will pick up X number of customers from his competition for the same reasons he lost his. If the general manager has this attitude, avoids you, and does not seem to want to satisfy your complaints, it is time to see the factory representative.

The Factory Representative. In a dispute between the customer and the dealership regarding warranty work, the factory representative (rep) is just about the final word on whether the work is covered and whether the factory will pay. The rep can also arbitrate seemingly hopeless mechanical problems (perhaps a cash adjustment) and authorize out-of-warranty work or work not normally covered—that is, when you can talk to him. He can be more elusive than a general manager, because the rep floats from dealer to dealer and not necessarily on a set schedule. If your dealer is derelict in advising you when the factory rep will be at his dealership to handle complaints, call or write the zone office nearest you to set an appointment. It may even be possible to resolve your problem over the phone.

The factory rep is not someone you can butter up, sway easily, or otherwise sneak one past. He is trained to listen patiently to your problems, never to become rattled, and to save the factory money. Every time he says *no*, the factory saves money. Every time he says *yes*, it is only because he must. He knows exactly what is covered and what is not at any given time in the warranty life, what secret warranties are in effect and apply to your case, and exactly how to handle the borderline, reasonable-doubt cases. A reasonable-doubt case could be a question of time; the warranty on the problem expired 2 weeks ago but you insist that you have had the problem since the day you bought the car. He must decide whether to accept your word and give you the claim, argue it out, reason it out, or tell you *no*. If it is a borderline case, he will try to dissuade you from pursuing the issue and convince you to give up the fight. Again, if he can convince you not to push the issue, the factory saves money. If he feels that you really plan to pursue it aggressively, he may decide to yield to your persistence. If he can say *no* and maintain your good will as a customer, he will do so.

How does he know he can say *no* and get away with it? Mostly by the way you present your story to him. A display of confidence weakens his position. Act as if you do not doubt your position and as if you firmly believe that the work should be done by the dealer and paid for by the factory. If you approach him meekly and are hesitant to ask for what may rightly be yours, he will take advantage of you. Be calm, but be firm.

Do not use words such as: "Could you" or "Would you" to ask for a remedy to your problems. This is a negative, closed-end question that expresses doubt and makes it too easy for him to say, "No, I cannot." Use instead words such as: "When can you? When can the service department fix this?"

Do not use your salesman as a runner. The rep can tell him anything and later deny it. He can also say *no* more easily to the salesman than to an irate customer. If you have taken the time to work things out and have been unsuccessful, it is time to seek external recourse. But before you do, tell the top man with whom you have been talking what you plan to do and give him one last chance to produce results. Do not threaten or tip your hand until you get a firm *no*, and if you get a firm *no*, give him the worst you can put together.

GUIDELINE FOR COMPLAINING

1. Try to resolve your service problems at the service-department level.
2. When you receive no satisfaction at that level, go to your salesman, then to the sales manager, then to the general manager or owner of the dealership.
3. Present your case with supportive evidence (records), and keep it brief and to the point. Get the general manager to agree with you that you do have a valid complaint. Let him know exactly what you expect him to do about your complaint, what will make you happy, and when you expect it done.
4. Never threaten unless you are prepared to take immediate action. If you threaten legal action, the general manager may call your bluff and tell you to sue him.
5. Be prepared to continue to return to the general manager with your complaint until it is satisfied. Put a time limit on his commitment—"How soon?" Have him put any past broken promises in writing and sign them. Each time you must see him, go through your entire complaint, start to finish—wear him out by talking.

14
External Recourse

DOES IT DO ANY GOOD?

EXTERNAL RECOURSE for the consumer is sometimes difficult to obtain. The agencies are there, the addresses are available, the people exist to whom you can talk, but by the time most people pursue a recourse it is too late to really achieve any reasonable form of satisfaction. At best, your complaint registered with the proper agencies can help protect someone else.

The best recourse available to you is preventive. Simply put, check everything out before you buy. If you have done all that and you have still encountered a problem, an avenue of release is needed to alleviate the frustrations you are experiencing—and to resolve the problem when and if possible.

Consumer protection and action agencies and groups are not always the panacea to your problems. They do not—and cannot—guarantee results, and relieving the burden of the problem from your mind may be the only satisfaction you receive. It may be necessary to resort to legal measures or militant tactics to get the satisfaction you want and deserve. For simple matters of irritation when you want to tell someone but do not want to become involved in a court battle, the following agencies are at hand to assist you.

AGENCIES

Better Business Bureau (BBB). The BBB is your best prepurchase preventive medicine. This Bureau will give you, for the most part, basic information about which businesses are legitimate and which you may want to avoid. It can usually give you a history of the business, who's who in the business, and, most important to you, how many complaints have been registered against the company by dissatisfied customers.

The BBB works only if people use it. Those who have already suffered problems with a business need to report them to the BBB so that those who have not yet bought have something to investigate. When a complaint has been filed, the business in question naturally has the right to defend its position, so there is a balance to the system all the way around.

If there is no BBB in your town and you must make a toll call to a nearby town to register a complaint or investigate a company, do it. It may cost a few cents for the call, but it will be worth the investment.

The BBB is also involved in arbitration settlements between the consumer and the business. However, the business has the option not to participate. Both parties agree before hand to abide by the decision of BBB. The abitrator then hears both sides of the story and makes the decision. (Records help.)

Consumer Protection Agencies. Similar in effectiveness to the Better Business Bureau, the consumer protection agencies are more concerned with consumer safety than poor business practices, although they do become involved. They will act as mediator between consumer and business in areas of financial loss and customer dissatisfaction, but their primary concern is protection before the fact, not mediation after the fact. Consumer protection agencies are found at local, county, and state levels. Check your phone book.

Federal Trade Commission (FTC), Washington, D.C. 20580. The primary concern of the FTC is fair trade practices. Although it does not handle individual cases, the FTC can be a great source of consumer information on warranties, installment contracts, and guidelines and is a complaint-lodging medium though no assurance of individual follow-up can be given.

National Highway Traffic Safety Administration (NHTSA), 400 Seventh Street, SW, Washington, D.C. 20590. The primary concern of NHTSA is new-car safety-related items. If your problem is a safety-related item, you can call a toll-free number to report it: 800-424-9393 (in Washington D.C., call 426-0123), or write.

National Advertising Review Board (NARB), 845 Third Avenue,

New York, N.Y. 10022. The concern of the NARB is for truth and accuracy in advertising. If you suspect fraud or misrepresentation in advertising, advise the NARB by letter; enclose a copy of the advertisement if possible. The agency will investigate or redirect your complaint.

Automobile Consumer Action Panel (AutoCAP). Contact information may be obtained from your library, courthouse, or the Center for Auto Safety, address below.

AutoCAP is a consumer-action panel composed of citizen laymen and members of the automobile industry. It will listen to your problem (verbal or written), make recommendations, and take action as warranted, either by panel, industry committee, or single mediator.

Local Consumer Organizations. Local organizations for consumers are usually staffed by local volunteers acting on consumer-interest issues. Not every area has one, but you can send details of your complaint to the Center for Auto Safety, 1223 Dupont Circle Building, Washington, D.C. 20036, which will forward your letter to the group nearest you.

ONE STEP BEYOND

Most dealerships do not want adverse publicity in newspapers or on the radio and television. Most areas have a consumer-action line or help line that works through a local mass-media communications system—television or radio. When it becomes necessary to solicit help from agencies, you might as well get everyone involved. If the problem is serious enough, you may even get a news camera crew and a reporter on the scene.

Nothing will rattle a dealership more than a well-organized picket. If possible, get others who have had a bad experience with your dealer to join your peaceful protest. Begin by learning local regulations regarding picketing and obtaining permission or a license to picket. Call the police chief or courthouse. Find out whether a license is necessary, and even if it is not, advise local law enforcement officials of your plans for a peaceful demonstration. Certain areas may restrict the size of your group and the hours you may walk. Print placards with three- or four-word slogans that sum up your protest—"SOLD ME (US) A LEMON," "SERVICE STINKS," "MERCHANDISE DEFECTIVE"—large enough to be read by passing motorists. Type a one-page summary of your problems with the dealership, itemizing what you bought and when, your problems with the car, how many times it went in for service, and the attitude (in your opinion) of the dealership and have photocopies made—fifty should do. Pass these out to customers entering the dealership, but do not force a copy on anyone. Customers have the right to come and go unmolested. Be prepared to march until you get the results you want—the service you deserve. Have at least one person walking during every legal hour; split the duty up among your group so no one person is marching all day long.

LEGAL STEPS

Some problems will absolutely have to go to court to be resolved, but it need not be expensive. Most areas have a Legal Aid Society or Legal Services Agency offering assistance to those within certain lower income ranges. For a small sum of money (it is not free), you are given the name of a participating attorney, an appointment is usually set for you to talk to him, and he will let you pour your heart out. He will then advise you of just what rights you have in the matter, the probability of going to court, what it will cost you to instigate legal proceedings, and your chances of walking away victorious. For the dollars invested in this way, it is well worth it just to find out where you stand legally, and what recourse you may or may not expect.

If your attorney advises you to file suit under the Magnuson-Moss Warranty Act, let the Federal Trade Commission know. Write to Warranties Project, Bureau of Consumer Protection, Federal Trade Commission, Washington, D.C. 20580.

Small claims court, found in every state, offers legal relief usually without the expense of an attorney, but there are limits that vary from state to state. Your local courthouse can advise you whether you fall within minimum/maximum dollar amounts and whether an attorney is required. The maximum ranges run from $300 to $3,000, and the waiting period for resolution runs from 3 weeks to 3 months. Again, the better your records, the better the results.

LETTERS

Any letter of complaint should be no more than one page in length, typewritten if possible, single-or double-spaced. When someone is holding two or three pages in his hand he has a tendency to scan the letter to pick out the important parts and read just enough to get the general drift of the material content. Keep it as simple as possible, but be thorough.

When you send a letter to a district office for action by a factory representative, explain the distribution: one copy to the district office, one copy to the manufacturer, one copy to the dealership. The manufacturer will then contact the district office, the district office will contact the dealership and/or you, and your problem should be on its way to a solution. Manufacturers normally send their dealers report cards monthly that state the number of complaints, the names of the complainants, and the nature of the complaints. Even so, the manufacturer allows the dealers a percentile factor of complaints before becoming really upset with a particular dealer. So do not send just one letter and expect miracles. Persistence pays.

SAMPLE FORM FOR COMPLAINT LETTER

On ———— I purchased a ————, serial number (————),
    (date)   *(year, make)*

from ————————, located at ————————. The purchase
  (dealership name)   *(address, city, state)*

price was: ————.

These problems existed at the time I took delivery and were to be taken care of by the dealer (or his salesman).
1. ————————————————
2. ————————————————

I have had the following problems since purchase and received service or lack of service on these dates:
(Itemize the problems and dates):
1. ————————————————
2. ————————————————

The service department has (choose one or all): failed to remedy the problems properly; created excessive and unnecessary delays; charged me for service rendered that was covered by warranty; been rude and discourteous; caused a great deal of worry and anxiety; used my car for errands; put excessive mileage on my car while it was in for service; misrepresented; broken promises; lied (or whatever else the dealer may have done to you personally).

Efforts to negotiate a settlement have failed. I have talked to: ———— and ———— and have received no satisfaction to date.

I want the following to resolve these problems: $———— cash

settlement; parts repaired/replaced; work done on the (engine, transmission, other); mediation to establish a fair settlement.

(If a warranty was issued in writing, enclose a photocopy with your correspondence. If a verbal warranty was given, detail the promises made. Include photocopies of anything you signed—contracts or agreements. The more complete your information, the better the results.)

MANUFACTURER CONTACT INFORMATION

Chrysler Corporation, 12000 Chrysler Drive, Highland Park, Michigan 48288-1919. Telephone: 313-956-5252.

Ford Motor Company, The American Road, Dearborn, Michigan 48121. Telephone: 313-322-3000.

General Motors Corporation, 767 Fifth Avenue, New York, New York 10009. Telephone: 212-418-6100.

Pontiac Motor Division, Div. General Motors, One Pontiac Plaza, Pontiac, Michigan 48058-3484. Telephone: 313-857-5000.

Cadillac Motor Car Division, Div. General Motors, 2860 Clark Avenue, Detroit, Michigan 48232. Telephone: 313-554-5147.

Import manufacturer contact information is available at your library.

The ball is in your lap. What you do in an individual situation is entirely up to you. If you choose to be docile about your problems and not to pursue a remedy to the end, it is you who must live with the results and suffer through the problems, and it is your responsibility to take actions necessary to obtain results. Never feel that a problem is too small to warrant remedial action. Never feel that since you made a mistake in judgment while buying your car that you must now live with that mistake. Never shake your head in resignation and say, "Well, they got me that time; but I'll know better next time." Dealerships rely upon these consumer attitudes to skirt the issue and take them out of the line of fire.

Every time a consumer says, "Forget it; it is too insignificant or too late to pursue," the dealership cash register does a little jingle. Stand up for your rights and be persistent.

Best of luck to you.

Order Form

To order additional copies of this book, check with your local bookstore, or order from Publishers Book and Audio Mailing Service, P.O. Box 120159, Staten Island, NY 10312-0004.

Please send _____ copies of *How To Buy a Car* @ $4.99 U.S./$5.99 Can. plus postage and handling charges of $1.50 for the first book and 50¢ for each additional book to:

Name _____

Address _____

City _____ State _____ Zip _____

Send check or money order only—no cash or CODs. You may charge with your Visa, MasterCard, Discover or American Express card. Please allow six weeks for delivery. Payment in U.S. funds only. New York residents add applicable sales tax.

Index

BESTSELLING BOOKS FROM
ST. MARTIN'S PAPERBACKS—
TO READ AND READ AGAIN!

NOT WITHOUT MY DAUGHTER
Betty Mahmoody with William Hoffer
_____ 92588-3 $5.95 U.S./$6.95 Can.

PROBABLE CAUSE
Ridley Pearson
_____ 92385-6 $5.95 U.S./$6.95 Can.

RIVERSIDE DRIVE
Laura Van Wormer
_____ 91572-1 $5.95 U.S.   _____ 91574-8 $6.95 Can.

SHADOW DANCERS
Herbert Lieberman
_____ 92288-4 $5.95 U.S./$6.95 Can.

THE FITZGERALDS AND THE KENNEDYS
Doris Kearns Goodwin
_____ 90933-0 $5.95 U.S.   _____ 90934-9 $6.95 Can.

JAMES HERRIOT'S DOG STORIES
James Herriot
_____ 92558-1 $5.99 U.S.